My brother, Jim Sloan, worked with
Commandant Thad Allen as his assistant
commandant for intelligence and investigations
for over five years. He died at the age of sixty-two
from Lou Gehrig's disease, or ALS, in 2009. Prior
to that, Jim served as director of FinCEN; retired
honorably from the Secret Service; and honed his
investigative skills as a homicide investigator in the
Union County, New Jersey, Prosecutor's Office.
He became a second lieutenant in the U.S. Army
Signal Corp at the age of twenty; he was brilliant.
Jim loved the Coast Guard. Though Jim was a
civilian, those that worked with Jim loved and
respected him. Commandant Allen relied on Jim
to the day he retired. The Coast Guard honored
Jim at his own home in Annapolis, Maryland,
in a ceremony attended by all Intelligence
Directorates. When Jim died, the Coast Guard
gave him a twenty-one-gun salute as he was laid
to rest. Dedicating this book to the Coast Guard
is the least I can do to recognize one of the best
organizations in the United States.

The Donning Company Publishers
184 Business Park Drive, Suite 206
Virginia Beach, VA 23462

Lex Cavanah, General Manager
Barbara Buchanan, Office Manager
Anne Burns, Editor
Rick Boley, Graphic Designer
Nathan Stufflebean, Research and Marketing Supervisor
Katie Gardner, Marketing Advisor

Barry Haire, Project Director

THE
DONNING COMPANY
PUBLISHERS

Library of Congress Cataloging-in-Publication Data

Sloan, Tom, 1952-
   Bratva's rose tattoo : a novel / by Tom Sloan.
      pages cm
   ISBN 978-1-68184-005-5
1. Hijacking of aircraft--Fiction. 2. International
relations--Fiction. 3. Government investigators--Fiction.
4. Secret service--Fiction. 5. Suspense fiction. I. Title.
   PS3619.L6284B73 2015
   813'.6--dc23

                              2015035855

Printed in the United States of America at Walsworth

BRATVA'S ROSE TATTOO

A Novel

by Tom Sloan

ACKNOWLEDGMENTS

I am grateful beyond words to my good friend Dennis Lynch, former U.S. Marine and Secret Service agent (retired). He helped me tremendously and would be annoyed with me if I went further. My sisters, Ann McGovern and Dr. Elizabeth Power, reviewed my book, giving the support to keep on writing. My son, Dan, prodded me to become a better writer early on and my wife, Gail, gave me the best advice to show, don't tell. My good friend, and mentor, Christopher Reich, himself a New York Times best-selling author, told me writing was re-writing. Boy, was he right! He believed this story would be a best seller. Diane Machalek and Evangeline Bozzuto were a big help in reviewing the book. Finally, my good friend Gerry Cavis went beyond friendship to ensure this book would find a hard cover. Thanks to all.

CAST OF CHARACTERS

Sultan Al-Tamini Saudi air traffic controller, Riyadh

Abdullah Rehaimi Saudi air traffic controller, Jeddah

Horace Corbin Special Agent in Charge (Sims's boss)

Tom Eddie USSS manpower supervisor

Steve Armey USSS, Eddie's assistant

Billy Sims USSS, Kuwait lead advance agent

Mary Walsh White House lead staff advance

William Burch USSS, Kuwait transportation lead agent

Velma Corey U.S. Ambassador to Kuwait

Colonel Aalim Maudud Kuwait Military (Sims's counterpart)

Carly Strain (nee Carly James) USSS, Cyber Squad leader

Maksim Valdimirovich Dostoevsky aka: Max, super hacker

Jose Riera Max's ultimate fighter (UFT) opponent

Ron McKenzie UFT commentator

Gary Maher UFT commentator

Arlene Baker Mary Walsh's advance assistant

Will Strain U.S. Coast Guard Commander (Carly's husband)

Stuart Kiehne Villanova lacrosse coach (Carly Strain's coach)

Vitaly Rubin aka: Shorty, Max's best friend

Tanya Ovseenko Max's stripper girlfriend and cocaine addict

Torre Max's American Terrier

Ivan Valdimirovich Dostoevsky NHL hockey star (Max's father)

Bratva the Russian brotherhood operate out of Brighton Beach, New York

Ekaterina "Kate" Petrov Max's mother

Gerry Veit Ranger Hockey Club representative

Arvydas Belov Bratva's chieftain, former KGB operative

Miguel Sanchez aka: Diablo, drug dealer

Brad Thallen Commandant of the United States Coast Guard

James F. Keegan USCG Assistant Commandant for Intelligence

Gerry Coffman USSS White House Detail manpower rep

Alexei Bratva thug

Tim Bowser Lexus dealership manager, Diablo's client, cocaine addict

Jack Halvey DEA agent

Jim O'Brien lead DEA agent

Kenny Reed DEA agent

Xavier Cordeleone Taboo Luzz cyber villain

Tom Dooley DEA Acting Special Agent in Charge (SAC)

Shane Gergich Assistant U.S. Attorney

Angelo Suarez Young Floridian hacker

Steve Austin USSS, NYFO, cyber squad agent

Brian Gallagher USSS NYFO, Special Agent in Charge (SAIC)

Mike Sinnott USSS agent, Newark office

Billy Fieldstone Diablo's fake name used at strip club

Jelly strip club bouncer

George Hamilton Carly Strain's first USSS Special Agent in Charge

Barry T. Moskowitz U.S. Magistrate conducting Max's criminal hearing

Richie Deschak USSS, young agent escorts Max to criminal hearing

John Blake Assistant U.S. Attorney prosecuting Max in NYC

Sergey Arkhipova Max's defense attorney

Frances Larosa U.S. Air Force, C5M Loadmaster

Colonel Javier Robles U.S. Air Force, C5M pilot (Andrews to Ramstein leg)

Special Officer Jimmy Warwick retired Marine Corp Sergeant Major

Brigadier General Jack Tuttle U.S. Air Force, Commander of Ramstein Air Base

Tatiana Bratva member, former KGB operative

Gamera Bratva member, former KGB operative

Colonel Daniel Riggs C5M pilot, Robles's replacement

Peter Baubles Director of National Intelligence (DNI)

Gerry Cavis Carly Strain's counterpart on C5M and Counter Assault Team (CAT) supervisor

Frank Larkin Jr. USSS, CAT member on C5M

Rick Caesar White House Situation Room operator

Dan O'Riordan USSS, CAT member onboard C5M

Major John Baer USMC, HMX pilot onboard C5M

Admiral Donny Merz U.S. Navy, Deputy DNI

Jon Bramnick White House Chief of Staff

Garcia Santos Keegan's USCG aide

Larry Cassell private sector Chief Security Officer (CSO), former USSS Director

James P. Fitzpatrick USCG supervisor escorting Max to Kazakhstan

Commander Nelson Keyser U.S. Navy, F-18 Navy fighter pilot

Harry Wilde USSS, Sims's assistant agent at Kuwait airport

Frank Larkin Sr. Yellow Taxi cab driver at Brighton Beach, father of slain USSS agent

Patrick McMurray USCG, Chief Petty Officer, met Larkin's cab at Newark Train Station

Commander Mike Mudd USCG, Blackhawk helicopter pilot, flew Max to USCG HQ

PROLOGUE

"Jeddah Center, this is Riyadh Center. We are no longer receiving the SAM143 transponder code," a calm-voiced Sultan Al-Tamini said into his microphone.

Al-Tamini sat upright at his assigned console location wearing a headset, its wiring dangling loosely, which connected him to a shared server. A half-filled coffee cup sat off to his right, the liquid contents too cold to drink, ignored. A large video screen before him displayed an array of multi-colored electronic blips. He grew aware of the missing blip.

"Roger. Nor is Jeddah Center," Abdullah Rehaimi, his distant air traffic controller counterpart, responded. On air, Rehaimi's vocal composure mimicked that of Al-Tamini. Neither betrayed their professional calmness.

At approximately 1400 hours, three hours from the Kuwait International Airport, a U.S. Air Force cargo plane, known as SAM143, ceased to communicate its proprietary four-digit code separating it from other aircraft in the region.

"Do you have any recent voice transmissions?" asked Rehaimi.

"Standby, Jeddah Center. I will replay the timeline," Al-Tamini replied.

Each of the Saudi National Area Control Centers (ACC) had been recently equipped with the latest generation of an advanced recording system developed by the Swiss Company Schmid Telecom AG. It was no small effort, but the House of Saud decided was necessary to keep the kingdom's avionics relevant. If the SAM143 had attempted a mayday, it might have been picked up and could be audible on a replay. Al-Tamini entered the aircraft identifiers in the Riyadh systems' voice recording search screen. Results were usually returned instantly.

"Jeddah Center, we have no history of voice distress calls from SAM143. Its transponder signal 0143 is no longer being received, and I don't have a timeline of when it actually terminated," Al-Tamini's said, his voice now an octave higher, a hint of strain in his normally controlled vocals.

"Okay, Riyadh. Jeddah will make notification to GACA and request search and recovery assets be placed on alert."

The Jeddah operative looked over at the distinctive red phone. It was a dedicated drop line to the Saudi Kingdom's General Authority of Civil Aviation. The phone was placed within arm's reach of the Jeddah operative. It was not used often. In fact, it was rarely used. When it was, it meant the conversation was serious; a communication no one would foresee as ending well.

"This is General Authority, how can I help you?"

"Sir, this is Jeddah Center. We have a problem."

ONE

The BBC reported on Sunday, the 24th of February, 1991, that Allied forces had launched a combined ground, air and sea assault against the Iraqi army, overwhelming its forces within 100 hours. Allied troops swept into Iraq and Kuwait from several points along the Saudi Arabian border. By Tuesday, the 26th of February, Iraq had given notice that it was withdrawing its forces from Kuwait, although still refusing to accept all the UN resolutions passed against it. Iraqi tanks, armored vehicles, trucks and troops fleeing the Allied onslaught formed huge queues on the main road leading north from Kuwait to the southern Iraqi city of Basra. Allied forces bombed them from the air, killing thousands of troops in their vehicles. The event became known as the Highway of Death. An estimated 25,000 to 30,000 Iraqis were killed during the ground war alone.

"Where the hell is Markaz al Abdali?" asked Supervisory Agent Tom Eddie. He twisted uncomfortably in his swivel seat at the manpower desk located on the eighth floor of United States Secret Service Headquarters. Here, in an area of the building separated by thick, internal walls, he coordinated the movement of 1,500 field agents who were available for temporary protective duty.

"Not a clue, replied his sidekick, Steve Armey. "Let me check the Internet. I'm sure it's between midway and nowhere."

The two men had just received an official notification from the agency's elite White House Protective Detail. "The President of the United States will visit Kuwait to commemorate the twenty-fifth anniversary of its liberation. This is scheduled for the last week of February 2016," read the text message.

Eddie carried the title assistant special agent in charge, as a headquarters mid-level supervisor. The thankless hyperactive assignment had taken its toll on him; he knew he needed to move to another position inside the agency. "I need to bust a move soon, and get back to the field." Eddie, or "Fast Eddie" as friends and co-workers knew him, earned the moniker while in Secret Service school. He was the fastest to complete the mile and a half run during physical fitness training.

"These past eighteen months have been the worst of my career." He and Armey absorbed the wrath of field office managers who complained to them about the constant agent tasking.

"This job sucks," said Armey. "Do these guys think we get paid more than they do?" He sat slumped in front of his solo, grey cubicle, photos of his wife and two young boys the only adornments. "The field assholes just don't have a clue what we do for a living."

Despite his constant complaining, Armey actually kept the field office noise out of his head slightly better than Eddie, but not by much. Taking potshots at the field office managers helped him feel better somehow.

"You know Eddie, it sure would improve our relationship with the field guys if we didn't have to travel them on the cheap," Armey lamented. The cheap route involved the use of Air Force cargo planes to transport agents to where they were needed to support the protective mission. Many agents felt like they were the cargo; some complained, but most did not. For some, the travel by cargo plane conjured up a sense of adventure, seeding the accounts of legend for a generation to tell. The planes that ferried the presidential vehicles had become part of agent lore. Most of the legends were car-plane stories involving mechanical failures or breakdowns that left agents stranded in distant parts of the world often without food or drink.

Sitting in front of his twenty-inch color monitor, Eddie focused on the White House request for the Kuwait trip. Country music radio played softly in the background, Garth Brook's *The Dance*, his only diversion from the looming logistical chore. He began the ritual of contemplating from which offices the new manpower would be drawn and which of the field supervisors he'd piss off.

Armey hated country music, though he never complained. He understood Eddie's need for it, ameliorating an otherwise drab duty. The music didn't keep him from talking over it. "Did you ever think this office was designed intentionally so we are forced to focus our attention on this shit? There are no fucking windows; who designs rooms like this?"

Eddie tried in vain to shut out Armey's incessant complaining, but he too experienced the frustration and responded, "If I had known what a pain in the ass this assignment would be, I never would have put in for it. Not even for the promotion."

"At least you got the fucking promotion," Armey responded, slightly irritated. "The only fucking reason I took this job was I believed it eventually would pay a dividend for me. All I want now is a transfer back to the field. Headquarters can keep their promotion."

Eddie glanced at him with mock disdain. He knew Armey still wanted a promotion. Ignoring the self-pity he said, "This will be a seventy-plus agent manpower request. We'd better give the Mil Aide's office a heads-up. They're gonna need to put all of them on a large car-plane. I hope they use the C5M. We're gonna need the room."

Armey smiled in an attempt to soften his rhetoric and said, "I suspect you're right. Especially with the president's limos and helicopters on board."

TWO

"Good morning, Boss!" shouted Senior Special Agent Billy Sims to the weathered gentleman sitting behind the enormous walnut-colored wooden desk. The desk looked strikingly similar to the famed "Kennedy Desk," made from the timbers of the HMS *Resolute*, the decommissioned British frigate. The weathered gentleman was Special Agent in Charge Horace Corbin. Distracted only momentarily by what he considered an overly energetic greeting, Corbin resumed marveling at the rays of sunlight streaming through the Old Executive Office Building window and onto the classified Kuwaiti trip file lying on his desk. Corbin had summoned Sims to his office for a final intelligence briefing before Sims's departure for a Middle East assignment.

Sims was pumped. He had been selected to be the president's lead advance agent who would manage the Secret Service advance team in Kuwait. Everyone on the Presidential Protective Detail liked Sims, and the feeling was mutual.

Sims displayed an infectiously attractive smile. "How's my favorite 'Bullet Catcher?'" Corbin glanced at his young protégé and shook his head in feigned disgust. An FBI buddy of Corbin's had coined the name "Bullet Catcher" earlier in Corbin's career, and it had stuck. It was a tribute the FBI agent paid to his Secret Service counterpart for grabbing a loaded gun from a potential presidential assassin. Corbin's entire career history hung on his office walls. Personally inscribed and autographed presidential photographs from the last twenty-five years silently testified to his dedicated efforts.

Corbin moved his head slowly left to right, then took off his reading glasses with his right hand carefully placing them on top of the briefing document, and stood up. "Come on in, Sims. Have a seat. You want a cup of coffee?" Sims knew not to move beyond a certain point in the office, the boss's "comfort zone" the agents called it.

"No thanks, Boss. Just finished my third cup in the White House mess."

"Sims, this Kuwait trip is a sensitive one for the president. His chief-of-staff, Jon Bramnick, asked for you personally. He said only a well-groomed agent like you would give the president the necessary confidence to handle all the nuances involved. Bramnick is not talking about you not having 'a hair out of place.' He is complimenting you for your reputation for not leaving the smallest detail unchecked. I know you won't let us down. It's his last year in office; I think he could use some good publicity. The president understands you will have to contend with Mary Walsh on this trip, and he knows she can be a handful, but he has equal confidence in her, too. He says he can't afford any more bad press and she knows how to work the media message."

Security plans frequently collided with the administration's political message. Corbin knew the White House staff advance, Mary Walsh, would be demanding, even for Sims.

"I appreciate your confidence, Boss. I know the last thing the Service needs now is blame for destroying the political message."

His thoughts turned to the make-up of his advance team. "Boss, may I have your permission to hand-pick my team?"

"Of course you can," said Corbin. "Your special talent is your ability to get along with people. And I can honestly say I've never supervised anyone who has the ability to extract from others the support this detail needs like you can. What I particularly like is the way you raise everyone's game."

"Thank you, sir. I learned it from guys like you."

"Nice try, Sims, but save your sucking up for someone who believes you. You're such a peckerhead." They laughed, shook hands, and said good-bye.

THREE

The AP reported that on January 17, 1991, a five-month buildup called Desert Shield became Operation Desert Storm. Allied aircraft attacked Iraqi bases and Baghdad government facilities. The six-week aerial campaign climaxed with a massive ground offensive on February 24-28, routing the Iraqis from Kuwait in 100 hours of battle before U.S. officials called a halt to the operation.

The White House advance team arrived in Kuwait City under the lead of Mary Walsh and gathered together for a quick meet and greet, her first countdown meeting. The countdown meetings were used to gather and coordinate various elements of the advance team: White House staff, military, and Secret Service. Through these meetings she could hone the message she felt was needed, and also ensure the entire group was working in unison.

Before the meeting began, Billy Sims told his team, "The primary site for the president's speech isn't much more than a small customs post. It's called al Abdali and is located about thirty miles from the Persian Gulf. The post was formerly used by the military to 'stand watch' over a stretch of highway known as the Highway of Death."

Walsh, standing nearby, overheard his statement and grew irritated. "It's the Highway of the Future," she announced to all who could hear her. She wanted to set the tone early in her first countdown meeting in the Sheraton Kuwait.

"This is not to be about the destruction of fucking Iraq military vehicles. We need to celebrate the success in the region and that will be the message from this White House. I don't want to hear it spun any differently."

Walsh was known as a dedicated, loyal White House operative. Individual staff members assigned to her knew not to cross or criticize her. To do so would earn a ticket home.

During the recent presidential campaign Walsh had taken on a young male staffer who had the audacity to disagree with her in front of her team. Not a wise move. She reduced him to tears with an epic tongue-lashing, using every foul word in her extensive lexicon. The incident further enhanced her reputation as someone who takes no prisoners.

The presidential advance team arrived ten days ahead of the so-called celebration to organize and establish a logistics plan. Walsh arranged for the White House staff to be housed in the Sheraton Kuwait located in the heart of the city's commercial center. She put the VIPs on the elevated floors so they would have an optimal view of Shuwaikh Beach leading to Kuwait Bay.

Members of the overflow support team, which included the Secret Service jump team and the accompanying press, were housed in the smaller Four Points by Sheraton Hotel, one block away.

"Our guys won't have a problem with the smaller hotel," Sims told her. "As long as they have access to the Shahrayar Restaurant and the fitness center in the larger Sheraton, they'll be happy."

"Sims, I really don't have the time to worry about your agents' comfort," said Walsh.

Sims let this sink in for a second or two then mustered a less than enthusiastic smile. "Understood," he replied curtly.

He realized her comment, made within earshot of his agents, did not endear her to them. "Don't worry guys, at some point she will need us for a logistical favor. It will be ours to give or not. It would be a whole lot easier to give," he quietly told them, "if she wasn't such a bitch."

Walsh was the agents' least favorite White House advance person. But they understood the reason she was in charge of the trip—she got things done to shed the best possible light on the president's agenda. "Let's get the meeting going. Sims, tell us about the security plans for the president's hotel."

"The hotels are only six miles from the Kuwait International Airport. We will secure both with Secret Service Jump Team agents once they all arrive by car-plane. The presidential motorcade will be accommodated along Fahd Al Salem Street, leading to the president's hotel. We will keep the secure package inside the hotel garage."

The secure package referred to the armored vehicles being flown into Kuwait to support the president. They, along with the additional agents and military, would be on board a C5M, the Air Force transport plane.

"Sims, I think we can stash the remaining vehicles out of the way on Abu Bakr Street around the rear of the main hotel," said Agent William Burch, in his heavy Southern drawl.

Burch hailed from Birmingham, Alabama. He had a terrific sense of humor and told off-color jokes. His accent contributed to their homespun imagery. Sims had handpicked Burch as his "TS" agent, shorthand for transportation agent, not because of his story-telling abilities, but because of the confidence he had in Burch's logistical decision making.

"The chosen presidential route is one of the more sensitive decisions in the advance process for many reasons," Sims told Walsh. The route had historical significance that Sims and Burch appreciated.

"The White House chief-of-staff will have to sign off on the president's motorcade along Highway 80, and I want to make sure we can live with the route once Walsh and her staff advise us as to their anticipated sites," Sims reminded Burch.

Burch, who heard Walsh's Highway of Death admonition, annotated his official map of the Highway 80 location with "Go fuck yourself." He didn't like her.

"Walsh, as far as the rest of the security plan, we will wait to see what the White House plans for visuals along the highway," added Sims.

"Yes, we will show the president proudly celebrating this historic Middle East success for which he can take credit without rubbing it in the faces of the fragile Iraqi government. We will display colorful banners in broad Arabic messaging along the route, highlighting the presidential visit. Some of the banners will feature the president and the king standing shoulder-to-shoulder, trumpeting the two countries' close relationship," Walsh displayed a slight smile.

Burch wanted to puke.

"Judging from the local news, every Kuwaiti citizen is overjoyed with the occasion of this presidential visit," Walsh said at the next countdown meeting.

"That may be true, " Sims offered, "but most Kuwaitis have no memory, or at best only a distant memory, of the Iraq invasion. The social dynamic here now is much different, especially in view of recent Middle East events. We in the Service need to account for some of the extremists who continue to reside here and, either support al Qaida, or are sympathetic."

"I don't need to be lectured about the Middle East. This is no different than having to deal with some of our own Tea Party zealots," Walsh replied, dismissive of Sims's brief.

"Understood." Sims speculated the event's high-profile publicity had the potential to work against his team's planning and execution. It could bring forward al Qaida sympathizers or Iraqi nationals bent on revenge who had the ability to blend into an otherwise friendly crowd. He didn't want to waste time and effort convincing her. "I will work around her naiveté," he thought.

After the meeting came to a close, the teams broke into their separate sections. Walsh spied the local U.S. ambassador, Velma Corey, who had arrived late, sitting in the back of the room and moved forward to her.

"Madam Ambassador, it is a pleasure to meet you and work with you to promote the president's message, which will hopefully present the USA in a most favorable light."

"Thank you. The embassy will support you as best we can."

"We are determined to highlight the president's contribution and competency in balancing the region," Walsh offered.

"Like I said, the embassy is here to support your efforts, not distort them. We will do our best to present the president, as you say, in the 'most favorable light.'"

Walsh, barely disguising her annoyance that the ambassador had arrived late to her countdown meeting, responded curtly. "I know. We expect nothing less. I look forward to receiving the help."

Ambassador Corey nodded affirmatively, "You will have it."

Walsh thanked her then turned and headed for the exit door.

Sims sat in the front row of the meeting room. As a seasoned lead advance agent, he had earned the proximity to the White House lead. He didn't like Walsh's brash presentation, but understood she held a stressful position. Walsh didn't intimidate him, but he felt her initial countdown meeting was not the place to stake his ground. He planned to keep his powder dry until he was ready, if necessary, to put her in her place.

Sims was not a newcomer to Kuwait. He had been an Army ranger in the early 1990s and had participated in Operation Desert Storm under General Norman Schwarzkopf. Returning to Kuwait was a thrill for him, but the stakes were clearly not the same. "Protecting the president may be a frenetic exercise, and it's obviously important," he told himself. "But it's nothing like riding the coattails of someone like the General into battle."

"She's way out of line if she thinks this is anything but a celebration of the military kicking some Iraqi ass," Sims whispered to his colleagues. Sims dismissed her comments as the flawed perspective of a young idealist trying her best to show her president in the best possible light.

"This is as much a U.S. military celebration as it was an opportunity for the president to pump up his chest. They earned the right to wave their hard-earned battle pennants. The current president had little to do with the success of Kuwait's continued independence. The military knows its proper place. If it means letting the president hype the event and take credit for the relative calm the military helped create in the region, then so be it. The military will still wave its pennants proudly," Sims continued.

"What does work in our favor is the support the Emir of Kuwait has invested in the twenty-fifth anniversary celebration," Sims briefed his team. "The Kuwaiti Emir sees the event as an occasion to bolster national pride and brag a little about how its own citizens assisted the coalition forces a generation ago." Sims wasn't surprised at the slight slant on the true history of the invasion.

Burch held up the local newspaper that displayed the Emir's quote. "Our brave and courageous Kuwaiti fighters contributed to repelling the invaders twenty-five years ago, and we consider the Americans' return to Kuwait a tangible sign of enduring friendship between the Kuwaiti and American governments."

"Well, it is better to have them with us than against us."

"We will meet the Kuwaiti security on the tarmac at Kuwait International Airport first thing tomorrow morning," Sims said. "There, we can outline our intentions and fill them in on what to expect when our assets arrive." The largest plane in the U.S. fleet was the reliable C5M, tasked with delivering presidential vehicles and helicopters to international sites for over five decades. Sims and his team expected SAM143 to arrive safely and on time.

The next morning Sims and his team arrived without fanfare at the burgeoning Kuwaiti International Airport. The airport had finalized plans for the construction of a new terminal, due to begin in 2012 with projected completion by 2016. It would be built to the south of the current terminal complex with new access routes from Seventh Ring Road to the south of the airport compound. It was designed as a three-pointed star, with each point extending six hundred meters from the star's center. Two airside hotels were planned to form part of the new building complex.

"The Secret Service will 'run' the intended presidential routes, using the same vehicles that are on board the C5M. Every nook and cranny along the highway will be inspected," Burch explained to his Kuwaiti counterpart.

Sims, seeing a puzzled facial expression, hastily explained to his Kuwaiti counterpart, Colonel Aalim Maudud, what Burch meant.

"Colonel, what Agent Burch means by the word 'run' is this. We use the same presidential vehicles during the practice runs that we do on the day of the visit to ensure the cars fit in all the places they will be used."

"Agent Sims, the Kuwaitis cannot suppress our excitement at the upcoming arrival of your Air Force plane," Colonel Maudud related. "We view the arrival of your car-plane as the first installment of U.S. logistical commitment toward our grand celebration." He appeared to be giddy with anticipation.

The arrival of the White House advance contingent fanned their excitement. "Agent Sims, this is the first visit by a sitting U.S. president to the kingdom since President Clinton's visit in 1994. To the Kuwaiti government, the fact the president is on his way to our homeland is a testament to our sovereignty."

"Hey Colonel, what does your name mean?" Sims asked with his trademark wide, toothy grin.

"Oh, Mr. Sims, you are a bit insolent, but I like it," said Maudud. My first name means *learned*. My family name means *friendly*."

"Well, Colonel, that certainly fits. Probably why I like you so much."

"The feeling, my friend, is mutual." Maudud reached out to shake his hand, grasping it firmly and placing his left hand around the back of Sims's extended hand. "We will work well together."

"I see your press corps is here and waiting patiently, Colonel."

"Yes, they hunger for any snippet of information. A sharp contrast from the Western media, I imagine. They will remain patient, and most obedient, to observe your country's unique arrival of armored cars and helicopters coming off the huge cargo carrier. Who else does this, my friend? Who else has the planes to move such equipment?" Maudud asked.

"The Russians do and sometimes the Swiss Guard for the Pope," Sims responded. "It's very expensive. The Russians do it to show they can. The Vatican does it because it's necessary to reduce risk to the Holy Father. They like having an armored Pope Mobile."

"I understand, my friend. The Secret Service is lucky to have such resources."

"Well, Colonel, the last time we had a protectee visit here in your country, al Qaida tried to blow up his motorcade. So this is a no-brainer for us. It means we don't take anything for granted based on our unfortunate experiences. You must remember former President Bush's visit here to Kuwait in the early nineties when al Qaida attempted to blow up his limo?"

"Of course, I do. We will ensure this doesn't happen to your president, Mr. Sims."

Back in Washington, Tom Eddie became aware of an emerging opportunity regarding the presidential visit to Kuwait. "Hey, Armey! I'm thinking of calling New York to see if Carly Strain is available to be one of the car-plane managers for the C5M. What do you think?"

"Sure. But what's the deal? Why Carly Strain?" Armey asked.

"Carly's husband is the Coast Guard military attaché to Kuwait. They've haven't been able to see each other for some months now." Eddie responded.

"Well, it's about time we made somebody happy. Let's do it."

"You know, I like it when we can help our guys out. She won't have much time on the ground with her husband, but it'll be a thrill for her anyway. I am sure for the both of them. I'll reach out and see what she thinks."

FOUR

A little over two hundred miles north of Washington, D.C., Madison Square Garden is the host to the most dynamic sporting, musical, and cultural events in the nation. Tonight the arena is host to the Ultimate Fighters Contest or UFC.

One of the two contenders is Maksim Valdimirovich Dostoevsky, known to his friends as Max. The handsome brawler with the blue eyes, blonde hair, and chiseled body describes his devotion to the sport for the commentators.

"I love fighting. When I'm in the cage, I feel free. I love the thrill of the combat, relying on my will to win."

His opponent is the more low-key of the two. When interviewed prior to the fight, Jose Riera looked at the commentators and offered only a wink, electing to remain silent.

Max thrills in the drama of violent physical competition, man against man, just like the father he never knew who came to the United States from the Soviet Union in 1990 to become a National Hockey League standout. Max inherited his father's intense focus. He is a physical and cerebral standout, in and out of the ring.

The UFC sponsors had promised the fight card would generate local interest, and it had not failed the city's expectations. It is late January and the days are growing longer, but nightfall still arrives early enough to mask the intoxicated arrival of thousands of fans who have come to witness the championship fight. Some fans have spent hours before the contest drinking in the bars surrounding Madison Square Garden. The promoters are salivating at the huge revenue this fight will command.

During the past twelve months, Max has participated in similar bouts around the country, building up a loyal fan base. His fans are excited by Max's speed, strength, and confidence. They recognize talent and perceived early on that he would likely land in the championship finals. But he isn't a household name—yet.

Commentators Ron McKenzie and Gary Maher were eager to begin announcing the fight. They've done their research, and they are ready to describe the live fight scenes, using technically correct terms while applying an enthusiastic narrative without catering to one fighter over the other.

"Max is the total package," McKenzie blurts into his UFC microphone. "He has studied a variety of fighting attack approaches and woven from them the most effective elements. His awe-inspiring approaches have sent intimidating messages to the most talented in the UFC fighter pool."

The UFC's first 2016 match-up features the son of a Russian émigré against the son of a Brazilian immigrant from Belo Horizonte.

"Both are young, but not physically equal. Max, at 6' 2", overshadows the young Brazilian by four inches and has larger and longer limbs," McKenzie continued.

"You are 100 percent right on that, Ron," offered Maher, setting up the color commentary. "Max loves the lateral drop combined with his efficient Greco Roman throws to get his opponent to the mat. And he's got five rounds in which to get it done. Five minutes in each round. Max is in tremendous physical shape, Ron. He's prepared for twenty-five minutes of high altitude combat."

"Gary, this kid has gone undefeated in his quest toward this championship; he's never tasted defeat in the UFC. But his younger years were a different story. He grew up in the tough Brighton Beach section of New York. His dominant skill came from not just hard work but by being knocked on his ass more than once while growing up. He learned to be a fighting machine."

"That's correct, Ron, and in contrast to that we have his opponent who has had his share of professional losses, but has succeeded through sheer determination to get to this final bout. Apparently, he has good study habits. He doesn't have to be taught twice. His defeats were learning lessons."

The announcers quieted as the combatants entered the octagon separately; blaring music and screaming fans cheering each on, some reaching out the to touch each fighter as he and his entourage pass through a gauntlet of humanity. The arena is filled to capacity. The earlier fight cards have stimulated the crowd to near hysteria. Neither Max nor Riera seem aware of the crowd's presence. They are focused on the looming battle. Finally, face-to-face, Riera eyes his opponent, trying to size up his strengths and weaknesses.

"Gary, the Russian never makes eye contact with his opponent. I hope Riera doesn't take that as a sign of weakness or a lack of confidence."

"But Max has to be careful too, Ron. Riera may be eyeing him, but he's also beginning to gauge his initial fighting range. He'll try to control that distance and execute takedowns, putting Max on his back quickly. Riera will try and control the pace and space of the fight, but he will soon find that Max is unpredictable," continued Maher. "He's going to use low kicks, high kicks, sidekicks, and most effectively, Ron, he will use his quick elbows. He has the quickest and most effective elbows in the octagon."

Riera starts round one in a boxing-centered attack. Max immediately recognizes the position and confidently counters with his signature leg kicks. The Brazilian has fluid movement, but soon runs into trouble while attempting to counter the high leg kicks.

"Max is famously swift in his kicks. He is instinctive. He knows how to analyze Jose's body language and remain outside of harm's way," says Maher. "But the kicks are frustrating his attempts to close in on him."

Max lands a devastating front kick to Riera's right knee, who retreats, limping in pain.

"So many elbows, spinning kicks. It's is hard for Riera to know what's coming next."

McKenzie responds, "Riera can't stand on the perimeter of the octagon. He needs to get inside the center of the ring if he's going to fight effectively. After that knee kick, he looks worried."

Maher jumps in, "Worried? No, he appears to be in a state of fear and now unable to strike back. His fear may prevent him from finding a way to strike back. These kicks will keep him trading jabs and kicks with Max, who's just faster, stronger, and has more reach."

"Riera can't win with animated head moves," McKenzie shouts over the roar of the crowd. "He needs to take some dramatic action to turn the tide of failure."

Suddenly, Riera attempts to pull guard on Max.

"I'm afraid that comes too late in the round to be counted," Maher added.

Riera survived the first round, but barely. As he sits in his corner the cut above his left eye is attended to by the fighter's corner cut man. The wound threatened to close the eye and end the fight. His breathing became labored, and his eyes no longer focus on Max's corner. The cut man laces the swelling wound to relieve pressure, and then pinches it to stop the blood flow, finally applying Vaseline as a stopgap measure, giving him another five minutes to fight.

"You got to find a way to get within range! You got to throw leg kicks!" As the bell rings and Riera returns to the mat, his manager shouts encouragement and instructions before the fighter resumes the battle with his opponent.

Riera thrusts forward toward Max, throwing an effective lead left hook. It connects, sending Max into a stunned retreat. He senses that a stumble on Max's part as a result of a single punch would change the fight in his favor. He begins to mix it up, no longer content to remain one-dimensional in his attack. As the taller fighter retreats to recover, Riera lands a punch that appears to connect. Max effectively moves out of immediate harm's way and shakes off the stun.

"The fight could end this quick, Ron," observes Maher. "Riera looks to have some momentum. He's come out this round much more aggressive, much less tentative."

"His confidence is truly reborn as Max drifts off balance toward his corner. He better make his move and get within range if wants to take the fight to the ground."

"There he goes!" In an instant, he shoots for Max's left leg. Entering Max's personal zone is a dangerous move, but he decides to go in full throttle, too late to stifle his momentum. Max sees it coming. He surges forward with a devastating flying knee to Jose's chest. He drops to the mat with Max closely following.

"What a blow, a stunningly effective knee to the chest," McKenzie exclaims. "He's now applying a neck lock, his right arm moving underneath as he sneaks his left arm in position as well. Look, Gary! He's thrusting his hips forward to flatten him up. He's got the choke. He's got the choke!" Max leaves his opponent no choice but to tap out.

"There it is, Gary." The experienced octagon referee moves in quickly once he recognizes the universal tap for relief and removes Max from his conquest. And not a second too soon. Max's noose was applied to deprive oxygen to the brain and render his opponent physically impotent. It was acute and complete.

"What a spectacular, flawless performance," Maher gushes to McKenzie, wrapping up the fight commentary. "Our viewers just witnessed an efficient, powerful fighting machine. He's one of the smartest, quickest fighters I have ever seen, bar none.

"He's going to be a force to reckon with for a long time to come. This kid's skills are already at the master level, and he's only just begun his career."

"Absolutely Gary, he is going to have a lot of pressure on him going forward, especially considering the toll it takes on a person to handle all the promotion. I hope he has someone who has his back."

FIVE

Billy Sims was alerted by the knock on his hotel room door. His room, by request, while not a suite, was larger than the standard hotel room, one of the few exceptions headquarters would approve. He needed to accommodate the many agent meetings he expected to host over the next ten days. It is during these meetings the advance process comes into focus and the security design is tailored to meet the risk. Occasionally, something happens which gives the lead advance agent "heartburn," distracting the agent from the important planning duties. Tonight, it happened.

Mary Walsh knocked anxiously on his hotel room door. "Sims, I need to talk with you privately and thought your room to be the best place for that." Sims observed her demeanor to be timid. He sensed some distress.

"Well sure. Let's go to the lounge and grab a beer. I could use one myself. It's been a long, hot day."

"Sims, I'd prefer if we could just talk in your room. This is a sensitive issue, and I can't take the chance that someone might overhear us."

Sims looked into her eyes and nodded affirmatively. He thought, "I hope this is all it is." He had no desire to romance the staff lead. His bride back in Boca Raton is more than enough for him, "one life, one wife."

"Come in. I'm sorry my room looks like a storm hit it." Sims moved some of his documents out of the way to free up a chair. He had ESPN playing on the room's flat screen television set, showing highlights of the latest NCAA men's basketball results. "March Madness" was a month away and it was his favorite time of the year. He grabbed the remote control and lowered the sound. He sensed his room was about to become a confessional.

"Sims, one of my female staff was found in a compromising situation by the Kuwaiti moral police."

Copulating on a public beach may be a disorderly conduct offense in the United States, but in Kuwait such salacious behavior can land the carnal couple in prison, without the benefit of a trial.

"Arlene Baker is one of my best advance operatives. I received word from the U.S. Embassy that she is now sitting in jail somewhere in Kuwait City. Apparently, she met some guy downstairs in the lounge, had a few drinks, and went for a walk. Other people on my staff said the guy was good looking with what sounded like a Russian accent. Baker likes anything Russian. I don't have a fucking clue what to do and the embassy doesn't sound like they are sufficiently compassionate. In fact, they think she got herself in trouble for being stupid. I told the embassy to stand by until I've had a chance to talk with my people and to keep it fucking quiet. Sims, I desperately need your help."

Sims surmised Walsh's major concern had little to do with Baker's actual dilemma, but rather had everything to do with detracting from the message crafted for the president's visit. Walsh moved closer to Sims and placed her head on his chest, whimpering as an act of submission. Sims gently pushed her back.

"I'll take care of this. But once we locate Baker, you need to put her on a plane back to the States. That is the only way the Kuwaitis will be comfortable adjudicating the situation."

"I will do that gladly. I can't even begin to express my gratitude. It has affected my ability to concentrate. What can I do for you? I am available to do anything you want."

Sims was growing uncomfortable. The last thing he wanted was to be seduced by her faux vulnerability. He was also concerned about the guy Baker had casually met, and then screwed, who had a Russian accent. Sims made a mental note to advise Commander Will Strain, the U.S. military attaché in Kuwait, of this fact when he briefed him on repatriating the young lady back to the States.

"If I am going to be of any value to you, I need to start getting my contacts moving immediately to help get her released. Time is of the essence. I need to jump on this right now, so if you can let me know where I can contact you in about an hour that would be helpful."

Sims began to nudge her toward his room door. She turned toward him and gave him a hug and left the room.

Sims "owned" the staff lead. There would be no further obstacles to his security plan if he pulled it off. He was counting on his relationship with Colonel Maudud to execute a plan to get Arlene Baker out of the country.

"Ah, my dear friend, it appears the American female got a bit horny in an inappropriate location. Not good for her. I will get her back to your hotel in the next hour."

"Colonel, you are the man. I will never be able to thank you enough."

"Yes you can. Get me a West Wing tour of the White House," he laughed.

Sims flashed a grin and said, "Colonel, that is a done deal. One last thing, is there any way we can interview this Russian guy who was found with the young lady?"

"I am sure he was just trying to get, as you American's say, lucky. His mistake was not taking her back to her room. This is a man's world, young Mr. Sims; the Russian got a freebie. Your young lady got a ride home. And, thank you, my dear friend, for making sure she leaves Kuwait before her obnoxious behavior becomes known."

"Can you tell me more about this Russian?" Sims asked.

"The Russian managed to talk his way out of the problem. You may want to debrief the young lady before she flies back to the United States. It is my guess he is a member of the Bratva, the Russian brotherhood, or as you may say, the mob. The Russians keep their eyes and ears everywhere. The young man's involvement is a coincidence, I suspect, which has nothing to do with the president's visit."

"Or, does it?" Sims thought.

SIX

What Carly James heard about the Secret Service intrigued her, and she applied for the job. At her panel agent applicant interview, three agency veterans asked her a series of questions to determine her interest in being an agent. More importantly, they sought to gauge the likelihood of her acceptance within their ranks—a likeability test delivered by a panel of her future peers. If the panel was not impressed, the process was over.

"Who in your life has meant the most to you and why?"

"My mother meant the most to me," Carly James said with a warm smile. "She always, always had time for everyone else. She never had a bad thing to say about anyone, and she never complained about what life threw at her. Not even losing her husband, my father, to ALS—more commonly known as Lou Gehrig's disease. My mom accepted the illness, tended to my father with love and respect, and gave his dying the dignity the disease tried to take away."

The admission surprised the senior agents, who were impressed with the genuineness of her answer. Candidates were often too nervous to come close to such a personal response. She connected on that one. The final question went to the heart of their interest.

"If you found yourself with two other agents in the evidence vault and observed one of them stealing cash, how would you handle it?"

The senior agents knew the question to be loaded with complexity. Some applicants try and read what they think the panel wants to hear. That practice is fraught with jeopardy. A spontaneous response can be too raw. Take too long to answer, not good, shows evasion. It is a question that tests the applicant's thinking and honesty. This question has gotten many an applicant in trouble and quickly passed over for a "better qualified applicant." End of story, no further discussion. There were as many right answers as there were wrong answers.

James didn't blink. "If the agent has the balls to steal the cash from an evidence vault and has the balls to do it in front of two other agents, then he better have the balls, assuming it's a guy, to resign before I kick the shit out of him for putting us in that position."

The interviewing agents sat in silent awe. Forget that she was attractive; these journeymen interviewed a lot of attractive applicants. James, they immediately became aware, was as genuine a prospect as they had ever encountered, and they already knew she was a high-caliber applicant.

"Bravo to you," said one of the three interviewers, an unusually rare utterance of acceptance from the panel. James did not receive any additional resistance during the remainder of the applicant process.

Carly James was tall, almost six feet, and not an ounce of butter on her. She wore her dark brown hair in a ponytail, except when she went out on the town and then she let it flow freely. It was said she could wear a low cut dress better than a Wall Street broker's wife. She could cause a stir when she wanted to, sometimes even when she didn't.

She had been an attorney in a previous career, but had grown bored with personal injury cases, working the municipal and county circuits. She was eager to find something more adventurous than her legal career.

She was encouraged to apply during a serendipitous meeting with a plaintiff's son, himself a Secret Service agent. James had always been more than just an academic standout. She played lacrosse at Villanova University and was considered a top player. Some of her teammates said she could have played for the men's team. She was that fast, that powerful, and that determined. She knew how to score goals. Despite her athleticism and aggressiveness on the field, James was very much in touch with her femininity. There was no better looking homecoming queen.

Her college paper, the *Villanovan*, ran a story on her, quoting her old mentor, Coach Stuart Kiehne, "Carly put more lacrosse opponents on their butts than they did to her. She had her share of bruises, but she never complained. I really admire her composure, strength, and courage."

"Mom? I just received a call from the Secret Service. They offered me a position as a special agent. I'm going to take it. I love you, Mom." James left the message on her mom's voicemail. She looked forward to a new chapter in her life.

James cut her teeth as a new agent in the Service's Newark field office. She excelled at credit card fraud investigations, particularly West African fraud, that is, financial crimes committed by multi-national groups from Nigeria, Cameroon, and Benin. She knew them to be the most intelligent fraudsters the agency encountered. They were seldom, if ever, violent. But they were wily and given the chance, might run. Unfortunately for them, James could outrun and out-think most of them.

She loved the adrenaline of executing warrants and relished the moment when the fraudster knew she outsmarted, outguessed, and outmaneuvered him. Her success as a field investigator proved ephemeral. Headquarters loves winners; her time to transition to a protection assignment had arrived. As a young agent she had hungered for the opportunity to protect the president close up. But after five years in the field with so much investigative success, she had second thoughts about leaving for a protection assignment.

"Too bad," puffed her field office supervisor, George Hamilton. The no-nonsense Newark field office agent in charge hardly looked at her. "PPD doesn't want slugs on the detail, Agent James. Fortunately for you, your reputation precedes you. Headquarters called; you're going to the White House Detail." The White House Detail was Hamilton's alternate reference to the prestigious Presidential Protective Division.

Hamilton had given the pep talk countless times, but it was a much different talk than the one he was accustomed to giving to agents who were picked for the less desired family details. In these circumstances, he tried his best to make the smaller detail assignment at least sound palatable, but his efforts generally fell short. Younger agents tended to go for the smaller detail because it fit their family needs or perhaps they wanted to attend graduate school, but it would never match the experience of the White House Detail.

"You dress well and you work hard. You shouldn't be surprised you got picked up for the 'Show' assignment."

Hamilton's Secret Service career spanned a generation. He was "old school." Anyone who pissed off the boss, or didn't perform field office chores to his satisfaction, went into career oblivion. This was how Hamilton managed his agents. Privately, he was proud to send his agents to the president's detail. He took similar enjoyment in sending those he had no use for to the boredom of a small detail. In the world of the Secret

Service, the Special Agent in Charge, or "SAIC," controlled an agent's personal life.

"You fuck with me, you're fucked" was an expression every agent in the office was familiar.

"Look James, I expect you to do well in Washington. The Secret Service has changed in the generation I've been here. You 'girls' are now part of the team, I get it."

James nodded respectfully, recognizing Hamilton's clumsy admission was as close as it would be to him appreciating females working successfully in the Secret Service.

"The way I see it if we get enough females like you as the new standard, the Service will have a good chance at remaining an elite organization. I like your spunk, your drive, and the way you carry yourself." Hamilton stopped short with his remaining thought about her nice ass, something he would have blurted out with ease in a prior generation.

During 2012, as she began her presidential assignment, standing tall, protecting the most powerful man on earth, James allowed herself to privately gloat. Standing along the white-walled colonnade between the West Wing and the White House residence, she glanced past the Rose Garden toward the Ellipse and savored a brief private thought, which she shared later with her family.

When she called home, James boasted how special it was to work on the detail. "How lucky am I to work in such a historic setting? Mom, the president of the United States walks by me, nods hello, and continues on to the Oval Office, and in a way that makes me feel like I belong here. He makes me feel that what I do here, standing my post, is important." A slight smile graced her face.

Over the next two years James moved up the detail experience ladder, and by her third year, she was assigned the most coveted role on the detail, lead advance agent.

It was during one of her advances she met Commander Will Strain. He was assigned to the Coast Guard Headquarters' Intelligence Directorate, a tour designed to prepare him for the elite assignment in Kuwait. His deployment began in mid-2015 and was to last for two years, operating out of the United States Embassy in Kuwait City.

Meeting Carly James didn't change his appetite for an extraterritorial assignment, but it changed his stance against marriage. It was love at first sight for both of them. After a short courtship, James wore an engagement ring, followed as swiftly by a small, private wedding ceremony. There would be time for a reception later—too much career work to get done first.

"We talk all the time on the Internet," the now Carly Strain told her Mom. "But when he's away from the embassy, there are periods when he's out-of-pocket in Kuwait and we don't get to talk. That's when I miss him the most. I'll be moving from the detail soon to accept a promotion in the New York field office. What do you think of that?"

Her mom answered, "Honey, you have a gift for making the decisions that are best for you. If you are comfortable with the idea then I say go for it."

"It is time to move on, Mom. With Will's deployment to Kuwait City, the new assignment will keep me focused on something new. And it comes with a promotion. I will be taking over the office's Cyber Crimes Squad." What she didn't tell her mom was she needed the new assignment to keep her loneliness at bay.

"Honey, that's terrific and you will be closer to family. I know it is hard on you and Will but it will pay dividends," her mom quipped.

But she missed her husband. She didn't like being lonely. "I think the transfer will help a lot, Mom. I will give you more details soon. Love you!"

SEVEN

The U.S. Government warned: "Internet crime has increased significantly within the last several years. Starting in the late 1990s, and increasingly over the last few years, this criminal element has used malicious software, or malware, to penetrate financial and government institutions, extract data, and illicitly traffic in stolen financial and identity information."

Newly crowned UFC champion Max and his friend Shorty left Madison Square Garden in Shorty's blue 2012 Honda Accord soon after the fight ended and Max had taken a hot shower. The champ moved without an entourage to the car.

Max was a foot taller than his buddy, but what he may have lacked in size he possessed in spirit. Max adored that in him. Shorty was the smaller kid everyone knew in high school who got bullied for just being the little man. Over time, that turned out to be a mistake. Shorty picked off the bullies one by one. Mostly, he resorted to attacking them from their blind side. The bully never saw it coming, but soon learned who was responsible. The bully always lay below Shorty standing over him. Each conquest strengthened his confidence.

"You ever come near me again, I will cut off your fucking balls." He didn't know for sure if he meant it, but it sounded good each time he said it, and they got the message. Those he knocked unconscious, he just urinated on after the attack. Others he just kicked in the balls for effect. Not one of them ever retaliated.

"Shorty, maybe you should have taken a shower, too."

"Leave me be, Max, or I'll kick your ass," Shorty laughed. He couldn't suppress his giddiness. His best friend was now the UFC Champion.

Max opened the passenger door and adjusted the seat to its full recline position before sitting. He looked awkward sitting adjacent to Shorty in the car—a stark contrast between the body types of the two friends. Shorty sat as close to the steering wheel as he could. His legs could not reach the accelerator and brakes unless he closed the distance. This was a visual Max could not resist exploiting.

"Good thing this ain't a stick shift, Shorty, or you'd be fucked," Max teased his friend.

With the passenger seat fully reclined, Shorty had to turn his head sharply to the right to look Max in the eye in order to make a talking point. By then, Max had slipped into private thought. Riera had been a formidable competitor and left him to deal with physical aches and pains he had never felt in prior matches. Though he was hurting, Max didn't show it. Shorty expected that. "He never complains," he thought.

"Hey Shorty let's stop off at the 7-11 and get a 12-pack of Amstel Light and celebrate." The store was not far from Max's Brighton Beach apartment. "And Shorty, while you're in there buy some chips, too. Tanya never went shopping. I have nothing in the kitchen."

Max's girlfriend, Tanya, was a Ukrainian stunner: tall, curvaceous—a fat-free dancer who knew how to charm her customers with a wink and a naughty grin. She was a lap dance professional, peeling the twenties from her lonely conquests with ease. She always left them never wanting for anything less than a change of pants.

Max didn't like the fact that she danced, but he did like her devotion to him—he always got the last dance when he wanted it. He also liked the space he had while she was out of the house much of the day and late into the night. It gave him time to work his keystrokes on the computer.

Tanya showed off her Victoria's Secret body at Stilettos, a gentlemen's club in Carlstadt, New Jersey, while Max honed his grappling skills at the gym or stayed home working his computer keyboard magic. His formidable computer skills nurtured an international criminal enterprise, communicating globally and anonymously, amassing hundreds of thousands of credit card numbers.

Shorty, or "КОРОТЫШКА" in Russian, was born Vitaly Rubin, the son of a Russian émigré whose father knew Max's dad back in

Moscow and then in the United States when his dad was an NHL player. Max always had the sense that Mr. Rubin, Shorty's dad, wanted to share with him something about Max's father, but held back. Something haunted him.

Shorty's temper was predictable and Max had to pull him out of more than one skirmish when he got the urge to defend his small frame. "He ignites way too easily," Max once told Tanya. "I've told him he has to be more disciplined or else he will meet his match one day and get hurt."

"Shorty, you're going get your little ass whipped if you continue to blow your cool," Max reminded him. "It's all about control, brother, control. I know it sounds cowardly, but even I need to know when to walk away."

Shorty's computer skills were non-existent, but to Max it didn't matter. Shorty was a loyal friend, and he knew never to breach the confidentiality Max shared with him. Though he rarely understood all Max's cyber drabble, he knew better than to talk about it.

"We are just days from success, Shorty. Soon we will have more money than we'll know what to do with." Shorty saw that Max, who intentionally avoided looking directly at him, wore a devilish grin.

"Will we have to leave the country?" Shorty asked.

"Now Shorty, if we play this right, we will be known as 'The Boys of Brighton Beach' and will never have to work another day in our lives. We will have homes, boats, cars, wives that adore us, and more money than we can spend. Trust me, I will take you there." Max loved him as a brother. "Shorty, do you know when most hackers get in trouble with the cops?"

"Haven't a fuckin clue."

"It's in their sloppiness and arrogance in attacking the big banks and then embarrassing the banks' security groups by bragging about it in online chat rooms," said Max.

"I don't even know how to get into a chat room."

"You don't have to. You and I target banks and their computer systems without them even knowing they've been compromised. We take their money out of their accounts, place the proceeds in dormant accounts, and set up the finale for transferring the money to our friends in Russia. We don't need to get greedy. We only need to get rich. We go slow, steady, always building our shadow network in a way that allows us to pull the plug. The money will electronically flow to us when and where we want it. You and I determine which banks to fuck with, to maximize our ability to extract data and store the proceeds of our efforts elsewhere. It's not personal. It's business. We don't brag about it and piss them off."

Max liked talking to Shorty about his ideas. Max had a lot of patience with his best buddy. He knew Shorty would not appreciate what he meant when he described the "exfiltration" of funds, the process of extracting electronic data to illegally withdraw other people's money. He knew his little best friend didn't understand what he was talking about and that gave Max comfort; he knew Shorty couldn't compromise him.

"Why do you waste your time explaining all this to me?"

"Because you are a good listener and won't repeat what you hear."

"That's because I'm too dumb."

"Shorty, you're not dumb. You can read people better than most and you have the heart of a lion."

Max, global hacker extraordinaire enjoyed gaining covert entry into network systems, and not for its own sake, but to make money. The endgame for cyber criminals, according to law enforcement sources, is to take full control of a computer system and use it to help carry out online thefts and scams. True for most hackers, but for Max the cyber experience was much more. His "operations" into secure systems—credit card processors, online banks, e-businesses, and the less lucrative but very seductive, government systems—had become folk legend.

For Max, the primary hacking community soon became boorish. He needed to progress to something greater, something that would satisfy his quest for a big payday on a level no one else had ever achieved. He also had a need to run solo and make an impression on the world.

"The more financially rewarding an operation, the better," he told Shorty.

Max used each keystroke to push forward his goal of one day being wealthy. This was not an arrogant goal. It was rooted in a strong confidence forged by a superior mental and physical agility. He studiously worked to develop and nurture a global syndicate that engaged in a systematic downloading of compromised credit card data. His dedicated online site, or carding portals, provided him with the forum he needed to post his compromised "goods and services."

The Russian hacking sites were known to be the best; the most sophisticated hackers relied on them. These were portal sites or carding sites that openly advertised their services. Max knew them all. Displayed on these portals were thousands of openly posted announcements that offered to buy or sell stolen credit card data, or credit card tracking data for white plastic cards used simply to exploit the stolen data still resident on a virile credit card.

"I hate these asshole hackers who screw with the United States. It's one thing to go after the money but some of these Islam groups use the Internet as a tool to attack the United States. They suck." Max told Shorty. "And they make my life more difficult with the Feds."

The cops knew about "anonymizing technologies" that allow hackers like Max to be virtual or "one step ahead" of them—cyber jiu jitsu. Max knew this game well.

But Max was not yet on their radar. Unlike other hackers who had made the mistake of operating openly on the Internet, providing law enforcement an opportunity to exert "official scrutiny," Max managed to evade their interest.

"There has to be something bigger," he thought. "This is mere chump change." The carding site soon became banal for Max. He dreamed of a greater opportunity to make money exponentially. He wanted a greater revenue stream from his next cyber triumph; the one he had mentioned to Shorty after the fight. He began to mentally develop what it would take to write the needed script that, once injected into a thousand banking systems, would translate into big cash.

As Max sat at home in front of his keypad, he heard Shorty in the kitchen of the Brighton Beach apartment.

"Shorty, grab me a beer out of the fridge. I think we need to dream a bit more."

Shorty brought two beers, handed one to Max, and then bent down to pet Torre, the fighter's pit bull.

Max had an enormous advantage his competition lacked. His sites supported both the English and Russian languages.

"Shorty, my portal site is the premier choice for the former Soviet Union states, particularly Romania, Kazakhstan, and the Ukraine. You know why? Because I offer my stolen data in both languages familiar to the fraudsters in these countries." Max exclaimed. If Max had a problem with someone's association with his global cyber enterprise, the unlucky individual was sanctioned, and, if necessary, attacked through his brand of cyber martial artistry, a merciless denial of service attack that would shut down a victim's site completely. The Champ brought the same level of intensity to his cyber defense as he did his fights. Other international carding portal administrators knew better than to inflict any strife upon Max or his site, at least not intentionally. By reputation, other successful hackers knew Max as someone who, if he caught up with you, would dispense a brutal cyber asskicking.

"If I want to fuck with them, I anonymously report them to the federal authorities of the country in which the hackers operated. If they operate outside the code of acceptable conduct, then they face my wrath," preached Max. He used United States and Russian Federation law enforcement authorities to frustrate his competitors. He was an anonymous snitch.

"You're kind of a bitch," said Shorty.

"Shorty, you know what bothers me more than these idiots trying to compromise my hard-drive?"

"Nope."

"Remember what I just said? These bastards use cyber to harass the United States. This is my fucking home." He didn't brag about his retaliation to anyone but Shorty, but he routinely sent his custom malware to international sites to disrupt critical infrastructure in countries that hated the United States.

"Fuck'em." He had a particular distaste for Al Qaida's use of the Internet, particularly when it used denial of service against a U.S. interest.

"They're pieces of shit, Shorty. Cowards."

When Max retaliated, the credit for the attack often went to a non-complicit Western government alleged to be screwing with an Iranian or Syrian electrical or nuclear grid. Max had no desire to be hailed as a patriot for fucking with the enemy of the United States.

"Let Israel, Denmark, or the United States have the credit," he thought.

On the criminal side of the house, it was different. It was easy to frustrate the United States and Russian investigators. He knew they did not possess the necessary cyber investigative skills to keep up.

He was cautious, at least sufficiently enough to keep ahead of the threat of capture, avoiding law enforcement's suppression grip. Like any good administrator, he kept his web pages separate from other cyber activities around the world; routinely deleted his log files to avoid detection; and, used proxy servers whose owners never became aware of his co-located presence. He used anonymous servers to guarantee the botnets he used would never be identified and direct attention back to him. The bots containing his malicious software were encrypted and the corporate systems he targeted were fooled. Their security systems' intrusion detection monitors were rendered meaningless. His signature cyber-strike at targeted banking systems allowed him to execute an overpowering code, giving him control and local privileges of the system he penetrated. He thought like a fighter, instinctively seeking to disrupt the adversary's command and control function, his brain.

"Botnets are customized to deliver my unique malware, hacker code. I send it out to attack a computer system on the low side and high side. Kind of like with boxing. I make sure my code enters a bank's system by injecting multiple codes, much like the millions of sperm that seek to fertilize an egg. All it takes is one sperm to be successful. For the rest, it's no more than a blow job." Explaining to Shorty the nuances of his cyber activities could sometimes be frustrating, but he did it with patience, and simple metaphors were helpful.

Shorty just stared at his best friend, not willing to betray his lack of understanding. He rarely asked Max for clarification.

"I operate in secret cylinders of excellence," he explained. "That's how I stay ahead of the American posse."

Shorty thought Max talked in riddles. "What the fuck does a cylinder of excellence mean?" he thought.

Just then, Torre alerted to the sound of fumbling keys at the front door. Max bent over and stroked her neck fur. "It's okay Torre, it's Mama," he said, as Tanya walked into the apartment. Shorty didn't like Tanya. He took her arrival home as his signal to leave.

"I gotta go," he said to Max. "I'll see you at the gym in the morning."

As Shorty grabbed his leather coat from a living room chair, he moved toward the front door, never making eye contact with the "bitch." She could not have cared less. Seemingly unaware he was even in the room, she went right for Torre to give her an affectionate rub. Torre was the only commonality between them.

Shorty thought one day the stripper would bring Max trouble. He wasn't sure exactly why, and never mentioned it to Max, but he remained suspicious of her.

Her drug use also pissed him off. He and Max didn't talk about it, but he was sure his buddy knew. "Max doesn't need a girlfriend who is always high. I wish she would just go away."

EIGHT

In cherished, pensive moments, Max thought of the father he never knew, Ivan Valdimirovich Dostoevsky, the young hockey protégé from the former Soviet Union. As a child he had watched videos of his dad playing professionally at the famous Madison Square Garden. There were the old VCR video highlights his mother had saved and put away for him to view as he grew older. But once he had memorized the dull grey action he no longer required them to recreate his father's greatness. In daydreams he added the color that made his dad special in his memory.

"Your dad was an honorable man," his maternal grandfather told him. "From what I have been told from his family in Russia your dad had an amazing work ethic. An ethic that made him a national Russian hockey star. His destiny realized when his hard work was awarded with a larger prize. He became a National Hockey League player."

Max yearned to learn more about his father and his legendary work ethic. He wanted to find out everything he could about his father's quest to be the best hockey player possible.

In truth, the son's desires were no different from those of the father. Max worked beyond exhaustion to hone his skills as a martial artist. He worked equally hard to attain his status as a global cyber boy wonder.

"Someday when you grow up to be a young man I will have told you enough about your father and his legacy to help you keep his memory alive in thoughts." Max deeply appreciated his grandfather's time.

The grandfather continued. "From what I have been told, your dad proved he could absorb the grind of endless training sessions and internalize the experience. He became skillful, fearless in his game, and determined in his quest for greatness. He reveled in the prospect of one day being not just among the Soviet Union's best, but being the best. Himself alone. His family in Russia was so proud of him and he did not forsake them. He sent monthly monies to them. You know something, young Max? You appear to have inherited your father's genetic superiority, his imposing height, broad shoulders, and a substantial chin."

What the grandfather didn't speak of was Ivan's dark past. Like many on the older Russian teams, players made extra cash performing "mule'" assignments for the local mob syndicate, the Bratva. Ivan knew the members casually. The Bratva paid the players enough to keep them wanting to do it, and it didn't use up all that much of their training time.

Running numbers would be the closest Mafia activity Americans would recognize. It gave him and his mates some spending rubles, enough to pay for some equipment and some vodka on occasion.

The Bratva took special interest in the team from a distance. It had its eye on several teams in the area, waiting for one to emerge as superior. When one did, the Bratva would swoop in to take advantage of the team and make some easy money.

As Ivan's team morphed into a legitimate contender in the Moscow suburb, the Bratva reminded them of their previous payroll association. They expected the players to remain loyal, and from time to time, throw a game. That's how the mob made money, a lot of money. Ivan never liked this obligation and respectfully resisted. He hoped his teammates did too, but he
wasn't sure.

Once, after a win, they went out on the town and consumed more vodka than they were entitled to drink. Ivan didn't remember much of the night, but the following morning he bore a rose tattoo on the left side of his chest, a Bratva symbol. He didn't remember it hurting, but it looked like it had bled.

Only the Bratva wear this particular tattoo design. He knew he had crossed the line. The mob would not take kindly to him wearing it without having earned it. Ivan did not flaunt it. Any attention the tattoo promoted would not bode well for someone not affiliated with to the mob.

"You can't have it both ways with them. You will offend them and then you will always be in danger of getting hurt by them," his family told him.

Ivan paid little attention to geopolitical issues, but he was a nationalist. He remembered the humiliation of the 1980 Soviet Union hockey team's loss to the United States in the semi-final game of the Winter Olympics. The superior Russian team wasn't supposed to lose hockey games, particularly to the neophyte U.S. team. But they did.

While the loss stung his teammates, it especially hurt Ivan. He didn't harbor a lingering hatred toward the United States; he just hated losing with greater intensity. His fortunes, ironically, would change as a result of the Soviet Union breakup. Russian hockey players were now able to cut their own deals to play internationally. Ivan's prowess caught the eye and the interest of the New York Rangers. He accepted an offer from the Rangers and began planning to migrate to the United States. He and his family were ecstatic. The Bratva was studiously aware.

When Ivan arrived at JFK airport in May 1989, he was hopeful he could earn the respect of the New York fans. He had no idea how thin the New York media's patience could be.

His Russian buddy told him, "In New York you have only two options—you either perform well, or you don't, and are disparaged daily in the local newspapers."

Ivan's second goal was to gel quickly with his Ranger teammates. He naively thought his athletic prowess would satisfy both concerns.

Ivan had previously only flown on small planes, traveling short distances around the Moscow area to play other teams, so his journey on board Aeroflot was his first international flight. The Aeroflot aircraft seemed spacious by comparison.

He stayed awake the entire flight, too excited to sleep. His excitement increased as the plane's wheels met the tarmac. Ivan mimicked the other passengers as he looked about the cabin and observed everyone unfastening their seatbelts, not waiting for the aircraft to come to rest alongside the ramp door. Once the plane stopped at the gate he stood up and grabbed his Moniker leather bag from the overhead storage area. The bag was a farewell gift from his Russian teammates.

He had checked his oversized bag prior to departure, but the leather bag contained every important personal treasure he possessed. His mother had carefully wrapped family photographs in plastic. The gold necklace he liked wearing with his open-collared paisley shirts was placed in a small box and wrapped with a rubber band. It lay next to the Walkman cassette player he used when he wanted to avoid socializing with his coaches and fellow players as he grew increasingly bored with them.

He collected his bag, got through immigration and customs without issue, and cautiously made his way outside the international arrivals area to the exit, where he had been instructed a Ranger representative, Gerry Veit, would meet him.

Ivan had also been told Mr. Veit knew limited Russian, enough to get him in a taxi and on his way to his new apartment. Ivan saw the sign held by Veit, welcoming him to the United States with his name listed prominently below.

Veit greeted him in broken Russian, but it was enough to make Ivan feel comfortable, and steered him to a dedicated limo. The limo driver took Ivan's large bag and placed it in the trunk. He directed Ivan to the right rear seat. Veit shook his hand and told him the team would be in contact with him soon, but he should rest and get situated in his new apartment in the meantime. Ivan smiled broadly, any attempt to mask his enthusiasm lost.

"Wow," said Ivan, taking in his surroundings. "This is great. Much better than a taxi. And it has leather seats." He looked out the window and smiled. "Welcome to America," he chuckled to himself.

The limo driver looked to his left and then sped onto the exit roadway to escape from JFK and onto the Van Wyck Parkway for a short stretch before getting onto the Belt Parkway where the limo would find itself in bumper-to-bumper traffic. It would be a slow ride to Brighton Beach.

"Welcome to the United States, and Happy Saint Patrick's Day," said the limo driver with a deep, raspy Russian accent. "My name is Mr. Arvydas Belov. I am happy to have the honor to drive you to your new home. You will feel welcome among the residents at Brighton Beach."

Ivan was pleasantly surprised, but did not know the meaning of Saint Patrick's Day. He began asking Mr. Belov to explain the sights he was seeing for the first time along the highway.

"Ah, I can see the marvel expressed in your face." Belov had seen this expression in the faces of other recent émigrés he had picked up when they arrived for the first time in the United States. Most were other Russian or Ukrainian arrivals.

One of the first things to catch Ivan's eye while riding in the limo was the number of vehicles on the New York roadway. "These cars are all so colorful in appearance and so many of them."

"Yes, here in the States, there are many options as you will discover."

Belov had arrived in the United States only a few years earlier. It could have been a lifetime ago to Ivan. In his eyes, Belov was a seasoned immigrant. The way he carried himself and his apparent confidence gave Ivan the impression Belov fit into this new homeland comfortably. He intended to emulate that confidence.

Belov helped to raise Ivan's comfort level, and he appreciated the instant familiarity. He wanted to be more inquisitive on the ride to Brighton Beach but resisted, instead savoring the ride to his new home. There was much
to see.

It was only a fleeting moment, but Ivan suddenly had the feeling Belov somehow knew of him in some other way, something separate from the NHL connection. He soon dismissed the thought.

The limo drove slowly onto Brighton Beach Boulevard. Ivan soon noticed he was amid a thriving Russian community. It appeared lively, yet simple. Its Slavic citizens moved about more casually, less stressfully, than their counterparts in Russia.

It was a Sunday afternoon, a sunny, slightly cool day. At the time, Ivan didn't know the significance, but it was March 17, his limo driver's favorite holiday. That explained why Mr. Belov greeted him earlier with "Happy Saint Patrick's Day." Ivan quizzed him about the day. He had never experienced one, but had heard New York had a large Irish population and a rich Irish history. Their Fifth Avenue Parade was considered second to none when it came to filling the city with excitement, and also filling its pubs.

"Hey, maybe soon, it will be the Russian's opportunity to have a parade to celebrate," he joked to Mr. Belov. His expectations of the United States were limited, so talk of the festive parade was exciting.

Belov drove to the corner of Second Street and Brighton Beach Boulevard and parked within a short walk to Ivan's new apartment. Belov hopped out and hustled around to the passenger side rear door to open it for the new arrival. Ivan grabbed his leather bag as he stepped from the limo and stood straight up, throwing the bag carefully over his left shoulder.

Ivan's apartment door was street level, another bonus. He left Belov to grab the oversized luggage and walked toward the grey, alabaster lions sitting sentinel in front of his new address. Each lion's right paw was raised to signal a welcome to the new occupant. Ivan displayed a cautious, appreciative smile as approached the place he would now call home. "My God," he muttered upon entering the pre-arranged apartment. "This will be sweet." By Russian standards, his apartment was overly spacious. It was clean, smelled friendly, and was already furnished. Ivan felt guilt. He wished his family were here to savor his success. He thought, "I will move them here one day."

He left Belov at the door after apologizing for having no local currency to give him as a gratuity and thanking him profusely for the ride. Before leaving, Belov told him he also lived in the community and would make a point to come speak with him after he was settled. Belov gave him his business card and told him his limo was at his disposal. Ivan would soon rely on both Mr. Belov's card and his limo.

As often occurs with diaspora communities, organized crime elements become integrated into the daily lives of the new immigrants. They were not much different than the Irish in the 1800s who dominated the streets of lower Manhattan's "Hell's Kitchen."

The new organized crime syndicate in town was the Bratva. And the new kid in town, a top hockey player with talent and drive that would soon make him an NHL star, was under the lingering eye of this formidable Russian mob. They took notice of him in Brighton Beach and sensed opportunity with the new hockey protégé. The Bratva, as Ivan would come to learn, had begun their seductive recruitment in the United States with a limo ride to his new home.

Ivan was introduced to his future wife at a community fundraiser held at the Café Restaurant Volva, located a block away from his apartment. His NHL status lent the local fundraiser some luster. She was a stunning beauty. Ekaterina was her first name. It means "pure." And when Ivan saw her, his thoughts couldn't have been farther from that meaning. Her last name was Petrov. It means "rock." Ironically, Ekaterina was from Saint Petersburg, formerly Leningrad under the Soviet Union. Everything about her was honest, special. When she was introduced to the NHL player, her friend said her name was Kate. Ivan even liked that. Smitten at first glance, he asked her out. Kate initially balked at the invitation, but with a slight nudge from her friend she nodded, "Yes."

Ivan was making good progress skating for the NHL. The league or the players did not intimidate him. But he was intimidated by the idea that if he didn't marry Kate in a timely manner he would soon be the loneliest guy on the planet.

They were married within six months and elected to remain in the Brighton Beach apartment, the same apartment Ivan first saw after being delivered there by Mr. Belov. It was all the more incredible knowing Ivan had not yet been in the United States a full year.

The next year, 1990, Kate gave birth to Maksim Valdimirovich Dostoevsky, a towhead full hair. A handsome little boy the young parents called Max. "The only U.S. citizen in the family," joked Kate.

Ivan cried in sheer joy as he realized how far he had come in the eighteen months since the Rangers recruited him.

NINE

Tanya Ovseenko immigrated to the United States for the sole purpose of making it big, an American success. She was a well-paid stripper who liked cocaine. She met Max through a friend in the lobby of a gym after one of his UFC bouts. Her physical assets attracted him. When he learned she danced in strip clubs, his interest piqued even more. He did not know of her fondness for coke, or if he did, he elected to ignore it.

"What do you think of her, Shorty?" he had asked his buddy.

The sidekick's facial expression gave him up. He wasn't impressed with the dancer. "You could do better."

"I have no interest in marrying her. I just want to get laid, and she seems fair game. We've got a date tomorrow night, so stay away from the apartment. I may bring her home."

"Wear protection, she looks like she's dirty," Shorty retorted, his facial expression not betraying his dislike for her.

Max liked what he got from her when they arrived back at his Brighton Beach apartment. She moved in the next day.

"It's okay, Shorty. Tanya dances so much she will be no bother to me here. I will continue to get my workouts in and do my enterprise stuff without her pestering me."

"She makes me uncomfortable, Max. So when she comes, I go. You know that."

Tanya stoked the club's clients for as many lap dances as she could. She never did the Full Monty with a customer. "That would come too close to cheating on Max," she rationalized. It was just business, to include a hand job or occasional blow job when the customer paid to go behind the curtains. Max didn't need to know all the details. Behind the club's curtains where she attended to her customers' carnal desires, she proved her boobs were the real thing. The customers paid well to feel them. She liked the attention.

Moreover, Tanya needed the attention. She felt good when she impressed the customers. Max rarely told her how attractive she looked these days. The customers were different. They provided a steady stream of positive feedback. Once she had hooked them with her body rub, she moved on to a seductive whisper and slight puff in the ear. She would feign excitement, deftly swiping her tits along their noses and lips. It worked liked a charm, and she did it well. Well enough to bring in the cash necessary to support her other devotion, one that made the job fun—her daily consumption of cocaine. Her habit was something else about which Max didn't need to know all the details. She wasn't sure if even he suspected.

Tanya liked arousing, and then dousing, the losers who frequented the club. She offered customers a tease at the possibility of further intimacy, always with the intent to finesse their cash along the way. She raised their comfort levels, and something more for most of them. She was proud, and at times amazed, at her ability to trigger the extraction of cash from the club's ATM with only a few suggestive whispers.

"I will be a little late getting in tonight," she told Max in the early afternoon. Sitting behind his computer console he simply nodded to her. She grabbed her purse and left for the club. After a few months of living with Max, the routine had already set in. She liked him. He got laid when he wanted, and she had a place to call home.

Tanya especially enjoyed getting off her nightly shift and scoring her own relief, her cocaine. Next to love play with Max, she most looked forward to her "incentive," a few fat lines of blow.

Tanya was known to hustle out the club's back door most every night with Diablo, her provider of choice. Miguel Sanchez was his real name. He was a seasoned drug dealer who came up the ranks fairly unscarred by the violence usually associated with the trade. Diablo's signature handout, the "banano," was his custom-made marijuana cigarette laced with cocaine. It was quite the charmer.

"What will you do for me tonight, Tanya?" Diablo asked. He held a packet in his right hand. He wasn't looking for money tonight.

TEN

"Commander, you have been selected to be one of the Coast Guard's new military attachés. You will be assigned to Kuwait City. We are pleased you will represent the Coast Guard in this new role in a critical region of the world. I understand the difficulty it will place on you, considering your recent marriage, and we will do what we can to help support you in any way we can. I understand your wife is a Secret Service agent in New York. You may want to talk with her to confirm you're both on board with this assignment."

"Sir, my wife is a princess. I can assure you Carly is on board with this assignment. So I can tell you right now, sir, I accept."

"Roger that, Commander. Your swift reply doesn't surprise me. By the way, the president is expected to visit Kuwait City early next year to participate in the twenty-fifth anniversary of the liberation of Kuwait. I am sure the ambassador will request your assistance. You will be there during an interesting time."

Commandant of the United States Coast Guard Brad Thallen had his eye on this young commander named William Strain. The commandant's attention piqued when he became aware of Strain's willingness to take on the toughest assignments.

Commandant Thallen sought to implement the Coast Guard's new intelligence mandate to deploy its own military officers from its Intelligence Directorate to strategic ports around the world as military attachés. Following all the post 9/11 changes, the U.S. Coast Guard stood out as a Department of Homeland Security success story, and the DHS secretary convinced the president that the Coast Guard ought to be vested with greater duties and responsibilities.

The commandant then began a subtle recruiting initiative, identifying selected officers who could be encouraged to accept military attaché positions at critical ports around the world.

Commander Strain accepted a stint at the United States Embassy in Kuwait City as the Coast Guard's first military attaché. It was easy to understand why the commandant wanted him.

William Strain, "Will" to buddies, graduated from the United States Coast Guard Academy in 2003. He majored in international affairs with a minor in Russian. His first posting upon graduation was to the Pensacola Naval Air Station for helicopter training, which he completed within the normal twelve-month period. He was subsequently assigned to the U.S. Coast Guard's Helicopter Interdiction Tactical Squadron, known as HITRON, at Cecil Field in Jacksonville, Florida, home to the squadron's ten MH65C helicopters, used to intercept fast-moving powerboats bound for the U.S. mainland with illegal drugs and other contraband.

He soon shaved his head of the blond locks that had attracted many a young co-ed, and even developed a swagger that seemed appropriate to the elite assignment. He was tasked with tracking down the "go-fast" boats from the Americas that were illegally transporting cocaine.

This Coast Guard unit was authorized to fire upon suspicious boats. Even the U.S. Navy didn't have that authority. The engines of many a smuggler turned out to be easy fodder for the tactical team's weapons.

The young ensign loved to maneuver his M240 machine gun into position, aiming his shots to the front of the bow of the go-fast boats. He enjoyed the action-packed days and looked forward to repeating them. Strain loved his assignment and the excitement of the "gentlemen's war" against the drug smugglers. But he wanted to expand his profile.

After his initial assignment, Strain became aware of a new Coast Guard initiative. The newly installed civilian, James F. Keegan, assistant commandant for Intelligence and Criminal Investigation, was interested in developing a SEAL-like program for his department's Homeland Security posture. The U.S. Navy was willing to conduct the training for them, provided the trained operators served the Navy's interests for two years. The Navy, to its credit, wanted to ensure the new operatives were representative of the difficult training their own SEALS went through.

The Coasties agreed, understanding SEAL-qualified trainers had to be SEAL-trained to develop their own cadre of Coastie trainers. They were appreciative the Navy would even consider helping them. The Navy never looked at the Coast Guard as a threat; rather, the Navy perceived it as a little brother who had gigantic balls.

Strain jumped at the opportunity. He had had enough of flying for the time being, and his desire to expand his effectiveness, both physically and intellectually, was deep-rooted.

Young Lieutenant Strain went to Basic Underwater Demolition School (BUDS) training accompanied by a dozen of his colleagues, mostly young, athletic enlisted men. The USCG screened the applicants for mental and physical stamina and prowess. They wanted to ensure as many of them successfully got through the grueling BUDS training as possible to avoid inter-agency embarrassment, but more importantly, to develop their own core of trained operatives as quickly as possible.

While at the Coast Guard Academy, Strain excelled at baseball. He was a golden glove fielder by anyone's standard and a pretty good hitter too. He always kept himself in top physical condition. By BUD's standards, he may have been an old man at twenty-six, and a bit of an oddity as a Coast Guard officer, but he was as fit as the proverbial fiddle and disciplined in his physical training. Maintaining top physical condition was a lifelong habit he had begun to nurture as a youth.

Strain could have had a successful Coast Guard career without SEAL training, but he understood that by expanding his professional profile he could create greater opportunity and develop more career options. His father, who was remembered as a powerful sage in his mind, had a dozen favorite axioms, each one more meaningful than the next. "Two guys went to college. One had good study habits, the other had determination. They both made it." This paternal admonition was usually followed by, "You get ahead in this world by having other people say good things about you."

His dad stoked in him a belief that a multi-disciplined training program produced broader options. His dad was right. Strain wished his father had been around to revel in his success as a Coast Guard officer, but he had succumbed to colon cancer at an early age.

With Strain's experience as a Navy SEAL shooter behind him, he was ready and eager to come back home to his beloved Coast Guard and engage in a more academic mission. He wanted to do something that would let him capitalize on his knowledge and skills—international studies, his harrowing helicopter feats, and the overall finesse he developed as a SEAL.

He didn't want to be just a trainer. He wanted something more cerebral. Then he received a serendipitous phone call from his boss, Assistant Commandant James F. Keegan, on behalf of the commandant.

ELEVEN

"Hey, is Coffman in today?" asked Billy Sims. He had a special bond with Gerry Coffman. They were buddies in the Service and their families were tight, spending many a holiday together.

A new agent answered his call. Sims knew the kid was probably overwhelmed with busy lines and he did not want to overload him.

"Negative, sir. He stepped away for a bit. Can I help you?"

"I want to pass on my manpower numbers for the trip and get some personal identifiers on those who are coming. I would like to do it with Coffman, if you could track him down."

Sims had called the White House logistics office to provide the number of agents he would require in Kuwait to support the president's visit. By his calculations, the multiple security perimeters at different Kuwait locations would require seventy-two agents.

Two of the agents will serve as jump team supervisors; upon arrival those two would be assigned to the relatively cushy command post in Kuwait City. Some of the remaining agents would be used to cover the president's arrival at the airport, tactical motorcade positions along the highway, and the motorcade itself. Most of the agents would be assigned to defend the president's speech site, the most problematic part of the trip. The logistics office knew better than to question the numbers of the highly experienced Sims.

"Well sir, truth be told, he's in the head, and he said not to bother him even if the president of the United States called."

Sims laughed out loud.

"Coffman certainly has his priorities straight. Okay, just have him call me. I'll be in my room for a while working on reporting instructions. Tell him I need to know the tail number for the C5M coming out of Johns."

"Will the agents have to double up in hotel rooms, or is that even an issue?" the young agent inquired.

"No. No, don't even go there, young man. I would never have them double up on my watch. But jot this down for Coffman: let the jump team supervisors know that liquor will be an issue, or I should say lack of it." Sims wanted to make sure the off-duty agents didn't come off the plane carrying six packs. "The hotel has a lounge where it is legal, but elsewhere it is dry. And one more thing, tell Coffman to have headquarters issue the agents passports that have no Israeli visa stamps. Kuwaiti immigration may balk at those that do, and I don't want to be held up on the tarmac trying to resolve the issue. We have to get right on the road and begin running routes."

"Got it, sir," responded the young logistics agent, beginning to feel a bit more comfortable with the highly regarded advance agent. "I will pass on the info. Let us know if there is anything more we can do for you, sir."

Sims's Secret Service advance team had arrived in Kuwait City via commercial aircraft a few days earlier. His team traveled with members of the White House staff, White House Communications (WHCA), and various military components. They were allowed to use Air Emirates, an unusual exception. Usually, the policy required the agents to use a U.S.-based airline, but it was not an easy route to get to and they were granted a very welcomed exception. The advance agents were overjoyed, as Air Emirates coach was as good as any U.S. Airway's business class.

Sims spent much of his time on the flight to Kuwait sitting with the White House military aide, commonly referred to as the mil-aide. The mil-aide worked closely with the Service to arrange for manifesting agents on presidential support aircraft. It was wise, always, for the Service guys to take good care of the mil-aide. He or she always had a prime seat in their follow-up or spare limo, was never distant from the president, and always kept the "football," the mysterious briefcase with the codes required by the president to throttle up the military complex. The football needed to be in close proximity to the president.

For Sims, the hour was late, the day was long, and he was running on adrenaline. The room phone finally rang. It was Coffman, the can-do logistics savant, who had a demanding assignment. It required long days, day after day, and an even temperament. The reward was usually being fast-tracked for promotion. "Hello, Sims?"

"Where the hell have you been? Don't you know we are trying to protect the president of the United States? Can't you schedule your shits for some other time, mister?"

"Fuck you, Sims. I heard you needed seventy-two agents. Lucky you. I will pass that on to the manpower guys. We'll have names for you later today."

"Hey, I do have a special request of the headquarters guys, though. The American Embassy Military attaché is United States Coast Guard Commander Will Strain. The Commander has been assigned to us to facilitate our requirements from the U.S. Embassy here, and he has been an ace. And guess what? His wife is Carly Strain from the New York office. You may know her as Carly James. He hasn't seen her in a couple of months, not that he's complaining, but you may know what I'm thinking already, Coffman. He's supposed to work the intelligence part of this trip once POTUS arrives, so he'll be with us for the duration."

Coffman laughed. "I know what it is you want, Sims. Eddie and Armey have already passed that request to the New York field office, and they are confirming her availability now. I know she manages the Cyber Squad. Her squad has been 'rockin and rollin' lately."

"I hope she's available. This guy Strain is a real can-do guy. He's actually a former SEAL by training and now works for Coast Guard Intelligence on port security. I had no idea the Coast Guard had this reach. They remind me a lot of us."

"I know it's late for you there in Kuwait. Is there anything else we can support you with? Or your family, or any of the families of any of the team?"

Sims thought about what Coffman just asked. It wasn't that he asked it, it was because he asked it. It was a big reason why he liked him.

"Nothing additional just yet, Coffman, but thank you. I still have to write up my reporting instructions for the agents and find a place to print them. But as soon as you hear from the Investigations boys about Carly, please let me know."

"Roger that, Sims. Will do. Talk to you tomorrow."

TWELVE

During his first year with the NHL, Ivan settled into a comfortable rhythm with the Rangers and was preparing to go on the road for several weeks. He packed his clothing to ensure he would have enough suits. In the 1990s the players were still required to maintain a dress code. He knew three suits would do it. He usually wore one suit at least three times, so the three suits corresponded with the nine games he would be away from home.

Kate did the laundry for the small family, never failing to have clean underwear and socks ready for Ivan's road trips. "Soon, I will have someone do this work for you, Kate," promised Ivan.

"And soon you will have someone to pack your clothes for you, Ivan," she countered with a smile.

He called Mr. Belov for a ride to the Teterboro Airport, where the team's charter airplane waited for departure to Montreal.

Ivan felt reasonably satisfied with his contributions to the team's success thus far. He thought the Ranger organization was happy with him, as well. He appeared to be well grounded, having married so young and already with a young son.

Ivan was nervous about his flight to Quebec. He wasn't the best flier. To expend energy he became compulsive in anticipation of the limo's arrival. Peering periodically out from the front window, Ivan pushed the window treatments aside to see if the limo had arrived. It finally did.

"Well, what do you think?" Kate asked as Ivan let the curtain revert back to its proper hang balance.

"About what, honey?" Ivan replied.

"About the curtains you just pushed aside and paid a lot of money for. You said you wanted more privacy in the room, so I had the double rods installed and bought the solid white sheer curtains while you were out this week. They put them up yesterday. Pretty good looking style, right?"

"Wow, I guess I've been so consumed with preparing for the trip I just didn't notice. Sorry honey, they look terrific!"

Just then the limo arrived. "Kate, my limo is here. I'm going to say goodbye to Max, grab my bag, and get going. I'm really going to miss you." With that he gave Kate a lingering hug and kissed her on the lips before getting his bag.

He moved his bag to the front door and put his leather satchel over his left shoulder before turning back to Kate to give another hug goodbye. "How lucky am I to have you," he whispered.

"Call me when you get to Montreal," she said.

"I will call as soon as I get to the hotel. I love you."

Ivan was out the door and walking to the limo where Mr. Belov met him. He relied a great deal on Mr. Belov, his limo driver of choice, and even recommended him to some of the other East European players.

Mr. Belov grabbed his larger bag and placed it in the trunk. Ivan kept his leather bag. All of his closely personal items were in it, including recent photographs of his wife and son—the loves of his life.

"I always place them on my nightstand in the hotel room," he confided to his wife. He got such happiness from them. They helped him get through the loneliness of the road. Most of his teammates went out after each game and partied. They considered Ivan a loner, but respected his decision to stay in his room with his photos.

Ivan moved to enter the limo through its right rear door. He always did this with the limo. The limo drivers liked their passengers to sit there; easier to see the passenger in the rearview mirror, he imagined.

He watched Mr. Belov hustle from the car's trunk, where he just placed Ivan's bag, to hold Ivan's door open. "Good to see you again, Ivan," Mr. Belov said.

"It doesn't seem that this man should be opening and closing doors for people like me," Ivan thought to himself. His instinct was correct.

Tonight, he was caught off guard. Mr. Belov took his seat behind the wheel in the driver's seat and for a second didn't move. That's when Ivan noticed for the first time someone else sitting in the right front seat, his head obscured by the headrest.

Ivan didn't know the man. He observed he was dressed in a black sports jacket and black shirt. He couldn't see the rest of his clothing, but his visible apparel had a sinister feel.

"Good evening, Ivan. My name is Alexei. I am a colleague of Mr. Belov. During the short trip to Teterboro I have been asked by my Russian brothers to request something of you. As you may know, our community in Brighton Beach is a close-knit, cohesive family. It is no different than the brotherhood you knew in Russia and for whom you proudly wear the rose tattoo on your left chest."

This last statement angered Ivan. "Who does this guy think he is revealing my tattoo in a conversation?" he said to himself.

"We know what is going on in our community at all times. We support one another when times are difficult. When asked to support our 'community's civic programs,' we expect our brothers to do so. You are uniquely situated to help us and here is our proposal."

Ivan didn't understand what the man was talking about. He had lived in the Russian community a short time and rarely ventured outside his immediate area. "Hell, it was a miracle that I met my wife at the local restaurant social when I did," he would laugh to himself. "How did he know I had a tattoo on my chest?" Ivan wondered. He grew concerned, but did not want this dark-shirted man to sense his agitation.

"Ivan, I am sure you know of our brotherhood, the Bratva. Here in Brighton Beach we prefer to think of ourselves as a civilly minded organization raising money to help our brothers and sisters. From time to time, the Bratva places a substantial wager on the outcome of various professional sporting events. It is a marvelous way to raise funds for the Bratva. Over the next week we will take some large financial positions betting against the Rangers when they play the Montreal Canadiens. We need you to help throw the spread. It will all be on the hush. No one will ever be the wiser, and you will make a lot more money than you currently make with the team. You will also be helping out the brotherhood. I realize this is abrupt and no doubt a rude introduction for you, but it is time for us to bring you back into the Bratva, to those who need you. We are aware you wear the Bratva Rose," Alexei said.

It was a purposeful, second reference to the tattoo.

"We want you to feel better about wearing that sign of our fidelity. Helping us to assure the outcome of a few hockey games is a good start."

The limo had not yet arrived at Teterboro.

"Mr. Belov," said Ivan sternly. "Pull this car over and let me out. I have no idea who this clown is with you, but if he is serious, and since he is sitting in your front seat I believe he is, I am no longer interested in using your services or complying with his outrageous request."

Ivan began shaking, not out of fear, but anger.

"Ivan, calm down. This is all very normal here in our community. We help each other out to raise the funding that is shared equally among the community. It helps to keep our girls from having to be hired out as dancers. It helps to keep people like your wife, Kate, and son, Max, safe while you are traveling. Look at it as community policing."

Ivan realized immediately this complete outsider, Alexei, was someone whom he wanted to keep his distance. Ivan also sensed Belov was more than just a limo driver; he was someone he no longer liked.

"Pull this car over now. I am getting the fuck out."

Belov pulled his limo off to the side of Route 3 and turned into a Holiday Inn parking lot. "I will get your bag out of the trunk," Belov offered, but said nothing more. Ivan took the bag and looked directly into Belov's eyes. It was momentary look of disgust. They were not far from the Teterboro airport. Ivan could easily taxi from here.

Ivan strode into the Holiday Inn's hotel reception area, passing a seemingly inebriated guest slumped off to the left side on a couch. The snoring grew obnoxiously louder with each inhalation. He approached the counter and asked if the receptionist could contact a taxi that would take him to the airport as soon as possible. He threw down a twenty-dollar bill to facilitate his request. "I know you," said the clerk with an admiring grin. "Good luck with the upcoming road games."

Belov and his front seat passenger sped away, each with a different perspective on the meeting. Alexei thought they would have work to do with Ivan. Belov thought not. Apparently, Ivan had not yet received a briefing on what to expect when you're a son of Bratva.

"I think we can convince him," Alexei said.

"It is doubtful," Belov responded. "It may be too late for him." He didn't think he would ever cooperate. "Ivan needs to be taught a lesson, perhaps even a severe one for his insolence."

The Bratva did not like "no." The request to Ivan to throw NHL games was serious and planned. It was not a simple request Ivan had the option to refuse. That "no" would have consequences. Belov knew his relationship with Ivan had undergone a permanent change once the proposal to throw the games was made.

After a few moments Belov reconsidered. "I will reach out to him upon his return and give him one last opportunity."

The Rangers' road trip resulted in six wins and three losses. Ivan was thrilled to be returning home. His plane would land at Teterboro in less than an hour.

Meanwhile, Belov waited in his limo for the Rangers' team plane to arrive at the terminal. A small cash bribe to the parking attendant helped him acquire a spot in the security lot. He positioned his limo near the lounge area the players would use to exit the terminal.

The team did not have to go through customs upon arrival, as it played its last game in Detroit. Once deplaned, the athletes moved as a group toward the charter airline's lounge exit. The rookies knew to remain in the rear of the gaggle. Ivan was the last of them to exit. Belov spotted him before he came through the door and bolted from his driver's seat in Ivan's direction.

"Ivan, I need a moment to explain what happened before you left. Please afford me a few minutes. I took the liberty to arrange to transport you one last time. Please."

Ivan was skeptical, but he was willing to give Belov an opportunity to explain. Besides, it was the quickest way for him to get home to Kate and Max. He also noticed Alexei was not with him.

"Fine," he said. "Let's go. I want to get home fast."

Belov loaded the larger bag in the trunk, but Ivan kept his leather shoulder bag with him and remained outside the limo. Belov came around to him rather than take his driver's seat.

"I do not want to repeat Alexei's request because I know it is disdainful to you. But, as a Russian brother, I encourage you to at least reconsider your relationship with the Bratva. You have a lovely wife and a new son to take into consideration."

Ivan took the statement as a veiled threat. He felt his temper beginning to flare and reacted immediately. "Can't do it, Mr. Belov. Alexei's original request haunts me to this day. I feel I must go to the League and report it. I don't want to get involved in the type of conduct your friend has proposed. I don't care how much money there is to be made. It is not me. It is not the legacy I want to leave for my young son. I have worked too hard to get where I am and have too many good people wanting me to succeed. Please don't ever, ever bring this subject up to me again. And, Mr. Belov, I will no longer need your services. Please retrieve my luggage."

Belov remained expressionless. He did not respond, but merely nodded, dropped his head down, and backed away. Ivan's bag was placed behind the limo for him to collect.

Ivan grabbed the bag and retreated into the terminal to arrange other transportation as Belov drove away.

While waiting for another limo, Ivan decided it would be best to keep this to himself. He was fearful an internal NHL investigation by the security office might taint him. He remembered the security presentation he received when he started with the league and didn't want the attention it might bring if the press got it.

As Ivan reflected on what had just occurred, he felt good about his decision. He had done the right thing in his refusal to compromise his principles. "I will move from Brighton Beach and distance myself from Belov and his people," he thought. He decided to move his young family out of the enclave to a suburb in New Jersey or Connecticut. "I have the money. Yes, I will do it soon."

Belov picked up a brick-sized cell phone lying next to him on the front seat and telephoned Alexei as he departed the terminal.

"He thinks he can divorce himself from the brotherhood. It is too late. He elected to be tattooed as a young man. He should have been aware of the consequences of wearing our symbol on his chest. Alexei, have the rose removed and tend to the bride as well."

Alexei needn't any more direction. He knew what he had to do. The limo driver was "the man." Ivan had made a deadly mistake. He had disrespected Bratva and was about to learn what happens when the Bratva is denied.

Belov quietly said to Alexei, "I will arrange for the child to be cared for." Alexei grinned. He loved killing. He was just given a license. It thrilled him. He relished tracking his victim down. Ivan was to be an easy catch.

The *New York Post* ran the story on its front page. It told about the murder of an up-and-coming NHL star. "The New York Rangers lost a franchise player," it reported. "Ivan Valdimirovich Dostoevsky was returning from a successful two-week road trip, but never made it home."

The New Jersey State Police Department and the NYPD were working in concert to piece together his movements after he landed home with the team at Teterboro Airport.

"Dostoevsky's body," read the official police statement, "was found by New Jersey state workers along the Passaic River between Kearney and Newark. He had been shot once in the back of the head and his left chest area had been mutilated." What the official police statement did not describe was the brutality of the murder. Alexei shot Ivan behind his right ear. The forty-caliber projectile efficiently entered his brain from short range and exited his frontal lobe with such facial destruction it distorted his appearance, rendering him unrecognizable to investigators. The bullet traveled an unknown distance upon exiting the skull. In fact, the effort to locate the bullet would prove hopeless.

As Ivan lay mortally wounded on the ground, Alexei knelt down next to him. The mobster struggled to place his gun between his overhanging belly and belt. With both hands free he ripped open Ivan's coat jacket exposing a starched button-down shirt. With one hand, Alexei tore the hockey player's shirt from his chest displaying a Rose Tattoo, located to the left of his well-defined, but silent sternum. He drew a switchblade from his left coat pocket and snapped the knife into position. Like a surgeon he inserted the blade an inch deep into the chest and carved menacingly around it as if repairing a divot on a golf green. With the heart stopped, bleeding was minimal. The faded dermal amulet lost its perceived, magical power to protect. It was now no more than Alexei's prized possession to be brought back to Belov as proof of death. Alexei grinned with delight as he lifted the detached pigmented skin from the corpse. He stood and walked briskly to his car.

The investigation of the bizarre homicide also led to the discovery of an apparent suicide by his wife, Kate. The NYPD found her body hanging in the Brighton Beach apartment when they attempted to notify her of her husband's death. It confounded them. Why would the young wife of a young, promising NHL hockey player seemingly end her life? Why would the devoted mom leave her young child to fend for himself? Did her love for her husband supersede her motherly duties causing her to grow so distraught as to end her life and forsaking her maternal responsibilities? To the investigators, it didn't make sense.

Sources who wished to remain anonymous said law enforcement authorities on both sides of the Hudson believed there might be a Russian mob connection. The *Post* also related the wife's parents were to care for the couple's young child. The child's name was not mentioned due to the baby's age.

Belov knew the baby's name. He read the newspaper account without emotion, treating the incident as purely business. His attention turned to baby Max's grandparents. They would now care for the young orphan. During the joint wake for the young parents, Belov approached the grandparents. "The Bratva will now financially support you as you raise the child." Belov pledged to them their grandson would nurtured by the local community, and he, as a community leader, would take personal interest to ensure Max received a proper education.

"I mourn for your loss. The whole neighborhood mourns too. We will derive great satisfaction in helping you raise your grandson into a fine young Russian boy." Kate's parents were grateful.

The grandparents did not know the full background of this self-described community leader privately planning for the boy's destiny. Actually, few did. The truth Belov kept close to his small cadre of loyalist was he trained as a former Russian KGB operative. He was trained in long-term preparation. Brighton Beach would come to know his plan soon.

THIRTEEN

Gerry Coffman picked up the dedicated drop line that ran from the White House Logistics Section directly to the Office of Investigations' Manpower Desk at Secret Service Headquarters. When the Investigations' phone alerted, Tom Eddie answered.

"Tom, this is Coffman. How are you?"

"Great. We've been expecting your call. We know you've got a lot going on out there." Eddie knew this call meant work for him and Steve. And that meant chipping manpower away from the various field offices located around the country. "It is getting so fucking old," he thought.

With the New Year holiday behind them, the use of field office agents would heat up, as the president, who had remained cloistered at Camp David, was now itching to begin travel. Besides, it was the best way for the president to disengage from the scandals and the mid-term losses that had beset him in his second term.

"I want to give you numbers for the upcoming Kuwait trip," said Coffman. "The car-plane is expected to depart Joint Air Force Base on February 21. It's coming out of Maguire Air Force Base empty and will load up pretty quickly. We'll need the agents' names by the sixteenth in order to get them all visa'd up for Kuwait. Looks like the advance team will need seventy-two agents. Two of them, of course, will be the designated jump team leaders. By the way, I know you received the request for Carly Strain. Did you have any luck getting her for the trip?"

"Coffman, when have we ever failed to make you guys look good? We got her. You know, her name has been mentioned quite a bit here at headquarters the last few days. Apparently, her squad knocked off a big cyber hacker from Brighton Beach's Russian enclave. The news said he is one of the world's super hackers. Anyway, I'll call her directly and find out if she can still do this."

"Thanks, Eddie. Talk soon."

FOURTEEN

"Mano," Tim Bowser said into his cell phone during his call to Diablo. Bowser fancied himself a linguist of sorts, and he was practicing his art by bastardizing "hermano," the Spanish word for brother. Diablo viewed him as a silly gringo. He wasn't sure if Bowser was mocking him or trying to impress him. He didn't care.

"*Necesito algo esta noche. Necesito mi dulce.*" Diablo had no trouble understanding Bowser was looking for cocaine.

Since the 9/11 attack on the Twin Towers, car dealerships had avoided selling vehicles for cash, in fear they would risk federal scrutiny under the U.S. Patriot Act and its mandate to trace terrorist funding. The act sought to bring many of the non-traditional businesses into compliance, particularly those engaged in large cash transactions, such as high-end auto dealerships.

Not all car dealers complied. The Lexus dealer, Bowser, freely took cash and took it without compunction. He knew the game and how to launder the money. Diablo supplied him with coke daily.

"Luck be a lady tonight," Bowser liked to sing when he got what he needed. Usually, he scored his cocaine with cash; however, at times Diablo provided it with the promise to make good.

The Colonial Lexus dealership sat prominently on Route 1, a busy commuter highway near the Woodbridge Mall, within the confines of Edison, New Jersey. The company's trademark beige alabaster storefront bore a sign that read "Bowser's Lexus of Woodbridge."

Bowser was one of two sons who worked at the luxury car dealership owned by their father, Peter Bowser Sr. He was the location's sales manager, and he was known for his aggressive temperament. If his sales team didn't like the idea of having to sell cars that practically sold themselves, they could move on to some other job. Or, as Bowser quoted, "Let them go lift their fucking weights, that's what most of them want to do anyway. Lots of muscle, little brain." He blamed his father for hiring them.

He actually enjoyed calling a delinquent salesman into his office for poor failure. It made him feel omnipotent. He enjoyed it even more if the target of his wrath was one of the muscled-up men his father hired from the nearby Gold's gym. They all had a chiseled, reality TV show appearance. If the cars didn't sell themselves, Bowser believed, these steroid guzzling boy wonders would have a difficult time making a dime.

The Lexus dealership did well in spite of the lackluster performance of Bowser's sales team. "Most of our profit comes from the service department, which my son Peter manages," his father bragged. "I place the best talent where it means most, which is why Tim ain't there."

Bowser overheard the comment and resented his father's devotion to his older brother, but kept his feelings in check. As long as the dealership made money, he made money. "Life is good," he thought. He needed the money to support his addiction. He began to spend more and more time with his dealer.

"Fine. When and where?" Diablo snapped. He didn't want to waste an entire night dealing with Bowser.

"Can I meet you on the turnpike?" asked Bowser, his bravado not at its usual sales level. Diablo sensed a timid tone in his voice, almost close to a desperate beg. Diablo had seen this despair in other clients and grew concerned. "Begging is not a good sign," he said to himself. "That's when mistakes get made."

"Sometimes, I think the only reason you tolerate me is because of the car I give you."

"Yes, that's it, I need you to take dutiful care of my car," the coke dealer responded sarcastically.

Bowser had arranged for Diablo to obtain the rare Lexus Future Advance Roadster, known as the "LFA." Possession of the hard-to-acquire vehicle was no coincidence. As long as he dealt Bowser the coke he needed, he was the car dealer's top priority. Bowser made it known among his service representatives that LFA took priority. When the LFA needed servicing, it went to the front of the line. Similarly, when Bowser needed servicing, he would find himself in front of some white lines. It was a classic symbiotic relationship.

"I am more faithful to this car than I am to any of my bitches. If they did as good a job staying down low on the road as the LFA does, there would be a lot more happiness for men in this world."

Bowser, desperate to score some coke, held his phone in his left hand, whispered into his cell using his right hand to cup his mouth. "I can meet you on the turnpike. I am up north at Shakers on Route 17 enjoying the girls, and I want to reward one of them tonight."

Shakers was a non-nude New Jersey go-go pub, not far from the famed Soprano's "Bada Bing." The girls were mostly East European or Brazilian, not a bad-looking one in the bunch. Bowser, a regular customer, was known to share his coke if a dancer got extra frisky with him.

Diablo chose a midway point he believed might serve both of them. It was 9 pm, and he wanted to get to the Lace Club by Giants Stadium for his own purposes, which usually meant a blow job from one of the girls. He had already put in a full day in the city, selling most of what he had.

"I am not far from the New Jersey Turnpike's Vince Lombardi rest stop, about two miles south of the New Jersey Turnpike's last toll. Meet me there." The location was convenient, and it would probably just be a quick hand off. Diablo could be back on the turnpike and on his way to Lace in minutes.

Diablo exited the fast-paced roadway, weaving his LFA into the rest stop bearing the name of the NFL legend Vince Lombardi. With the elevated New Jersey Turnpike perched high above the rest area, the LFA came to a slow crawl, its engine softly growling as Diablo downshifted to a reduced speed. From the lot, the turnpike presented as an intimidating, massive concrete structure. It provided an unattractive impression for a first-time visitor to the Garden State.

Diablo drove slowly through the expansive truck lot and chose a space bordering the Sunoco gas station, just past the dedicated car lot. He backed the LFA into a slot that allowed him to observe who came in and out; he especially wanted to avoid the attention of any suspicious New Jersey state troopers.

Diablo reconsidered his position and felt it was too conspicuous—a rare Lexus parked next to a busy public highway. He made a 360-degree survey of the lot and chose a place farther from the illumination of the powerful rest stop lights.

He felt he was now in better position to escape notice by gawkers or the state police. He saw only hurried travelers, coming and going into the vendor shop to relieve themselves. They were too busy, he hoped, to notice or care about him or his car. The Empire State Building's tower was prominent in the eastern nightscape. The surrounding swamp appeared to be the only physical impediment between the iconic building and himself. He turned to focus on vehicles coming into the lot.

"Stay focused," he muttered to himself, as he sat with his seatbelt unfastened while sipping a Red Bull energy drink and waiting for the slick car salesman to pick up his package. The "cat's pee" Diablo called it. Crack cocaine. "He must have some pretty bitch in mind so wants the more potent stuff. Looking for a more potent blow job, I guess," he laughed to himself.

Diablo's cell phone rang. "Hello?"

"I'm two minutes away from the rest area," said Bowser. "I forgot to mention I don't have cash, but we can settle later this week. Okay?"

"Okay, but be cool brother, you didn't have to call me!" said Diablo. He prayed Bowser wouldn't bring one of the bitches with him. He should have mentioned that condition and grew uncomfortable with the prospect of one coming along. He reprimanded himself for not being more cautious. "This is how people get in trouble," he fretted.

He sat upright in the driver's seat and glanced around the lot a second time, trying hard not to give away body language that would send signals to those whose job was to read them. He didn't want to attract the attention of any trained observers, like cops, or bad guys for that matter, who wanted to rip off other bad guys. He saw no evidence of any state cops around, not even nestled in some nook to write a report, read a paper, or nod off.

The closest vehicle that caused him a bit of concern was two hundred feet away. It was a dark black Suburban with tinted windows, parked in the corner near the Vince Lombardi entrance by the truck lot. It was positioned head first, just as the parking sign commanded. The entrances to the vendor shops—Nathan's, Burger King, and Popeye's—were all located midway between him and the Suburban. Patrons casually came and went.

"Shit," he chided himself, suddenly realizing he had just made another mistake by parking tail in. Diablo began to think too much. "I could switch spaces and park head in," he thought. "But that would just draw more attention."

"Stay put," he commanded himself. Just then he noticed Bowser arriving in a Lexus 470 SUV. "No passenger, that's good," Diablo thought. He thought about flicking his headlights to alert Bowser to his presence, but caught himself. "Another stupid idea. Even thinking that way makes me think I'm slipping. What the hell's wrong with me?"

Bowser pulled up next to Diablo's car. Driver faced driver. Diablo nodded as Bowser exited his car and moved to the LFA's passenger door to get in. The LFA still had that new car smell, an aroma Diablo was about to give up. "Never smoke in your car," Bowser cautioned him.

"Let's do this quickly. I want to get out of this fucking lot. It spooks me. I've got some personal business to do." He didn't say where he was going.

Bowser looked around casually and saw nothing spooky. He thought his buddy Diablo was being a bit of a "drama queen."

Bowser was relaxed. He had already knocked back a couple of beers and was starting to feel pretty good. Diablo handed Bowser a plastic bag. Once he had the goods in his hands, Bowser's thoughts immediately returned to Shakers. Now he had the leverage to make a dancer happy. She in turn would make him happy.

With the coke delivered, Diablo tuned out whatever Bowser was saying and started to think about the girls at Lace. He hoped Tanya was working. She was his favorite. When she didn't have the funds to support her addiction there were other ways she could make Diablo happy. A proper good night ending could reduce any debt owed him.

He didn't know Tanya's boyfriend personally, but he had heard a few things. If Max's reality was even halfway close to his reputation, then he never wanted to have to explain to Max why Tanya was servicing him.

"When you settle with me, it may be best to never tell your man it was with a blow job," Diablo once told Tanya. "I wouldn't want to have to shoot his ass." Tanya scoffed at the suggestion. Keeping her thoughts to herself, she knew Diablo would be quick prey before he could draw any weapon against Max. She let the comment pass. She smiled sweetly and took the coke. She never waited for Diablo to even zip up his pants.

She would immediately snort a couple of lines and prepare for her return to the stage. Ready for the next dance.

FIFTEEN

DEA agent Jack Halvey sat in the rear seat of the black Suburban, peering out through the rear window, his high powered 8/42 WP Huntmaster binoculars at the ready. His knees grounded his elbows as he depressed the button on his wrist transmitter to advise the surveilling DEA agents the subjects in the LFA had handed off a bag. When the Lexus pulled into the space next to the target, Halvey had to adjust his position angle slightly within his vehicle to get a better visual.

"The driver passed a plastic envelope to the target sitting in the passenger seat," Halvey said, displaying the calm of an airline pilot announcing his plane had just leveled off at 33,000 feet.

"Roger that," responded Jim O'Brien, the DEA case agent. O'Brien was trained to be cautious. He wouldn't give the signal to move in until, and unless, they had the observations necessary to justify an arrest without a warrant. He had to build on the probable cause before he could bust a move.

"Do you see them passing any cash?" inquired O'Brien. Halvey continued to focus his binoculars on the activity inside the LFA, letting the refractive lenses do the snooping, capturing the proof the DEA needed to justify swooping down on the targets.

"Negative, Jim." Halvey swiftly described his observation to O'Brien. He knew O'Brien's decision as to whether to make the arrests depended on what he was being told, so he wanted to make sure he reported what was going on inside the luxury Lexus in an accurate and timely manner.

"Arresting these two mutts will be a good week's work," O'Brien replied. He appreciated having the experienced Halvey along. He had the "eyeball" to help make the case against the Lexus dealer. A prosecutable case against this high-end car salesman would be a feather in the agent's cap.

SIXTEEN

Max felt things were looking good. He continued to target the big banks, setting them up for a big score. Max used a variety of intrusion models, but his ace model used a pre-hack event, a malware injection into the system, to bypass company controls which would allow a future major breach to occur.

Most of his pre-hack events involved breaches caused by malware introduced by him through a simple phishing process to capture customer banking credentials. Max hoarded this information; he didn't sell it to others like most hackers do in their online forums or chat rooms.

Max was a disciplined planner and looked at the larger picture as he systematically violated thousands of computer systems. Max was gearing up to make a financial killing when Carly Strain entered his life.

To someone like Max, the hacking was never personal. He never knew his victims. He didn't care. To him, it was about redistribution of wealth. Max never worried about prosecution in his pursuit of the big money. He was confident he was too good at covering his cyber tracks.

Max developed a slick SQL injection ability that assumed ownership of ten million user accounts associated with thousands of mutually exclusive servers. SQL is computer slang for "structured query language." Ask a hacker what SQL actually means and most probably would not know. Max did.

The SQL tool gave hackers like Max the ability to manipulate proprietary databases. The level and experience of the hacker determined how effective the manipulation of the database could be. Max was a better scriptwriter than most hackers. His computer language was written to such a high degree that his ability to inquire about other systems' data management and retrieve that proprietary information when needed to further his "exfiltration" of data was fluid. It was what made him more prolific than anyone else.

When Max penetrated a system, he left no trace. He was Russian, and Russians don't leave calling cards. As a prolific code writer, Max was known to develop malware that could wreak havoc on the most sophisticated corporate information security, or "Infosec" as it is also known. Max never screwed around with the public sector systems. In an oddly patriotic way, he felt he shouldn't be messing around with Uncle Sam.

Max had a fierce devotion to his cyber acumen work. His self-taught skills allowed him to penetrate private systems at will. He conducted reconnaissance on the banking targets like a super sleuth, breaking into their networks and depositing his malware in them. He extracted valuable data with the skill of a surgeon and maintained a hidden presence within networks, erasing his actions like a caddy repairing a sand trap.

He relied on finding a system's flaws, its vulnerabilities. He would analyze the assembly code, dissecting how the code was written within a system's own SQL, and then exploit it. This would allow him to discreetly extract customer banking data for his own nefarious use.

Max aggregated user passwords with the efficacy of an NSA Cyber Section chief's largest server. Most hackers use a simple "app" tool, the MD5, readily available to crack passwords. App is a small piece of software that aids the hacker to perform a specific job. In this case, the app helped Max to gather passwords. In fact, Max needed to gather them exponentially, so he altered the app script and told Shorty he made one "app on Viagra." The data flowed his way. He knew system administrators would take months to recognize their servers had been compromised by the vulnerability that allowed him access. The delay provided Max with ample time to gather victim accounts for his grand cyber finale.

Max was intent on making the final dump of cash equity into his JFOT the largest in cyber history, amounting to billions of dollars. JFOT was a hacker's abbreviation for Just Fucking Out There, a reference to the data floating freely in cyber space. Few in the Bratva knew of his defalcating goals, but those who did were eager to benefit.

The young super hacker envisioned a coordinated attack against every major U.S. bank. He planned on utilizing a thousand bot masters, deputized fellow black hat hackers, for a massive "man-in-the-middle" attack. Each would get a piece of the pie for his efforts. Many would have done it just for the chance to be a part of cyber hacking history.

Max's cyber scheme centered on a previously unknown piece of malware, an offshoot of the Z-Trojan, which, once injected, would transmit details about a compromised server to Max's command and control server. All the compromised servers would then, in effect, be cloned. When the customers' IP addresses were simultaneously pinged, they would provide Max with online bank account data, and he would begin the process of exfiltration, which would send the customers' bank funds directly to him.

The Bratva coffers would soon be overflowing with electronic gold, thanks to Max. He was an advocate and user of Bitcoin, a virtual currency.

"Why do you only go after American banks, Max?" Shorty had once asked him.

"Because they are easy, lazy, and greedy. Besides, banks don't want to inconvenience their customers, so they only employ the basics in security prevention."

SEVENTEEN

Agent O'Brien was a five-year veteran of the Drug Enforcement Agency. He had graduated from Seton Hall University in Newark, New Jersey, with a business degree. He had toyed with the idea of going into investment banking. He had also considered going into the hedge fund business. He found it fascinating and was intrigued by the fast pace. A chance meeting with his best friend's brother, a Secret Service agent, changed his mind. He had considered going for the FBI or the Secret Service. They were always the first two agencies to come up when recommendations were being made. But the Drug Enforcement Agency began to emerge as his clear choice. O'Brien saw it as an opportunity to make a difference, not in the lives of others, but in his own life. He saw it as a pathway to satisfy his craving for the wild side, plus it was legal.

Halvey gave word that something had indeed been passed, but also blurted, "I don't see anything else."

O'Brien considered the situation for a very brief moment, then concluded he had enough probable cause to make arrests. After all, his group had been trailing Bowser for the better part of the week and had made similar observations of him passing drugs to a variety of women. Now the DEA had sufficient probable cause to arrest the drug supplier. They had been tailing Bowser for a while, knowing he would eventually lead them to his source. He didn't disappoint them.

"This will make for a good night," O'Brien said to the surveillance team. "Let's go," he commanded over his car radio.

With that broadcast, three DEA vehicles positioned behind the Vince Lombardi rest area shifted into drive and moved in what appeared to be a choreographed symmetry toward Diablo's Lexus, surrounding it with no escape possible.

The DEA agents exited their vehicles with guns drawn, fingers off the triggers. Training always dictated such a disciplined response. Their fingers were trained to quickly engage the trigger if either occupant were to move in a threatening manner.

"Put your hands on the steering wheel and don't move them," O'Brien counseled Diablo, his Glock, Model 27, .40 caliber pointed directly at his head.

The agent's calm confident command inspired Diablo to comply with the verbal order. It didn't matter if the agent was actually using his off-duty, back-up weapon. Diablo meekly sat up upon hearing the command. O'Brien's partner, Kenny Reed, gave a similar command to the car's passenger. Bowser complied without resistance. Reed thought Bowser might have pissed his pants. He grinned at O'Brien. It all felt really good.

Caught red-handed at the Lombardi rest stop, Diablo struggled to control his thoughts and maintain a level of logical appreciation for what was happening. His available options slowly took form in his mind.

"How the hell do I get out of this?" thought Diablo. "I just gave this fuck two packets of crack cocaine and now I am going to jail." He was still frozen in place, trying to come to terms with O'Brien's directive.

"How fucking stupid is he? He led them here! How fucking stupid am I for fucking letting him bring the fucking cops on me? Fuck. What an asshole!" he thought, trying to keep his racing thoughts and emotions in check while silently berating the sleazy car dealer.

"Keep your Lexus service 'puta!' You just got me busted, and you have no idea what I have to lose!"

He hoped the DEA agents would not recognize the value of the vehicle they had just taken into custody. Almost as soon as he had the thought, he realized the pointlessness of his line of thinking. The car offered him no leverage any longer. The car now belonged to them by virtue of the drug transaction they had just broken up.

O'Brien knew the value of the soon-to-be-forfeited car. The prized roadster was to be confiscated. He knew the U.S. government was not obligated to return it.

"It was his decision to drive his prize to this venue. He should have been smarter," O'Brien told Reed. "It's ours now."

Bowser's focus narrowed immediately. His tunnel vision corrupted any chance he might have had to develop a plan to deal with the gun-toting federal agents. He saw no option other than to comply.

As he looked into Reed's eyes, he quivered, barely able to mumble a coherent response.

"What's going on? What's this all about?" Bowser said, his voice cracking. Reed had heard this reaction and response many times. He had no patience for this type, especially when the subject had just betrayed his family.

Reed maintained his grip and continued to train his duty Glock at Bowser's head. "Put your hands on top of your head and interlock your fingers."

Reed reached for the passenger door and with his free hand opened it, grabbing Bowser by his right arm.

"Get out of the car, fool!"

Reed had seen many reactions to his drawn gun over the years. Bowser's response did not disappoint him. Now and again, the pointed gun would elicit bodily excretions from the suspect that exasperated and frustrated the most experienced DEA agent. But not Reed. He thought it amusing that he could have such impact.

Reed had learned long ago not to place a suspect in the back of the G-car, the federal police vehicle, without adequate barrier protection to the rear seats. As a standard precaution, he would stow plastic bags and paper towels in his car trunk. They would be needed to deal with Bowser's soiled pants.

The agents positioned Diablo and Bowser against the side of the two-seat roadster and patted them down, while other DEA agents covered them. No New Jersey State Police were apparently in the vicinity and none had responded to the arrest. The event had occurred spontaneously. It had happened so quickly it would have been serendipitous for a trooper to be present.

O'Brien ordered one of his back-up agents to call the local DEA office and have the duty desk make a "standard" arrest notification to the turnpike's New Jersey State Police command center and alert them to the arrest activity at the rest stop. It was a courtesy call, nothing more.

"With luck, we'll be long gone before any troop car arrives," O'Brien said. He intended no disrespect. The DEA guys didn't have time for niceties every time they arrested a two-bit drug pusher. Time was of the essence. They needed to squeeze the arrested men into talking when they got them back to the office. O'Brien and Reed began a systematic pat down for weapons. None found.

They cuffed the two suspects and put them in the rear seat of the G-car. "No plastic bags or towels required this time," O'Brien said. Reed wasn't so sure.

After placing the two men in the DEA vehicle, O'Brien looked at his partner. He raised an eyebrow and grinned at Reed. "Did you get a look at what that guy was driving?"

Reed looked back at the Lexus for a moment. He shrugged and looked back at O'Brien with an empty expression. "So?" Reed was fully aware they had an interesting vehicle in their possession, but he played stupid. He enjoyed teasing his young partner.

Reed and O'Brien had confiscated dozens of vehicles over the past few years, many as a result of similar investigations. To these seasoned agents, the arrests of Diablo and Bowser were nothing more than another day at the office. Process the arrest, document the seized property, and hope it translated into some positive asset forfeiture money to help fund the agency's non-budgeted priorities. But every now and then the seizure of a unique car, like Diablo's LFA, piqued everyone's interest.

Reed knew playing coy about the car would frustrate O'Brien. The junior agent flashed him a look of incredulity, then immediately realized he was being had. "You're a peckerhead, a real dick, Reed." He laughed and shook his head. Reed looked down and grinned.

O'Brien directed one of his backup agents to drive the LFA from the turnpike lot to the local DEA office in Newark, New Jersey. "Be careful. The boss is gonna want first dibs on this one, so no scratches." O'Brien winced as the agent smoked the tires, then tore out of the lot. He shook his head and sighed. "Your career, pal. Don't blow it."

O'Brien couldn't stop thinking about the LFA. "Reed, this car we just confiscated is the Lexus luxury prototype. Every advanced feature you can think of is integrated into this car. Do you know how much fun this car would be to drive?" O'Brien was giddy with excitement at the prospect of giving the DEA special agent in charge of the local Newark office news of the seizure.

When they arrived back at the DEA garage in Newark, the car was there waiting, safe and sound. O'Brien turned to Reed. "Look at the damn thing. It reeks with performance power. I can see myself using this car in a future undercover operation."

"Yeah, sure you can. As long as the bosses don't want it," Reed said.

Diablo was about to lose the car of his dreams. Its interior was a composition of carbon fiber, leather, alcantara (a synthetic leather suede material), and slick metal surfaces. Its design boasted an elegance that would stand the test of time.

The LFA had a powerful V-10 engine that would redline at 9,800 rpm. It was constructed of forged aluminum, with forged titanium rods and solid titanium valves. The car had a sweet twelve-speaker sound system, a virtual recording studio. Its design had but one purpose: to achieve premium aerodynamic performance. It was Diablo's jewel. Was! It would soon belong to the DEA.

O'Brien and Reed exited their G-car and took their night's catch up a dedicated elevator directly to the DEA's Newark field office where they began processing the two arrested men. There was no further conversation, not with the arrestees, anyway. The agents intentionally avoided talking with them, an action designed to make both Diablo and Bowser sweat a little.

Back in the office, Diablo was desperate for an opportunity to negotiate with O'Brien. Trying his best to affect puppy dog eyes, he tried to gain O'Brien's attention. "I have information I think the Feds would like to hear."

O'Brien had frequently heard this come-on during his five-year career. Sometimes it paid off, but more often than not it was merely a suspect looking for immediate relief with little to actually offer in return. Nevertheless, O'Brien always thought it a good idea to listen. He never foreclosed investigative options.

"Is it too late?" Diablo asked, careful not to let Bowser hear him. He hoped to offer enough of a biscuit to the DEA to allow for a possible reduction in his exposure to the law.

"Never too late, my friend," said O'Brien. He always appreciated hearing a suspect's entrée. Diablo had bought himself a temporary reprieve from the DEA's holding cell.

Bowser was on his own as the DEA sought to press charges against him. To the DEA, Bowser was a throwaway. Sure, he could be used to testify against Diablo in federal court, if necessary, but the DEA had no other use for him. His life was about to implode. He was going to lose his job and his family. With nothing to offer, Bowser sat idly in his chair. He had unwittingly led the DEA to Diablo. He had become a DEA target when the Financial Crimes Enforcement Network, known as FinCEN, became suspicious of his increasingly blatant efforts to launder money gleaned from the dealership's cash deals.

FinCEN was receiving Suspicious Activity Reports, or SARS, from a variety of financial institutions, detailing Bowser's burgeoning deposits of cash. Drug activity was also suspected and FinCEN sent the aggregated intelligence to the DEA office in Newark for further investigation.

Diablo, on the other hand, had gotten O'Brien's attention and established some temporary bona fides. He had, he believed, one card to play in his effort to convince the DEA he had worthy information with which to barter. He was going to do his best to use what he knew about Tanya, the dancer, and her boyfriend, Max, to avoid jail time. His gamble was riding on the hope he could give O'Brien something bigger than himself and lessen his legal woes.

"Mr. O'Brien, I can tell you about a computer hacker who is about to screw with the world's banking system. His bitch buys from me. She loves what I sell. She's a high-class stripper. I can take you guys right to her." Diablo realized his situation remained dire unless he could convince the DEA he had something bigger.

O'Brien thought Diablo displayed too much temerity and too little humility. "What do I care about cybercrime?" he snapped. "My interest is drugs and money laundering, not some keystroke freak."

O'Brien moved closer to Diablo's ear. "Shit, give me a better tease than that," he said in a lowered tone. "I can't do shit for you if you don't have something more than me missing some sort of fireworks." Diablo was disappointed by the response. He sat back. His eyes glazed over as he reconfigured his approach.

O'Brien was not sure where Diablo might go next, but not wanting to forsake the opportunity, he played along. "*Dígame, que tiene que me interesaria saber? Pronto!*" Diablo glanced up at O'Brien. He was mildly impressed with O'Brien's Spanish. He had been told to come up with something interesting, and to do it soon, or the conversation was over.

"I can give you information about the computer crime of the decade," Diablo said. He licked his lips nervously. "It involves the Russian mob too. The hacker's girlfriend is a cokehead. Her name is Tanya. And I can set her up for you. She needs me nightly for coke and I can arrange to let you have her. She likes to brag about all the stuff her boyfriend is up to, and if it's even half true, her boyfriend is about to make off with more gold than you got at Fort Knox."

O'Brien wanted to hear more. "Interesting, but there are a lot of hackers out there. Some are better than others. Some are just trying to make a statement. You and your car dealer buddy are all I really need tonight. You guys are going to jail."

O'Brien knew the value of a good lead. It could jumpstart the case of a career. But tips that didn't pan out risked wasting other agents' time and the night was already late. He needed more substance.

"She says he's involved in something big going down real soon. It involves him working with the Russian mob. She calls it the Bratva. They work out of Brighton Beach. The dude's name is Max, and he's about to cash out. She says he's some sort of hacker extraordinaire. Her words, not mine. She says he's about to launch some sort of global fraud operation that's going to redistribute wealth to him and his Russian buddies."

O'Brien nodded and said, "I'll think about it." It had been a long day and he didn't want to keep the other agents working longer based on such limited information. He thought it best to let the two arrestees sit in a jail cell overnight and resume the questioning in the morning after the two had time to absorb the gravity of their situation.

After processing the two suspects in the Newark office, O'Brien let the other agents go home for the night while he and Reed drove Diablo and Bowser to the Union County Jail in Elizabeth, New Jersey. The jail was the designated lockup for the Feds to house their short-term federal arrestees. Diablo knew the place well, and many of the current prisoners were familiar with him.

Bowser remained silent during the ride from Newark to Elizabeth. He was scared and nervous about being placed overnight in the county jail's general population. He contacted his attorney while in custody at the DEA office. The attorney said he would meet Bowser at his arraignment the next morning before the U.S. Magistrate in Newark and instructed him not to say another word to the DEA.

Diablo believed he would not have to worry about an attorney. He hoped the DEA would work a separate deal with him the next morning. He was confident they would want to hear more about Tanya and her boyfriend.

EIGHTEEN

"I love to manhandle networks and systems, and I do it better than anyone else," Max told Shorty, "but when hackers try to fuck with me, it's personal. It really pisses me off." When he felt it necessary, Max would quickly retaliate for attacks on his cyber hacking enterprise, and he did so without remorse.

Max was a cyber-genius who easily grew bored and restless, usually a signal it was time to ratchet up the ante and go for a larger score.

Most of his likeminded "friends" were cyber acquaintances. He never met them personally, but he quickly assessed which ones he liked and which ones he didn't like. He encountered a diverse crowd online. The ones he couldn't stand were the Al Qaida sympathizers.

Profit was the name of the game, not destruction, not taking down systems, unless it was an occasional Al Qaida-inspired propaganda site. Then he had no qualms disrupting them. Max was only ten when the World Trade Center was attacked and the daily flow of broken families and heartbreak affected him even as a young person. It was then when he most missed the parents he never knew.

When he first met the self-proclaimed "hacktivist" called "Taboo" online, Max was encouraged to join forces with "Luzz Sec," a loosely formed hacking group. He declined. "Why would they waste their time pursuing foolish disruptions to computer systems without monetary reward?"

Max wanted money, not hacking fame. Wealth, he believed, led to power. Fame led to getting caught, or worse yet, getting pinned by the law enforcement authorities, losing the cyber fight to them.

"Taboo, why does Luzz spend so much time retaliating against companies and government agencies when there is so much low-hanging fruit for us to grab and make us wealthy," texted Max. "Is it an ideological or purely political thing? What a waste of time." He felt contempt for the group.

In early 2012, Max demonstrated his hacking prowess, making him a cyber savant in the eyes of Luzz Sec. The global hackers were impressed with his ability to hack into an array of financial systems for profit, disrupt network television for fun, and less often, retaliate to defend his hacking empire.

But that was the old Max. He had grown, matured. Hacking groups were competitive, and for an up-and-coming group, someone like Max as a managing partner could provide Luzz with a tactical, and strategic, advantage against other hacking groups with whom it globally competed. For Max, belonging to such a group would be only a short-term relationship. "They have no discipline," he thought. He felt a more sinewy group would be a better partner for him. But for now Luzz would serve the purpose of aiding his desire to analyze a group in a larger global footprint. He would study them and then move on.

Xavier Cordeleone, known by his cyber handle Taboo, was eager to recruit Max for his own emerging hacking emporium. His group was known to the world as "Luzz Sec." This was to be Max's first stab at developing global relationships and international camaraderie with similar-minded hackers. He was not impressed. He thought Taboo was a flake who talked too much and wanted to know too much too fast. Max suspected something was awry with the management of this hacker group. He felt Luzz was a deceitful organization, one not to be trusted.

Taboo continued to recruit him. "With your talent, the Luzz Security Group will reign supreme," Taboo texted Max with the hubris of an older brother. Max was ill at ease with the invite in the wake of their persistence. "Dude, you already got the talent for money and fame. We look forward to you coming with us. You can make a big impact on world events as a Luzz partner."

Max responded, "I hope it makes us all wealthy. I will do my best to earn your respect through hard work, long hours. I will sweat. I will bleed. I will remain diligent and never give up pursuing success."

Taboo thought Max was joking with him. He had no idea it was how Max approached everything he did. He hadn't become a successful mixed martial arts fighter by being lucky.

"Take a breath," Taboo texted. "This ain't a fucking war."

But Max always saw his pursuits through a prism of a physical challenge. He didn't want this guy Taboo to think for a moment he would be less than devoted to being the best he could be. Max, the fighter, kept his hands up and looked for an opportunity to notionally take Taboo to the cyber mat. He kept his texting brief and offered little to help Taboo come to know him personally, other than his determined personality. But he did want to probe Taboo more. So he continued. "Tell me, how do you reduce risk to your activities?"

Taboo responded quickly. "No risk with Luzz. We run way under the radar and are loyal to each other. We tolerate no Benedict Arnolds."

"Anyone can become a Benedict Arnold. Arnold's ego caused him to betray his country. I don't need to get arrested for pure ideological shit because someone's ego was bruised."

"You sound a bit timid to me," Taboo responded.

"Not timid, it just seems to me that Luzz spends too much precious time on social issues and is not devoted to establishing wealth. I am in the game to make money. Fucking with people only pisses them off and makes them work harder to retaliate. We need to pick our enemies carefully. Luzz, from what I have seen, spends too much effort attacking systems that don't produce wealth. Obtaining personal information from a local PBS television station is small potatoes. PBS doesn't have shit in the bank and its donors probably don't have much either. They're all idealists. They don't save money, they spend it, particularly other people's money. Just look at how much the idealists in this country have put us in debt. My point is it would be a waste of time compromising PBS."

Taboo did not respond in a timely manner, so a petulant Max got another text volley in. "Don't you think you ought to be using your time to go after the big fat cats with the money? This Occupy Wall Street shit is pointless."

Taboo didn't like the new guy questioning him in such a pushy fashion. It was unbecoming behavior for an FNG, an abbreviation he adopted from the FBI guys, who referred to their new recruits as "fucking new guys." From Taboo's perspective, Max's focus on wealth did not appear to fit the Luzz social charter. For Luzz, it wasn't about making money; it was about fucking with the cultural institutions or causing disruption to the governmental order, whether local or federal. It was about sending the Wall Street pricks a message. They are the ones who epitomize big fat cats with money, he believed. So when Taboo finally responded, he sent a calculated message. "Max, I will get back to you. We want you in the Luzz Security Group big time, as a brother and major technical contributor. However, I am concerned your global appreciation of politics isn't as sophisticated as it should be. We can work with you on this, but it can't be just about money, dude."

Taboo didn't realize the young Russian-American would take immediate exception and reject the recruitment.

"What a fucking jerk-off," thought Max. "Fuck him. Fuck Luzz, and fuck all that Occupy Wall Street bullshit. For me it's about the money. These guys may be good, but I'm better. Why waste my time with them?"

Max knew how to manipulate vulnerable computer systems as well as Luzz did, to meddle, or even cripple them. "I don't have time to be a social savant," he thought. "The cyber shit changes too fast. To survive is to know when to check, when to parry, and when to strike. These boys focus too much on people, particularly the Feds, who know how to block, pivot, and parry, too. An association with Luzz will only get me targeted and arrested. I will play along only long enough to learn the Luzz operational structure and then detach myself."

NINETEEN

Not long after Jim O'Brien secured the prisoners in the county jail, he dialed his boss on the phone and began to describe the night's work. Tom Dooley, the acting SAC for the Drug Enforcement Agency's Newark office, expressed an interest in learning more from O'Brien about the investigative intelligence Diablo had offered up.

O'Brien eagerly briefed his boss about Diablo's assertions. He knew Dooley took great satisfaction in collegiality with his federal counterparts and entertained any opportunity to give a major league criminal referral to the head of another federal agency. Dooley felt it enhanced his chances to be permanently appointed to the agent-in-charge position. A growing reputation for inter-agency cooperation would help him garner that support.

"Bring the arrests to the attention of the U.S. Attorney's Office first thing in the morning," Dooley advised O'Brien. "After their initial appearance we can talk about this Diablo's assertions."

O'Brien deferentially concurred with his boss and agreed to comply. He didn't need to be told what to do, but if the boss needed to demonstrate his managerial prowess, then so be it. O'Brien was satisfied that his managers allowed him to make the street calls, so it didn't bother him to appear slightly obsequious. O'Brien operated on the theory that it is best to let your work speak for itself, and so he strived to present himself always in a compliant and professionally pleasant manner. He remembered an earlier boss's axiom, "It's not how fast one goes; it's how far."

The next morning O'Brien placed a call to Assistant U.S. Attorney Shane Gergich about the Diablo-Tanya connection. O'Brien's plan was to successfully record enough incriminating detail during a drug deal to get her to cooperate and help them track Max. Gergich authorized the DEA to "wire Diablo up" and secretly record his conversation with Tanya. They were scheduled to meet later that day as she arrived at the strip club.

"We need to alert the Secret Service's New York field office and ask if they want to be part of the investigation," Gergich suggested. "If it pans out she can help lead to Max, indicating a complex hacking scenario, then having the Service involved up front will help expedite things." Gergich knew from his past prosecutions the Service would have an investigative interest.

During 2003–04 he had managed the prosecution, and more precisely the "handling," of young Floridian hacker Angelo Suarez, who became an influential informant for the U.S. government. He helped the government peer into the global operations of three super hackers. The government, through the Secret Service investigation, learned much about the cyber enhancement world from these super hackers, and it scared the crap out of high-ranking government officials.

"My God," Gergich would acknowledge off the record, "if these bastards start working for foreign government cyber terrorism or espionage groups, we're all in a world of shit."

He continued with O'Brien. "Should this case spin off into a greater cyber issue, and if Tanya's boyfriend becomes a significant player in a broader global hacking enterprise, then it makes a lot of sense to include the Secret Service to take the investigation to the next level."

O'Brien took no offense with Gergich's recommendation. He liked the "Secrets" and felt comfortable with their participation in the investigation. "I will ask acting SAC Dooley to make the call."

TWENTY

Just as Max stopped texting, Tanya entered the living room. She found him in what appeared to be a trance, indicating a deeply pensive, analytical state. She had no deep knowledge or understanding of Max's cyber sprees or affiliations with hacking groups, except that he spent an inordinate amount of time working at his keyboards. She preferred he spend his time honing his mixed martial arts skills. He was less agitated when he engaged in physical training. Besides she thought, Max needed to be in top shape as a contender for his next event. At age twenty-six, he was in his prime and was a legitimate Ultimate Fighter contender. She knew he yearned to honor the memory of his father by winning the championship.

Tanya walked up behind Max, normally not a smart move in consideration of Max's reflexes. But Tanya's heavy perfume alerted Max's olfactory senses and awoke him from his catatonic state. Tanya put her hands on his shoulders and squeezed tenderly.

She whispered in his left ear, "When you are silent, you are incredibly and deliciously attractive." Max tolerated her attempt to relax him, but he did not return the attentions she so desperately craved. Instead, in a measured emotionless tone, he shared with her, "A new hacking group seeks my technological talents, but I am afraid accepting their invitation would be too exhausting and time consuming on issues I have no passion to pursue. But if I am to grow intellectually, I must learn as much as I can about how these groups operate so that I may be prepared one day to defeat them if necessary."

Tanya wasn't entirely aware of what he was talking about, but she understood that when his talk grew businesslike, she just needed to listen. She conceptualized in her own seductive way how she could capitalize on it, but it didn't work. He wasn't interested tonight. Tanya shifted her thoughts to her other love, cocaine, as she left Max in the room alone. He wouldn't notice. She had to go get ready for work and retreated to her bedroom without saying a word. She was confused by his rant. It was not the Max she thought she knew. But now she had to concentrate on herself.

Her need for his affection was not satisfied. No matter, she would get to work and have more attention than a girl could ask for. Her job as a stripper took care of that need.

Then she heard Max's epiphany. Max continued to negotiate with himself, speaking loudly enough for Tanya to hear in the other room.

"This guy Taboo is not good. He is too much an ideology guy. I am a greed guy. I like greed guys. They fight for something of substance, not an idea hanging out there with twisted perversions trying to get the rest of society to pay attention to them. Greed guys like money. They like to live. They constantly seek to move forward. The ideology crowd is always tearing things down. They seek destruction. Well, I seek opportunity. I want to be a champion, not some slug sitting on the side of a sidewalk with a handwritten cardboard poster. They're fucking assholes. They're no better than those Al Qaida assholes. I got no time for them or their radicalism. I have no time to dream about diverse ideologies, sending political messages to corrupt governments and businesses. Now is the time to create wealth for me. I need to make a statement by making money. I can do that by winning UFC fights, which will show the world who I am physically. And when the world is thinking I am just a moron fighter, I will be busy re-distributing their money my way, cracking into a thousand of their bank accounts, siphoning off their dormant funds. Then they'll figure out how stupid I am."

Max went silent again, almost trancelike, as though he had talked himself into a catatonic state. He sat alone, strategizing his upcoming cyber event.

Tanya showered quickly, dried off, and then pulled on a pair of cutoff jeans and a tight-fitting tank top. With no bra, she was sure to attract plenty of hungry stares when she arrived at the Stilettos nightclub. She liked to wear flip-flops to work, putting her heels in an oversized personal bag that matched her dance outfit. With flip-flops she felt she could blend in easily at the local shopping mall and not appear slutty or too glamorous. There would be time for that later at the club.

Tonight she needed to shop at Victoria's Secret and pick up some sale items. She couldn't resist the Victoria's Secret offer for free lace cotton hip huggers and a free pink getaway bag. The sales come-on offered $10 off push-up bras. She didn't actually need any, but felt compelled to get one just to cash in on the freebies. Besides, she rationalized, the promotional bag could be useful for carrying her dainty dance outfits.

She handed the store associate her discount card, which had arrived in the mail a few days earlier. It made her feel like she belonged to a special club. Moreover, Victoria's Secret just had to know that she represented their wear as it should be truly worn.

Once she arrived at the strip club, she disrobed and changed into one of her new outfits. She had purchased a red and white Christmas outfit that got her through the holiday season, but now that it was February, she had tired of it. So had the customers. No more holiday garb for her. She had lost her seasonal spirit long ago.

Tanya preferred to wear all white—if not all white, then a combination of red and white or red and black to contrast with her well-developed tan, which she maintained at a tanning salon near Max's home in Brighton Beach. With the money she made as an exotic dancer she couldn't care less about the president's tanning tax. Her tanning salon remained open despite the additional tax.

She learned from the other dancers to wear the briefest of apparel. It was about revealing as much skin as possible, but leaving enough to the imagination to maintain the tease. Tanya usually preferred not to mix and match her outfits like most of the other dancers did. She thought it professionally tacky; it was a feeling to which she clung tightly, as it gave her a heightened sense of self-esteem.

Her two favorite outfits attracted a lot of attention from customers: a white long-sleeved fishnet dress and a chemise dress with slash detail over a matching thong. Now and then, she covered her athletic figure with a naughty schoolgirl look. The red and black plaid never failed to attract the old perverts and their cash. She occasionally wondered if it really mattered how she dressed. Her outfit would come off eventually and her ogling customers would probably not remember what she had been wearing anyway.

Max rarely knew what she wore. "He's the only one I really care about seeing me," she lamented as she packed her studio bag with several stage outfits and stiletto shoes.

On her way to Carlstadt, New Jersey, Tanya reflected on her fleeting attempt to give Max a shoulder massage. His loss of attention and desire for her had initially pained her. Now she had no more tears to fight back. Max's non-responsiveness had left her dangerously close to emotional bankruptcy. Living with him was no longer fun. She felt unwanted and found it increasingly difficult to entice his interest. She had grown more aware that he was distancing himself from her, and it made her anxious.

The stress of her home life with Max was exacerbated as he became more obsessed with his daily workouts at the dojo. When he came home he dedicated himself to the lost horizon of the Internet, usually until early morning, and even then he barely slept.

"I don't know how long he can go on with this lifestyle," she thought, aware of one thing for sure; there was increasingly less time for physical intimacy. She didn't necessarily need physical interaction as much as she needed confirmation that he still had desire for her.

Oddly, while Tanya felt left out of Max's emotional sphere, she did not feel totally abandoned by him. He was on his way to greatness, and if she could survive the temporary loneliness, the interpersonal relationship might improve. She clung to that notion. She was comforted in knowing she was his one and only. She was all he needed, although he didn't seem to need her much these days. She counseled herself to remain patient. During these desperate internal admonitions, Tanya sought to stem the loneliness. That's when she needed her coke. She could mask a lot of emotion once she had met with Diablo and indulged.

She departed Brighton Beach for Stilettos in her 2015 Jeep Wrangler, a four-speed stick shift. It was a feisty vehicle even with a four-cylinder engine. Tanya expected Diablo would be there to replenish her depleted emotional long days and longer nights. Then she would be satisfied. It carried her through the day and the night. Tanya chuckled as she drove to the club, thinking how funny it was she was now deriving most of her happiness from a guy who went by the name of the devil.

Approaching the club she silently prayed to the "Baby Jesus." It was a prayer taught to her by her mother as a youngster while still living in the Ukraine. She compartmentalized the drugs and the dancing while keeping Jesus in her life to keep her internal conflict at bay; it worked. Praying gave her comfort. Her mother had taught her that the Lord would always forgive, and if she sought forgiveness she would receive it. She desperately believed if she kept the faith, she would always be in God's hands and it would keep her from going to Hell. Tanya needed that assurance. She preached Jesus to her customers in a bizarre effort to remain in God's good graces.

"God bless you, Sweetie," she would say. The client rarely acknowledged the blessing or comprehended why she would even invoke it. In her twisted logic it kept her in good grace.

Tonight it was time for the Devil. She was to meet first with the source of her comfort, Diablo, and pick up a larger than usual supply of the cocaine.

"I hope he has what I want," she sang to herself while driving into the club's lot. She didn't have the money to pay him tonight, but he would understand. He sounded pretty itchy to meet me tonight, she thought. "Probably wants a blow job since I don't have the money. I may have to give him one. Damn! I hope he showered."

TWENTY ONE

Brian Gallagher was the highly regarded special agent in charge, or SAIC, of the Secret Service's New York field office. The Secrets always add the "I" to their abbreviation, indicating the head of the field office. This differs from Justice Department agencies, which use the economical three-letter version.

Gallagher sat drinking his morning coffee in the Brooklyn office overlooking an especially clear Manhattan skyline. He was contemplating how good he had had it for the past twenty years in the Secret Service.

Gallagher managed the Service's flagship office and was considered by many to be a candidate one day to replace the Service's director. Truth be told, he never wanted that position. Being SAIC of the NYFO was enough for him. His office managed many of the agency's largest complex criminal investigations and hosted the larger annual security events, which included virtually every known head of state in the world.

During Gallagher's term in office, none of his agents had been shot; nor had any made the front pages of the New York tabloids. Also, none had ever resigned. His agents had great respect for him and his leadership of the office.

"Is it time to consider retirement?" he had begun to ask himself. Gallagher was a hot commodity in the New York area. There were half a dozen corporations that would love to have him as their chief security officer. That's what he wanted one day, but not today.

Gallagher's desk phone rang. It was the DEA Newark SAC. When that call ended, he made another. He contacted his Cyber Crime Squad supervisor, Carly Strain, to brief her on the DEA telephone conversation.

"Carly, please have a seat," he said when she arrived at his office. Strain took the seat directly in front of Gallagher's desk. She had been in the office many times and was never disappointed in the view overlooking the Manhattan skyline. Regardless, she shifted her attention immediately to the boss.

"I just got a call from SAC Dooley from the DEA, Newark Division. He told me his guys arrested a mid-level drug dealer last night who wants to provide information on an impending cyber-crime. He said the dealer sounded credible. They don't have much more than that, but they are going to wire the suspect up and cover a meeting with the hacker's girlfriend in New Jersey late today to see what develops. The U.S. Attorney is onboard and aware of the wire. I would like you to work it, so contact our Newark field office and be sure to have one their agents with you so we can avoid any territorial bullshit."

Later that day, Jim O'Brien met with Kenny Reed from the DEA, Secret Service Supervisor Carly Strain from the New York Field Office Cyber Crime Squad, and Special Agent Mike Sinnott, a representative from the local Secret Service's Newark office, at the Sheraton lot along Route 3, just across from Giants Stadium.

"Our guys will wire up Diablo. He'll attempt to engage Tanya in conversation. Once we have probable cause, we'll go in for the arrest." Strain was in her element. She welcomed the invite from the DEA. Her husband, Commander Will Strain of the U.S. Coast Guard, was a military attaché in Kuwait and worked often with the DEA in the Middle East theatre. She liked the DEA guys and trusted them. She was also confident in their investigative abilities.

Sinnott knew he was brought along to ensure the interests of his office were represented. It didn't bother him that the larger field office would take the lead. From the New York office's perspective, keeping their Jersey field office in the loop was a demonstration of collegiality.

TWENTY TWO

"Text Tanya. We'll need to know if she intends to work tonight. If so, tell her you'll meet her at the club after she arrives," O'Brien said. Texting was Diablo's normal manner of communication with all of his clients. She wouldn't be alarmed
by it.

Diablo's text worked. "I'll see you when I arrive. I need a little extra tonight, Honey." Tanya's response indicated to Diablo that she wanted five grams.

"With five grams she faces a minimum of ten years behind bars," Kenny Reed said. To O'Brien that was good news. It would be well into the felony range as a purchase—a Class A felony.

O'Brien had Reed bring the Lexus to the hotel's parking lot for the pending deal.

"Hey Carly! Look what we confiscated last night from Diablo," he said. O'Brien's smile gave away how excited he was about the car. For the moment, Diablo was going to drive it to the Stilettos Club, where he would meet with Tanya.

"We want to keep things as normal as we can so as not to spook Tanya. If he didn't have his car she would probably notice. I just hope he doesn't scratch it up," said O'Brien. "My boss would be very disappointed."

In the confines of the Sheraton lot along Route 17, the agents checked the distance at which Diablo could still be monitored while wearing a transmitter. O'Brien drove his G-car a one hundred yards from the rest of the group to test its range. A Sheraton security officer observing the activity drove his security jeep over to the loitering group, his rooftop yellow lights blinking. As he got closer, Reed pulled out the badge he carried on a chain around his neck from inside his shirt and displayed it at chest level for the security officer to see.

"If this doesn't work," he told Strain, "I'll bray like a donkey until he backs off." Fortunately, it did work, and the jeep and its driver returned to their post outside the hotel's entrance. The security guard could see the "locals" were up to something that was not his business. He was right.

"The radio frequency from the surveillance equipment works well, Jimmy. We have good reception well over a hundred yards."

Reed transmitted over the G-car's radio. "Thanks Ken. Let's depart for the meeting and get this going." They wanted to arrive and set their observation posts at least thirty minutes before Tanya arrived for her nightly shift.

Sinnott drove, with Diablo sitting in the right front seat. Strain rode with O'Brien. Reed drove the LFA. O'Brien wanted to limit the time Diablo would have access to the LFA.

With Sinnott trailing, Reed found a spot he liked. It was located in a parking lot across the highway from the strip club at the Meadowlands Fuelstop on Paterson Plank Road. O'Brien set up closer, situating himself in a driveway adjacent to the strip club, but separated sufficiently by a thicket of small trees and brush. The position gave him maximum cover while offering a great line of sight, and more importantly, a clear and distinct radio signal. The agents were not concerned that Diablo could be in any danger. They wanted only to monitor and record the conversation that would support Tanya's arrest and lend credence to Diablo's tip.

Tanya was expected to arrive at Stilettos about 6 o'clock. The agents observed little customer pedestrian traffic into the club at this early hour. As they had discussed back at the Sheraton lot, once she arrived, Diablo would drive the LFA from the gas station lot to the strip club, exit the vehicle, and personally approach the stripper. O'Brien knew the risk in trusting Diablo with the keys to the LFA, but the four agents would have a pretty good "eyeball" on his movements at all times. "Besides," he thought, "Diablo is clinging to the hope that when all this works out he might still get his LFA back." He chuckled softly to himself, "Not a chance, Diablo. Not a chance."

Reed left Sinnott alone in the G-car as he walked over to the LFA. He opened the passenger side door and sat next to Diablo. Reed brought Halvey's powerful binoculars to the scene. These were the same binoculars used the previous night to observe Diablo passing the plastic envelopes to Bowser.

The two passengers were close enough to observe Tanya's arrival. She usually parked behind the club where Diablo could meet her and give her coke, hopefully for cash. "When cash is tight, I sometimes exchange the drugs for oral satisfaction," Diablo told the DEA. O'Brien hoped for cash.

Diablo, disappointed his relationship with Tanya was about to change so dramatically, consoled himself with the idea that his cooperation might get him out of serious trouble with the Feds; perhaps he'd even get to keep the LFA.

TWENTY THREE

Prior to meeting with the DEA, Agent Strain had directed her cyber squad to conduct some preliminary background checks on Diablo, Max, and Tanya.

"Carly, this guy Diablo is on record with the Secret Service for credit card fraud back in the 1990s. He 'pled out' and received one year of probation. Tanya has no record," reported Steve Austin, her squad deputy.

"We have this guy, Max, listed as a person of interest in a hacking scenario the Service became aware of while monitoring a Title One investigation," he added, referring to the government's legal monitoring of a hacker's keystrokes and listening in on a subject's telephone conversations.

Many, if not most, hackers were out of work or made very little "legit" money with normal jobs. It was not unusual for hackers to find themselves communicating with other like-minded individuals, which would explain how Max's conversation was intercepted on someone else's wire.

"Carly, it appears from the database that Max never incriminated himself, but did talk knowledgeably about electronic money transfers involving e-gold accounts and something about reverse cash deposits to dormant bank accounts."

Strain responded, "Okay, so it looks like we didn't have enough to open an investigation, but we have enough to list him as a person of interest. I got it. Thanks for all that, Steve."

Over the years hackers have developed increasingly better evasive techniques to keep law enforcement at bay. The preponderance of hacker

IP addresses, the Internet Protocol identification that allows for tracing the origin of the computer, were determined to originate from Eastern Europe. This fact was not surprising to the Secret Service. Strain's cyber squad had successfully tracked and prosecuted many high-tech criminals, and industry and law enforcement experts attributed the increase in prosecutions of cyber-criminals as an effective deterrent to large-scale efforts by the criminal hacking community to attack the large company computer systems.

"Hackers aren't stupid," Austin often lamented to Strain. "Their tactics constantly change in response to the increase in prosecutions, and I think they are moving from massive breaches to smaller, less risky heists. The better hackers adapt to our methods and the whole circle begins anew."

TWENTY FOUR

"I think we need to give her about ten minutes to get situated at the club before I go inside and talk to her. She usually needs time to go to the dressing room and pretty her face up. If I go in there too fast it might spook her, because I'm not following my normal pattern," Diablo suggested to Kenny Reed.

Reed agreed. "We'll give her some time to settle down. No problem."

"Diablo, why is she looking for so much tonight?" asked Jim O'Brien

"Probably for the other dancers. Her boyfriend doesn't do drugs."

"She's arrived and is parking her red two-door Jeep Wrangler behind the club. New York registration XXX-69," Reed transmitted over his two-way radio.

"Must be a vanity plate," O'Brien replied. "I'm surprised New York allowed that one to slip through. Make sure you call it into the office for a motor vehicle check and have the duty desk conduct an NCIC check as well to see if the owner has any criminal history."

"Roger that, Jimmy. I'll send Diablo over to the club lot in a few minutes. We want to let her settle down inside first." Reed didn't have to explain further. O'Brien trusted Reed to make the correct call.

The agents didn't know exactly what would come from the recorded conversation, but the little background Diablo had given them had made the monitoring effort worthwhile. He had related that the dancer was hooked on coke, and she had a boyfriend who was potentially a well-versed hacker who could lead them straight into the world of the

Russian mob in Brighton Beach. Drugs, hacking, and racketeering often led to a satisfying night for the boys with the badges.

"Okay, you can depart now and go slowly, no speeding. We don't need to get pulled over at this point," admonished Reed.

"No worries, sir." Diablo arrived at the strip club and parked his LFA near Tanya's Jeep. "Keep it normal," he thought. He knew his every move was being monitored.

Diablo stepped purposely into the bar. Jelly, the bouncer, knew to scratch in a false name. He usually wrote down some variation of W. C. Fields for Diablo. Tonight it was Billy Fieldstone. He passed by the bouncer, who gave him a simple nod, an acknowledgement that he didn't have to sign his name on the form mandated by local ordinance.

"This is such a silly thing," Jelly thought. "Who in their right mind is going to put their real name on a club's list?"

Jelly was anything but jelly. He got his nickname from the girls because of his fondness for peanut butter and jelly sandwiches, sometimes triple-deckers with heavy doses of grape jelly. Jelly was a weight lifter by day and a bouncer at night.

"I've got the perfect job. I get free pussy anytime I want, plus the job is fucking easy."

Most of the work involved looking like a tough guy. His chiseled physique sent out the intimidating message loud and clear. The patrons tended to stay in line, and when confronted by Jelly and told to keep their hands off a dancer, they always complied.

The rest of the job required him to keep the dancers dancing. Sometimes that meant tracking down a girl in the deep recesses of the club, where he would usually find her snorting coke, a big no-no by club rules. Even worse, sometimes he would find one of the girls screwing a customer or letting the customer "finger blast" her.

The club owners only cared about this behavior when they weren't getting a cut of the action. Depending on the girl, Jelly might or might not enforce the club rule. Those who tipped him improved their status with the club enforcer. The tip didn't always have to be money. Jelly was just as happy when the payoff was a blow job. Or better yet, sometimes the girl would offer to share her stash of coke.

"I thought he was going to meet her out back," O'Brien said to Reed over the radio. "His transmitter is sending a lot of static. And who is Jelly?"

"Stand by, Jimmy. He should be rendezvousing with her outside by the Jeep shortly."

Diablo took a seat in front of the elevated dance floor, not far from the dancers' personal dressing lounge, and watched two topless dancers actively engage in a feigned devotion to each other's pudenda. He knew if he wanted to, he could break the duo up with a facial expression that implied he was offering free cocaine.

Tonight was not the night for that. The dancers all knew him and would favor him when he signaled, even if it meant dropping a current patron. However, he was on a different mission this night and needed to remain solo. Tanya came out of the lounge dressed in a see-through blouse and cutoff jean shorts. She had yet to change into one of her signature outfits, designed to showcase her Victoria's Secret form. She sat next to Diablo.

"We need to go outside," she whimpered. She looked down and away to imply submission. To Diablo, this usually meant she didn't have money for the coke she desperately needed, or worse, didn't have the money or the time to devote to Diablo should he demand some attention. Tonight Diablo could handle it either way.

He swiftly complied with her suggestion to go out back, mostly to satisfy his new handlers and get her out to where the wire could pick up their conversation more clearly. "The more they get on her, the better it is for me," he thought.

He didn't need to convince her to talk. She always talked. He hoped he could steer the conversation toward Max and his impending criminal operations. He wanted to impress the Feds. He leaned in close and whispered in her ear. "Let's go through the lounge and out back. I have what you need."

Tanya nodded. Her relief turning to anticipation, she took the lead. She grabbed his right hand to lead them both through the dancers' dressing lounge. Jelly was still stationed at his chair by the front door screening customers. He would not have cared if Diablo walked into the girl's lounge. He knew it could only benefit him later when he got a share of the girl's coke.

As Tanya and Diablo entered the lounge they saw only one other girl present. She paid no attention to them as they hustled through. The girl was barely able to keep awake, her elbows perilously close to the edge of the lounge's only mirrored table. If her hands slipped her head would strike the mirror. The anemic-looking dancer appeared to Diablo to be more than exhausted, probably strung out. "That girl needs more sleep and less partying. Long night for her," he said to Tanya.

"Fuck her," said Tanya. "She never pulls her weight around here. Jelly should just throw her lazy ass out the door. Besides, she's too freaking ugly to work here. She gives the rest of us the creeps when she does show up for work. She's so dirty. Look at her hands. They're filthy. She hasn't taken a fucking bath in days. She's gross."

Diablo chuckled to himself. "How self-righteous they can be." He almost made a comment about Tanya's own addiction, but caught himself. He didn't want to jeopardize his opportunity to impress the Feds.

"This night is all about escaping," he thought. He needed to be "libre," free to do his "negocios drugos," the business that kept him living in his current lifestyle. He was ready to give up Tanya.

In the parking lot behind the dance club, Tanya leaned against another dancer's new blue BMW convertible. It was her way of establishing territory at the club, plus it was a convenient place to seat her superior ass and not mark up her own Jeep.

Tanya had parked her Jeep at an angle, taking up two spaces. She wouldn't give the other dancers an opportunity to scratch her car as they pulled into or out of the lot while all coked up.

Once she was settled in on the side of the BMW, she pulled Diablo in close. Her buttoned down blouse was now anything but. Her ample cleavage was inches from his face. Her shirttail hung over her cutoff jeans, trimmed intentionally to show off the barely concealed buttocks that led to her long athletic legs, providing perfect symmetry to her dancer's figure. Four-inch spike heels added to her aura. The surveillance team took notice.

"Honey, I have no money and can't spend time with you right now. I promise I will make it up to you soon. But I need my coke." As she got closer, Diablo grew worried Tanya might feel the transmitter that was attached to his lower back, sending signals back to the surveillance vehicle where their conversation was being recorded. The agents had duct-taped the device, a standard agency "kel-kit," to his back and laced the twenty-four-inch wire, tipped with a small microphone, up his back and around his neck, securing it to the inside of his silk t-shirt.

Diablo didn't want her to get too close and notice the small bulge in his collar. But he also didn't want to appear overly cautious. The agents had done an effective job of concealing the microphone. The signal was strong and the hovering agents were listening to an audible conversation.

He gave her a smirk, a non-verbal message to let her know he was receptive to her request. He slowly backed out of her arms' reach, but not so far as to break up the conversation. He wanted to pivot the subject of the conversation to Max.

"Baby, you seem to have a lot on your mind lately, and no time for Daddy." Diablo began his stroking. The agents listening from their vehicle were interested to learn how he intended to manipulate the conversation, but were more eager to hear how the deal consummated so they could arrest her. The agents knew that they, not Diablo, were more adept at the interrogation process. They preferred Diablo not stoke any other topics, and not get too cocky. "Just stay focused, man," O'Brien was heard repeating. Nevertheless, they had no other choice but to monitor the conversation until she had the coke.

"I'm tense probably because Max has been so obsessed with his bank job. I think he's about to do something really big, because he spends all his time now with his computers and on his headset. He's been so consumed by it all. I just hope he makes a lot of money so I can get the fuck away from here." Tanya reached out with an open palm in a gesture to Diablo to hand over the cocaine.

"Here baby, you pay me when you can, any way you can, but make sure you don't leave the area without telling me should your hombre bust a move after he makes his billions," Diablo skillfully prompted. "I can get you all the coke you need when Max becomes a rich man. For now, take the coke on credit."

Tanya took the bag and kissed Diablo on his right cheek.

"Thanks, Baby. I have to take care of Jelly tonight, so the little bit extra helps." Diablo wasn't sure, but he thought the agents had heard enough to make their case.

He was right. Within seconds, Sinnott and Reed pulled into the lot from the right side of the club, leaving Strain and O'Brien to make their appearance from the left. No lights, no sirens, just a calm approach.

No one in the club, especially Jelly, had an inkling as to what was going on. For the second time in two days, Diablo found himself in handcuffs. Only this time it was a staged arrest to lead Tanya to believe he was caught "mano roja," or red handed, that is, involved in the drug transfer; it was a classic law enforcement technique to give the informant plausible deniability.

Sinnott cuffed Diablo and placed him in the G-car. His cuffs were not as tight as they had been the day before, a DEA concession in light of Diablo's cooperation.

Diablo was confident he'd done his part and looked forward to getting relief. For him that meant freedom. His face went flush as he considered what Max could do to him if it ever came out he had set up Tanya, and now Max, to the Feds. He sat back in the agent's vehicle and stared out the window as he watched O'Brien cuff Tanya, while Carly, who was backing up O'Brien, moved her hands up and down Tanya's torso to pat her down for any secreted weapons. Once the pat down was completed, Carly led her to a waiting DEA vehicle and guided her into the seat. She secured a seatbelt around Tanya's waist and firmly pushed the car door closed. Diablo grinned, "I wish I could have done that, my hands would been all over her." The agents' cars deserted the lot as quickly as they had arrived. For the moment, no one inside the strip club was aware of what just happened.

The DEA could come back later for the Jeep. O'Brien thought it best to leave it alone for the time being and let the club owners figure out for themselves where Tanya might have gone. For all they would know, he reasoned, she might have left for a short time with a client. The LFA was another matter. O'Brien had Reed drive it out of the lot. "Didn't want to lose it," he said to Reed.

The whole arrest scenario took less than one minute. As the second Fed car left the lot, the rear door of the club swung open. The filthy dancer peered out, but saw nothing. She took a puff of a cigarette that dangled from her lips and shrugged at the non-event. The commotion she thought she heard was no longer present. She exhaled, gazed fondly at her new BMW, smiled, and returned to her mirrored table.

In the DEA vehicle, Tanya had been securely placed in the back seat with her safety belt fastened. Though her hands were cuffed behind her back, she did not seem to be uncomfortable, unlike most arrestees who complain quickly that their cuffs are too tight. It was a tactic usually intended to delay, to slow things down and try to figure out what to say when the inevitable questioning begins.

Tanya may have been pissed off, but it was not because she feared questioning. She wanted and needed the cocaine, and now it was not to be. She was agitated.

"Fuck me," she said to herself while in transit to the DEA office for processing. There she would be most vulnerable to the agents' interrogation. The more experienced agents got the niceties out of the way while the arrestee was being transported. It was not uncommon for suspects to be so chagrined that their spontaneous utterances flowed freely, providing the investigator with talking points to chip away at any alibi.

Agent Strain sat in the right front seat of the DEA government car and after securing her own seat belt, turned to read Tanya her Miranda rights.

"You have the right to remain silent, the right to have an attorney present before you answer any questions, the right to have an attorney if you cannot afford one, and if you answer questions these answers may be used against you in the court of law. Do you understand these rights?"

"Fuck you, bitch. I didn't do anything wrong," Tanya snarled. Carly chuckled. Tanya's custodial condition was so pathetic, and she presented no threat unless she started spitting. Strain was prepared to let her curse.

"Okay, Tanya, but you may want to tone it down a bit," Strain replied calmly, exuding the confidence of an experienced agent. Tanya's stance was a welcome opportunity. The seasoned investigator wasted no time and began to whittle away at Tanya's attitude.

"Tanya, you just purchased five grams of cocaine. You will go to jail for a long time. If that is truly what you want, then so be it. Keep that chip on your shoulder. But there are options, and you ought to calm down and listen; otherwise, you're facing ten years in jail. That's a long time for a pretty young lady." Agent Strain put on a matronly demeanor when talking to Tanya. It came easily.

Strain instinctively knew she would need only a short time to turn Tanya and convince her it was in her best interests to give up some information. She wanted to do it without Tanya requesting a defense attorney.

Her Miranda rights were long forgotten by the time Tanya arrived at the DEA office in Newark, New Jersey. Strain's tactical reading of her rights so soon after her arrest, she hoped, would reap benefits, ultimately resulting in Tanya's cooperation.

The DEA and Secret Service agents took Tanya without fanfare into the DEA office. No newspaper photographers, just a lonely walk between two federal agents into a dull, grey asphalt building garage, then directly to a dedicated elevator that would take Tanya anonymously to their office.

The elevator allowed them to avoid the "perp" walk. Parading a defendant can prove embarrassing and may destroy any goodwill initiated between the arresting agents and the new defendant.

Tanya now sat alone inside the DEA's interview room, a spartan setting featuring nothing more than a rectangular table, four white folding chairs, a round digital clock, and what appeared to be a mirror. The mirror was actually a one-way observation window that allowed the agents an opportunity to read the suspect's body language while he or she was being interviewed.

Tanya sat slumped at the table. Strain uncuffed Tanya's right wrist and secured it to an eyebolt screwed into the cinder block wall. She wasn't concerned about her bolting. She wanted to keep the pressure on.

If the threat of federal incarceration didn't impress her, the DEA could have her charged locally, that is, have one of their local counterparts in Bergen County, New Jersey, charge her with "drug purchase with the intent to distribute," a bad omen for any defendant facing time in state prison.

Federal custody was perceived as country club time; State prison time was considered "hard time." The comparison was a productive interrogation technique used to get suspects to talk. Once suspects realized that going local was a possibility, there was a tendency for them to become chatty.

Tanya grew increasingly nervous, borderline scared. She began to appreciate her dilemma, realizing perhaps she would be off the street for a long period of time—no cocaine, no Max, a completely inverted world. She didn't like the feeling.

After just several minutes in the room, Tanya seemed to have an epiphany. She started to get it, to understand the gravity of her situation. Strain's job was about to get a lot easier. "I know what you want and I will give it to you."

The room went completely quiet for a few seconds. In the room with Tanya were Agents Strain and O'Brien, who exchanged sideways glances and nodded, acknowledging the prospect of her cooperation. O'Brien assumed a deferential posture, letting the Secret Service Cyber Squad leader take the initiative.

"I'm all ears, Tanya. Do you want a cup of coffee?" Strain now concentrated on building a relationship.

"You can't be just interested in me. This has to be about my boyfriend, Max," Tanya said.

"Yes. You are right, Tanya. And we would be interested in helping you should you have information that may help us, but I can't promise you anything until I hear more."

Strain was pleased to see how quickly this was unfolding. She knew she had to keep the momentum moving forward and convince Tanya the key to overcoming her situation was full cooperation.

Thanks to her squad, Strain now knew Max was a major player in the hacking community. She needed fresh information that Tanya could produce to satisfy the legal requirements for a search warrant. She needed Tanya as much as Tanya needed her.

"If I tell you about my boyfriend's interest and what I think he is up to, will I get the hell out of here?" Tanya asked.

"That depends on what it is that he is doing," Agent Strain replied. "Tanya, you are in big trouble right now. If you provide us with solid and verifiable information on Max, it will go a long way, as I just told you, toward reducing your exposure to jail. I can help, but you have to begin providing something of substance if you want that help."

"Agent Strain, I do want to help myself out of this problem. My boyfriend is into hacking and fighting. He spends his days practicing mixed-martial arts and his nights working his computer network dominance." That was not her word. She had heard Max use it many times while bragging to Shorty about his exploits.

"He's planning to pull off something big. Bigger than anyone has ever seen. He says it will be earth shattering." Tanya became introspective as she attempted to recollect Max's comments. "I know he is close with the Bratva, the Russian mob, but I don't know if he is a full member. He tends to be his own boss."

Strain encouraged her. "You don't have to be an expert. All we ask of you is to allow us to gain access to your apartment when he is not there to familiarize ourselves with his computers. Tanya, if you let us visit you in the apartment, we can accomplish what we need to in order to understand what Max is up to, and leave you out of the equation. Max doesn't have to know you provided us with any support. He may not find out that you were even arrested. You help us and we'll help you."

Tanya put her head in her hands and began to cry softly. Then both hands drifted down to her lap as she raised herself up straight, sitting up like a newly crowned beauty queen. She ceased crying and wiped away the legacy tears. "I will help do that. Just tell me what do I have to do." Her face was no longer contorted. She began to look calm and confident.

Strain glanced over at O'Brien, his body language signaling he was merely observing her. She continued with her questioning, a nod to O'Brien affirming the progress that had been made thus far. Tanya's cooperation was about to provide the vital intelligence on a shadowy figure who frequently came up on the Feds digital screens, but who they had previously failed to identify.

TWENTY FIVE

Carly Strain answered her husband's call. It was the first time she heard from him in a week, and she fretted as she sat at her desk in the New York field office. "Hi, honey, I miss you so much. I wish I could be there with you. There is so much going on here with my hacking investigation. DEA gave us a great lead and it is developing so quickly. What's going on with you?"

"You won't believe this but we're going to have a presidential visit here in Kuwait," Will responded. "Are you aware of that?"

"Honey, not only am I aware of it, but I have been notified I have been selected to be a jump team leader on the trip thanks to the Secret Service guys on the ground in Kuwait who worked a deal for me to see you."

"I have been working with an Agent Billy Sims from the White House Detail. He is a fantastic person. He has impressed not only me, but the Kuwaitis too. They love him. The embassy has assigned me to work with the White House advance lead on logistics and then transition to my traditional intelligence role while the president in on the ground. It looks like I may be able to be on the tarmac when your plane arrives. I can't wait to see you."

TWENTY
SIX

Carly Strain fingerprinted Tanya at the DEA office. Normally another agency doing the fingerprinting defied protocol, but this served as a testament to Strain for establishing a relationship with Jim O'Brien so quickly. He trusted her. So did Tanya. Another DEA agent sat down with Tanya to collect her personal information while O'Brien and Strain returned to his office to develop a strategy to target Max.

"If we contact the U.S. Attorney's office and explain the importance of letting Tanya go this evening on her own recognizance, they may go for it. I'm not sure we have enough to convince Gergich that she won't run on us. She may want us to get Tanya arraigned first and post bond. The problem with that is it will definitely alert Max and ping his radar. That'll screw things up and make it near impossible to get access to the apartment."

"I agree, O'Brien. I think if we are going to pull this off we need to get it done now. If she were to let us into the apartment, we wouldn't need a warrant," said Strain. "We get into the residence, insert our proprietary thumb drive into Max's computer to inject our coded script and get out. With the thumb drive it shouldn't take more than a day's activity to get a good footprint of what he's doing and where he's going. My squad can then pen a draft for a search warrant for the U.S. Attorney's Office, specifically for Max's hard drives."

O'Brien agreed. They walked into the processing room and he nodded to the agent standing with Tanya. The agent got the message and quietly left the room. Tanya felt alone.

"Tanya, are you thirsty or hungry?" Strain asked.

"Just a little thirsty," she said. O'Brien got up and retrieved a plastic water bottle from the office refrigerator next to the interview processing room. "Thank you," said Tanya. She was now more respectful in tone and had taken on a more subdued manner.

"Tanya, we want to move forward with Max, and we need to know we can count on you," said Strain. "We can arrange to have you released on bond as early as tonight, but we have to convince the U.S. Attorney you are trustworthy. That would mean we take you back to your apartment and you allow us to be inside for fifteen minutes and have access to Max's computers. It would mean that in exchange for our help in getting the drug charges minimized, you say absolutely nothing about helping us. Is that clear, and is it something you want to do?"

Strain was about as straightforward as an agent could be. She believed in her gut Tanya could be trusted to get the cyber-trained agent in and out of the apartment without detection.

"I can do that. Max is actually staying in midtown all day tomorrow, participating in a full mixed martial arts fight card. He said he wouldn't be home until late in the evening."

The last comment stimulated Strain's investigative juices. Though the DEA would take a backseat role in all this, she appreciated their help. Strain knew the key to understanding the degree of Max's criminal intent would be to get the Secret Service's proprietary application, or "app," introduced to his computer. The device would allow the Service to monitor his keystrokes and gain access to the "inner sanctum" of his hard drive.

"Tanya, we're going to take you back to the lounge to get your car. After you explain to anyone at the club who happens to ask that nothing more happened tonight, it was all a misunderstanding, you need to go home. We'll make sure you get there and stay there. You're being released before judicial action, but you will be monitored. If your cooperation falters, the deal between the DEA and yourself will evaporate. You will then go directly to jail. We will need to meet you tomorrow as soon as Max departs for midtown. Is all this clear to you and do you still want to do this?"

"Yes, I do," Tanya answered.

Strain was eager to conclude business with Tanya for the night. She needed to get Tanya back into her normal rhythm so as to not raise Max's suspicions.

The next morning Tanya called Strain as requested. "Good girl," thought Strain, exhaling a sigh of relief. She had been up most of the night reviewing the information the Service had acquired and placing the pieces of the puzzle together. She sensed Tanya had had a rough night too.

"I had a bad night's sleep," she confided to Strain. "But I am eager to get on with this."

"Terrific. I didn't get much sleep either. Did Max leave yet? We're ready to do this, but want to make sure we don't get interrupted."

What Strain didn't mention was the Secret Service already had enough probable cause to obtain a search warrant for the residence, but Tanya letting them into the residence voluntarily would make it much easier. The agents would be able to gather a greater understanding of the layout of the apartment for tactical entry to actually search the residence and arrest Max.

Strain didn't tell Tanya they intended to install a Kingston thumb drive and inject the sophisticated sniffer onto Max's server. She saw no need to share the additional information. The agents would simply wait for a serendipitous moment to attach, download, and then extract their thumb drive, taking no longer than the time it takes a nurse to give an allergy shot. Tanya's job would be to let them in and point them in the direction of Max's hacking lair, exposing his main CPU, his computer processing unit.

About one hour later, Strain and her senior cyber case agent, Steve Austin, arrived at Brooklyn's Brighton Beach. During the warmer weather visitors could find matronly Russian women sitting out front on their porches speaking no English, clinging to their lingual heritage, and studiously observing the "foreigners" who walked uncomfortably past their doorsteps. But on this day in mid-February it was too cold to be outside, so most remained inside, occasionally peering out their front windows.

Strain and Austin parked their government vehicle a good block away from the target location to avoid unnecessary scrutiny. The target residence, an apartment, was situated not far from similar multi-tenanted apartments that dominated the neighborhood. The long line of apartments on the street lacked imagination. Each apartment was as nondescript as the one on either side. If it weren't for the house number on the outside door, the post office would have a difficult time with its mail delivery.

Strain found the entrance to the municipal lot after she made a left turn off Brighton Second Street, taking a quick right into the municipal lot—a good place to stash her government car. She knew from experience to bring coins to feed the meter. Usually she didn't care about getting a ticket, but this day was different. Of course, she could avoid a ticket by placing her NYPD-issued placard on the G-car's dashboard, but that would draw attention.

Strain gauged correctly that the more attention they attracted, the easier it would be for them to be recognized as intruders. In this Brighton Beach neighborhood word would quickly spread about any unusual behavior. She scanned the lot and found several empty parking spots near the boardwalk. "Minimize your presence," she whispered to herself. She especially didn't want to have to fend off some outraged parking lot master for taking an inappropriate parking space. The lot was a pay-and-display parking facility at twenty-five cents for ten minutes.

Strain estimated the time inside Tanya's residence would be no more than twenty minutes. She turned to her passenger, "Here's two dollars' worth of quarters. Feed the meter. That should give us enough time to come and go with plenty of time to spare."

For Austin, it was a rare occurrence to feed a city meter for a government car. "Do you get reimbursed for this?" he asked, wincing as though it pained him to pay.

"Don't fret. I'm sure the Secret Service can handle a few cents."

Strain thought Austin's comment would come in handy one day when the opportunity arose to tease him in front of his colleagues, perhaps at the transfer party for his next assignment. She stowed it in her memory bank. Austin had a reputation as a classic "short arms, deep pockets" kind of guy, a trite reference to his frugal habits.

Austin returned from the pay machine with a receipt, which he placed on the driver's side dashboard. He and Strain started out on foot. They crossed Brightwater Court and headed straight out the lot entrance toward Third Street, moving northeast toward Brighton Beach Avenue.

A white desolate beach lay behind them. "No lifeguards today," Strain thought as she looked back. This time of year the beach was closed. A sign in both English and Russian read "Please, no Swimming or Bathing." Another sign warned, "Ocean beaches are affected by strong currents and sudden drop-offs that contribute to drowning."

Strain had no intention of visiting the beach, but she remained impressed with the large white-capped waves that rhythmically pounded the shores. No one was present to witness nature's musical beat other than an occasional pedestrian wearing the preferred wardrobe of the Russian male émigré, a black or blue running suit with large white stripes along the arms and legs. A large, standalone boardwalk sign, erected at the end of the enormous wooden structure, stated in Russian, "No Smoking on Boardwalk." The phony looking fitness buffs ignored it.

During the summer months the Brighton Beach area took on a completely different appearance. Its Russian diaspora flock to the sand, dotting it with a colorful array of umbrellas, chairs, and towels. It was not much different than most other American beaches but for the fact that little English was spoken, and Bratva Mob business deals were being consummated.

Strain loved the water and the drum beat of the waves. It gave her a sense of calm. She took a deep breath, inhaling the fresh salt air as she and Austin walked on toward their visit with Tanya. She held in her pocket the thumb drive that Austin would insert into Max's hard drive.

She needed to be cognizant of the chain of custody issue should the download be successful and the case against Max blossom. As a former law student, she had learned the discipline of evidentiary law and the United States Attorney's requirements for a solid case. So as they got closer to the apartment, she reviewed in her mind how Austin would use the thumb drive to install the investigative app and then withdraw it, and more importantly, how she would later retrieve it. She made a mental note to record time, date, and location within the apartment when it was transferred and retrieved. And then she would "memorialize" that action in her report. A good defense attorney would closely scrutinize every aspect of the investigation. The thumb drive could be an important factor in the defense counsel's efforts to taint the prosecution's case. Strain would not allow that to happen.

"We can't afford to screw up the search warrant. So make sure we verify the exact address and start thinking about how we will describe the location in the application," said Strain, ordering Austin to commit the experience to memory. For law enforcement, a screw-up, such as entering the wrong address, would certainly diminish the confidence of the United States magistrate, and the prosecutor, for future cases.

"Relax. I have my recorder right here, and I've already been documenting what we'll need. I'll leave out the waves you've been looking at, or else the judge may think you've been daydreaming." Strain smirked in appreciation of his observation.

Both agents wore heavy winter coats. Strain put the coat's hood over her head to help disguise her appearance. Austin wore his usual Yankees baseball cap, more to cover his bald head than to hide his identity.

As they crossed Brighton Beach Court, Strain took note of the handsome tan and white brick apartment building to her left. She noticed an array of CCTV, closed circuit television, and Pelco surveillance cameras positioned strategically around the apartment building. "Probably static cameras, not pan, tilt or zoom," she thought. Most likely erected around the complex, she reasoned, for legacy purposes rather than real-time surveillance. To her right she observed a brick building painted blue with an alternating yellow alabaster siding. What seemed strange to her was the graffiti that adorned the first floor. "I wouldn't want to be the person responsible for that and get caught by the Russian landlord," she thought.

"Let's make sure we tell our guys to cover their faces to avoid being picked up by these cameras. They're all over the place." The search warrant team would take up static positions at the same intersection the two agents just crossed to ensure that no vehicles made their way up Brighton Third Street after the team's arrival.

Agents Strain and Austin walked the perimeter of the block to assess the neighborhood. About a half block from the apartment they walked past Primorski's Restaurant near the corner of Brighton Beach Avenue and Brighton Third Street. The lively restaurant was a well-known community location, one of the more popular eateries on the block, and was patronized frequently for its generous menu. Despite its reputation for good food, non-Russian patrons were not welcome. Strain had no intention of antagonizing the neighborhood.

At many of the restaurants in the Russian enclave, outsiders could count on rude, sometimes even hostile, service. Restaurants like Primorski's serve as a de facto Russian town hall, a gathering place, mostly attended by the Bratva.

"We need to hustle past this place to avoid their attention," Austin said. "In fact, let's cross the street and continue on."

"You're right. Let's keep moving. I'll let Tanya know we're a minute or two out."

The Bratva, they knew, had eyes and ears everywhere, particularly here in the heart of Brighton Beach. The area had been an enclave for Russian émigrés since the Russian Jews immigrated there in the 1960s.

Once embedded, the community made the process easier for later émigrés arriving in the United States from Mother Russia, people like Max's father, to feel an immediate homeland connection. Even the drive to Brighton Beach from the Belt Parkway would give the new émigré the sense he was in a section of Moscow, as the area featured many similar drab-colored, multi-tenanted housing developments similar to those in Moscow.

Fortunately, the cold winter day offered some protection from curious onlookers, keeping tenants inside and away from their front porch stoops.

Strain called Tanya's cell phone, "Tanya, this is Agent Strain."

Tanya answered quickly. "Agent Strain, I am ready for you. The door will be open upon your arrival."

Strain wanted to limit their exposure to the curious few Russian onlookers on the streets. She did not want to be left waiting outside. Tanya greeted the two of them as if she were one of their specially trained operatives.

"Good girl," Strain said to herself. The two Secret Service agents entered the apartment and stood by as Tanya double-locked the front door behind them.

Tanya, clearly nervous, expressed her concern about Max coming home unexpectedly. "Tanya, we will be done and out of here in a few minutes," Strain said, sensing her mood.

The agents quickly scanned the layout of the apartment. It was moderately furnished, not unattractive, but devoid of ambiance. The living room walls were unadorned, other than an assortment of cheap portraits of mixed martial art bouts in tawdry frames.

The aroma of leather filled the room. It emanated from a recently purchased brown leather upholstered sofa couch, with matching chair and ottoman. In front of the leather couch, a glass top coffee table, served to display one of Max's first place UFC trophies. A cocoa-stained sisal carpet covered most of the wood flooring; it was a hardy weave that could conceivably outlast its owner. The couch faced directly toward a fifty-five-inch flat screen monitor, sufficient for a sport aficionado like Max and his friends to savor the many repeated viewings of recorded UFC contests.

Suddenly, and much to the agents' surprise, a red-nosed pit bull appeared. It was an American Staffordshire terrier, whose dark, short-haired coat blended into the carpet as she sat obediently on the living room floor. Austin instinctively placed his right hand on his service weapon while maintaining his focus on the canine.

The dog's wagging tail calmed Strain immediately. Austin's feelings were not so quickly assuaged. Strain, a consummate animal lover, greeted the dog affectionately. The Cyber Squad supervisor's body language signaled to Austin that it would not be necessary to draw his service weapon.

"Awe, what a good looking dog you are." Strain made a mental note to factor the dog's presence into her raid plans. "Austin, we must advise the squad not to take the dog out when they enter the apartment."

"Not take the dog out? Don't you think it will need to pee on a tree?" he asked.

"Shut up, Austin!" Strain feigned anger.

"Tanya, you didn't tell us that you had such a surprise for us. What's her name and how old is she?"

"Her name is Torre. Max got her about a year ago and adores her. She doesn't have a mean bone in her body, but the neighborhood is scared shitless of her. He says let them continue to think it. We don't like the neighbors knowing our business anyway."

"Well Tanya, let me caution you that NYPD officers routinely encounter dogs like Torre, and their reputation as attack dogs in some low-income housing projects precedes them. The police are prepared to take the animals out if an owner sends them on an attack mission," replied Strain.

Strain didn't want that to be the case with Torre. She hoped the dog would not overreact when the agents entered the apartment with the speed and force that usually accompanied such a ballistic event. She thought about asking Tanya to remove the dog and then reconsidered. "No, I can't do that," she thought. "Better to not take any chances on jeopardizing the warrant and tipping off Max." Changing the fundamental routine of the apartment was a bad idea. "Tanya, can you show us Max's room? More specifically, the area where he does his computer work?" Tanya led them to one of two bedrooms.

Before entering the room, Strain, the experienced criminal investigator and now Cyber Squad supervisor, whispered to her colleague. "If the guy is this good, let's be mindful of any countermeasures he may have left to defend his computer room, particularly any electromagnetic trip wires he may have used to wipe his hard drives clean and leave them unreadable."

Strain referred to her knowledge that some of the more sophisticated hackers would design and use a modified electromagnetic pulse-generated device to protect their work areas from being compromised by law enforcement authorities. Government professionals, like Strain's squad, or the CIA, employed a Rasket Device, which would electromagnetically erase all digital data evidence. Similarly, a hacker like Max would likely use a jerry-rigged contraption that mimicked a high-powered microwave weapon designed to deliver high-intensity radio waves in milliseconds, which would disrupt the electronics on the hacker's hard drive and erase much of the forensic evidence the search warrant was intended to obtain.

"Yeah, I wouldn't be surprised to learn he had nothing. I bet he is no different than the rest of us. Here you and I are in the security business and probably have no meaningful security features in our own homes. It's human nature, not sure why, but true."

"That's right; the cobbler's children have no shoes."

"What the hell is a cobbler? A turkey?" Austin asked sarcastically.

"It's a shoemaker, silly." Strain had grown up differently than Austin. Her mother had often used that proverb to describe liberal activists who spent their time worrying about the poor of the world while their own children were nutritionally deprived. Strain always found it interesting that different environments and experiences provided different sayings, and what those sayings revealed about people's perception of the world around them.

Austin led Strain to the door of the bedroom. Both of them scanned for devices prior to entering. Comfortable that none had been observed, they entered the room slowly and methodically, continuing to mentally catalogue the room's contents. On top of the makeshift desk, which was a piece of four-by-eight foot plywood supported by two Home Depot plastic sawhorses, sat two keyboards and two twenty-inch color monitors. Wires led to several CPUs below the makeshift desk, with a single lamp placed on the far corner of the plywood desk. A lone swivel chair was the only traditional piece of furniture in the room. In front of the keyboards lay a headset. The headset featured a microphone that extended from the right side. Max wore this to issue his commands.

"This is a regular operations room," Strain thought. "Information comes in, Max massages the information he receives, then sends it out to his minions to act upon." This was his war room. This is where he would delve deeply into the cyber space he controlled. It was nothing fancy, just a jerry-rigged system of monitors, wires, and mental gymnastics.

Austin's task was to immediately recognize which one of Max's CPUs would deliver the most effective results after the injection of government malware. "How ironic," he thought, "that I get to legally compromise the super hacker's computing system." Turning the tables on this guy was an investigative thrill, and Austin enjoyed the moment. "Here's a guy who spends a large number of his waking hours as a 'Bot-herder,' attacking large corporate systems, like banks and mega financial enterprises, targeting their proprietary data. Now I get a chance to see him do it in real time."

Austin thought of himself as a "White" Bot-herder. He legally used simple, structurally repetitive, written software. The software would run automated tasks over the Internet and allow the Feds to receive Max's data real time when he used it to manipulate other computer systems from his makeshift war room. The injected thumb drive would deliver the legal code and turn the tables on the super hacker.

Max's command and control structure would not be blocked, just monitored. The Secret Service did not want to shut his operation down. On the contrary, they wanted him up and running in order to capture his data in real time and build a strong legal case against him. Thanks to Tanya, her boyfriend was about to get the equivalent of a Secret Service cyber arm lock and the Secret Service was lucky, he wouldn't realize it until it was too late. For Austin and Strain, having gained access to the apartment and close proximity to the one of the world's best super hacker's equipment was the ultimate investigative achievement.

Austin placed the small finger-sized drive into the USB port located at the rear of the CPU. He restarted the computer to allow the device to quickly download and infect its operating system. It was an action no different than what the defector, Edward Snowden, had suggested the Intelligence Services did to the Iranians in 2011 to disrupt their nuclear program. The Stuxnet Virus was a classic data-disrupting event that provided the "good guys" with the extraordinary ability to alter the code that ran the Iranian nuclear systems.

"It's important the thumb drive delivers its application and then deletes itself after successfully compromising the computer," Austin later explained to the new agents on the Cyber Squad. "The goal is not to alter what the hacker is doing, but rather to capture and identify what he was doing, to accumulate enough incriminating information to obtain a search warrant, and if lucky, an arrest warrant," he continued. "It's important to us to inject into Max's operating system a script that disguises itself in order to function surreptitiously and not suggest to him our presence." There was always a chance Max would discover the app before they had what they needed.

"I am sure Max employs information security, or countermeasures, and he probably does so on a daily basis," Austin told Strain. "But I don't think he will detect this in time to stifle it; it is advantage to the Feds." He made no attempt to suppress a devilish grin.

While Strain distracted Tanya, Austin completed his task and removed the thumb drive. "Okay, let's go."

Before leaving the apartment, the ever-conscientious Strain began to scan the rooms in order to determine points of ingress for the raid team. She saw a rear door through the kitchen—the only other option to enter the apartment. She also noticed all the windows had a grill-like insert, ostensibly to deter or stop burglars. She grinned, thinking what it would be like for a burglar who might enter Max's place while he was inside. "Good luck to you, asshole," she thought, contemplating the scenario of a face-off against the UFC champion. Then she turned her attention to Tanya.

"Tanya, it is important you keep your cool and not give Max any indication you are cooperating with us; otherwise, this will not work, and you will be turned back over to the DEA. Are you able to get away for a while?"

Strain wanted to be sure Tanya knew what was at stake. "It is crucial you not be here when we come back. I can't tell you exactly when we will return, but it will be soon."

"I know what I have to do, Agent Strain, and I won't let you down. I dance most afternoons and nights and will let you know when I am gone. How can I get a hold of you?"

Strain slipped her a piece of paper with the agent's cell phone number on it. She didn't want to leave a traditional business card for fear Max would see it or Tanya would use it in the future as a reference. Strain suggested she use her cell phone to call or text once she was out of the residence. They left the apartment quickly without attracting attention. The entire visit took less than twenty minutes.

TWENTY SEVEN

Steve Austin's injection worked. By seven o'clock that night the Secret Service technicians started capturing data. The feed began to paint a picture of someone immersed in massive cyber fraud. A quick analysis of the data flowing their way soon revealed Max's modus operandi. They learned he employed a variety of search engines to deduce where large sums of money resided, mostly in a variety of banking institutions. More important to the investigators was how he schemed to get it. Aghast, they saw he was in mass production mode. Time appeared to be of the essence.

Max wrote his own malicious software, which was delivered by his Trojans to vulnerable company computer systems. For him, script writing, developing new code, was second nature. The difference between Max and other hackers was his exponential ability to target multiple victims simultaneously. He identified his victim institutions from previously successful penetrations. He entered easily and aggregated customer credit card and banking data daily, mostly in contravention to the companies' contracts with issuing banks, that is, the large credit card processors.

From Max's viewpoint, companies that failed to maintain basic countermeasures were lazy. "That's their problem," Max had said. "If they want to leave the data for me to pick, like low-hanging fruit, shame on them. I feel no guilt."

Max designed his script to siphon off as many banking credentials as possible from thousands of unsuspecting customers whose digital pedigrees resided on the servers he infected. Once his malware captured the victims' banking credentials, his next step consisted of programming the banking computers around the United States to send billions of dollars into proxy bank accounts, which he had previously established and meticulously maintained.

A major obstacle for the successful hacker was to figure out how to employ mules, or low-level operatives, to take the money extracted from the targeted accounts and transfer it to a variety of overseas accounts. Max thought this element of the process was too cumbersome and fraught with potential failure. In his early days, he considered using Hasidic Jews as his mules. They could be deployed to a thousand locations, eager to take a percentage of the stolen revenue. But using so many Hasidic mules at ATMs was something Max envisioned as problematic. Their unusual attire and hairstyle would invite unwanted observation by anyone in a non-Hasidic neighborhood. Furthermore, it would take too damn long for them to perform the transactions necessary to achieve financial success.

"Why should I even think of sharing the proceeds with the Hasidic community?" he thought. "Too many people, and too much headache." It was taxing enough to have to commit a portion of his receipts to the Bratva. At least being a member of the Russian mob had some meaning. One either shared with them or died. But belonging to the Bratva also had its privileges. It gave him the early resources he needed to train and nurture his career as a mixed martial artist and also the funding he needed to purchase the hardware for his hacking activities.

The Bratva guys liked to tell him, "You're on scholarship." There was nothing fancy about the relationship, but the Bratva would eventually expect its share. No debate. Just an expected assessment, which must be paid. Even Max appreciated from his early childhood that the Bratva was too powerful and far-reaching a foe to "fuck with."

As Strain's clandestine efforts with the thumb drive began to yield data, her squad's detective work in sniffing out Max's plan yielded the story of how Max intended to harvest proceeds from his massive digital crime spree and electronically send them to his JFOT account, hacker parlance for "just fucking out there."

"We need to shut him down soon, and we need to do it before he can transfer the proceeds to his accounts and out of our grasp," Strain told her squad. "If he can pull this off, it won't reflect well on us."

"I think we got lucky with the DEA arrest, otherwise we never would have seen this coming," Austin chipped in.

All indications from the Fed's data mining suggested Max was a day away from pushing the button to extract the funds. Everything he needed to execute his plan appeared to be in place. The malware had been injected, his reconnaissance was successful, the victims had been tapped, and the compromised banking servers were ready to submit the needed banking credentials. Billions of dollars were about to be sucked out of the victim banks in a cyber-swoop, and they would then evaporate into the Ethernet. Max's exfiltration was set for the next day.

The Cyber Squad's efforts to piece together the collected data meant it had sufficient narrative to support a search warrant. Knowing the imminent time of Max's intended strike added to the squad's excitement.

"Austin, develop an action plan to hit Max's apartment sometime in the next twelve hours," Strain directed. "As soon as the magistrate signs the search warrant, we move in."

The Cyber Squad loved her style. It didn't hurt she was attractive. She turned heads. The guys in the squad were proud to be managed by someone who was held in such high regard by both peers and managers. But there was one reality they all shared: none of them stood a chance with her. She was very happily married. Regardless, it didn't stop them from flirting with her.

TWENTY EIGHT

"How did it go at the magistrate's office?"

"We had no difficulty. The magistrate even said the affidavit for the search warrant was aces," said Steve Austin, wearing an ear-to-ear grin.

"Well, I'm not surprised. You put your heart and soul into it, and I thank you for that," said Carly Strain. She was relieved. Time was now on their side.

The "Secrets" had gathered more than the probable cause necessary to justify a breach of the Fourth Amendment. All agents knew the amendment by heart, having memorized it during their Secret Service school. As an attorney, Strain was particularly sensitive to remaining faithful to this particular constitutional edict. For her, the sacrosanct document required a devotion not dissimilar to that which she demonstrated in her efforts to protect the office of the president. Any action that might tarnish the document would be contemptible, and an agent who didn't do his or her homework and ended up rendering a search or arrest warrant defective would welcome God's wrath over Strain's.

The Cyber Squad prepared in earnest to execute the warrant early the next morning. Strain received a text message from Tanya letting her know her situation. "Agent Strain, I will not be home overnight. I will be staying with my mom. Max will be alone throughout the evening. Torre is there, too. Good luck. Tanya."

The raid team calculated they might encounter a violent response. Max was not your usual hacker. He was up at all hours and was likely to be active upon their entry. He slept little and didn't seem to need it. The team was aware of the dangers involved, and they planned carefully, taking into consideration the likelihood of a violent confrontation.

They prepared a dynamic raid plan to include their use of heavy weapons, flak jackets, and battering rams to take down the secured doors. They even included an NYPD Emergency Services Unit, better known as "ESU." It was NYPD's version of Special Weapons and Tactics. This was a multi-disciplined group of men and women who responded daily to city-wide calamities, ranging from ledge jumpers to suspicious powders to cats in trees. The ESU teams prepared for it all.

"Okay, everyone listen up," shouted Agent Austin to get the attention of the raid team. The agents and the ESU detectives had arrived at the New York field office in Brooklyn at 0400 hours to go over the final to-do lists for the warrants. The New York Electronic Crimes Task Force, NYECTF, pride of the Secret Service, was ready to execute its search warrant on the Brighton Beach residence in hopes of preventing a mass cyber theft.

Agent Austin noticed he seemed to have everyone's attention, so he continued. "The name on the search warrant reads, Maksim Valdimirovich Dostoevsky. To his family and friends, he is Max. Our target is the son of a Russian National Hockey League player, born in New York City. He is six foot-two, has blue eyes and blond hair. We are passing out his photograph we obtained off of social media. At age twenty-six, he is already a dominant mixed martial arts fighter here in the New York area. This kid is reported to be a masterful physical specimen."

"Sounds like you have a special feeling for him," one of the team members said, generating a few chuckles from the room. Austin maintained his composure, only acknowledging the commenter with a sideways glance. "The reports we've received about him say he thrills in physical violence. He pursues his physical interests with a consuming ferocity. He is almost immune to pain. At least he never admits to feeling it."

"And that's why we're bringing ESU," said Strain. "The ESU will also be tasked with breaking down the front and rear doors with their breaching materials." This usually involved the simultaneous use of massive sledgehammers. On some occasions, ESU even relied on shotguns and small quantities of C4 to breach stubborn locking mechanisms.

Austin continued, "For this mission, the Secret Service will assign each ESU team one of their Cyber Squad agents to enhance the communication between agencies. Most hackers are typically docile, faux intellectuals, relying on their wits, as it were, to execute their fraud." Austin spoke from experience. He and Strain's squad had arrested dozens of these characters.

"This guy is a different breed," said Austin. "He is considered the most formidable hacker of the day: smart, greedy, and dangerous. He lives with his girlfriend, Tanya Ovseenko, a Ukrainian beauty. We know she will not be present in the apartment." Austin didn't share with the mixed group that Tanya was the informant in the case.

"We know him to be operating the most sophisticated hierarchical carding group in the world at this time. His hacking group owns most of the Internet chat rooms, which provides a global reach, and more importantly, anonymity."

"What the hell is a chat room?" asked one of the ESU detectives.

"Seriously?" said Austin. "Okay. I'll speak slowly. It's a cyber location used as a legitimate forum for Internet users to communicate with each other, but in this case it gives Max and his operatives cover to do their own communicating, usually about the lucrative world of credit card fraud."

"Got it," responded the detective with a smirk.

"It's where the target sends out his commands to his ground team," Austin added, trying to get the detective's buy-in.

"We don't expect anyone other than Max to be in the apartment." Austin knew Tanya wasn't going to be there, but decided to include her in his briefing. "We believe while the target works his keyboard magic, nurturing his international criminal enterprise, his live-in girlfriend dances nude. And again, I have no idea how they know that." A few agents stifled their chuckles while others merely cleared their throats.

"Too bad she's not likely to be there," said Strain. "Sounds like she could get the ESU guys to slam those doors down a bit more quickly."

"No, Strain, we're doing this just for you, and you don't even have to dance for us," someone shouted. Strain looked over at the ESU supervisor, a hint of crimson in her cheeks.

"Okay, that does it," said Austin. "If there are no questions, let's depart and set up at our pre-determined locations and await the command to execute."

About forty-five minutes later the radio crackled, "Strain, this is Austin. We are all in position and have all ingresses into the target residence covered. There are very few pedestrians on the sidewalks at this time. Over."

"Roger that, Austin. At 0600 hours let's hit the residence," Strain said. She had her assets in place to strike Max's apartment pursuant to the search warrant the magistrate had signed, describing the location in detail and the assets to be seized.

The warrant, written broadly to permit the agents to seize as much information and data as possible, would allow them to go into closets and drawers without fear of losing evidence through a legal technicality.

"All responding units, remember to use caution with the pit bull terrier and avoid, if possible, having to eliminate it. Her name is Torre." Strain knew this was a dicey request. The safety of the agents and ESU detectives were paramount. If the dog sought to protect its master, the inevitable would occur.

"Fire in the hole," one of the ESU officers blurted out over the common police-operating radio frequency. It was the signal the door to Max's apartment was about to be breached with a small explosive charge, of fabled C4 composition. The charge served two purposes: to breach a point of entry for the raid team and to stun and incapacitate. ESU decided to use it after hearing the Austin brief, indicating the potential for a fight from Max.

The Secret Service New York Electronic Crimes Task Force agents drew their standard Sig-Sauer 229s and burst through the newly created openings of the apartment, compliments of the NYPD.

Max had been sitting in his living room, catching a few moments of sleep. It was a technique he practiced which allowed him to briefly refresh while remaining active for long periods of time. When the blast decibels reached their maximum level, his mind immediately shut down the pain, and he instinctively grabbed for his trusted .40-caliber Glock, Model 27, and prepared for battle.

He reacted to the small charges and the deafening noise in less than a second. His initial instinct was to inflict pain on his unknown attackers when the front door blew open. He was ready to blast the intruders with a full clip of hollow points, with three extra clips at the ready for reload. He had practiced this scenario in his mind many times. He could unload and reload in less than a second. The Service, however, had also trained its agents to be prepared for such moments.

When the front door blew open, it masked the back door's ballistic slap to the floor. Max had a fleeting moment of appreciation for the intruders' flawless execution. It was not dissimilar, he thought, to one of the arm locks he applied to his opponent in an all-out mixed martial arts match.

Torre, the loyalist, reacted as quickly to the sound as did her master. But the two doors simultaneously hitting the floor confused her, and her reaction was suppressed until she could figure out which threat to defend her master from first.

Max grabbed Torre's collar as he lowered his weapon to the floor, but not before a Secret Service agent had pointed his shoulder weapon, a Remington 870 shotgun, at him and chambered a round. Max alerted like a hunting dog to the characteristic crackle, the chambering of the number four buckshot round into a shotgun's short tube. It was a sound understood and respected by law enforcement and criminals alike.

Strain followed the lead raid agents into the apartment and suddenly found herself within arm's length of the target. She pointed her .357 automatic Sig Sauer 229 directly at Max's head, a distance no less than two feet from the end of her gun's barrel. For Max, this would not normally be a threatening situation. If the two were alone, he knew he could easily dispense with the hand weapon and reverse the position, but he realized that would be foolish now. As strong, fast, and lethal as Max was, he knew was outgunned. He also knew he didn't want half his head plastered against the living room wall, particularly by a female agent, but that would likely happen if he elected to raise his weapon at the trained agent. "How embarrassing would that be?" he chuckled to himself. Max was a smart man. He would live to fight another day.

Max still had Torre by the collar. Torre didn't overreact, sensing her master was not in immediate danger. She sensed his calm demeanor, but remained alert at his side.

"Don't even think about the Glock, Max," said Strain. "Put your hands up over your head and interlock your fingers. Stand up slowly. Now!" Max began to slowly move into a standing position.

"Leave Torre be, and I will take her," said Strain. She was relieved, but trying not to display her emotion that Torre had safely survived the breaching of the apartment. "It's okay, Torre. It's all okay, honey," said

Strain. She whispered assurances to the nervous dog while not letting her eyes stray from the suspect.

Max smirked. He slowly lifted his arms up, placing his hands on his head. "I guess this is not your first time visiting my home," said Max. "Did Tanya introduce you to my Torre or do you have an existing affection for Brighton Beach pit bulls?" Max's mind continued to swirl with speculation. "How did the cops get to me? Did Taboo outflank me? Was it Shorty? Did I piss off the Bratva? Did Tanya forsake me? Or is this some attempt to disparage my championship fight win?" He didn't let the confusion show on his face.

Tanya became his primary Judas suspect. "So this is how you support me, you little whore?" he thought to himself. "Wonder what they had on you? Drugs, no doubt. But how the fuck could that have led to me? I don't touch the stuff and never had it here at home. There's no way they have any information on me or what I had planned. No fucking way, unless the bitch did the real stupid thing and let these bastards in. Of course, she let them in, and of course they know what I am up to. I got too fucking comfortable and spent too much time on the fighting, taking my mind off defense. I didn't even have my own back."

Strain placed her Sig Sauer back in its holster and grabbed her cuffs with her free hand, a procedure she had mastered over the years. Max was now facing the wall with his hands over his head. He would not resist. Strain applied the cuff to his left wrist and snapped it in a locked position. Taking his left arm down behind his back she then reached for his right wrist and firmly guided it to the small of his back and snapped the remaining cuff in place, securing his arms and hands.

"Stay in place, Max. And no offense, but we will be placing leg irons on you. You can still walk, but you won't be able to raise your legs much. I'm sure I don't have to explain why."

TWENTY NINE

"Today was to be different," said Fast Eddie. He would get to play the good guy for once and send some field office agents on a decent foreign trip with some good ole' American flag waving, a place in the Middle East where they actually still liked Americans. But Fast Eddie knew better. The field agents had disparaged him so often, and for so long, he knew most of them no longer believed that crap. Everyone was tired of the extensive travel.

"All the presidents since George H. W. Bush have traveled so much, there are no good trips anymore," he told Steve Armey. It didn't matter the agent population was larger now than it had been in the eighties. The Service now covered more protection duties and with an agent population strained beyond logic. But his next call was to be different, at least he hoped it would be. He dialed Carly Strain direct.

"Carly Strain? This is Tom Eddie from the manpower desk. How are you?" Eddie knew Strain only by reputation. He had heard about her through the informal agent network. She had a good reputation, which meant she could handle herself on the street and didn't embarrass anyone doing advance work while assigned to the White House. "We are sending a jump team over to Kuwait for the twenty-fifth anniversary of the liberation of that country. The president will be there. How would you like to be one of the supervisors?"

"I would love the chance to take the jump team to the Middle East," Strain responded, almost gleefully, to the headquarters' manpower supervisor. Her enthusiasm was not the norm for these calls. A call from the "Drain," as most of the field supervisors referred to the manpower requests from Secret Service Headquarters, was not normally considered good news. They sapped the field office of its agents in order to fill temporary protective assignments around the globe, taxing the ability of the field office's criminal squad to effectively sustain major criminal investigations and get the cases on the front burner with overloaded and sometimes reluctant prosecutors. This time it was different. Agent Strain emotionally and physically needed this trip. She desired to be with her husband.

"This is perfect for me, Tom. And good timing too."

Eddie liked that Strain felt comfortable calling him by his first name. He was the current poster boy for what the field perceived as the Secret Service manpower drain. But today, he was Strain's salvation. He was the key to some long-sought, long-needed relief—a way to see her husband soon. She couldn't wait to see her husband for a lot of reasons.

"Did you know my husband is assigned to the region?"

Strain asked the question as though headquarters may have, for once, been more prescient than she could ever have believed. She couldn't imagine that this was just a huge coincidence. Her husband, Commander Will Strain, the Coast Guard military attaché assigned to Kuwait City, had been gone much too long. She needed to see him soon.

"The PPD advance agent, Bill Sims, personally asked for you. He's in Kuwait City with your husband. I'm glad it will work for you. By the way, what kind of investigation is it you have going on that has headquarters all abuzz?"

Agent Strain had rehearsed her response to this question many times, and she was able to rattle off an executive summary of the case with ease. "It is the mother of all hacking cases. Our target is the most colorful, effectively dangerous hacker in the world. He is in constant animation and has only begun to exercise his skill set. He's one dangerous fucker, and we anticipated a handful when we executed the warrants, but it all went down peacefully, thank God."

"Where is he now?" Eddie inquired.

"He's about to be appear before a magistrate in the Eastern District." Strain referred to the federal courthouse located in Brooklyn, a stone's throw from the New York field office. "He's a Russian mob protégé, and I'm sure his arrest has stirred up some shit in Brighton Beach."

THIRTY

Agent Austin gave Max his Miranda warnings, although he knew them by heart. They had been drilled into him during his days in Glynco, Georgia, where, as a young recruit, he had gone through basic criminal investigator school before attending the more demanding Secret Service Academy located in Beltsville, Maryland.

"You have the right to remain silent," Austin began. Sometimes he thought it sounded silly, as most defendants don't talk anyway, but now it was ingrained in all law enforcement for fear of losing a case because a sharp defense attorney could grill you in court to disclose exactly how you presented the warnings. If an agent failed to provide the Miranda warning before questioning, any statements then made by the defendant would be ruled inadmissible as evidence. The agent's reputation with the prosecutor, not to mention your agency, would be damaged. It was easier to go through the ritual.

"I know my rights. You don't need to give them to me," said Max.

"Too bad. You're getting them. And then if you want to talk, so be it." Austin gave a rote, emotionless recitation of the rest of the warning. He was not deterred or intimidated by Max's celebrity. Austin wrapped it up. "Do you understand your rights?"

"Yes, sir," said Max. "Any chance you could loosen up the cuffs on my wrists? I think they are stifling the blood flow to my hands. I am losing feeling in them." Max stooped down as Agent Austin began to place him in the G-car. Austin held him up and Max remained in respectful mode. Austin realized he was feeling some degree of compassion for the defendant. This guy was not your average catch. He was a super hacker and a mixed martial arts champion. This guy was special. When and if he weathered the judicial storm, he would go free and probably go on to fame and fortune.

"Remain still and keep facing the car," Austin said, just prior to placing Max into the G-car. "I'll give you some relief. Don't try anything foolish."

Max was still wearing leg irons, so any attempt to make a dash to freedom was out of the question. "No worries, Agent. If I wanted trouble I would have kept my Glock." Max looked up toward the open sky and took a deep breath. He had no intention of trying anything. The agent had nothing to worry about. He had lost this round. He made a quiet attempt to express his appreciation for the loosened cuffs. "Thank you, Agent. And thank you for the respect. I won't do anything that will piss you off or threaten you. Where do we go now?"

"We're taking you to the Metropolitan Correctional Center in lower Manhattan where you will be searched and processed by the U.S. Marshal's office as an overnight federal prisoner," said Austin. "First thing in the morning, we'll come back for you and take you to our office in Brooklyn for additional processing: fingerprints, photographs, and additional personal data."

The Secret Service agents were no longer concerned that their presence in the Brighton Beach apartment might attract attention. On the contrary, this was the time to let word get out and send a message to the community that one of their own had been taken down for violating federal law. The agents departed with their trophy arrest while their colleagues continued the mission's search exercise.

Austin didn't want to give up custody of his charge, even for the short overnight stint, but he did so, albeit reluctantly. He decided to stay at the field office overnight in order to remain nearby. He could take a morning shower there before retrieving Max from the jail and taking him to his arraignment, which would be just a few blocks away at Cadman Plaza in Brooklyn.

Cadman Plaza is a judicial enclave of local, state, and federal courts, a one-stop judicial option. "It is totally convenient, dudes," Austin would tell the new agents at the field office.

The next morning, Strain met Austin and Richie Deschak, one of the new squad agents, in the courtroom of Magistrate Barry T. Moskowitz. Once there, Strain updated Assistant U.S. Attorney John Blake on the latest information gleaned from the search at the Brighton Beach apartment.

Blake knew Strain from his own days in the Secret Service. Unlike her, he had elected to attend law school while juggling a career as a New York field office agent. As fate would have it, the office needed a full-time midnight communications supervisor. The job was perfect for him. It allowed him to work the midnight shift and attend law school during the day. Once he graduated from Brooklyn Law School, he left the Service to take the job as a federal prosecutor.

Strain felt relieved with him handling the initial appearance. He understood the complexity of the case and would convince the magistrate of the need to keep Max in custody without bail.

Magistrate Moskowitz had a traditional federal courtroom. The walls were covered with walnut paneling floor to ceiling, with the magistrate's desk perched about three feet higher than the prosecution and defense tables, adding to the imposing presence of the judicial authority. The Great Seal of the United States hung on the wall directly above the judge's chair. Judges or magistrates generally would enter via a dedicated side entrance from their administrative offices, which gave an air of mystery to the ceremonial, but deadly serious, workings of the court.

Austin and Deschak arrived fifteen minutes early to pick Max up from the federal jail and deliver him to the court in time for his appearance before the magistrate. For Austin and Deschak, this was a big deal. Word had gotten out about Austin's prisoner, and Austin observed the oddity of seasoned deputy U.S. marshals paying more than cursory attention as Max was led through the court's security apparatus that morning.

"You'd think he's a rock star," Austin said to Deschak. "Look at the way they're ogling him. I guess they think this one's pretty important."

Max realized he was being stared at, but he was used to drawing attention. How could he not? It was just a matter of time before any random person on the street would recognize him. He kept his thoughts to himself as he observed the processes unfolding around him. The one thought that kept nagging at him was Tanya. "How did I not see her potential for tripping me up with the Feds?"

"I'm glad they think he's important," said Deschak. "Look how fast we got through the checkpoints."

Usually, the marshals made the agents jump through hoops, just to piss them off. Not unusual behavior, really—just the normal tribal rivalries between law enforcement agencies. The Secrets were not immune to this behavior. They owned the White House and made the other Feds jump through the same hoops. The United States Capital Police did the same thing. So did the NYPD. So did everyone.

Deschak wondered how anything ever got done. He was amazed it did. But this morning the message seemed to have spread around the courthouse to not fuck with the Secrets who were escorting their prisoner to his arraignment.

Upon arrival at the Brooklyn courthouse, the two agents presented Max to the U.S. Marshals Service, which took administrative custody in a well-practiced procedure. Based on separation of powers, the executive branch had now turned the defendant over to the judicial branch.

"Austin, why do we need to have the marshals take custody?" asked Deschak. "Seems redundant."

"There's a reason for everything," said Austin. "It's the responsibility of the marshals to deliver him to the court and secure him until he's either released with bail, on his own recognizance, remanded to federal custody, or in some situations, given back to the custody of the arresting agency for further investigative action, and used as a confidential informant. But while he's in the judicial bucket, they control the custody."

The room had an unusually large number of attendees present, particularly for an arraignment. Blake turned to look at the gaggle of courtroom personalities for clues as to who they might be. "Nothing different," he noted. "Just more of them."

Some of the attendees were the same old bored retirees who showed up when they smelled something special in the courtroom. They would arrive early each morning and chat with each other to decide which of the day's judicial actions would be the most exciting to observe. Something about the super hacker attracted them to this courtroom.

In the back row sat a well-groomed, but weathered-looking, man who appeared to be Russian. He was dressed in a dark suit, white shirt, and solid red tie. Blake's quick scan picked him up. He assumed the Russian was associated with the defense attorney, Sergey Arkhipova, who was standing only feet from him at the defense table. "Or maybe he's the defense attorney's driver," the assistant prosecutor thought to himself.

Both attorneys awaited the opportunity to address the court. Several large, bulky marshals led Max through a door opposite the magistrate's door. He was still handcuffed, but this time his hands were in front. The handcuffs were secured to a chain around his waist in order to limit his arm motion. The leg irons remained in place to prevent him from running.

Blake watched as Max entered. He saw him glance to the rear of the courtroom, where he made eye contact with the Russian, and gave him a slight nod that carried an air of confidence. The marshals escorted Max to a seat just to the left of Arkhipova, the defense attorney, where he sat down.

Agents Austin and Deschak hustled to meet Carly Strain in the magistrate's court prior to Max's appearance. They slipped into their seats less than a minute before the deputies escorted Max into the courtroom.

"All rise. Court is now in session, the Honorable Barry T. Moskowitz presiding," announced Deputy U.S. Marshal Paul Scanlon with the putative authority derived from the majesty of a federal courtroom. "The matter before the court today is the United States versus Maksim Valdimirovich Dostoevsky."

"Good morning, gentlemen," said the judge. "Please be seated. We are here this morning for the arraignment of the defendant. Is that correct, Mr. Blake?"

"Yes, your Honor."

"What are the charges the United States brings forth?"

"Your Honor, the United States this morning is charging the defendant with twelve counts that include Conspiracy to Engage in Computer Hacking, Computer Hacking in Furtherance of Fraud, Conspiracy to Commit Access Device Fraud, Conspiracy to Commit Bank Fraud, and, your Honor, Gross Aggravated Identity Theft." Blake recited the charges with confidence borne from experience.

"Thank you, Mr. Blake. And Mr. Arkhipova, knowing this is only an arraignment and not the forum in which to explore the evidentiary merits of the case, how does your client plea?"

"Good morning, your Honor. Mr. Dostoevsky respectfully pleads not guilty to all charges."

"Very well, sir. Mr. Blake, what is your recommendation on bail before we discuss a date for the next hearing?"

"Your Honor, due to the egregious nature of the offenses and the real threat of flight that Mr. Dostoevsky presents, we respectfully request the defendant be remanded and this court hold his passport until judicial action is complete," Blake said. He made the request for rcmand based on information Strain had developed overnight, which indicated the defendant was linked to the Russian mob, the Bratva. It could post bail and have Max ferried out of the country to either the Ukraine or some other former USSR satellite state within a day or so.

"Your Honor, we have information that the defendant is well supported by organized crime, Russian organized crime to be specific, and if he were to be released from custody, we would likely not see him again. Further, your Honor, the defendant is alleged to have aggregated wealth beyond imagination and maintains it somewhere in cyber space. The government is still in the process of forensically researching this issue, but there is no guarantee we will find it."

Defense Attorney Arkhipova rose immediately. "Your Honor, this is not the crime of the century. I think remanding my client without any opportunity for bail is excessive and, quite frankly, a constitutional issue. The government, sir, has no information to support these charges, and all of this is no more than a gross harassment of an innocent man. They have kept my client leg-ironed since his arrest. This, sir, applied to someone who has never been arrested, is an honorable citizen, a role model to thousands of sports fans, and who the government now seeks to incarcerate without cause other than the unsubstantiated word of a hooker."

Max raised his head and looked at his defense attorney. "What information do you have that you have not shared with me about Tanya giving me up?" he thought, but did not ask.

The magistrate responded, "Thank you, Mr. Arkhipova. As I told you, sir, this is not the time to address the court with a response as to the merits of the case, but rather a time to provide a factual basis for assuring this court of your client's continued availability for future judicial appearances. In due time, you will have the opportunity to present your defense, but not today. In light of the government's legitimate concerns, the court is sympathetic to the government's request to remand the defendant without bail until a further hearing can determine the likelihood he will not likely flee the jurisdiction. I wish to set a date for the near future. Any other issues relating to this, Mr. Blake?"

"Your Honor, if it were to please the court, it will be necessary for Agent Carly Strain to be present to provide testimony during the defendant's next hearing. However, the United States Attorney's Office is now aware she will be out of the United States for about the next five to seven days in order to support the president of the United States on his trip to the Middle East. So, if possible, could the court schedule the next hearing on or after Monday, February 28?"

"That makes the court curious, Mr. Blake, as to the nature of her business in regard to the president. What makes this "business" so compelling that she can't be present?"

Strain began to feel uncomfortable. Her cheeks burned with embarrassment that the discussion about her forthcoming protection assignment was taking up the court's time. But the court seemed to relish the discussion involving the president of the United States. The usual courtroom visitors who showed up daily to observe the courtroom drama were certainly interested with the unusual topic.

"It is my understanding Agent Strain will be in charge of a large number of Secret Service support personnel who will arrive in Kuwait prior to the president via an Air Force cargo plane delivering the president's vehicles and helicopters."

"Very impressive, Agent Strain," Moskowitz said, his attention directed at her. "You have an interesting job, investigating crime one day, protecting the president the next. Not that the court needs to know, but one can only imagine how this affects one's family life. When do you leave and when do you return?"

Now the embarrassment Strain felt began to dissipate. Her lawyer training was kicking in, and she realized the judge was giving her some wiggle room.

"Your Honor, we are scheduled to depart from Joint Base Andrews in Maryland this Sunday, February 21, with the president's cars and helos and should return by week's end." Strain saw no need to mention she was to meet her husband in Kuwait, the first time she would see him in months. She felt it would detract from the professional nature of the assignment. "The priority is to support the protection of the president. It is not about me," she thought to herself.

Judge Moskowitz knew he was taking liberties by discussing the issue of Strain's trip to Kuwait, but the discussion in his courtroom remained unique, so he allowed himself one more unrelated question. "How does the cargo plane fly all the way to Kuwait? Doesn't it need to refuel?"

"Yes, your Honor, it does. We will stop briefly on Monday morning the 22nd at Ramstein Air Base in Frankfurt, Germany, for a refuel and then be on our way."

While the judge engaged Strain, Blake noticed the defense attorney glance back to the Russian man located in the rear of the courtroom. It seemed to Blake that he sought some affirmation as to whether he should further object or comply with the judicial process. He knew the attorney had represented Russian mob members in the past, but he had not known of him handling anyone in the hacker community. Hackers were a very different lot.

"Thank you, Agent Strain. The court hopes you have a safe trip, and we appreciate your service to the country, especially when juggling your various assignments. Mr. Blake, unless you have something further I will render my decision."

"No, your Honor. The United States has nothing more."

"Mr. Arkhipova, do you have anything to add before I render my decision?"

"Yes, your Honor. If your decision is to agree with the government, I respectfully request you consider allowing my client to travel within the continental United States to continue his quest as an Ultimate Fighter and participate in its championship contest later this month. This is his only form of income."

"Thank you, Mr. Arkhipova. The defendant will be held without bail until the next hearing. The court also requires that his passport be turned over to the United States marshal for the duration of the proceedings. I will schedule the next hearing for Monday, February 28." Moskowitz looked at both attorneys. Neither offered further objection.

Strain took a deep breath. She could now manage all the aspects of her Secret Service duties and get "lucky" with her husband in Kuwait City. "Sweet," she thought.

As the judge stood up in his courtroom, the daily observers slowly rose to their feet, followed by everyone else in the courtroom; a traditional sign of respect for the court. He entered his suite as the deputy U.S. marshals escorted Max away from his attorney while still secure in cuffs and leg irons. The courtroom's side door was purposely built to lead defendants to the fingerprint processing area. His attorney was not allowed to follow. Blake studiously watched Max's attorney while his client was led out of the courtroom. Whoever the Russian was in the back of the courtroom, he had Arkhipova's attention.

Blake remained curious. The Russian came forward to talk with Mr. Arkhipova. Blake leaned over to Strain and whispered, "See if you can identify the man talking with Arkhipova. There's something going on between the two that may affect the status of our defendant."

"No problem. I can have Austin and Deschak check the ledger, located by the courthouse metal detectors, that lists the names of the visitors coming into courthouse. Do you want them to conduct surveillance?"

"No," replied Blake. "Just get some background on who he is and what his interest in Max may be."

Strain nodded. "I'll get back to you shortly." She gave Blake a firm handshake before joining up with Austin and Deschak.

Back in his office, Blake answered his phone. It was Strain. "His name is Arvydas Belov. A name check with the Office of Foreign Assets Control indicated he is a prolific Russian arms dealer, mostly ferrying his wares through the Middle East. He is said to enjoy the Saudi royal family's protection. The Saudis obtain a great deal of their weaponry through back channels and maintain a close working relationship with Mr. Belov and his clan of weapons' dealers. Furthermore, he is knee deep in the Bratva. We confirmed through 'Worldcheck' that he has numerous connections with money laundering associates and their operations globally. What he was doing in the courtroom today is anybody's guess."

"We'll keep an eye on him. I know Max is a prolific hacker and a member of the Russian mob, but why they have such a heavy hitter to monitor this judicial action is a puzzle. Make sure Austin keeps me up to speed on the investigation while you're overseas. I have a feeling you guys may have only touched the tip of the proverbial iceberg. Have a good time in Kuwait."

THIRTY
ONE

The special air mission took off from Maguire, the U.S. Air Force base, in Burlington County, New Jersey, en route to Joint Base Johns to pick up her special cargo. Loadmaster Frances Larosa's primary responsibility was to calculate the cargo weight and passenger placement within the aircraft and report it to the pilot.

"The pilots need to know the plane's internal configuration in order to provide him or her with a stable aircraft, and maintaining a center of gravity throughout the flight is your primary duty," her instructor told her in lead loadmaster training.

Upon the plane's arrival at Joint Base Andrews, Larosa peered out the circular window aft of the cargo hold to observe a handful of casually dressed operatives milling around the tarmac. "The Secret Service contingent," she reasoned.

Standing by their staged vehicles, members of the group focused on Larosa's cargo plane as it slowly approached their location on the tarmac. The small convoy of limousines and SUVs represented the Secret Service "vehicle package" that Larosa would help transport to Kuwait to support the president's visit. All four vehicles were armor-plated, mechanically primed and cleaned, sitting almost majestically, awaiting the arrival of Larosa's C5M from Maguire. Their tanks were filled with only enough gas to get them on and off the big bird, to be topped off only after they arrived in Kuwait City. Not far from the vehicles, Larosa observed two HMX Marine Helicopters, blades folded. Standing at attention next to the birds were on-duty Marines, armed and serious. No one came in close proximity without authorization.

"Where are the Marine pilots?" Larosa thought. "We need to load and go."

"I know what you're thinking," said a man from her crew, sensing her anxiety. "The HMX pilots are probably in the Joint Base Andrews operations center prepping for the Kuwait arrival. They go operational as soon as the C5M arrives and are probably studying the weather."

Larosa nodded in appreciation. "I'm okay. Just got the jitters for my first SAM. Look at these vehicles. I hope we don't scratch 'em."

"That'll be the least of our worries. Let's just get 'em there." Her crewman walked away to help prepare for the opening of the cargo door.

The C5M landed gracefully on the base runway. Her crew, all reservists out of Maguire Air Force Base, took special pride in the moment.

"No one should think of this crew as playing second fiddle. Our mission to support the president is top priority," Colonel Javier Robles had told his crew before their departure. He demonstrated a flawless approach. The giant air ship slowed to a near stop after banking left onto an isolated parallel strip. Once there, it taxied its way to the waiting vehicles and HMX helos.

Robles, a civilian attorney, satisfied his Air Force reserve time for the year with a two-week assignment that featured this special air mission to support the president of the United States. "Not too shabby," he told his wife before departing from home. "More war stories for the clients when I get back."

Robles attended the Air Force Reserve Officer Training Corp, or ROTC, program while at Kean University in Union, New Jersey, graduating in 1986. Most of his ROTC courses were actually taken at the New Jersey Institute of Technology in downtown Newark. He welcomed the opportunity, as it allowed the fervent sports fan to attend many of the sporting events held at the nearby Prudential Center, or the "Rock," while skipping ROTC classes he thought useless. It didn't hurt him; he absorbed enough of the curriculum to get through the program, obtain his degree, and receive a second lieutenant commission.

He attended flight school in Colorado and Arizona, where he qualified to fly most of the cargo planes during his active duty: the C-130, C-141, and C5. He never got certified to fly the workhorse for the Air Force, the C-17, used heavily during the gulf wars in Iraq and Afghanistan. His remaining active duty missions were all aboard the C5.

Anticipating the day he would muster out of active duty and enter the Air Force Reserves, he had applied, and was accepted, to Seton Hall Law School, attending classes in Newark. The rigors of law school required Robles to divert his attention from sports and focus solely on his legal studies. "This is fucking harder than flying," he confided to his classmates.

When he graduated from law school he returned to his Reserve service, working his way to the rank of colonel. "Why do you bother staying in the Reserves?" his wife has asked him. "It's not the pension, Babe. It's more the psychological benefit. It allows me to break from the tedious law practice from time-to-time and do something exciting. Flying the C5 gives me a welcome respite from the book work," he said.

Larosa opened the side hatch door and lowered the stairs onto the tarmac about fifty feet from the vehicles. Dressed in a form-fitting green flight suit, accented with spit-polished black boots and Oakley hundred dollar shades, she slowly stepped down each stair rung, all the while surveying the equipment, followed one-by-one by her crew. Once all seven of them had deplaned, they stood in place, waiting for the loadmaster to make her move then give the nod to deploy and prepare the plane.

Larosa said, "Now this is what it's all about. I can do this. Two Marine helos and four armored cars, plus eighty souls. It's gonna be one for the books." Larosa enjoyed the challenge. "This is what I trained for," she thought. "The Air Force has the confidence in me to do the job, and I'll get it done." She was a newly minted loadmaster on her first POTUS special air mission out of Maguire Air Force Base. She was not to be intimidated. Her first challenge: the lead Secret Service special officer. She was going to have to rein that one in quickly. "They always think they're in charge." She felt the immediate need to convince him and his crew that taking care of the cargo was her job. She was in charge. Larosa intentionally caught the special officer's eye, raising her left eyebrow as she tensed her lips. She hoped to send him the not-so-subtle message that she was to be dealt with respectfully. Her crew referred to it as her "whale eye."

Special Officer Jimmy Warwick, a retired Marine, took no offense. He had seen it before with other loadmasters. From here on out his goal was to survive the flight in the most comfortable way possible. Getting along with the young female reservist was his means to that goal.

"It's your ship, sir. Just tell me where to park our cars," Warwick belted out as Larosa approached. He was too well schooled in the art of situational power to let any reservist get under his skin. The former Marine sergeant major had his career plan worked out. Working with the Secret Service agents and support personnel was building equity so one day he and his bride of twenty years could enjoy retirement on the Maryland Eastern Shore. But for now, driving around in the president's limos was a treat. "My neighbors think I'm the coolest dude in town," he thought.

"Sergeant Larosa!" Warwick bellowed. "Do I have a deal for you!" Warwick wanted to tee up the loadmaster with a gift—a hat, shirt, or challenge coin—chum; it usually worked. He hoped to convince the loadmaster to allow him and the other special officers to sit in the limos during the flight. A fifty-fifty proposition at best, he knew. If he could pull it off, it would be the equivalent of a first-class ride to Kuwait.

"Not right now," said Larosa. "I've got a short timeline to get these vehicles locked down and choppers disassembled and tucked in for the trip." For the reservist it was now about the chains, straps, and integrated cargo locks applied in an orchestrated lockdown to secure the precious cargo. She was all about business first. Talk could come later.

"Roger that, Madam. I'm here to serve." For Warwick, the bargaining had just begun. "Just a matter of time," he thought to himself. He knew the time for his charm offensive would come soon enough, and it would seal a deal for sitting inside the limos. Dealing with his Marines was going to be a different story. The HMX guys would hear of the sergeant major's presence on board, and he would need no introduction. "If only it were that easy with some of these Air Force twits," he said to himself.

Colonel Robles and his co-pilots disembarked the plane and headed for the air base operations center to assess the weather en route to Ramstein. Robles and his two young reservists, both Air Force captains, would complete their part of the mission once the C5 landed at Ramstein Air Base, earning them ample reserve flying time with the oversized cargo plane. Once Robles and his crew arrived at Ramstein they would be relieved, catch up on their sleep, and be available to take the cargo plane back to the States after the presidential visit concluded in Kuwait. It was all very symmetrical.

When Larosa saw the colonel, she took it as her cue to climb back on board and work her way up to the cabin, where she would begin the process of raising up the aircraft's entire nose assembly for the loading and securing of equipment on board.

THIRTY
TWO

Ramstein Air Base, a relic of the cold war, has served the needs of the United States military for decades, with major operations in the Middle East theatre. Situated in the German state of Rheinland-Pfalz, it serves as headquarters for the U.S. Air Force in Europe. Located near the town of Ramstein, in the district of Kaiserslautern, Germany, it remains a significant North Atlantic Treaty Organization installation.

Brigadier General Jack Tuttle, first assigned to the base as a young, single, Air Force lieutenant twenty years earlier, ran the place now. "My command supports twenty squadrons. Each stands ready to respond with rapid mobility and agile combat support for military operations in the region, which includes the Middle East theatre," he is often quoted as saying. "I loved living here twenty years ago and am overjoyed to be back. I love the citizens who live in close proximity to the base and many who work here at Ramstein." Tuttle managed more than 16,000 United States citizens in addition to 6,000 trusted German workers on the base. He had known some of them twenty-plus years earlier, and when he returned he quickly became reacquainted with a number of them.

But General Tuttle had a problem—he liked women, a lot. And when tempted to dally, he did. He trended to the "dark side," as he called it, from time to time. With the power of his command came pretty women. He was a married man with a loose interpretation of the vows he took, but he skillfully avoided the appearance of inappropriate social or sexual relationships. His dalliances seemed to never interfere with his career or promotion opportunities. He had thus far been lucky, and he knew it.

As a young captain, Tuttle had had two favorites: Tatiana, who was of Russian descent, and Gamera, a Ukrainian. The two young women were as athletic as they were beautiful. What he didn't know then and never found out, was both were operatives who had been recruited when they were very young by the KGB operating out of East Germany. They both spoke fluent German and English with little accent. Their KGB tasking was to compromise Western assets, specifically high-level military officers. If they were lucky, a Western embassy staffer would fill the bill. At the time, the young lieutenant was not a high-value target on their radar. But things had changed.

When the Berlin Wall tumbled down, opportunities to migrate to the West and seek work became the most lucrative option. Many of the KGB personnel remained in contact with one another. Tatiana and Gamera elected to remain with their old handler, Belov. Belov said that one day they would be useful in the new unified Germany. So they packed small bags with only essential dress and toiletries. They brought no wall photos, no personal memorabilia, and only enough cash to get an apartment and enough time to find employment near the U.S. Air Force base at Ramstein. They knew how to survive. Jobs in a newly re-minted German nation would be scarce they reasoned. They knew the Americans wouldn't disengage too quickly, at least not until there was Teutonic fusion between the separated Germanys.

Their beauty opened doors at the airbase, where they first assumed cleaning jobs. The jobs paid little, but it was enough to keep food on the table. If they needed to augment their income, they knew how to discreetly work the street. If absolutely necessary, they could reach out to Belov.

They shared a cheap apartment early on, but as life moved forward an increasing accrual of funds slowly changed their condition. The real goal was to remain dormant until, and when, Belov needed to activate them.

The women ingratiated themselves with the air base brass, eventually taking on administrative duties and moving closer toward acquiring a trusted clearance level that would allow them access to any area of Ramstein Air Force Base. They got lucky, they thought, when they met the handsome young lieutenant, Jack Tuttle, and began to socialize with him. He was immediately smitten with both of them, but it was Tatiana, especially, who caught his eye. More than once he had been caught gazing at the well-defined symmetry of her ample cleavage. He had no knowledge of their background. All he knew was they were two very attractive women who were struggling in a difficult German economy.

"Shit," he mumbled to a friend. "Those girls could make it anywhere, just on their looks. But there's something about 'em that separates 'em. They really carry themselves well. I just can't get a fix on it. But they are special."

The three partied together on a regular basis, but he only crossed the line with Tatiana. He had feelings for her and even considered an extended tour until his more powerful career instincts convinced him otherwise. His promotion to captain made his decision to transfer back to the States a no-brainer. There was an occasional letter back and forth, but he became too busy with his rising career. Now he had come full circle. He was back as the air base commander. He was delighted to learn Tatiana and Gamera were still there and working on the base.

"You both look great!" Tuttle gushed when he reconnected with them.

"We may, General, but we are all a bit older and it takes more effort, and you don't look bad yourself," Gamera retorted. With the KGB gone, their old master, Belov, would have demanded nothing less from them than to maintain their usefulness to him and the Bratva. Both were eager to retire to their homelands after twenty-plus years working on the United States base. They found life in Germany comfortable, but there was always a lingering desire for home.

Neither had married. Both had had love affairs that could have sidetracked their loyalty to the Bratva, but didn't. The women, like their male Bratva counterparts, may not have always been faithful, but they were always loyal. They would never have even considered crossing Belov. If he learned of a potential breach in trust he would eliminate the perpetrator. This held true even for valued operatives like these women.

Tatiana and Gamera had remained low maintenance during the ensuing years, dormant even, not asking the Bratva for much, but they knew where their bread was buttered. Their bank accounts had swelled in the last few decades and not from working at Uncle Sam's air base. The women inherited their wealth while on the Bratva dole, benefitting from a lifelong membership, surviving as silent members of the mob. Their chests dared to bear the characteristic red tattoo testifying to their allegiance, fully aware that no one left the Bratva except through death.

Over the years the mob had relied little on them, but like other mob members, they remained on the payroll and were prepared for a Bratva assignment when one came their way. The Bratva took on the KGB culture to cultivate resources around the world and use them when needed. It faithfully kept track of its assets, regularly tending to a long-term investment that was there for any "just-in-case" missions. Now was their time. On Saturday, February 20, the call came.

"Tatiana, this is Belov. I am so happy to have the pleasure to speak with you. It has been awhile. I am sorry I can't take much time for pleasantries, but what I need is of the essence, and we must act quickly to set things in motion and take advantage of relationships we have cultivated."

Belov was calling from his residence in Brighton Beach, Brooklyn, not very far from where the Secret Service had executed its search warrant and where Carly Strain had taken Max into United States custody. Belov had just left the courthouse where Max had his initial appearance and where he learned what he needed about Max's next appearance scheduled by Judge Moskowitz. Belov would work quickly to prevent the hacker from having to appear again. He unveiled his plan to spring Max from custody to his German protégé.

"Tatiana, the Bratva needs you and Gamera to take on a daring task that will require your full attention to detail and apply all you have learned these last decades; all you were taught by me in the KGB."

Belov explained to them the importance the Bratva placed on ensuring Max got released from U.S. custody expeditiously.

"There are no quick options here. Max is incarcerated in a federal facility, the Metropolitan Correctional Center. It is an impenetrable fortress. It leaves no ability to extract him forcibly from the authorities."

Tatiana did not say a word, listening intently. What he laid out as a plan excited her latent talent in the silent world of intrigue.

"You must use every social engineering skill you have to facilitate your way onto the C5M the United States is to use to transport the president's vehicles. It is scheduled to land at the Ramstein Air Base on the 22nd in the early morning for refuel prior to departing for Kuwait City to support the president of the United States."

Tatiana was not surprised Belov knew the totality of detail concerning the president's trip to Kuwait or the fact the Bratva would use such leverage to extricate Max from U.S. custody. KGB operatives were schooled in matters of compromise, developing specifics and details on targets. Information was never discarded on high-profile targets, but filed away and used when needed to conduct operations.

"Tatiana, today, we face the nation we once loathed. We are about to take on the U.S. government. It gives me chills up my spine, a feeling I have not felt in a long time." Tatiana continued to listen, surprised at the admission she had just heard from the normally reticent boss. He relished connecting the international dots, awakening the sleeping giant, remnants of the once formidable KGB, for one more grand international assignment. As a proven tactical and strategic thinker, Tatiana listened closely as he described a plan of action. As the Bratva boss he was known to execute his operational plans using a matrix of operatives within the States and around the globe. He was considered a mysterious, mystical character. To the Russian mob, where he climbed the Bratva ladder quickly, he was the father of the black market. To federal law enforcement, he was considered a leading crime boss who managed and controlled mob activities globally. He was a suspected arms mover and was believed to be a major supplier throughout the Middle East. To Tatiana and Gamera he was a nostalgic figure to whom they remained devoted. The women were thrilled he had activated them for an operation.

"The Bratva is aware you still enjoy a relationship with the new base commander. We will need you to use that relationship to get on board the C5M. I need to know, do you still have the stamina to pull it off?"

"Yes, of course, Comrade. We can and will do that," said Tatiana. Many former Soviet Union citizens hungered for the old ways. They longed for Mother Russia to regain her former luster. They lamented the end of the Communist state but clung to their egalitarian salutations. Tatiana was one of them. Belov went into detail with her.

Bratva intended to exploit the new commander's prior sexual relationship with Tatiana, as well as his fondness for Gamera. They knew how sexually charged he had been from his activities of years earlier. They surmised he had not changed. Bratva was counting on his continued desire for lust. Tuttle had even put his career in jeopardy back then. What he didn't know was that after twenty years it would come back to haunt him. Belov's Bratva intended to use the commander as an unwitting partner and use his base authority to get the women on board the C5M; ostensibly to hitch a ride to Kuwait to observe the twenty-fifth anniversary of the successful coalition invasion of Iraq to liberate Kuwait. "The president of the United States will be there. It is a must-see event," Tatiana explained to the general.

The women had worked studiously the last two decades to groom an intimacy with the air base, achieving a degree of trust and confidence with the institutional employees who ran its daily operations. Daily access allowed them to avoid being subjected to an array of detection technology, usually metal screeners and X-ray machines. But their true ace-in-the-hole was that everyone knew the base commander liked them, and they were beyond suspicion. No one wanted to contravene the commander's orders and jeopardize their future promotion possibilities.

The two international thespians were going to act their way into the hearts of anyone who mattered, then act their way past the guards and aboard the cargo plane. Now was the opportunity to redeem years of service and retire in Russia as wealthy dames.

THIRTY THREE

The C5M needed every bit of the three-thousand-plus feet as it made its approach to Ramstein. The aircraft would not remain on the tarmac long; its mission was too important. Once it was refueled and the flight crew was replaced with fresh aviators, the plane would resume its mission, en route to Kuwait International Airport.

"Everyone listen up! During the refuel the agents and Marines will be allowed to deplane and stretch. It should only take an hour. Anyone interested in being transported to the military airport lounge to freshen up can hop on the grey bus. It will take you there and back, but you must make sure you don't get lost or we leave without you!" Larosa barked. Most of the passengers elected to remain with the C5M.

"Is there anything I can get you to drink or eat?" asked the Air Force private. He had been instructed to pay special attention to the general's guests. Tatiana and Gamera sat patiently in the military lounge waiting for the plane to arrive. "The C5M has arrived for refuel and the bus will arrive shortly to take you both to the plane to board," advised the private.

"No thanks," Gamera responded. "We're okay. Just excited about our trip and looking forward to seeing Kuwait."

"I wish I could go with you. I'm only twenty-one and don't even know much about the liberation of the country, but with the president being there I guess it will be exciting," the private exclaimed in a boyish Arkansas drawl.

"When you get to the airport lounge, you will meet Colonel Dan Riggs," the general had told the ladies prior to their arriving at the lounge.

"Riggs and his flight crew will be relieving the crew arriving with the C5M and will ferry the plane the rest of the way to Kuwait. He's a great guy."

Tatiana spotted the C5M agents as they entered the lounge from the airfield and tipped off Gamera with a nod. Simultaneously, the women's faces lit up with beaming smiles in an effort to disarm suspicion. There were no Marines with the agents. The HMX commander had them assume security posts around the helos to ensure no Air Force personnel got close.

Colonel Riggs observed the women and walked over. "Hello. My name is Colonel Riggs, and I am delighted you both have accepted General Tuttle's invitation to accompany us to Kuwait City."

Tatiana didn't like the fact the colonel had surprised her and Gamera. They had been focused on the arriving agents and he caught them off-guard. "Not good," she reprimanded herself. Gamera read her mind. Colonel Riggs continued to flash his toothy grin. His fellow pilots kept a deferential distance, allowing Riggs to schmooze his passengers. Besides, they didn't want to interfere with the base commander's interests. To them, these women were potential career busters. But they all noticed the U.S. flag was emblazoned on Tatiana's left breastplate, conveniently positioned in order to direct the eyes toward her ample display of cleavage.

"We have our own van. If you are interested in riding with us rather than waiting for the airport bus, you are welcome to join us. I think the agents will be here until the end of the refueling operation," Riggs offered.

Tatiana pulled her carry-on bag closer to her mid-section. "That would be wonderful," she responded.

THIRTY FOUR

Saudi Arabia, February 22, 2016

"Is everyone secure?" Riggs transmitted over the intercom to Larosa.

"Roger that, sir. All souls secured and equipment chained down," she responded.

With the plane refueled for its final leg of the trip, the pilots prepared to taxi for departure. The original Maguire Air Base crew had reached its maximum allowable time in the cockpit and had been replaced. The loadmaster and her team did not have the same mandate and remained on board to continue the trip.

General Tuttle personally selected the young colonel to relieve Robles and his crew. This was an unusual, but accepted, practice. It also made it easier for the women to get on board without being questioned. Colonel Riggs would look the other way when it came to security "hygiene."

The C5M, and its elite cargo, departed the air base, needing every bit of the runway to gain lift. The aircraft seemed to struggle as it labored up to its cruising altitude of 33,000 feet, but to the pilots it was a normal takeoff. Once it leveled out, it vectored toward its destination at 475 miles per hour. The lumbering green hulk had traded a cool, wet German day for the dry, hot Kuwaiti desert.

"Most people don't know this, but the plane you will travel on has been a loyal flying workhorse since the late 1960s," Tuttle told the women. "It's one of our safest airplanes, but our crews refer to it fondly as 'FRED,' an acronym for 'Fucking Ridiculous Economic Disaster.' The truth is, it's only been involved in two crashes. One resulted from ground fire and one was from damage sustained while on the ground. I hope that comforts you. We don't expect any hostile gunfire."

"We are not worried, Colonel. We trust you completely," replied Tatiana. "But why all this expense to move these vehicles? Can't your president use cars and helicopters from Kuwait?"

"It's way too complicated to explain. But the Secret Service relies on us to do the mission, and we do. They have priority. The Marines do as well when they support the president," he said. He stopped talking in order to avoid boring them.

What the general didn't tell them were the identities of the other passengers aboard the C5M. It didn't matter. The Bratva knew. The women were to accompany seventy-two Secret Service special agents who were to be lodged in a confined upper deck, a non-ambient area, an area of the plane temporarily fitted with what agents refer to as "a poor excuse for airline seats." The seating compartment bore no resemblance to anything one would recognize as commercial passenger plane seating. The agents were packed on board in a manner that seemed to most of them like being stuffed into a large closet. They had no choice but to take it in stride, although some of them cursed the manpower guys for the assignment.

Most of the agents settled down for the last leg of their long flight, comforted with the thought, at least, that they would not have to spend the flight in the more traditional netted seats usually found on these Air Force transports.

"Who else has this kind of job?" asked one of the seventy-two sardines, a newly commissioned agent.

"Just get over it," responded one of the senior agents. "If you don't like it, quit. This is a long-ass trip and you need to make the best of it, otherwise you're going to have a long and tasteless career."

At Ramstein, seating was based on "barbershop rules." The older agents knew how to keep their seats dedicated as they disembarked during the re-fuel. They ensured they left their name-tagged equipment bags behind on the seats as ownership. One didn't move an equipment bag from a seat without consequence. So an occasional shoving match between a young agent who didn't mark his space and a nineteen-year-old Marine who needed to find a space became inevitable, and unfortunately for the young Marine, not usually favorable to him, as his Marine Corps captain would order him to stand down.

"Fuck these prima donnas," the Marine would whisper as he sought a seat in the rear.

"Pardon me, Private?" the captain responded.

"Nothing, sir. I was just praying I could find another seat."

The agents, drawn from a variety of Secret Service field offices throughout the country, received a briefing on the trip while at Joint Base Andrews. Carly Strain, the newly minted jump team leader, addressed the seventy-two agents. "Our assignment will be a five-day mission to augment the president's protective detail. The president's visit will involve a desert site, which I understand to be an old military facility not far from Kuwait City called Markaz Hudud al Abdali. There will be a lengthy motorcade, about ten miles from the site to the Iraqi border. Interestingly, the location is fifty miles from the Iranian border. So this is to be memory maker for us all."

Strain glanced around the room at the attentive faces, and then continued. "The U.S. military outpost remains a legacy to demonstrate the support the United States provided Kuwait in the first Gulf War in 1991." She went on to cite a report obtained from headquarters. "It featured a successful Combined Special Operations Command—a once-secret operation that injected operators into the belly of the beast—Saddam's once mighty production site for chemical weapons, just north of the Kuwaiti-Iraqi border."

Agent Strain knew it sounded rote to some of the old timers among the jump team, but felt obligated to give them the brief. "The outpost now enjoys present-day prominence as a joint operations command for what many believe to be a future invasion platform to render Iran nuclear-free."

Strain realized the latter part of what she had just read was classified SECRET, and she reminded the jump team it was such and should remain confidential, meant for their ears only.

"The remaining information is all open source," she said. "The commemoration site has been chosen by the Kuwaiti government to celebrate the twenty-fifth anniversary of the 1991 liberation of their country from Saddam's Iraq. And, of course, the reason for us to make the trip is to provide perimeter security for POTUS. Saddam didn't like the fact that Kuwait completely blocked his access to the Persian Gulf. His angst, no longer a concern, faded into the evil ethos along with his soul as he was hanged in disgrace by a newly constituted Iraqi government. That's the background. Any questions?"

There were no questions, but Strain then followed up with the obligation headquarters had imposed four years earlier on all jump team leaders. She reminded them all to stay away from bars featuring "live entertainment" and remember their obligation to refrain from alcohol for twelve hours prior to going on duty. Kuwait City had its share of loose women, who mainly operated within hotels to be less visible to the "Sex Police."

A young agent raised his hand. "Is Kuwait a dry country?"

One of the other agents answered, "What do you think she is, a weather woman?"

Strain responded, "Where there is a will, there is a way. All I'm saying is, if there is alcohol to be found, it'll be found. But you need to know that you need to be careful. I don't want to have to handle any issues with any of you getting 'jammed up' by the Kuwaiti authorities."

Strain knew from previous experience that the United States Embassy would have an ample amount of wine available along with plenty of spirits for the traveling U.S. delegation. But any drinking of alcohol had to be done privately and discreetly within the embassy compound. The Secrets couldn't afford to get into trouble. The frenzied news media traveling with the president would have a field day with such a story.

"It is best not to drink at all," Strain said. She knew that admonition would not be received well by the seventy-plus agents. "But if you must drink, keep it within the confines of an American facility."

With two of their VH-92A helos ensconced on board the C5M, the Marine pilots and their support crew integrated themselves on board the transport plane, commingling with the Secret Service agents. The Marines were all male, whereas the Secret Service contingent had an uncharacteristically high number of women, with ten female agents in its ranks—eye candy to most of the Marines. What may have seemed unusual twenty years earlier, sending women into the Middle East, was now an accepted notion. Headquarters had not even run a second thought by the manpower specialists back at Secret Service headquarters. Women now represented 20 percent of the agent population and the planners did not concern themselves with the sensitivities of Islamic laws or religious practices when deploying manpower. With the president traveling more than any of his predecessors, the manpower squeeze took away much of the discretion from the Secret Service managers. All field office "bodies" were equal and were to be made available to support the protection of the president anytime, anywhere.

The C5M departed Germany fully refueled to fly non-stop to Kuwait and was expected to arrive at 1700 hours Kuwaiti time. The agents would be met on the tarmac by Agent Sims and his advance team and be transported to their hotel. The Marines would reassemble their dismantled choppers and immediately do a practice flyby of the celebration site. It was important for them to nail down their landing zones, or LZs, and begin to understand the geographic threats to their aircraft at each arrival and departure site.

Not all threats were terror-related. Geography, natural or man-made, could present many hurdles. The power of the blades could wreak havoc on the most serene locations. By their very nature, the active helo blades were disruptive. The tranquility of selected sites was disrupted, trees distorted, tents uprooted, and umbrellas torn from weak grips. During this particular visit, there was the very real possibility of creating an unintended sandstorm, potentially a chaotic situation for those in close proximity.

The Marines didn't worry about food or sleep, or at least that's how the Secret Service perceived them. They were a self-reliant bunch, a real can-do group. They were also remarkably low maintenance. They would get the job done and move forward to tackle their next mission without fuss.

Many of the Secret Service agents came from the Marines Corps. "The mirror does not lie," some liked to say. The Secret Service saw the Marine Corps in itself, in temperament and in mission. The "Secrets" knew the Marines would get the job done. The agents had tremendous respect for the leathernecks. But, as with any close-knit family, there were times for quarrelling, and when it came to C5M seats, they often quarreled.

The Marine Squadron HMX-1 Nighthawks are based out of Quantico, Virginia, but the squadron maintains ready aircraft at their facility in Anacostia, Maryland, which houses the dedicated VH-92A, or "White-Tops," that seem to support the president's short-duration transportation requirements. The Marines were proud of the newly deployed presidential helicopters. Built by the teamwork of Lockheed Martin and Sikorsky engineers, the Kuwait visit would be the helos first foreign venture.

The helos are flown by the best of the best, tried and tested. Marine military helicopter pilots represented the country well. They were battle tested, but also performed admirably in the diplomatic missions that presidential or vice presidential transport demanded. This mission would have them ferry the president on short trips in which time and space were critical components of his itinerary.

Over the Mediterranean, Colonel Tuttle intentionally avoided Israeli airspace, electing to go the extra distance through Egypt before entering Saudi Arabia's territorial sovereignty. The Saudis demanded this arrangement from the Americans in order to create the international illusion that Israel did not exist. Upon entering Saudi airspace, Tuttle vectored for the Kuwait City International Airport. Tuttle anticipated the Saudi air traffic controller would accept the responsibility for communicating with the C5M and guide it to Kuwaiti airspace.

"Riyadh Air Traffic Control Center, this is SAM143, Do you copy?"

THIRTY FIVE

Sims's advance team and their Kuwaiti counterparts "married-up" to conduct an exhaustive review of the president's intended itinerary. Together, they inspected and sanitized the entire length of the Highway of the Future, or Highway 80, on which the president would travel in his enormous limousine. The Secret Service would eventually take the "Presidential Beast," as they called it, for a test drive on the highway, itself a dangerous endeavor, as they would become vulnerable to an attack.

Iraqi operatives still simmered with hatred from their embarrassing loss to the "Great Satan" and were considered threats to this president's visit. After all, they had tried to kill former President George H. W. Bush and his Secret Service detail in the early 1990s, but failed. It was a Saddam-directed event. His ultimate hanging was a welcome denouement to many in the United States, including the Secret Service agents who came close to their own demise at the hands of the late Iraqi dictator.

Agent Sims had already established a great working relationship with his counterpart. "Colonel Maudud, there are air interdiction assets I need to discuss with you. I know the request may seem over the top, but in order for us to feel absolutely comfortable, we need to know your Air Force has our backs with air security."

Colonel Aalim Maudud was not fazed by the request. He actually wondered why it had taken the affable U.S. agent so long to bring it up.

"My dear friend, the Kuwaiti Air Force will cooperate in any manner it can to ensure the beautiful Kuwaiti skies are free of the mal-intended."

"I thank you, my new friend," responded an equally appreciative Sims. "We absolutely want your air support to ensure the president can enjoy a no-flight area."

"The Kuwaiti Air Force, our Al-Quwwat al-Jawwiy, will provide the necessary air support to interdict any unauthorized aircraft, Mr. Sims."

"I thank you, Colonel. The requested no-fly area has been a standard security feature for the Secret Service since the mid-nineties. I realize it places a burden on your wonderfully adept Air Force, but the comfort it provides us is priceless." Sims knew how to make any request into something the provider would feel good about giving to him. Ironically, it was former Assistant Treasury Secretary and former New York City Police Commissioner Peter Baubles who suggested to the Secret Service that they engage Black Hawk Helicopters to ferry their specially trained counter assault teams and train to interdict small aircraft attempting to penetrate any designated no-fly zone. This capability went on to become a hallmark best practice for the Secret Service's National Security Special Events, and just as importantly, a feature for the PPD advance team to employ overseas to guard against an Al Qaida air attack.

"I can assure you we will do our best." The Kuwaiti Air Force was going to "infest" the airspace with its assets to ensure a safe and secure air and land arrival by POTUS.

Commander Will Strain, who had accompanied the Secret Service on this meeting, chuckled at the Kuwaiti's response. They were so eager to impress the Secret Service with their capabilities, they had promised every "bird" in the fleet.

The State of Kuwait was a constitutional monarchy, unlike its sister state, Saudi Arabia, which was a regular old monarchy. Its leader, the Emir, remained firmly in control of the kingdom, though the last decade had seen tensions arising from the "have-nots."

Kuwait was only slightly larger than the state of New Jersey, but it offered the United States and its partners a strategic location at the entrance to the Persian Gulf. Kuwait featured a dry desert, an intensely hot weather pattern for the summer months, cold winter months, and only short cool episodes. Kuwait was small in comparison to other states in the Middle East, but made up for it with its zest to partner with the West.

A sort of national glee fell over the country, as Kuwait anticipated hosting the president of the United States in the border town of Markaz Hudud al Abdali. The harsh memories and wounds of the war caused by the Saddam invasion in 1991, which encouraged the raping and pillaging of the populace, had not faded nor had they been forgiven. So when the Secret Service requested the Kuwait Land Forces, or KLF, deploy manpower to maintain outer perimeter security in advance of the president's visit, the KLF didn't blink.

"Agent Sims, you've made quite an impression on our host, Colonel Maudud. I don't know what you have, but whatever it is, you ought to bottle it and sell it," said Will Strain. He grinned at Sims.

"I like this guy, Strain." Sims thought to himself. "He has a nice way about him."

Commander Strain eagerly awaited the U.S. Air Force C5M cargo plane. It was now well known on the ground the Commander had a vested interest in the C5M; it ferried a special cargo for him.

Although Commander Strain was usually a cool operative in even the most stressful of situations, Sims noticed he showed signs of excitement in his demeanor on this occasion. Carly Strain was the love of his life. While separated from her for many months, his fondest image of her, the one that sustained him, was one of her with her dark black hair pulled back in a tight pony tail, dressed in a white buttoned-down long sleeve shirt, a tight pair of blue jeans, no belt, and a pair of flip flops that denoted a casual reflection of life. He hated not having her with him and found himself undergoing daily self-introspection. He now questioned whether his career was worth the separation.

Carly Strain was an up-and-coming Secret Service manager. She loved her career and enjoyed working and living in the always vibrant New York City. Although they were apart, the Commander never worried about her fidelity. He only wished they could share more time together. It was a thrill that she had managed to orchestrate a visit to Kuwait to support POTUS and see her husband too. He couldn't believe his good luck, being in a position to support the Secret Service Kuwait advance team. He felt sure the stars and the moons were aligned in their favor.

"Commander, I can tell you have an extra zip in your step today," said a grinning Sims.

"You betcha," he replied. "I am trying to contain my exuberance."

Sims turned his attention to the Kuwaiti support team present at the airport. "You have worked with the locals before on this scale?"

"No, not quite. But I can tell you that while their eagerness may end up making them look like the Keystone Cops, tripping all over each other, they mean well and want to impress you guys. I know the Kuwaitis to be genuine in their support of the Secret Service, but I also know that human nature can go awry in times of celebration, with professional folks doing very unprofessional things just to be part of the party, like dropping their post assignment to get a better look at the president."

"I will do my best to keep them focused," Sims responded. "I want to make sure you can stay focused on the arrival of your bride."

THIRTY SIX

In the aftermath of the sex scandal in Cartagena, Colombia, which allegedly involved rogue Secret Service personnel and military special operators taking prostitutes back to their hotel rooms prior to a presidential visit, new rules were put in place by headquarters. Secret Service managers like Carly Strain were placed on the car-planes to supervise the off-duty behavior of the agents. Headquarters intentionally placed as many female agents as possible in charge of the jump teams. This covered the Secret Service obligation to satisfy the likes of the lady senator from Maine who obsessed out loud about the alleged sexual antics of some agents. Her answer to the problem was female supervision. The senator believed female supervisors could curb the perceived male agent's proclivity for paid sex.

Strain knew this was bullshit. "Just more political correctness," she said. She felt if a guy, or a gal for that matter, wanted to "wander," they would, and no supervision, male or female, would change that.

"Guys are no different from us," she told her husband during the Cartagena hearings. "Perhaps the senator could pay more attention to her own house and rein-in her Cuban colleague, who is alleged to have paid for underage sex in the Dominican Republic. Hell, a female agent is just as much of a risk. They 'wander' as much as the guys do. What? Women don't crave sex? That's bullshit. We get just as horny as you guys do. We just don't have to pay for it."

As the C5M lumbered toward its destination, the special passengers engaged in a variety of distractions and internal vignettes in order to pass the time during the flight: playing cards, eating box lunches on the hood of one of the chained-down armored vehicles, and reading. Few passengers were interested in getting shut-eye during the early part of the flight.

Down in the belly of the C5M, a few of the Secret Service operatives remained in close proximity to the "Beast." The name was the latest moniker given to the most recent acquisition in the presidential inventory. If lucky, a persuasive agent could convince the loadmaster to allow some of the transportation support personnel, TS agents for short, to take positions inside the secure armored presidential limousines, creating the illusion, at least, of riding first class while on board. Persuading the loadmaster to allow seating in the secured vehicles was a difficult task and was usually only attempted by the most senior Secret Service representative. It was a very different mile-high experience, for sure.

The C5M was a unique experience for the Secret Service. On board, agents would find a seat, position their personal equipment in close proximity, check out their box lunches they pre-purchased from the Air Force, then get positioned to chat with fellow agents they hadn't seen in some time. It served as a sort of flying reunion for some of the seasoned agents. In an odd way, they liked it. The early hours of the long flight brought out their gambling instincts. Footlockers that were used for storing the extra equipment—M-16s, MP-5s, and Remington 870 Shotguns—were brought together to form a poker game platform.

Time begins to contract as the poker games and the novels bring on their intended consequence. The flight to Kuwait International Airport was long enough to provide time for sufficient shut-eye in order to be functional upon arrival, or at least alert enough to get through the agent briefing. After the card games, most agents tried to get some sleep.

In contrast, the HMX Marines took the flights more routinely. For them, it was about getting sleep. Once a seat was secured, it was simply time to get some "shuteye." Only the Secret Service transportation personnel had access to the front seats of the special vehicles on board. Most of the field agents on board had little or no idea one could sit inside the limo while it was being transported. It was not an entirely well-kept secret, as the experienced agents knew it to be an option. Yet, it was an option they kept close to the vest in order to ensure tranquility on board the flying albatross. The older agents saw no need to inform the younger agents. Let them earn their stripes. Besides, they weren't invited.

Agent Strain knew of the perk, but Loadmaster Larosa had her manifested up front in the pilot's cabin area along with her co-jump team leader, Gerry Cavis.

"Cavis, do you ever feel the slightest guilt about sitting up here?"

"Nope, the seating arrangement is a perk set aside for Secret Service supervisors," Cavis commented. "We get to bunk up front with the pilots and loadmaster. This is sweet. So, Strain, don't be foolish. We did our time in the back. Let them eat cake."

"Shut up. That is so bad to think that way," Strain shot back.

"I know. But someone has to sit up here, so it might as well be the best looking of the bunch."

"You're cute for an asshole," Strain said.

"Don't tell your husband you feel that way. He may get upset and kick my ass."

Warwick overheard the comment from the stair landing that led up to the supervisor's area. "No worries about the transportation guys who are assigned to the belly of the plane, Agent Cavis. We'll be just fine while keeping an eye on the vehicles."

"I'm sure you will!" Cavis shouted back down. "And don't worry about the field agents!"

"I won't. And I won't let them know about your luxurious sleeping arrangements either. I'll let them know you said to eat cake. Ha ha!"

Most of the younger agents didn't know any better, and they sat in the remote, cavernous compartment to the rear of the plane. For the junior agents it was standard practice for the car-plane detail. It was generational experience that provided more than an ample number of war stories for the young agents' rites of passage, giving them bragging rights and road stories that would last well into retirement.

Larosa turned the interior lighting off. Those who elected to read or play cards relied on battery-operated lighting. They were the diehards, as most on board fell asleep very quickly.

"What is it that the loadmaster's crew does downstairs?" one of the young agents asked a veteran agent while holding his cards close to his chest.

"The crew remains percolating inside this flying mammoth, engaged in routine maintenance of the aircraft, double-checking the tie-down chains to the vehicles and choppers, or stowing plane property," said the veteran agent. "Sometimes it may look like busy Air Force work, but let me tell you something, kid: you don't want to be on a plane with equipment the size of a fucking helicopter working its way loose."

"Why do you bother busting Warwick's chops?" Strain asked Cavis.

"I actually like Warwick a lot and just want to keep things loose. He takes and gives shit as good as anyone I know. We're lucky to have the old Marine with us to manage the vehicles."

Cavis was selected by headquarters to assist Strain manage her jump team. He would deploy his CAT while in Kuwait in order to provide tactical cover for the president. His team slept aft too, and they mixed in well with the field office guys. He constantly reinforced to his agents that they came from the field office and would one day return to that place.

"Don't be peckerheads or else the field will remember you and treat you accordingly," he advised.

Strain had an admiration of the highly respected team leader that stemmed from her time working alongside him during her PPD days. He was in his sixteenth year on the job, the last four as CAT team leader. He loved the field's criminal investigations and had sworn he would stay in the field for the remainder of his career, but then he was tapped for promotion to supervise the entire CAT program. He couldn't say no. He had a previous three-year stint under his belt as a young CAT member before he rotated off the assignment and went back to the field to resume duties as a criminal investigator.

Headquarters wanted him back on CAT to remedy a managerial problem. The available pool of candidates, or more specifically, competent candidates, was small. He didn't want to spend the rest of his career as a specialized agent, but didn't want to throw away an opportunity for promotion either.

"Strain, I very much envy your investigative success and in many ways wish I could have had a different career path that looked more like yours. You have a well-deserved reputation." He was aware she was married to a special operations guy in the Coast Guard and was careful to avoid being perceived as sending any flirtatious signals her way. She took the compliment as intended.

"Thanks, Cavis. That means a lot coming from someone like you."

On this leg of the journey they were to share cabin space with the two new passengers who had boarded after the refuel stop at the airbase in

Ramstein. They were told the general's "guests" would join them. The trip from Andrews to Ramstein had been spacious and comfortable, with only the two agents housed in the four-bunk cabin. Now they would be sharing the space. Cavis anticipated he and Strain would no longer have the lower bunk option.

"Hey, I'll take the upper bunk to give you a bit more privacy."

"This might get uncomfortable for you, sharing the cabin with three ladies," she shot back. He smirked, but said nothing.

Before retiring to their bunks, they engaged in some small talk with Tatiana and Gamera, mostly superficial chatter, just to be respectful. The supervisors were keen on getting some sleep and didn't have an ardent desire to make new friends. They knew they would be busy once they landed in Kuwait and were eager to get some sleep.

"I'll take the top bunk," Cavis offered. He handed out earplugs to the other cabin occupants.

"No shit, Sherlock. I don't want you looking up my ass from below, and since you don't have much of an ass, there's not much for me to look at. So yes, please, by all means, take the upper bunk," Strain said.

The women politely giggled at Strain's audacity. They didn't spend much more time being social, but eagerly waited for the two Americans to get in their bunks and fall asleep. Then their Bratva mission to deal with the pilots could begin.

Neither inserted their earplugs, as they wanted their hearing to be sensitive to the newly adapted environment not far from the pilot's cockpit. Each feigned sleepiness and assumed bunk positions, giving the appearance of settling down for the rest of the flight. Tatiana read a novel in the lower bunk opposite Strain, while Gamera played with her iPad. Neither spoke German or Russian in front of the Secret Service managers. They knew to do this from their KGB training. Keep as much off the table as possible. Don't give the enemy any data to contemplate or use to ask questions that could lead to detection.

Strain's last thought before dozing off was that the women were quite affable. "I can understand why the general likes them," she thought. With her head on her pillow she politely whispered to both of them, "You don't travel with much baggage."

Tatiana smiled politely. "In the old days, no one had much to pack, so that is just the way we were brought up." Strain had enough animation left in her face to return Tatiana's smile before falling asleep.

Cavis's thoughts focused on his five team members who were located in the rear of the plane. He hoped they were comfortable. "I'm sure they're doing fine," he thought. "CAT guys know how to adapt." Despite their reputation for being well trained and disciplined, some considered the elite group arrogant. Cavis occasionally reminded his guys to present themselves without pretense, particularly to the younger agents. His team loved him, and he loved them. The man who they called "the Good Shepherd" soon drifted off to sleep.

THIRTY
SEVEN

Warwick wasn't sure, but he sensed Loadmaster Larosa might have a thing for him. "Thank God the loadmaster is female," he chuckled.

Larosa knew it would be no easy task to get the presidential vehicles on board the C5M and chained down. The HMX helos presented an equal challenge to the new loadmaster. Warwick had experienced many chain-downs with the "Beasts" since being named the lead special officer. When he offered his help to the loadmaster for the helos, the loadmaster welcomed it. The Marines on board were not about to tell the former sergeant major to get lost.

Larosa made one last inspection of the cargo on board. She passed Warwick several times as she ensured the chains were properly fastened and taut. Neither made a comment to the other, but there existed within her an excitement she hadn't felt in some time. She allowed herself a flash of sexual attraction toward the former Marine. She tried unsuccessfully to banish the thought. It would not vanish.

She turned the overhead lower cabin lights off, leaving only two single low-intensity lights glowing from the forward and aft of the flying motel. They provided enough illumination to allow anyone still awake and moving around to avoid tripping on the chains. When the Air Force renovated the C5Ms, it integrated these new mini-recessed LED spotlights—high performance technology that used only one stingy watt.

Her crew members had already nodded off in their reserved webbed seating. They would be able to squeeze in a two-hour nap and had no problem falling asleep. The process was routine for them, and they slept without any chemical aids.

Warwick was standing between the two limos when Larosa walked toward him. She used a small flashlight to provide additional floor lighting. She had received the flashlight as a gift from a Weichert realtor the week before while looking for a new apartment in Lakewood, New Jersey. She thought it had worked remarkably well so far, but probably had a short shelf life.

"You don't need that light to make you look any more attractive," Warwick whispered loudly enough for her to hear.

"What was that?" Larosa responded. She eyed him quizzically.

"I said, you are the hottest looking Air Force loadmaster I have ever seen, and I want to get to know you better."

"You are way out of line. Now get in this 'Beast' before I throw your ass in there." She felt emotionally off-balance and a little light-headed. Whatever she was feeling, she liked it.

"I can't open the door myself and may need help," whispered Warwick. He pointed at the six-inch-thick armored and enforced door located to the right rear of the Beast. Inside, within the vehicle cabin, was the customary location where the president of the United States would sit.

"I'm not sleepy," said Warwick. "And the idea of having someone to talk with inside the limo is appealing. Want to sit with me?"

Larosa hadn't planned on sleeping either. She had planned on reading the rest of her Christopher Reich thriller, *Rules of Betrayal*, the third book of his successful trilogy, but immediately discarded that idea upon Warwick's invitation.

"Sure, get in. I'll sit with you. Shit, it may be the only opportunity I'll ever have to sit in a presidential limousine."

Larosa turned her penlight off and scanned the perimeter of the fuselage for any ogling witnesses. There were none. She entered the spacious limo as Warwick held the door open. As a security feature, the inside dome light was always turned off. It only activated when the president or Secret Service personnel inside the vehicle turned it on. Warwick slowly pulled the door closed, careful to make as little noise as possible. When the door mechanism locked shut, Larosa reached her right arm around Warwick's neck and pulled him in close.

"I thought we were going to talk," he teased. He said no more as Larosa's tongue entered his mouth and began to swish about searching for his. Her left hand found his package and his hardness prompted her to move to a new position, straddling him but never disengaging from the passionate open kiss.

Warwick began to unzip her flight suit. Larosa wore no undershirt, only a bra, which strained to contain her ample chest. He grew enthusiastic upon witnessing the Air Force sergeant's full form. Her erect nipples, responding to the erotic moment, titillated him beyond patience as he moved to suckle each of them. Warwick tried desperately not to come across as a newbie. He didn't want her to think he was some young lad who had never tasted a woman's bosom.

Larosa wasted no time undoing Warwick's buckle to gain access to his aroused member. The former sergeant major thought she was about to give him a blow job. With her flight suit off her shoulders and chest fully exposed, she aggressively pushed his pants down to the limo's floorboard, exposing his full erection.

Larosa slid the rest of her flight suit to her ankles. She appreciated that she could stand up in the rear of the limo. "There's enough room back here for an orgy," she said to Warwick. She then re-straddled her new lover, carefully sliding his cock inside her. Her juices facilitated the position and together they began to grind.

"You're so warm," Warwick whispered. Larosa had a different take on the moment, and she began to moan louder with each rhythmic thrust downward. Warwick escaped the passion briefly to scan the limo's surroundings. He didn't want any gawkers to catch the ecstasy. Comfortable that no one had been alerted to his first Beast experience, he returned his full attention to the moment.

Larosa was lost to her base instincts and sought to further the intensity of the feeling, which was already intensified by the location. She had no concern at the moment about the possibility of someone shuffling by the car and peeking inside. The idea of achieving orgasm inside the most secure vehicle in the world excited her to previously unknown heights. As she reached climax, Warwick moved his hand up to cup her mouth in an attempt to stifle her moans. She slapped his hand away and let go with continued cries of satisfaction. The intensity of her shudders caused Warwick to ejaculate, as he pounded her body between her writhing hips.

She felt his member retreat. It didn't matter. He had satisfied her.

The whole experience took less than seven minutes. She caught his eyes and laughed softly. "Okay, Warwick. Now that I own you, what are your plans for another mile-high fuck? You got anything on Air Force One?" She smiled, then pulled away and began to get dressed. She put her bra back on, then pulled up and zipped her flight suit.

"You don't wear panties under that flight suit?" Warwick asked. "Doesn't that get itchy?"

"The only thing that makes me itchy is watching you help me put these vehicles on board. I don't itch anymore. Do you?"

Warwick pulled his pants back up and buckled his belt. Out of the corner of his eye he caught a figure approaching the driver's side of the limo. "Don't move. Just sit quietly. There's someone approaching." Larosa sat like a cat stalking its prey, without moving a muscle. The windows were tinted to such a degree that anyone looking inside would be hard-pressed to discern any activity, particularly with the low light level.

Gerry Cavis walked past the two limos. He gazed intently at the ladder leading up to the agents' berth, located just beneath the mini-recessed light. He stared at the light as though it were a beacon drawing him toward it. Warwick sensed something was up. This was not about Cavis not sleeping. He had something on his mind.

"We have to get out of the car," Warwick told Larosa. "I think something is going down, but have no idea what."

"Okay. I'll get us a couple of bottles of water. We can at least talk while we have some time. Now that we've come to know each other, we ought to get to know each other better." Larosa wanted the closeness to last a little longer, but she saw that Warwick's direction of interest had changed. She told herself to just follow his lead and see where it went.

Warwick and Larosa opened the door and stepped gingerly from the "Beast." Larosa looked to see if either had left any items behind. Warwick hadn't used a rubber, but it didn't concern her. She'd been on birth control for the past six months. She stared at the president's seat to see if any traces of their activity had been left. None had, and she breathed a sigh of relief. "The last fucking thing I need is to be accused of leaving the president's seat a mess," she thought to herself.

Once outside the limo, Warwick and Larosa observed a second figure walking slowly and resolutely along the side of the fuselage and toward them. It was Carly Strain. She walked with her arms extended to maintain balance. One arm extended to the side of the plane's metal interior and the other touched the limos to hold her steady. The look on her face didn't betray Warwick's instinct. Strain had the same focused look on her face as Cavis.

"Strain, is everything okay?"

"I need to get the Marine leadership down here, and then advise you and Larosa about the state of this aircraft. I need to do it fast. Cavis is going to let the Marine officers know to come to me. He will brief his people up top."

.

THIRTY EIGHT

Tatiana nodded to Gamera. It was the signal to move forward to the cockpit and deploy the plan. Timing was critical. The threat had to be delivered at a time and place that would limit the pilots' options and encourage complete cooperation. Belov's plan required forcing the aircraft to the ground over Saudi airspace and in proximity to the dedicated airfield where the Bratva's Antonov 225 waited. The women could not waste another moment.

Tatiana took her rucksack off the floor and placed it on her lap. Carefully, she began to unzip the bag, leaving in plain view the KGB-designed cyanide petard, the Mubtahar. It was a gas weapon device used by Al Qaida to poison intended targets and had been adopted over the years by criminal and terrorist groups in one form or another. The Bratva used it extensively in parts of the globe to force compliance with their terms during negotiations.

Tatiana had grown confident after successfully bringing the petard on board without arousing suspicion. Her General Tuttle had made a career-ending mistake. "So be it," she thought. He would pay a price when the inevitable follow-up investigation ensued, and investigators discovered his self-absorbed breach of the air base security system. Tatiana could not have cared less about what would happen to the general. It was business. He was the current "mark," and his carnal desires clouded his judgment.

"KGB 101. The original social engineering practice continues to work," thought Tatiana. She had compromised the source and leveraged the opportunity to access the system, which was no different from what the hackers were doing with electronics. "KGB operatives remain relevant," she thought. "The general is expendable."

With the chemical petard on board, the ladies now needed to convey to the pilot and his crew what they were capable of doing to their plane and its human cargo. Belov had told the women, "If they're not convinced, it will have a devastating effect on them."

Intended for use in small confined spaces, the chemical petard is designed to release a lethal quantity of hydrogen cyanide, cyanogens chloride followed with chlorine gases. At a high dose the result is death, and it's not a pretty death. The petard's full release promotes loss of consciousness, convulsions and hurtful respiratory effects, and finally, cardiac failure. A long fifteen minutes of suffering would occur after initial exposure.

The plane would certainly go down, and the women were fully aware of the consequences. They had two plans to persuade the pilots to cooperate, and they were more favorably disposed to Plan B, the low-dose version. A Plan B release would be less deleterious to the passengers and crew, but would send a powerful message to all aboard, and quite frankly, scare the shit out of them.

The lower-dose release would cause symptoms that mimic poisoning from the toxic compounds, cascading from giddiness, to hyperventilation, to palpitations, to dizziness, to nausea, to vomiting. Finally, it would leave the victims with a terrible headache, not to mention a nasty case of eye irritation, but it would not kill them. Yet time was a major consideration. They had to quickly determine the crew's compliance levels. They brought individual air masks to neutralize the effects of a Plan B release and had one extra in their rucksack for the pilot.

Plan A would mean certain death for all aboard, and the masks would be useless in that scenario. The women were prepared for that, if necessary. The KGB had taught them to follow instructions regardless of the consequences, and Bratva insisted on it. They weren't suicide bomber types, but without a cogent threat to force immediate and unequivocal compliance, the ploy would fall short of its intended objectives. The women were warriors and were prepared to fall on their swords if need be, but they were confident it wouldn't come to that.

"We will control the head of the giant and not worry about the body. With everyone sleeping, we need only to control the pilots' chamber,"

Tatiana told Gamera. Their cabin was less than fifteen paces from the cockpit door. The task, while daunting, was doable, and Belov felt confident the women would pull it off. In fact, he felt so confident he began to initiate the rest of his plan to receive the hijacked aircraft.

"Belov, we know the plane's layout well, having worked at the Ramstein Air Base the last two decades. Both of us have been aboard them frequently," she assured the mob boss. "We are as familiar with the plane's layout as its loadmaster is."

Cavis snored lightly. Strain inserted earplugs before falling off to sleep, her left arm dangled limply from her side. Confident both agents were in a sound sleep, they furtively moved from their bunks toward the cabin door. First, their attention focused on the agents' personal travel bags containing their duty weapons. The woman didn't need the agents' weapons; they each had their own. They just wanted to ensure the agents would not have access. They grabbed the bags and exited. Strain and Cavis did not stir. The bags were hidden in a closet before the women arrived at their destination, the cabin.

The women had each strapped a small-framed Glock, Model 27, on the inside of their respective left thighs prior to arriving at the airport. If they were made to go through the metal detectors it would have been dangerous for all. They took the chance.

The pistols contained nine, .40 caliber rounds in the magazine, and with an additional round chambered, gave the weapon a total of ten lethal bullets. Their guns were ready to fire double action, single action if the hammer was pulled back first. The women knew how to use them. A guarantee in the event the crew didn't believe the petard's potency.

Colonel Daniel Riggs had graduated from the Air Force Academy in Colorado Springs, Colorado, in 1996. Riggs loved every minute of the academy and became enamored with Colorado from day one. His graduating class was honored by the presence of his commander-in-chief, President Bill Clinton, who shook hands with the graduates as they were commissioned second lieutenants.

Within thirty days of graduation, Riggs arrived at flight school, where he first met a young Captain Jack Tuttle. Tuttle, himself a pilot, had recently returned from a deployment to Ramstein, Germany. The two bonded quickly, and Riggs considered Tuttle his primary mentor.

It was Tuttle who orchestrated the "plum" assignment to fly the presidential vehicles to Kuwait City.

Colonel Riggs was awake, sitting on the right side of the cockpit. He was chatting casually with one of his co-pilots, as the engineer seemed to be engaged with calculations on a large yellow pad. They all looked up when the ladies entered and shared the same look of mild incredulity. The look on Tatiana's face signaled something was on her mind. The colonel spoke, "You two should be sleeping. What's going on?" Tatiana and Gamera entered the rear of the spacious cabin and shut the door behind them.

Tatiana held the petard in her left arm, snugged against her, just below her bosom. She raised her right hand and pointed her Glock at the colonel. He swallowed hard and stared. Gamera stood behind with her weapon pointed to the left of the cabin, covering the rest of the crew.

"Listen carefully, Colonel, and don't react foolishly to what you are about to hear," said Tatiana. "We are going to take custody of your plane at this very moment. As you can see, we are armed, but the device I am holding is even more deadly. It is a chemical device that will be activated if necessary. Let's hope it will not be." The crew members were fully alert and paid attention.

"Turn off the plane's transponder now. Any attempt to send out a distress signal will result in the termination of your crew and passengers." Tatiana was not in the mood to debate, her determined facial expression gave a clear "don't fuck with me." She had the crew's attention. "The transponder is off," said Riggs.

"No one will be harmed if you comply. Please know we are capable of the worst-case scenario should you elect to contact anyone from this time forward. The canister gets activated." Riggs, and his co-pilots, listened intently, but remained calm.

"The plane is on auto-pilot," Riggs said. "We will take no further action." The women were particularly alert for any attempts by the crew to send out distress signals.

"You will need to prepare to land this plane based on the coordinates we will give you. The airport is not listed on any reference you may have. So, don't argue," Tatiana said as Gamera handed a crew member a piece of paper.

"If you expect me to land this plane, I will need to ask you operational questions about where it is you intend to land this aircraft," said Riggs. He immediately recognized the threat to be real and did not want to dither around with "maydays." He surmised all souls on board would have a better chance to survive on terrain than in the air with two women who posed such a threat.

"We are over Saudi Arabia now. If we are to land here we will need information on the airports' runway, location, or its capabilities to handle our arrival," said Riggs. The colonel's facial appearance began to betray his composure, as beads of sweat aggregated on his forehead. To Tatiana it was a sign the colonel did not want to die.

"No worries," said Tatiana. She handed him a detailed description of the intended airport coordinates for its location and the landing direction and length of the runway.

"It's off. Now what?" Riggs asked.

"Just remain seated with your belts on, and please don't make any attempt to stop us. Cooperate and no one will get hurt. The supervisors from the Secret Service will be directed to convince their personnel on board not to do anything stupid. When we get on the ground all will be released. We only want the equipment." Tatiana knew this not to be true.

Colonel Riggs suspected this was not all about limousines and helicopters. He thought it had more to do with the president's visit to Kuwait, but was not sure what. He thought it best to focus on a safe landing until they were on the tarmac.

Tatiana withdrew a thumb drive from her shirt pocket, a Kingston DTVP/8GB, with plenty of space for its precious code. She moved between the pilots and inserted the simple bit packet into a port to introduce the new aircraft identification code. It consisted of standard language for the plane's Automatic Dependent Surveillance-Broadcast system, or ADS-B. The signal was global aviation's effort to automate the process by which aircraft transmits data to air traffic control systems as planes navigate airspace. The development of the ADS-B was supposed to eliminate human involvement and avoid screw-ups by air traffic controllers. All planes send out a specific code to inform air traffic controllers about a plane's position, direction or heading, and its velocity.

Belov made sure the Kingston thumb drive was discreetly delivered to Tatiana before the C5M departed from Ramstein, and more importantly, that she knew how to use it. It contained a simple code that once injected into the CPU of the plane's onboard computer would alter the C5M signals. Unfortunately for the ADS-B system, there was no encryption to overcome, and Belov and the Bratva were well aware of this. It would be an easy venture to dupe the air traffic controller with multiple messages, similar to a hacker's distributed denial of service attack on company systems. In this case, he hoped to confuse the controller and give the plane sufficient time to land without raising suspicion. The controller would be inundated with messaging and would not know who was sending what or whether a particular aircraft message was authentic, that is, whether the plane information was actually being sent from a specific plane the controller was tracking. The receiving controller would initially believe there were numerous aircraft in the air, based on the misleading code's work. Deciphering the codes and then eliminating what was real and what was "ghost" would consume the controller's immediate attention.

"This little device will allow us to mask the plane and get it to where we need it," Belov had told Tatiana. "If you accomplish this after convincing the pilot to acquiesce, then we will prevail."

The thumb drive did its job. This gave Belov's people additional time in which to take custody of the aircraft's cargo. The stowed personnel, now officially abducted, would not be aware of the situation until just prior to wheels down.

THIRTY NINE

"Can you tell me who the hell is taking us hostage?" asked an agitated Cavis. "That will be helpful when I explain the situation to my agents." He wanted to figure out who their new captors actually represented. Tatiana replied with a chilly stare.

While Gamera remained in the cockpit, Tatiana returned to the bunk area where she had left Strain and Cavis. With Glock in hand she gently nudged Strain first and allowed a few seconds for the barrel of the gun facing her to take effect. Strain nodded in compliance. Cavis turned in their direction, awakened by their whispers. Tatiana said, "Please listen and understand that you are in no danger as long as you both cooperate. The plane has been abducted and Colonel Riggs has been ordered to land. I need you to go to the plane's rear quarters and explain to all the personnel the rules of abduction and how they should conduct themselves in order to avoid a catastrophe. You will all learn more when the plane is on the ground."

Cavis looked about the cabin. "Your bags have been taken and placed elsewhere," said Tatiana. She read his body language and the worry it conveyed.

"My credentials are inside my bag. Will I have a chance to retrieve them? I am sure Agent Strain has a similar need."

"Yes, I will make sure you get them. I need you both now to make it clear that no one should attempt to stifle the altered flight plan. Once we are on the ground at the airfield, any attempt to resist will result in personal mayhem by an overwhelming force," said Tatiana.

"I will do my best to convince them," said a still stunned Agent Strain. She knew the only course of action was to remain in lockstep with the pilots, as the C5M remained their responsibility while in flight.

"I would like to speak with the colonel and get his direction," said Cavis. Tatiana responded. "I will take Agent Strain to talk with the pilot. You are to remain here until we get back." Strain gave him a stern look. He recognized the glance as a warning—this was not the time for resistance. She perceived the CAT team leader's testosterone levels to be in acceleration mode. She just wanted to keep everyone alive. "I will be right back," she said, as Tatiana led her to the cockpit.

About five minutes later, Strain returned to Cavis. "The colonel has surrendered his aircraft, and per his command, we are to follow the orders of the abductors. Let's get on the ground and once there we can consider our options. Lord knows we have the weapons to put up a good fight, but should we? No. You have to convince the CAT team, particularly your Frank Larkin, that this is not their fight. They are not protecting the president at this moment, and it's just the onboard equipment and us. We can get through this without a firefight. Tell Larkin we need to suck up our pride and go with the colonel's directive. We have to take these women at their word that no one will be harmed. This is not an 'Onion Field' situation." Strain referred to an infamous LAPD incident in which two detectives gave up their weapons in an effort to resolve a dangerous standoff, only to be taken hostage, brutally tortured, and ultimately murdered by their criminal abductors.

She was responsible for the safety of seventy Secret Service agents. Her husband would have counseled her to comply and come back to fight another day. She would appreciate him giving her that advice now. She missed him terribly. She needed him, but she knew what had to be done.

"Our people will pick up on this hijacking via their 'Sigint' (Signal Intelligence) and deploy Special Ops assets to support us," she said. She pondered the internecine consequences affecting the C5M passengers once they learned of the abduction and remained concerned, particularly in regard to the hard-charging Larkin and his team.

"Cavis, we need to first brief some of the senior agents as well as the HMX guys, so no one over-reacts. It needs to happen fast, as the plane will descend quickly and we can't let this get out of hand. If our senior guys can keep their people under control, it will go a long way toward getting us out of this scenario."

It was common for the HMX pilots to remain with their Marines up top rather than take up a cot behind the cabin in the front of the aircraft or remain in the belly. Strain and Cavis left the ladies and worked their way down the ladder from the front cabin through the fuselage to the agents and Marines.

"I'll brief the agents, Cavis. You let the Marine officers in on what's happening."

Cavis continued to make his way back from the supervisor's cabin to the aft of the C5M, all the while thinking aloud. "The unilateral takedown of a special agent mission. A fucking SAM flight for Christ's sake. This is surreal."

Halfway to the rear of the plane he encountered an energetic and highly agitated Frank Larkin, the proud, stubborn son of a New York City taxi driver. Cavis knew it was going to be a tough sell to get Larkin to agree to capitulate to some questionable authority. The idea of forsaking his teams' automatic weapons would be unthinkable to him.

Cavis made his way to the rear of the aircraft, where he grabbed the railings connected to the dull army-green ladder leading up to the seating compartment of the agents and Marines. He expected to find most of them sleeping, perhaps some reading a thriller, or find some awake playing cards on the top of an empty beer cooler. He wasn't disappointed.

Cavis had agreed with Strain that while he was explaining the hijacking to the agents and Marines, she would brief the Secret Service special officers manning the equipment in the belly of the aircraft.

Warwick and Larosa came around together from the side of the limo to encounter her. "Strain, are you looking for me? You should be sleeping."

"No. But I'm glad I've got you both together. I want you both to listen carefully. And Larosa? I speak for the colonel on this." Strain gave them a full brief on the plane's takeover. They accepted the information surprisingly well, embracing the seriousness of the threat, which allowed Strain to move up to the upper deck to support Cavis's agent brief.

Strain didn't want heroics on anyone's part that might provoke the women to detonate their doomsday bomb prematurely. She crafted her words carefully. She wanted to be clear and make certain everyone understood her orders, and those of the C5M pilot, were to be strictly adhered to. "It's his plane; he's in charge. We have a much better chance of survival on the ground than reacting while in flight," she told them.

"Do we know what the endgame is?" asked Warwick.

"No, we don't know the motive, but we are sure of their ability to execute their threat."

Strain felt confident Warwick and the loadmaster would do their part to rein in their charges as the situation unfolded in the next few minutes. She made her way up to the agents' cabin and observed Cavis and Larkin in a tense standoff.

"There's no fucking way we give up without a fight. We got the weapons!" Larkin hissed to Cavis, as several of his sleeping team members stirred in their seats, still oblivious to the takeover of the massive cargo plane.

"We've got no choice," Cavis replied calmly. His voice held no tone of exasperation, as he continued softly. He needed Larkin to cool down. "These bitches have us by the balls. If we take pre-emptive action now, we're dead men flying. It will surely prompt them to release the cyanide canister, and we all go down. We can't let that happen. Once we're on the ground, wherever the hell that might be, their directive is for all of us. The Secret Service agents, the Marines, and the Air Force personnel are all to disembark the plane without weapons, baggage, or any other equipment. I have no idea what this is all about, or how it even got to this point. But know this: we're still breathing."

Larkin, aghast, stared sternly at Cavis, unable to adequately gauge for the moment the formidable threat facing them. He seemed unable to digest the information he had just heard. Cavis's comment fueled his simmering anger.

"Who are these people exactly and how the fuck did they get on board this plane?"

Larkin had been around the Air Force long enough in his career to know there were times when a commanding officer would get what he wanted, even if that included adding cargo or even travelers, to a SAM without accountability. Larkin surmised that serving the personal interests of the local air base commander in this instance would soon come to haunt this base commander.

FORTY

"Sir, I have no confirmation, but I am picking up radio traffic that I think refers to the SAM143, and it is not good."

Will Strain's facial muscles didn't move. His arms and hands hung loose as he made his way to the operator. "What is it you think you have?"

After Belov's thumb drive disabled the C5M transponder, the Saudi air traffic controller didn't detect the loss of the transponder for almost ten minutes. Ten minutes lost to the intelligence agencies around the world that would have enabled them to put the pieces of the puzzle together and notify responsible parties that a hostile situation in the air had occurred.

The United States intelligence apparatus deployed in Kuwait City in support of the president's visit provided Will Strain, the Kuwait duty military attaché, with the real-time ability to monitor the hijacked flight's movement via the latest NSA generation software. While his staff was casually tracking the flight path of the aircraft that carried his precious cargo, they became aware of the plane's disappearance.

"The air traffic controllers are reporting the loss of the plane's transponder. Some sort of trash coding obfuscated the radar monitoring air traffic over Saudi Arabia. I am fairly sure they are referring to your wife's aircraft, Commander."

Will nodded to show his appreciation of the NSA operator's assessment. "Okay. Contact Air Ops at Kuwait International and see what they have. I'll contact Germany and see what their air traffic controllers have."

If the commander was worried he didn't convey it. He had nerves of steel, the calm of a monk, the intelligence of a prodigy, and the answers of a savant. He trained all his life to be cool under pressure and would not betray himself now. He would find the party responsible for abducting his wife and kill him on his terms.

Before his call went through to Germany, the NSA operator reported back to him.

"It's confirmed, sir. The C5 ain't squawking and hasn't for at least a half hour as far as I can deduce from the transmissions. It sounds like the GACA, the Saudi kingdom's General Authority of Civil Aviation, is just now beginning to mobilize."

The GACA, situated near the King Abdulla Airport at Jeddah, would activate aircraft resources to get airborne and begin wide-area grid searches. The Saudi response would be directed here should the situation escalate and a search and recovery effort ensue.

"Does it sound like they have a fix on an area for a search? It seems there has been a significant delay in recognizing the loss of their signal and that could increase a search field exponentially," Strain said, dissecting the situation with the precision of a surgeon.

Strain realized he no longer needed to travel to the air base. He would be best informed by remaining at the embassy's SCIF (Security Compartmentalized Intelligence Facility) where the intelligence gathering apparatus present at the embassy had been augmented in anticipation of the POTUS visit.

An unpleasant silence hung over the large scif, awaiting Strain's next move. He picked up the secure STE phone (Secure Telephone Equipment) to alert his headquarters, and he calmly explained to the duty officer the status of the C5M. There was no mention of his wife being on board. That wouldn't be professional or relevant. It was classic Will Strain.

"Please notify Assistant Commandant Keegan and advise him that he can contact me here directly via the Kuwait Embassy STE. Let the White House Situation Room know, too. I suspect this may be the first hint of a problem." Strain placed the phone back in the cradle and walked out of the room. He felt a tinge of emotion coming upon him and didn't want to share it.

FORTY ONE

The manpower room's dedicated White House telephone line, intentionally colored red for visual effect, hung prominently on the wall behind Tom Eddie. When it alerted, the room vibrated with a non-conventional ringtone to distinguish it from the other drop lines. In addition, a light-emitted diode, a red LED, illuminated brightly to ensure all personnel in the room was cognizant of who was calling.

"Can you imagine what it would be like if we actually had the technology the public thinks we have in here?" laughed Steve Armey. "It sure would make our lives easier to manage, having to handle so many personnel."

The LED was the only concession to technology that adorned the room, but when the electroluminescence activated, it got their attention. It was almost closing time, and Eddie thirsted for his first beer of the day. He elected to answer the alert phone.

"C2," said Eddie, giving the duty room's unofficial call sign for "command center."

What he heard next transformed his view of the windowless Operations Room into a narrow tunnel. His perception of the outside world was lost and his surroundings quickly closed in on him. Eddie stood up, capturing Armey's full attention.

Now on his feet, Eddie gasped, then took in a deep breath to regain his composure. He did not muster an answer quickly enough to satisfy the caller, who grew impatient, not knowing whether the agent on the other end of the line adequately appreciated the information just relayed.

"Agent Eddie, did you copy what I just said?" said Rick Caesar, the exasperated White House situation officer.

"Roger. I understand," said Eddie. He was barely able to give the acknowledgement. Armey continued to look in Eddie's direction, trying to figure out what news had just cold-cocked his boss.

Eddie took pen in hand and documented what he heard: "*Special Air Mission 143 reported missing over Saudi Arabia. Radio and transmitter lost. No further at this time.*"

"Caesar, I got it. But I have a couple of questions. What is the government's public response going to be? Do we need to keep this from families?" The answer to one would probably be the answer to both, he thought, but wanted to get the questions on the record. Eddie's mind raced, trying to think of any additional questions. He knew the worst would come when he had to formulate his own internal notifications. "This is going to be difficult," he thought.

"There is nothing more known at this time," said Caesar, his tone icy cold. "We are only now getting permission to enter Saudi air space to begin search and rescue operations. I will be here all night with this and keep you apprised. Until further notice, this is for your headquarters' ears only! Understood?"

Fast Eddie sat back down. He wished he had already been in the G-car en route to his first beer and this had never happened. He took a deep breath. He would be in the Operations Room for some time.

"Roger that. I will make all of our HQ notifications discreet," said Eddie. He hung up the secure phone. "Oh my God," he said softly. His mouth hung open.

Eddie sat in a catatonic-like state for what seemed like minutes, but was actually only seconds. Armey continued to study the concern on Eddie's face. He knew something serious had happened, but waited patiently for Eddie to compose himself.

"Is it POTUS?" said Armey, unable to contain himself any longer. "Has something happened to him?"

"No. It's the SAM. It's missing somewhere over Saudi Arabia," said Eddie, almost inaudibly.

"Fuck!"

Eddie, his thoughts skipping ahead, rehearsed the notification protocol in his mind as to who to contact first of the abduction.

"Armey," he said, "I have to formulate a message in the most succinct way possible and be able to tell some of these assistant directors that this is all we have, and no more. They are going to be our biggest problem."

"Just let the Intelligence Division handle that," said Armey. "You don't need to get involved with all of them."

There was a headquarters pecking order. The first call would always go to the Intelligence Division. Their duty desk was best equipped to circulate the message to all assistant directors and get the Secret Service's "8th Floor" Crisis Management Desk up and running. The director was top priority, and Eddie resolved to report the situation directly to him.

Fast Eddie took a deep, chest-expanding breath, then looked directly into his partner's eyes. "If this proves true and the C5M is lost, it will be the saddest moment in our Secret Service history, the most tragic event ever to affect us." He began to choke up, but caught himself and regained his composure. "Looks like we may be here overnight, so you ought to contact your bride and let her know you won't be home. But keep this information confidential, even from her."

Eddie's training kicked in, and he was able to rein in his thoughts. He distanced himself from the magnitude of the manpower loss, placing it in a mental silo, so he could become functional. He estimated there had to be at least another twenty-five to thirty Air Force and Marine personnel manifested on the ill-fated aircraft.

"Armey, this is a totally fucked-up situation. Not real," he blurted. "There have only been two or three of these fuckers that have crashed in the last forty-odd years, for Christ's sake. This can't be!"

He thought about Carly Strain and began to fear the worst. "Her husband may never see her again, and I sent her there."

The two men exchanged a meaningful glance and began to make the notifications.

FORTY TWO

Colonel Dan Riggs landed the C5M softly on a single runway at the unknown Saudi airbase. The passengers remained confined in the upper compartment as the massive cargo plane's twenty-eight wheels skidded on the tarmac. Though he had no choice but to take a steeper flight path to the airport with the coordinates given him by the women, he managed to finesse the landing and make it feel routine. Most on board may not have noticed.

The C5M's premature landing barely roused some of the passengers who had taken either a prescription sleeping pill or an over-the-counter melatonin, anticipating a longer flight duration. The doses and times at which they were taken were predicated on an arrival that was set for a few hours later, so it took precious minutes for the groggy effects of the sleep aids to wear off.

One by one the passengers awoke. Gerry Cavis, Frank Larkin, and some of the other agents who had been chosen to be "read in" to the imminent dilemma anticipated an angry chorus of questions erupting from the scores of type-A personalities on board. Cavis decided the best path forward was to be matter of fact. He reasoned they needed a few more minutes to become lucid. So he, Agent Larkin, and Major John Baer stood by momentarily in the front of the seating area before giving the passengers the news they had been abducted. Cavis didn't know Baer before the trip, but bonded with him immediately as the Marine officer digested the situation.

"Not much of an airport, boys," Riggs muttered.

"No sir. Looks like a long runway and large storage facility. Doesn't appear it expects a lot of passenger transitioning here."

"C5, move your aircraft to the north end of the field. You will see an Antonov 225 parked there. Assume a position perpendicular to its nose. Understood?"

"Understood!" Riggs assumed the voice was coming from the base operations.

"Colonel, look at the size of the 225. I have never seen one, but have read about them. It kind of makes us look puny, don't you think sir?" said Riggs's engineer.

"It's here for a reason. I suspect once we're all on the tarmac, we'll be heading to it, and then on to somewhere unknown."

As Riggs slowly taxied toward the location, the agents and Marines on board, most not yet aware of the circumstances, quietly quizzed each other for a possible explanation. They sensed something was amiss, based on the time of day.

"It's too early to have arrived in Kuwait City, so maybe we just hit a strong headwind and need gas," an agent speculated to the young Marine sitting next to him.

"Not a chance," the Marine responded. "We would have felt something like that. More likely, it's a mechanical issue. We'll find out soon enough. Hopefully, the loadmaster will let us disembark from this fortress and stretch our legs a bit."

Cavis walked up the ladder to the upper cabin and glanced about to assess the faces before him. He had quickly formulated the message he would give to convince the personnel to comply. It would be an incredibly difficult message for them to consume, understand, and agree to. He had asked Larkin earlier to begin waking them up and allow them some time to emerge from the fog of their sleep. "We've got most of them," he said to Larkin, "Let's do it." The noise from the aircraft's engines had abated, indicating to him he did not have much more time.

"I have something serious to say to you all, and I want your total attention," he said. "What I have to say may save our lives, so listen up."

"What a way to wake up," said one of the senior agents. Even the groggiest among them were alert to the jump team leader's presence and his grave countenance.

"In the last half hour, while most of you were asleep, the plane's captain received a compelling threat from persons on board," said Cavis. "Our plane is being hijacked; we are being abducted. It may seem inconceivable at first blush, given the weapons and ballistic capability we possess, but this is not a joke; it is deadly serious. We have been outflanked by two females up front who breached our manifest protocol at Ramstein to board the plane. They were not adequately screened and now possess what appears to be a potent chemical device, possibly a cyanide canister that is believed to be lethal to everyone on board. We are hostages without a shot fired."

Cavis wanted to give the group as much information as he could in the limited time they had before being called to the tarmac.

"What we know is the two females who presented the threat appear to be following a well-prepared script to get this plane down in an area of Saudi Arabia of their choosing. We can anticipate an armed force to be on the ground waiting for us to disembark. The colonel of this aircraft has ordered his passengers to disembark without any equipment. These women have assured us no one will be harmed or molested as long as there is no attempt to resist. We realize this is counterintuitive to everyone on board. We know we have weapons on this plane that could put up a difficult resistance to these people, and we know it is our instinct to fight. They, on the other hand, have the high ground. We are blinded as to what is exactly out there to fight, and that's a game changer. So, while we don't know what it is we will encounter outside the aircraft when we come to a stop on the tarmac, we do know it is in the best interests of all of us not to react in a way that will put us all in mortal danger. We don't know if this is a terrorist act. Somehow, someway, whoever they are, they have us by the balls and it ain't good. Since we are contained in this fucking tube they have a tremendous advantage. We don't have any answers right now; we have nothing more, unfortunately, than what we just shared. I suspect we will soon know the answers to our questions. We are directing you to remain calm. Do not go for the weapons on board in the secured lockers, and do your best to keep your wits and mentally record as much detail as you can for further use. If it comes down to it, we'll know when to take action." Cavis concluded when he noticed Carly Strain making her way up the upper cabin ladder.

The agents and Marines remained in a stunned silence. Some were standing; others were seated. Though their first thought was to grab their Sig Sauers, every one of them realized they were unlikely to survive an explosion inside the aircraft and preferred their chances on the ground. Disciplined and orderly, an unexpected collective calm permeated the group. Only minutes had transpired since Cavis conducted the brief, but that is all it took to get the group adjusted to the situational pivot. The silence broke when Strain emerged through the portal from the ladder below.

"Guys, you all know our mission has been compromised. The situation is bordering on the bizarre. Our C5M is now on an airstrip somewhere in Saudi Arabia. Cavis told you we are hostages, which I know seems inexcusably surreal, but that's the reality of the situation. They appear to be Russian but we don't yet know if they're criminals or terrorists. We will certainly learn more as we follow their instructions to deplane through the forward door, just to the rear of the pilots' location. This will mean walking the internal length of the aircraft. If you have any items that might be considered offensive to these people, this is the time to get rid of them while still on the plane. We have been told that once we are on the tarmac we will be given an explanation as to what is happening. Do not attempt to take any weapons or, in the absence of a direct physical threat against us, make any attempt to resist. This is a direct order from Colonel Riggs who is the de facto 'in charge' of us all."

Strain started to turn toward the ladder when one of the CAT members, Dan O'Riordan, spoke up. "Bullshit! We have our weapons, and we should use them!" he shouted.

Cavis glanced harshly in the direction of outspoken team member. "I will say this once. We understand your anxiety, your frustration, and your anger, and we appreciate your courage. Regardless, if the ladies were to detonate their cyanide device, we're all fucking dead. It won't do us any good if some of our guys decide to fight it out. Agent Strain is passing on Colonel Riggs's directive, and we will comply with it. He's in charge, and it is his command to surrender, not ours."

Strain looked Cavis in the eyes and whispered, "Thank you." She continued to provide the group with further instruction on how the captors wanted them to disembark.

"Once we exit, we have been told to aggregate on the tarmac in front of the C5's port side wing. Once we all get there, we will be informed as to what we can expect. Remember your training. Keep your dignity at all times."

Unease filled the air as they tried to come to terms with what they had heard and the unknown they were about to encounter. They began to move as directed, with Strain and Cavis in the lead. The group quietly made its way through the fuselage, passing the Marine HMX helicopters and the presidential limousines. The agents glanced at the footlockers positioned between the vehicles that housed their long weapons and side arms, feeling an emotional impotence.

Some of the agents viewed it as a death march. It was scary stuff, but Strain's encouragement in regard to maintaining their dignity meant something to each of them. Training for crisis situations had prepared them, and they maintained their composure. The military guys were similarly trained. So the group maintained a solemn composure as it moved to the hatch door, each climbing down five steps to the tarmac. Their first sensation was not the desert's afternoon heat, but rather the bright, unobstructed sunlight that temporarily blinded them.

One by one the unarmed passengers exited the hatch, carrying no personal items, no bags, no weapons. Colonel Riggs, Major Baer, and Cavis had been positioned at the foot of the ladder to provide subtle direction as to where they should move. The hostages were now aggregated on the side of the C5 just below the port wing. "Safety in numbers? Nope, not now," thought Cavis.

Belov's well-armed operatives were tactically deployed around the C5, approximately twenty-five feet from the hostages' position. Their weapons were at the ready, fingers off the triggers. Cavis believed their posture was either a sign of respect or just an understanding the hostages were not suicidal. Two ice coolers, filled with bottled water, sat on the tarmac immediately before the gathered group. The Bratva's mammoth Antonov, located adjacent to the C5, had a majestic quality, sitting silently with the Saudi desert as a backdrop.

"Looks like we may be going for another ride," Cavis whispered to Strain. She nodded affirmatively and continued to concentrate on the team that was disembarking the plane.

Tatiana and Gamera stood about twenty feet away, next to a large, burly man. As Strain glanced about she grew more than curious as to the man's identity. She knew instinctively he had to be an integral part of the new dynamic that had gotten them all here. Plus, he looked strangely familiar. She had seen him, or perhaps his photograph, before. "Perhaps very recently," she thought. She hoped the man would be the link to explain what was happening here in the God-awful desert heat. She turned to Cavis. "Gerry, I know that man with the women. He runs the Russian mob, the Bratva."

FORTY THREE

When Belov needed to change the dynamic and use the Antonov for something other than arms delivery, no one in the kingdom asked questions. The Antonov 225 was the world's heaviest fixed-wing aircraft; it made the C5M look diminutive by comparison. Operated by Antonov Airlines, a Ukrainian post-cold war carrier, the plane was marketed as a strategic airlift cargo aircraft. Its colloquial name was "Mriya," or "Dream" in English. The Ukrainians marketed the original Antonov as having a 290-foot wingspan, a 275-foot length, and a fifty-nine-foot height. But most importantly, it required an 11,000-foot landing strip. The plane was not designed for short-field operations and the Russian syndicate didn't intend to use it that way. They procured the plane for their own special mission. Now the Bratva had it lie in wait at the secret north Saudi Arabia airbase, which could handle the needed runway length. With more than eighty airports in the country, the Saudi kingdom offered a number of clandestine landing opportunities for sinister aviation, giving the Antonov ample opportunity for landing discreetly in parts of the kingdom in order to satisfy its sovereignty, their euphemism for arms trade.

For this mission, Belov had selected an airbase with a landing strip that could handle the long runway needs of his plane and the plane he intended to abduct. It was located up in the harsh, dry desert of the northwest region of the kingdom, just north of Ha'il. It was one of the most active airports in the region during the height of the second Iraqi war. Now, virtually uninhabited, the airstrip was too distant for meaningful use for trade or commerce, but was more than appropriate for a sinister rendezvous. While the runways were still functional, safety elements such as fire apparatus and control tower operations were almost absent. Even the region's naturally depleted water resources would not satisfy the basic fire suppression requirements for an active runway. The reserve water tanks were long gone. What remained was the ever-present threat of a ferocious sand or dust storm, but this was a perfect location for Bratva's abduction mission.

The airbase's existence during the previous Iraqi war was a closely held secret. It operated as a valuable transit location for the shipment of material and served as a staging area for most of the U.S. Special Operations groups. Few in the Saudi Ministry of Defense and Aviation Forces knew of its location or strategic use. Its perimeter was well defended by trusted elements of the Royal Saudi Air Force, the Al-Quwwat al-Jawwiya.

King Salaman bin Abdulaziz Al Saud, the reigning monarch, knew quite well the importance, albeit ephemeral, of keeping the airbase a secret, and the need for plausible deniability should its existence become known. The king could not risk alienating the Arab community in the region, particularly stirring up more hostility and paranoia with neighboring Iran. The region's stability was far too tenuous.

FORTY FOUR

"Where's Larkin?" Strain whispered to Cavis, subtly scanning her guys who were standing obediently on the tarmac with her. She felt beads of perspiration migrating down her forehead and into her eyes, stinging them. "This is not good," she thought. Strain wiped her brow and continued to account for her charges, always the shepherd tending to her flock.

"I don't see Larkin. He's not on the tarmac. He must still be on the plane. Shit. What is he up to?" Strain alerted to the leg emerging from the plane's hatch. She recognized the tip of an automatic weapon about knee level. She swirled her head to the pre-positioned snipers when she heard the unambiguous gunshot report. She and the other hostages instantly recognized the sharp sound. Their collective attention snapped sharply to the left, the focus of the origin of gunfire. The familiar sound, a single shot, had been heard thousands of times on the firing ranges at Secret Service training. It was a sound they would never forget.

Belov's sniper had positioned himself to observe the exiting agents and Marines and carefully monitor their movements as they deplaned, one by one. He first aimed his weapon's infrared laser at their chests, then moved it to their heads as they emerged. The gunman released his breath when he believed all of the manifested passengers were on the tarmac. He glanced over to Belov to get an indication he could stand down when he observed body movement coming from within the fuselage. He took a deep breath, released half his air, and engaged the target. Without command, the operative took aim with his Heckler & Koch 416 assault rifle. The Russian mob had adopted a weapon used by the Navy SEALS. The target wore a bulletproof vest, dark black BDUs, or battle dress uniform, and displayed what the sniper assessed in one-half second as a Heckler & Koch MP-5.

When Larkin lifted his weapon out of the C5's hatch door, the sniper reacted instantly, firing a single shot that struck Larkin squarely between the eyes. He fell instantly, his lifeless body draped over the hatch opening. His MP-5 clattered down the steps to the tarmac, while his right arm dangled over the short ladder extended from the plane's exit door, eerily twitching. Cavis's grip on Strain's right arm suppressed her desire to respond to the fallen agent. He could not permit her to be targeted by the sniper who had just tasted blood and would not hesitate to taste more.

No one moved. Everyone was aware of what had just transpired, but they were also aware of their own need to survive. They did not move to help their fallen comrade. Larkin had made a tragic mistake—a miscalculated, desperate move. The hostages were resigned, at least, for the short term, to accept their situation, knowing instinctively that the sniper's fellow operatives had spontaneously raised their weapons, fingers on their triggers, pointed directly at the group. No one moved.

Tatiana motioned for Strain to come to her. Strain looked over at Cavis, then toward Colonel Riggs and Major Baer. "I guess this is where we find out what the hell is going on," she said. She proceeded to walk in Tatiana's direction, aware that ninety agents, Marines, and Air Force personnel were focused on her body language. She had to appear confident and strong and use her body language to convey leadership.

"Don't show any nerves. Be strong," she told herself, her mind racing at full throttle as she attempted to figure things out. She hungered for an explanation. "It's just a fucking presidential support trip. Why do we have one of our CAT guys shot dead?" She turned to Cavis. "Have we just given terrorists the tools to harm the president in Kuwait?"

Cavis shrugged. "If we have, everyone in the group will be called upon to sacrifice their lives, if necessary, to defend the president."

Strain tried to keep her mental calm so she could work on the realities of the situation. "Who has the ability to plan an operation that can force a C5 down to a remote landing field? The enormity of what the two ladies have done here defies any rational explanation," she thought. She knew she was not exactly in a position to demand one.

"Agent Strain, my name is Arvydas Belov. I am sorry for the loss of your colleague. We did not want this to happen, nor did we expect your colleague to attempt to take the action that required us to neutralize him. It shouldn't have happened. I hope, dear God, it is not required again."

Strain held her composure, not wanting to show any emotion to the man, and directed her resolute stare at his eyes.

"Agent Strain, you and I have not met personally, but I am aware of your good work. I applaud you and your New York colleagues for your investigative achievements."

Strain didn't blink, but wondered if this was related to something she had, or had not, done. Then it struck her in the gut as she recognized Belov from Max's arraignment. Her thoughts raced to connect the events overwhelming her mind, as she tried to make sense of the scenario unfolding before her. She had to factor Belov into the event: an international gun runner, the use of the Saudi airfield, an Antonov 225 standing by at a Saudi secret airbase, the Bratva, the cyber ace Maksim Valdimirovich Dostoevsky, and now, herself, as one of Belov's hostages.

"Holy shit. This whole deal is to leverage Max's freedom," she thought. "How does anyone have the wherewithal to accomplish that in such a short period of time?"

Belov, encroaching on her personal zone, looked as though he read her thoughts. She speculated he realized she had just made sense of all the pieces. She did. Strain felt his close proximity uncomfortable. He extended his left arm over her right shoulder to gently nudge her in closer to him. "He's creepy," she thought, "his tobacco-laced breath is pungent and obnoxious." Belov's right hand casually brushed her ample bosom. Strain braced, but did not retreat. She stared directly into his eyes with a message, "Don't do that again."

"Agent Strain, let me explain quickly, as our time on the ground needs to be brief. It is vitally important, perhaps even a matter of life and death, to remove ourselves from this airport and get airborne. Once I have your people on board our aircraft I will be able to explain with more clarity why this is all happening to you and your colleagues."

Belov placed his right hand on her left shoulder to encourage her to move away from the group and toward the Antonov. "Your group will be secure and not harmed inside our plane while en route to the next destination," he explained. "My people will take selected equipment from the C5." Strain did not respond, but tacitly agreed.

"Once my crew has everything loaded, we will depart for a friendly country. Its identity is not important for you to know at this time. We intend to notify the U.S. government that we have you and your people, and some of your cargo and equipment are in our care. We will encourage your government to release one of our family in exchange for you all. I don't foresee this lasting more than a day, possibly two. It is, Agent Strain, that simple. Unfortunately, simple doesn't always guarantee that no one will be hurt. Your man did a foolish thing trying to repel us. It is my hope no one else will be hurt."

Strain did not want to leave Larkin's body behind.

"Mr. Belov, I want to take our agent home with us. May we have your permission to recover his body?" She had no idea how she maintained the composure to even ask the question, but she did, striking a sympathetic chord in the normally heartless Belov. He looked in her dark blue eyes and suddenly adopted a softer tone. "Yes. We will preserve his body for you."

Belov motioned for an aide to come to him. Strain heard him whisper to the aide in Russian. The aide sprinted away toward the Antonov and returned with a folded body bag. Belov understood her need, but not out of a sense of compassion; he wasn't known to be compassionate. For him, it was a pragmatic decision; he felt it would expedite the loading process.

Strain took the body bag and hustled over to Warwick. "I need you to retrieve Larkin's body. Can you take a few of your guys back to the C5 and place him in the bag? I have received permission for us to do so."

Sergeant Major Warwick looked about and saw the Bratva shooters in their same positions. "You think they'll withhold their fire long enough for me to zip him up? I like to think I can get home in one piece." Warwick had a Clint Eastwood presence—a dry confidence, not necessarily contagious, but comforting to those around him. It was rhetorical question. He nodded to Strain. "I'll get it done."

Strain returned to her group to ensure they complied with Belov's demands. The agents and Marines moved obediently in single file to the Bratva plane. Larosa's Air Force crew remained behind, tasked by Belov's men to remove the limos and the helos from the C5 and chain them down inside the Antonov. Larosa explained to Belov's thugs that the Air Force couldn't operate the limousines and needed one of Warwick's men to do it. The discussion became tense quickly as the men with machine guns directed them to move. Larosa held her ground and Belov's people grudgingly acquiesced.

"Fucking Americans. You are just being difficult. This is the kind of shit that can get you hurt."

Larosa responded quickly. "We are not trying to be difficult, but these vehicles are not normal cars. They are difficult to drive. The windows themselves take time for a new driver to adjust. The glass is several inches thick and distorts a new driver's vision. We only want to do the right thing."

"Okay. Get someone from the group to drive," said one of Belov's men.

After Warwick finished securing Larkin's body in the bag, Larosa's crew took it to the Antonov. Larosa then signaled to Warwick that she needed him. He had heard her conversation with the Bratva and was already heading that way. He positioned himself behind the wheel of a limousine. It was the same one in which he had been seduced. He worked with Larosa and her crew to slowly drive the vehicle off the C5's ramp. "Hey, I'm getting off twice in one day," he joked to Larosa as he eased the limo past her.

She didn't laugh but thought, "How could I have just made love with this guy? He has no sense of concern for what is happening. He's heartless."

FORTY FIVE

The Bratva members resided in much of what was the old Soviet Union and felt at home in the legacy satellite nations, especially Kazakhstan. So, when Belov's Antonov took off from the Saudi airport with its precious cargo, it vectored over Iranian airspace toward the comfort of Kazakhstan's coastal city, Aktau, located along the Caspian Sea.

The trip from the Saudi airport to Kazakhstan actually required the Antonov to fly over Iraq prior to reaching the northern tip of Iran before entering Kazakhstan's airspace and the Caspian Sea. Once there, the plane would land at its home airfield, located just south of the city of Aktau and north of Kazakskiy Bay along the Astrakhan-Atyrau-Aktau highway. Belov believed once the aircraft entered Saudi airspace and reached its cruising altitude, it would have a better than average chance of making it to its home airbase, where the mob, not the government, secured it. Once there, the former KGB operative's plan to exchange Max could unfold without jeopardy. Then, and only then, would he allow himself to take pride in his brilliant work.

"The Antonov will be in Iranian air space for an hour," his pilot advised him on the hot Saudi tarmac. "But we should move this operation a bit faster to ensure we get to the Caspian Sea as soon as we can. Then I will feel more comfortable."

"We will get it done. Just have your engines ready for a quick departure. I will make sure everything is buttoned down," Belov assured him.

Belov's avian workhorse enjoyed special status in the kingdom, where it was allowed to come and go over protected airspace with impunity. The Russian mob ensured the plane had unfettered access in order to satisfy the kingdom's insatiable appetite for illegal arms. With the Russian mob in the equation, certain nation states looked the other way. This plane flew unmolested.

Belov banked on the United States having no appetite for going public with the abduction news. The international ramifications attendant to a theft of such magnitude would be much too delicate for public consumption. The American public didn't need to know it had been had by a former KGB thug. Belov had the United States by the balls.

To the United States, Kazakhstan remained an unpredictable friend. While the country had tried to keep a lid on corruption and protect itself from an ever-increasing power grab by the Bratva, it had failed. The best it could do was to keep things stable. Ironically, the Bratva helped. The country enjoyed relatively low unemployment due to its extensive oil reserves, but it remained a popular locale for drug and weapons smuggling. Corruption in the ranks of the government was widespread and the mob owned large stakes in the nation's banks and police force.

"I will carry out my mission and there is nothing the government can do without suffering consequences," Belov told himself. Belov felt that he owned Aktau.

It took the Antonov six hours to make the trip. Its passengers were allowed to stretch, but that was it. "No bathroom breaks, no food, no drink. Just have them remain in place until we arrive," Belov had ordered his people to tell the hostages. "There will be time to take care of personal business when we arrive in Aktau."

Warwick's military experience had tempered him to where he could handle pretty much any situation. He had seen and done too much in his career to get riled. Once he got the limo into the Antonov, he moved in and around the fuselage, nonchalantly observing the number of hostage takers, their weapons, and how they positioned themselves within the plane. He convinced himself they were not intending to harm anyone else. He thought they seemed confident as they moved about their plane and inspected their captives, but Warwick didn't feel intimidated by them. He would abide by their admonition to stay put and wait until the plane landed before making a "head call." He saw they had a mission, and the hostages were a pawn to be traded, so he relaxed. When he saw Larosa settle into a webbed seat along the fuselage, he moved to sit next to her. "Hey there," he said, putting his hand on her knee to comfort her. "We'll be alright. With any luck the Special Ops guys will have us out of harm's way in less than a day."

The vehicles were secure, but not to the satisfaction of Larosa. She was concerned about the weight distribution during the entire trip and was relieved when the plane landed. "God knows where we are," she thought. She only knew it had taken six hours to get there.

"Why the fuck did they take the time to take us all? All the vehicles and the helos, all of us? This is fucking crazy," she said to Warwick.

"Not a clue. I'm just glad we're alive. Let's concentrate on keeping our wits," he said to her. "Let's see where this show goes. I don't know what the CAT guy was thinking, but it didn't turn out good for him. He shouldn't have tried to be Audie Murphy."

"I hope it doesn't come to that. I'm scared for us all," said Larosa. She began to sniffle. Warwick put his arm around her and pulled her in to his chest. The Bratva operatives looked at them but didn't react. Their guns were at rest. Most lit fresh cigarettes.

FORTY SIX

The U.S. Intelligence Directorates attempted to identify the actor who published the following threat against the United States of America:

"All souls on board the special air mission to Kuwait City in support of the President have been abducted and are being held at a secure location. We demand that Maksim Valdimirovich Dostoevsky be released from the Metropolitan Correctional Center within 24 hours, or else the hostages, starting with the Secret Service personnel, will be executed."

Rick Caesar looked quizzically at the screen. His right hand moved the computer's mouse, highlighting the script just below the threat quote.

"Who forwarded this?" he said to himself. "Did it come from the NSA?"

He saw the signoff as coming from a U.S. Coast Guard Intelligence analyst. "That's interesting," he whispered sarcastically. "They are sure getting more active with their intelligence alerts."

He continued reading the message, knowing he would have to synopsize the content for his boss, the DNI. The message indicated that a threat, populated anonymously over the FBI's Public Access Complaint website, had been received within the hour.

"What the fuck is a FBI Public Access Complaint site?"

He didn't immediately recognize the significance. The site operated as a completely anonymous and untraceable tip hotline for the Feds. The threat he read apparently couldn't be readily traced. The information had been transmitted over the Internet on a 4chan.org website, as an image-based bulletin board where anyone could post comments and share images. It was a simple, but brilliant means to route a message; users did not need to register a username. More importantly, the website's own analytics automatically recognized the stated threat and sent it to the intelligence community within minutes. An NSA analyst picked it up and treated it as an important tidbit of data to be passed on. A Coast Guard analyst working on the DC Joint Terrorism Task Force then spotted it and forwarded it on as urgent.

Back in the White House Situation Room, Caesar's desktop computer continued to alert. The latest read, "URGENT UPDATE ALERT."

This was one of a series of follow-up messages providing him background notes on the country where the Antonov was taking its hostages. It read: "The word 'Stan' means 'place of' (land of) in Persia." Five of the seven existing "Stans" were part of the former Soviet Union. Each one of them assumed nation-state status in the wake of the USSR's dissolution: Uzbekistan, Kyrgyzstan, Tajikistan, Turkmenistan, and Kazakhstan. There are more than one hundred ethnic groups in the seven Stans, if Pakistan and Afghanistan are included. Ethnic commonalities are dependent on the individual Stans' geographical proximity to Mother Russia. The closer the Stan was to the Russian border, the more Russian Orthodox; the closer to the south, the more Muslim.

Caesar knew he had less than a minute to get his intelligence report prepared and forwarded to the DNI. Anything more than a page pissed the boss off. He had to synopsize the threat. "I will need to hand carry this one," he thought. His heart grew heavy with the information.

FORTY SEVEN

"Peter Baubles, Director of National Intelligence" read the front page of the *New York Post*.

In this position, also known as the DNI, Baubles would report directly to the president of the United States. The DNI's primary duty was to manage the vast U.S. intelligence complex and make sense of all the signal and human intelligence gathering efforts among a quagmire of smart people often at odds with one another—an eclectic sixteen-member Intelligence Directorate.

His selection came in early 2015 following the disappointing tenure of the previous DNI, who had been blamed for a botched response to the Libyan scandal that was relentlessly investigated by an emboldened House Oversight Committee. The president had no choice but to pick someone more palatable to both sides of the political aisle. He needed some political space, as his second term never seemed to get any traction.

A former New York City police commissioner, who had little experience or training in military intelligence, now filled the job of DNI, typically held by an active duty commissioned officer from one of the branches of the armed forces. Nevertheless, the president, in his second term, wanted desperately to neutralize his critics, so he sought to alter the perception of the position.

To satisfy federal law, he filled the deputy DNI position with active four-star Navy Admiral Donny Merz. The president believed this would serve to blunt any criticism of his newly minted director lacking the acumen and experience to manage the mammoth intelligence enterprise.

"We will be working for a fucking police chief," Admiral Merz confided to his military aide. "I've worked in the intelligence field for over thirty years, and now I'll report to Barney Fife."

"Perhaps you need to talk to the president one on one before the confirmation proceeding begins and explain your concern," said the aide.

"You may be right. I think I will. At least then if Barney Fife fucks things up, I'm on the record as having voiced my concerns."

As he listened to the concern, Merz's aide worried the admiral might not be able to control his anger. "He didn't get to be a four-star by pissing people off," he reasoned. "It must gall him that he isn't in the West Wing with the DNI."

The admiral had little confidence in the former police commissioner's intelligence savvy, or lack thereof, but he wasn't politically suicidal. Sure, he knew the commissioner had what it took to keep crime down in a large city, but this was a big, ugly world with a lot more sinister actors lurking behind alabaster figurines trying to destroy the security fabric of the nation.

Merz carved out a few minutes on the president's Oval Office calendar the next morning. He had been in the office several times previous, but it remained an impressive, almost intimidating, setting. He entered through the door of the president's secretary.

"Admiral! Great to see you. Have a seat," the president said. "I'm glad you feel comfortable enough to come talk to me. What's on your mind?"

Merz took a moderate breath and then let it out. "Sir, it takes an investment in understanding geopolitical matters to know what to expect before shit happens. It takes an intelligence apparatus to predict the unforeseen. This guy you've chosen simply ain't got it."

The president looked him in the eye. "Take another deep breath, Admiral, and relax. You're on the team for a reason. You are my balance, and I will work with you to make sure this all works out. But I need your support."

"Baubles may be a big city personality, but that's it," Merz countered respectfully. "The world doesn't need a beat cop, it needs James Bond."

"Let me tell you something, Admiral. An old Army general, I think his name was Sam Wilson, said, 'Ninety percent of intelligence comes from open sources. The other ten percent, clandestine work, is just more dramatic. The real intelligence hero is Sherlock Holmes, not James Bond.' I'm going with Baubles."

"Well, at the end of the day, Mr. President, my loyalty is to you, and of course to the office of the DNI. It will be challenging to see how his level of global sophistication serves you and how capably he manages the intelligence issues that confront us. This guy, in my opinion, is not the person for the job, but I will live with it."

The president saw it differently. He viewed Baubles's resume as a testament to a commonsense view of the world's conflicts and relationships. The commissioner had been schooled in "estimative intelligence gathering."

During his initial interview with the president, Baubles explained his problem solving methodology.

"Mr. President, NYPD's success has been based on its ability to judge probable outcomes with basic, factual notions to gauge the current intelligence landscape—looking at what might be, or may happen; all based on computer models. This, along with making people accountable, is how we took crime down to record lows. I gave the precinct commanders the tools to do the job and then made them show results. Under my tenure, the Big Apple became an easy place to navigate safely. It is data, modeling, and executing, Mr. President."

"Peter, there is no question you have raised the bar, and that's why I want you here to do the same thing with our intelligence community. Make some of these ranking agencies more accountable. You're very intuitive. I want that here. I want you to manage the position and transfer your skill set to the larger global issues." He liked that Baubles was a superior strategic thinker, albeit on a local level.

After the Baubles's interview the president was sitting alone behind his mahogany desk when Jon Bramnick, his fifth White House chief of staff, walked into the Oval Office through the secretary's door. Few had access this way; certainly the Secret Service when needed, but most visitors had to be escorted through the main hall door. Bramnick was no visitor. He was the gatekeeper and sometimes the unwanted political conscious. He sensed the decision the president was about to make needed some context. "I am skeptical about appointing someone with little or no political savvy," Bramnick said in a controlled, yet oddly melodic tone.

The president finished initialing a directive before moving it to his out box. He looked up at Bramnick. "Yeah right, Jon. A city of nine million citizens and a police department considered the seventh largest standing army in the world, and who thinks this guy doesn't have the fucking credentials for this job?"

Bramnick nodded and looked down. "Okay. I know he's a savant when it comes to defending the city against criminals, but I think there will be some very interesting dynamics in play when this new sheriff comes to town."

FORTY EIGHT

"Typically, the DNI office is cloaked in secrecy. It's opaque to outside media search engines that attempt to explore its trending efforts. My man Baubles intends to bring down that obstructionist wall. He will encourage an extraverted website as a tool to manage the media's thirst for uncovering, and peering into, the deep vault that is filled with secrets from the government's perceived dark side. Getting them hooked is a more effective way to manipulate the media. Kindness first, gain trust, and then, when necessary, exploit the shit out of them," the president explained.

Baubles was no stranger to the bureaucratic tendency. He possessed an instinct for returning an agency to its common denominator. He accepted the position, pledging to the president he would make the office more accountable, he would extract top value from the intelligence community, and he would reduce the agency "fog." He relied on his experience and instincts as a former police commissioner to make each member of the department, throughout all the ranks, keenly accountable.

"It starts with the precinct captains," he told the president. "I will give them the tools to do the job. And I will let them know the job better get done or they can expect to be moved to a position more suited to their incompetence level, or even worse, be let go."

Baubles's ego needed no stroking. He was willing to relinquish command if it became clear to him and his boss that his methods were ineffective. The DNI's mission required the agency's "tentacles" be involved in every aspect of intelligence gathering. He had spent his days at the NYPD shaking things up. Creative in his process, one of his signature shakeups involved deploying his detectives around the globe to extend, enhance, and extract information with a greater data gathering capability, and thus, keep the city aware and safe. He liked the FBI but didn't have great confidence the NYPD was getting intelligence information in a timely, accurate manner. Without timely intelligence, he preached, decisions and actions of vital importance weighing upon the NYPD were in jeopardy of being greatly flawed. "A flawed decision can get people killed," he told his commanders.

The president said he wanted a DNI who could think outside of the box and trend the intelligence community toward a new way of looking at the geopolitical world. Trending, as in a sailor tacking his boat out of harm's way—moving it to a safe harbor during a storm but having it available to sail when the weather breaks. At least Admiral Merz appreciated the metaphor. Bad intelligence, like storms, makes for an uncomfortable sail.

"Admiral, one of your former colleagues, Bill Shedd, once said 'a ship is safe in the harbor; but that's not what ships are for,'" said Baubles

When made aware of Baubles's notion to provide the media with a government information website, Admiral Merz thought it dangerous. He said to Baubles. "The media should never be a part of the cloak and dagger world. I have to tell you honestly, I think this idea is naïve. You can't trust these people, and there's been a shift in the last decade. These guys are now sniffing around looking for the president's vulnerability in the wake of the NSA leaks. They'll build on that if they uncover too much more about our operations."

"I don't disagree," said Baubles. "But my style is to embrace, keep the adversary close, as they say. I want to shake things up with some of the intelligence directorates we manage. The big boys, like the CIA and the FBI, need a spanking. And I want to enhance, for example, the Coast Guard intelligence boys. They're a loyal and dependable bunch, and global. The president believes his intelligence community is academically corrupt, not in a fraudulent way, but an intellectual way. There's too much inter-agency rivalry and a lack of effective leadership. I'm here to change that."

FORTY NINE

The new DNI picked up his secure phone and placed a direct call to James F. Keegan, the young assistant commandant for Coast Guard Intelligence and Criminal Investigations.

The STE phone at Keegan's desk alerted and he answered, "Keegan." STE stood for Secure Telephone Equipment used to convey encrypted telephone conversations.

"Hello, Keegan. I guess we have a real cluster fuck on our hands."

"Looks like we have one dead Secret Service agent and about one hundred hostages, mostly Service. Also, looks like the Russian mob took the president's vehicles and helicopters. That must be this Belov guy's way of making some sort of statement. Probably something from his old KGB days, when they taught him to try and shove it up our asses."

Keegan was the type of intelligence leader Baubles felt he could count on to upset the existing applecart. Besides, it was Keegan's man in Kuwait, Commander Will Strain, who first alerted the government's intelligence community to what was known to be an active hostage taking of global significance, but was also a situation that had to be kept under wraps.

"Keegan, I need to see you to discuss a response to the C5M event. I want to explain to you how we need to handle the current incident."

Baubles suggested they meet for lunch at the White House where he could share his thoughts. Most who ate at the mess were mid-level staffers or their guests, but many considered it the place to be seen if you thought you were important. Though the DNI was a high-level official, he ate there because it was convenient; he could not care less about being seen. To him, it was just a good place to eat, run efficiently by the Navy. It was a stone's throw, or even less, from the famed White House Situation Room adjacent to his office. The Washington power elite, who almost never dined in the White House Mess, would be disappointed to find out it was not much bigger than a large living room. Many of the conversations that have taken place in the mess have been as cryptic as those in the Situation Room, worthy of a Vince Flynn novel.

"I can be there in twenty minutes, sir." Keegan was already out of his desk chair and putting one arm in his suit jacket. He had been a frequent visitor to the White House, and specifically the Situation Room, from his days in the Secret Service. When he became director of the anti-money laundering organization, FinCEN, he continued his visitation schedule to help develop a robust program to deter and punish money laundering.

"This is my first trip to the Situation Room under our new boss," he told his aide Garcia Santos as walked out of his office, still trying to place his other arm in the jacket's sleeve while making his way to the lockbox outside his office to retrieve his I-Phone. Phones of any type were prohibited inside the secure scif area (scif is short for secure compartmentalized intelligence facility).

"Hey, Santos, you think the new DNI will know how important I am?" Keegan said with a laugh.

"Yes sir, I think he will," said Santos. "If he doesn't know yet that you walk on water, I'm sure you'll tell him."

The non-commissioned status of Garcia Santos didn't deter him from returning the sarcasm. He and Keegan were joined at the hip. A bond had formed between them from the day they had first met a year earlier.

"Let's go," said Keegan. "We have to be there in twenty minutes." Santos led the way down to the garage and got into the G-car. He knew Keegan liked to sit up front and didn't like his door held open.

"Just concentrate on driving. I can handle the rest," said Keegan. He always said that when they got in the car. "I love this guy," Santos thought.

As the car departed, Keegan allowed himself a moment to recollect on past visits to the Situation Room, and he tried to remember what it looked like before its last renovation. The memories brought a smile to his face. He had provided the impetus that had led to the upgrade of the room, divesting the outdated, unreliable encrypted audio/visual equipment of the last century. Today, thanks to him, it was a more efficient 24/7 operation that used thirty operatives from the intelligence community, the Department of Homeland Security, and the various military branches. The Situation Room's communication capabilities had been greatly enhanced, moving the facility out of the twentieth-century IT architecture and into the twenty-first century.

"Not a single day I spent at the White House did I ever forget how much it meant to me as a citizen," Keegan remembered telling his younger brother, Bobby, who had never left their home state of New Jersey. "I believe working at the White House is an honor, and I owed it to my fellow citizens to do the best job I can for them while assigned there," said Keegan.

"Bravo," he thought to himself. Then his thoughts quickly returned to the current dilemma.

Santos approached Seventeenth Street from Constitution Avenue and turned right. Keegan looked up from his notepad and saw the South Lawn. His thoughts drifted back to the days when he guarded President Bush.

"Santos, you probably have heard me say this before, but the true significance of what Secret Service agents do is to ensure the continued preservation of that office, regardless of the person who holds it. Ensuring their safety and security is a means toward that end. It is this solemn responsibility few Americans will ever truly understand." Keegan believed this completely and would have given up his life to protect the office and serve his country.

"Yes, sir. I have heard you say it before. And just as eloquently. Do you think I need to hear it again, sir?"

"Oh, shut up, Private," said Keegan with a smile.

"Please, sir; this is the Coast Guard, not your beloved Army," said Santos. He made a right turn into the first of several vehicle interdiction points. Both of them now remained silent as a young female uniformed division officer approached the vehicle. She signaled to the booth to lower the delta barrier and waved the car through. The barrier was quickly raised, and Santos positioned the car inside what looked like a mantrap to be screened by the agency's K9 squad.

"Same procedure as when I was here," Keegan said. "Best trained dogs in the world for what they do."

The officer signaled the vehicle had been cleared, and she motioned Santos forward. Keegan saw Baubles standing between the Old Executive Office Building and the West Wing entrance. "There he is."

"Got 'em, Boss!" said Santos.

Baubles stood checking his secure iPhone in front of the West Wing's protective white canopy.

"Hey, Santos, you see that iron fence holding up that heavy canopy?"

"Yes, sir."

"That sturdy wrought iron fence is a remnant of a West Wing renovation long ago. It remains in place as an always-loyal Centurion, having no allegiance to politics, but remaining in place to defend its potentates silently and obediently. You should take a lesson."

Santos looked at his boss and raised his eyebrows dramatically. "Boss, what brand of Kool-Aid have you been drinking?"

Keegan winked and exited the car.

Baubles looked up from his iPhone and then broke away from the incessant stream of emails to greet Keegan. He put the iPhone in its belt case in a one-handed motion as he extended his right hand. "Hey there. Welcome back." He led Keegan through the West Wing entrance toward the White House Mess and quickly launched into discussion.

"It's no secret why I have asked you here. Of all my intelligence directorates, I find you the most credible."

Keegan thought perhaps Santos was right. "Maybe I really do walk on water," he laughed to himself. "I'll have to remember to tell Santos about this. "

"I truly look forward to developing you, and your directorate, as one of the more trusted partners within my office."

"Thank you, sir, and thank you for your confidence."

"I hope you're hungry. We can eat and talk and then head on to my office. The White House Mess menu today is especially generous."

"I am hungry, sir."

"Please call me Pete," Baubles said politely. He motioned for Keegan to follow him through the double doors past the Secret Service Uniformed Division officer manning the post, then suddenly among the neat cloth-draped tables of the White House Mess.

In a D.C. restaurant, heads would have turned upon their entrance, but in the West Wing, employees and their guests were given subtle encouragement to not give undue attention to other diners.

"This place could satisfy a reporter's lust for rumor and hearsay for a long time," said Baubles. "But we have no worries with this crowd today. But seriously, my beloved paper of record, the *New York Post*, could fill twenty of those 'Page Six' pages with one lunch visit here. Ha."

"Of course, sir; I mean Pete. But they'll not get it from me," Keegan said. He tried to stay in the middle of the road.

Keegan found the former police commissioner's demeanor refreshingly naïve in light of the normally stuffy White House social ambiance.

A White House steward promptly brought the menu and suggested the special of the day for their consideration. "Today, we have the chef's selection, which is a braised beef short rib with bordelaise mushroom sauce, spicy aji amarillo, mashed potatoes, fine green beans, baby carrots, and cherry tomatoes. Or . . ." Baubles raised his hand, stopping the steward in mid-speech. "That's enough. It's exactly what I will have today and with a glass of iced tea. How about you, Jim?"

Keegan, adjusted to the speed of the decision-making process, handed the menu back to the steward. "Just a Coke and a cheddar burger for me. Medium rare, please."

"I've learned about your efforts to streamline your directorate and have heard about your low-key management skills within the Coast Guard. I see you in me. You probably know I have been labeled as an outsider, a maverick, even by some across the street in the Old Executive Office Building. Well, it's true. And I hope to capitalize on it while serving as the DNI. I want you to understand who I am and how I plan to lead this intelligence community, and I believe you do understand intuitively. You will learn, and perhaps come to appreciate, how I operate. As you know, we have a situation now before us, the hostage-taking incident, which will be my first major test. The thing that has always kept me from getting myself in trouble, even though some think I shoot from the hip, is I always shoot straight. Jim, I want only solid warriors to build this new team, and I need you to sign on with me early. I hope you'll stay with me for the long haul, but more importantly, right now, I need your support for my decision to address this matter with a private sector solution. We can't allow the United States to be extorted by these mutts. But here comes our food, so let's talk more later. We'll discuss my strategy in my office."

The Navy steward promptly served the lunch and left them in relative privacy. The two men became aware of another trait they shared: both finished their meals way too quickly. "Must be a cop thing," Keegan thought to himself.

When they had finished eating, Baubles wiped his mouth with the pristine white cloth napkin emblazoned with the presidential seal. "Come with me. It's time to let you know why I've asked you here today."

Baubles had shifted quickly from his role as the gracious lunch companion and was now in full director of national intelligence mode. It was time to set in motion the signals that were to be sent to the Bratva, which would facilitate the return of the hostages without fanfare or unwanted publicity.

FIFTY

The two men walked in silence, covering a short distance from the mess down a hallway on the West Wing's ground floor to the Situation Room entrance. Once they entered, Baubles looked at Keegan, "Does all this look familiar?"

Keegan had been in the West Wing's Situation Room often enough to know how to get to the DNI's office, but he offered a polite response. "It does, but I never get tired of seeing it again."

"I just had my office renovated. What do you think?"

His office had that old familiar beige-textured look, Keegan thought to himself. Nothing too fancy, but comfortable. It was a quiet location where the DNI daily digested the complex intelligence briefs prepared for him. Hundreds of pages came across his desk daily. Unlike some government heads, he actually read them.

"It is a handsome office, sir."

"Well, that's quite the compliment. Better than calling it cute, I suppose. So, I guess you mean it has a masculine appeal? I like that."

Outside the office, activity was growing frenetic. The area was operating as a fusion center, as operatives massaged billions of bits of data and attempted to interpret and make connections with the material.

Baubles represented a new type of DNI, partly to counter the criticism of the last few years. Since the Snowden scandal, the White House had been forced to navigate toward a more acceptable process of data mining. The Rand Paul class action suit regarding the government's ability and authority to collect domestic phone data remained mired in the courts and continued to present a thorny issue. Baubles's job, as the president's chief of staff informed him, was to find a common ground that would allow the administration to regain some of its lost traction.

"Take a look around. As you know, this room never sleeps. Over there is my best analyst, Rick Caesar. I'm comforted when he's on duty. He has a very keen eye for what is important, and he produces the most sanguine updates. It was Caesar who notified the Secret Service that these thugs had kidnapped almost four score of their people."

Baubles offered Keegan a coffee before he hit the button on the side of his desk to "fog" the office windows. They sat in what was arguably the most secretive office in all of the government, but a degree of suspicion was ever present, and thus, the need to compartmentalize any discussion. Even the trusted Situation Room staff was excluded as a further precaution.

"We were both cops at one time, so I'm sure our concern for secrecy is born from our instincts to keep only those persons who need to know, in the know. When too many people know too much, it can compromise our ability to execute complex and dangerous missions with the element of surprise." Baubles had served during a time when he saw too many of his fellow officers injured or killed as a result of leaks to crime syndicates. He felt the situation was no different in the world of high-stakes drama and international intrigue. "The less some people know, the better."

"You won't get any argument from me."

"The U.S. government has a long-standing tradition not to negotiate with terrorists, criminals, or others in matters like this. The old saying is 'behavior rewarded is behavior repeated.' The bad guys, once they sense weakness, just keep coming back with renewed gusto. We can't get into that game. You and I didn't do it when we were cops, and we know better than to engage in that now. Since there's no way we're going to permit these Secret Service and military folks to remain as hostages, we have to figure out how to get them released without airing the perception that the United States caved in."

"Is there more to this than just the idea we don't negotiate with terrorists or criminals?" Keegan asked, thinking perhaps he was missing the point.

"The Russian mob is prevalent up and down the East Coast of the United States and in most of South America. They have their greedy tentacles well within the Russian, Israeli, and other former Soviet Union governments. They go about their business and rake in more money than most countries. They are deadly efficient, and as we have just learned, so well organized they can muster an abduction of one of our Air Force C5M aircraft on only a day's notice. The fucking United States military can't move that fast."

"I understand, but how will the United States manage to keep the lid on this information, particularly in light of the murder of one of the Secret Service team? I realize the media has been easier to manage these days, but that can change when it smells blood, particularly the FOX News Network."

"The president has decided we will release the hacker, Max, to the Bratva within the next forty-eight hours. We understand they used an Antonov 225 to ferry our people and equipment out and their plane has landed near Kazakhstan's west coast by Aktau, just off the Caspian Sea. The Kazakhstani government is handcuffed by the Russian mob, and though they have made international headway to distance themselves from Russia, the government of Kazakhstan will not intervene. They quite simply fear the Bratva more than they fear us. Luckily, they will give us the flexibility to operate there as well, in order to consummate. They just want the whole matter to go away. We will be given control of the Aktau airport, at least one side of it. The position of the U.S. government will be to disavow that a C5M is being held hostage. As far as anyone is concerned, it is merely a mechanical issue. I'm sure you remember from your SS days how often these planes break down. The rest of the cover story will suggest the Antonov 225 was brought in by our Ukrainian friends to help ferry the manpower and equipment to Kuwait. Once Bratva is assured that Max is on the ground at Aktau, the Antonov 225 will depart and deliver the personnel and equipment to Kuwait 'on our behalf,' as it were."

"I get it, sir. How do you see the private sector operating in this? Will our position be scripted for them?" Keegan thought the DNI had boiled this matter down to a chess game and was playing for a draw.

"I have already contacted someone I am sure you know and respect. Larry Cassell, the chief security officer for Data Now Corporation, has agreed to be our intermediary. He has only been partially briefed and is standing by to hear from you. In fact, he's expecting a call from you at the end of our meeting in order to discuss the logistics. You will give him additional detail on the players in this matter—basically, the background he'll need to bring it to a conclusion. After you've had an opportunity to review the information we have on Max, we'll get you out of here and up to the NYC area. Cassell is preparing to fly out tonight to meet with your military aide, Will Strain, in Aktau."

"I know it may appear to be an emotional conflict of interest, but Will Strain's wife is one of the jump team supervisors who has been taken hostage. Strange coincidence, but it is what it is."

"Yes. And you know what? It gets even more interesting. Agent Carly Strain is the Secret Service supervisor whose cyber squad arrested Max last week. I'm not sure Commander Strain is the right guy to assist Cassell in light of the emotional investment, but I will defer to your judgment."

"Commander Strain can handle his emotions. He is the one person who has a good sense as to what has happened. He first reported the missing C5M to the Situation Room."

"Okay. Let's get you going with the briefing material on Max and get you out of here and up to Cassell."

"Yes, sir. And thanks for the lunch. When this is all over, I'd like to reciprocate with lunch at Coast Guard HQ." Having the DNI to Coast Guard HQ would send a message to the intelligence community that the Coast Guard Directorate was an important cog in the DNI's wheel.

FIFTY ONE

Baubles had reviewed the Keegan file before he had summoned the assistant commandant to the White House. What he read had revealed Keegan to be more than a diamond in the rough. "This guy is the Hope Diamond," Baubles told Caesar after Keegan had left the Situation Room.

James F. Keegan's career spanned an incredible breadth of public service. As a nineteen-year-old college dropout, he was drafted into the U.S. Army. The Vietnam War was in full spin, so there was not a lot of opportunity for a boot camp novice. Early testing by the Army had tagged him as gifted, with an extremely high intelligence quotient. He was selected for Officer Candidate School (OCS), but that wasn't necessarily a good thing. Most of the OCS classes during this period were sent to Vietnam where they suffered high casualties. Keegan didn't factor that into his decision. He saw it as an opportunity to redeem himself from a poor college performance, so he jumped on it.

The youngest in his graduating class, Keegan was commissioned a second lieutenant just as he turned twenty. He didn't go to Vietnam; he received his orders for Germany—the luck of the Irish. He served a two-year hitch with the Army Signal Corps during the relative quiet of the Cold War. His primary concern was whether the then-Soviet Union would decide to flank the U.S. military in Europe with a lightning strike from the East while U.S. attention was focused on in Asia.

At age twenty-two, with his U.S. Army obligation completed, the lure of a promotion to captain didn't thrill him. Back home, the "bug" had bitten him. It was a family law enforcement tradition. Keegan hailed from a long line of law enforcement officers. After a brief stint as a "beat" cop, he was promoted to a county prosecutor's homicide investigator. By the age of thirty he knew there was a larger pond in which to swim. A mutual homicide investigation that involved a Secret Service counterfeit informant was where it started. The collegial association with local agents whetted his appetite for federal service and launched him into a career in which he reveled for twenty years. He began to make a big impression on higher ups. He became the Service's sole representative to the National Security Council's Counter-Terrorism Sub-Group. Here he met regularly in the White House Situation Room with top intelligence officials in the government and was privy to the compartmentalized intelligence not usually shared among law enforcement agencies. Keegan became recognized for his talents. He had an intuitive sense of what to do with the intelligence he had digested.

"You'd better bring your A-game when sitting at the roundtable with Keegan. He outsmarts most of the bureaucratic thinkers with whom he sits," said one of the Treasury attorneys. Keegan didn't attempt to intimidate, but he expected the same level of logic and homework from those he worked with as he expected from himself.

Keegan saw his opportunity to raise the Coast Guard's profile within the intelligence community. He was a smooth, non-threatening personality, so he was accepted quickly. He was determined to recruit the talent he needed from within the Coast Guard and personally worked to extract acceptable profiles from the Coast Guard Office of Personnel Management. If the Coast Guard Intelligence and Criminal Investigations Directorate were to accede to the next rung, he thought, it would only happen by infusing the directorate with smart, savvy people. Success for the up and coming group would come by selecting the right people and deploying them in strategically important embassies around the globe. The United States Embassy in Kuwait was one of his first to staff. From a mound of personnel files on his desk emerged the profile of Commander William Strain. Impressed, Keegan selected him for the assignment. Keegan noticed the commander was a newlywed and found himself wondering if the marriage would work.

"I see he's married to a Secret Service agent," he said to Santos. "This shouldn't be a hard sell; they're cut from the same cloth."

FIFTY TWO

"I perceive the Coast Guard as a giver, not a taker," Baubles told Keegan. "It exists to help its fellow citizens. You came on board with them right after Hurricane Katrina, and the way their helicopter crews conducted their rescue operations and established the agency's rescue prowess was singularly unprecedented in the homeland. I remember seeing the Coast Guard referred to as the 'New Orleans Saints' in a helicopter caricature that was going around."

"Thanks. It's why I love working here."

"What I really appreciated was the Coast Guard rescued more New Orleans rooftop victims than any other agency and did so without fanfare, without the bureaucratic bullshit red tape afflicting other government twits. Now you know why I want you guys in the mix to help solve this exchange."

"Thank you for the confidence."

As Keegan returned to his office, located on the west campus of St. Elizabeth's Hospital just off the Suitland Parkway, his mind began to race as he considered his marching orders from the DNI. Santos wasted no time exiting the southwest gate from the White House to get to Constitution Avenue. He knew all the shortcuts through District's maze of streets and had his boss back in less than fifteen minutes.

"Good job, Santos. I'll need you inside once you stow the car."

"Roger that, sir. I sense you've got a lot on your mind, and I'm sure it ain't that you had a bad meal." Santos took no offense when Keegan didn't acknowledge his attempt at humor. The boss was on a mission, and he was focused.

Keegan needed to make contact with Larry Cassell, chief security officer of Data Now Corporation, the world's largest third-party processor of credit card transactions and money transfers. Cassell was located in the heart of midtown Manhattan. While many corporations had gone to a VoIP (Voice over Internet Protocol) solution to protect their conversations Cassell was the only private sector CSO to have a coveted top-secret clearance and a secure, DHS-installed, STE telephone in his office.

"Santos, here's the telephone number. Please dial him now."

Keegan's trusted aide initiated the secure communication with Cassell. He dialed the dedicated number very deliberately and waited. Because he sensed the importance of the call, it seemed the few seconds that had passed since he dialed had taken much longer than that. When the telephone's bright red LED light indicated the STE had been answered, Santos spoke up.

"Sir, this is Tech Garcia Santos calling from U.S. Coast Guard Headquarters, Office of the Assistant Commandant for Intelligence. Are you able to stand by for Mr. Keegan?"

Cassell was well versed in the formality. "Yes, I am," he replied.

"Thank you, sir. Please insert your Crypto Ignition Key, press the secure button, and wait for the LED indicator to activate, which will indicate the connection has gone secure. Mr. Keegan will be on the line at that time. Have a good day, sir!" Tech Garcia then went "silent and deep," leaving the assistant commandant's office.

Cassell acted as instructed, inserting the key and pressing the secure button. He waited about two seconds to allow the call to go encrypted in order to prevent eavesdropping. He knew America's adversaries, not to mention the global hackers, would love to know how the technology worked, but the NSA encryption keys were held sacrosanct. The cryptographic algorithms remained a tightly held secret, unusual in an era of leaks and information sharing. The activated telephones were officially classified instruments of the intelligence community. Cassell understood it was a sign of respect that he had one.

"Keegan, how have you been?" Cassell quickly spouted, hoping to gain an additional second or two to consider what the call might entail.

"I'm doing well. Thank you. I wish this was a social call, but it's not. Let me get through the brief, then you can peel the onion back." Keegan wanted to set the tone of urgency quickly.

"Fair enough. Is anyone hurt?" Cassell couldn't hold his question in check.

"Yes, there is one fatality. But there are larger concerns." Keegan took a deep breath and proceeded with his methodical briefing. At the conclusion of his brief, he could sense Cassell's mental gears churning.

For the two old friends this was more than just an abduction—this was personal. Some of the "boys and girls" being held were the children of a previous generation of agents with whom they had worked during their tenure in the Secret Service.

"Cassell, I will follow up with you in an hour and give you the totality of the DNI's initiative. I will make arrangements to meet you face to face in Newark, New Jersey, with the classified concept of operation. Be well."

FIFTY THREE

Keegan called the DNI to update him. "Baubles, I will be meeting Cassell at the Newark Penn Station in New Jersey. It'll be convenient for him. It's only a twenty-minute train ride away from midtown and then onto Newark airport after our meeting. Also, it's really noisy venue." Keegan requested he be allowed to use his own techs from Coast Guard Headquarters. He knew his crew could protect information. He saw an opportunity to show what his guys could do.

"Keegan, you know I appreciate any effort to trim the sails of the other directorates. Go for it."

Keegan directed Santos to contact Cassell on the STE. "Cassell, I will be taking the Acela from Union Station and will arrive in Newark Penn Station in two hours. I have a 'package' for you. The meeting location is being made secure with our operatives now, and we will be able to speak confidentially."

"Not a problem, the sooner the better. I look forward to seeing you, my friend." Cassell's heartfelt tone conveyed a soothing, trusting quality. He had nothing but a brother's devotion for Keegan. "I will meet you in the train station's lobby."

Keegan's high-tech squads were capable of arriving anywhere in the United States in less than N + 6 hours, using the amount of time it took them to get to the airfield plus the time it took to get to anywhere in the United States. Upon arrival, the techs would promptly deploy their proprietary equipment to ensure against eavesdropping.

"Santos, tell me again what these guys will do. I just told the DNI we have the sophistication to do the job, but quite frankly, I'm not tech savvy like you, and there is no latitude for missteps here."

Santos chuckled. "They travel with state-of-the-art equipment that is easy to deploy and reliable. They'll use a spectrum analyzer, an AVCOM PSA-65A, to search the entire radio frequency spectrum for any listening devices. And, to assure a room's integrity, techs will then complement their search with an Electro Physics Electro viewer Model 7215 that detects use of any covert infrared or laser transmission devices. To detect thermal signatures of any hidden electronic devices they will employ the latest version of an EMX Thermal Imaging Camera. And, in a multi-tenanted environment they'll use their Kaiser SCD-5-Sub-Carrier Detector to detect carrier currents from devices left resident on power or telephone lines. The private guys don't usually get this sophisticated, but these days, with all the retired special operations techs out there who have been taught how to install this stuff covertly, nothing will be left for granted. How does that all sound, skipper?"

"Okay, professor. I got it. But wouldn't it be easier to just add a little buzz to the room to mask the conversations?"

"Sure. Isn't that what they did in the early part of the last century when you were a cop?"

Though smaller than the better-known New York Penn Station, the Great Hall at Newark is statelier in appearance. Its marble walls depict the evolution of the world's transportation metamorphous. Large alabaster engravings define the millennium's use of boats, ships, motor vehicles, and trains and highlight man's overarching travel as a game-changer in conquering the globe. The development of planes transformed that travel, bringing the globe's far corners within a day's reach.

The station, situated along the rehabilitated Passaic River, is a majestic representation of a once vibrant city. The Great Hall remains host to a confluence of visitors, commuters, and vendors who mingle daily in a choreographed social dance. The dance is a mosaic of the city's citizenry. The flow is sometimes disrupted by a vagrant population always ready to take advantage of the unwary traveler. The station's transit cops nudge the homeless to keep them moving and direct them from the hall to the outside courtyard. They know not to return until the unwanted attention of the officers has abated, allowing them to return for a bit of warmth in the February winter.

That afternoon, the long-timbered benches were clear, void of the disheveled, hooded-shirted vagabonds, as the techs entered. The transit cops had received a directive to rouse them from their daily afternoon siestas sooner than was normal. Privately disdainful toward the cops, the vagrants reluctantly began their migration to the outside venue. They knew better than to return until the cops grew more hospitable.

Keegan arrived in Newark and proceeded with haste to the wooden bench attached to the vacated transit police observation desk across from the Dunkin Donut kiosk. Coast Guard operatives sat on contiguous benches, dressed in various rumpled facsimiles of the displaced homeless residents who were normally there, but lacking their special odor. The transit cops deployed elsewhere. They didn't balk at an order received from their command, thinking it might pertain to a visiting dignitary with his or her own security personnel.

Passengers strolled through the station, oblivious to the tete-a-tete about to occur inside the station. The setting, artificially created to provide the DNI with a degree of comfort, provided an opportunity for his designee, Keegan, to meet and greet his old friend and pass on the intelligence and marching orders in person.

Cassel scrambled out of his Columbus Circle office and made his way to a waiting taxi, arriving at the New York Penn Station in less than ten minutes. He raced down the Madison Square Garden escalator off Seventh Street to catch a 3:40 pm commuter to Newark. He timed it to arrive within minutes of the assistant commandant's Acela. Cassel moved briskly from track one, taking an escalator down past the station's vendors and into the Great Hall. He spotted his old friend and slowed his pace.

Keegan was sitting alone when Cassell enter the Hall. He didn't move, but waited for Cassell to come sit next to him. He thought his friend had the confident gait of a gentleman, "If someone were observing him for the first time, their impression would certainly be one of admiration. He is so well attired." A slight smile signaled the fondness he had for his good friend, but it soon gave way to the serious information with which Cassell would be entrusted to take with him to Aktau, Kazakhstan, in order to get their people back.

"It is good to see you. I am sorry it has to be under these circumstances. You and I used to talk about how vulnerable the Secret Service was on board a C5, and how one day the Service could suffer a large loss of life while traveling on one of those planes, but we never anticipated it would due to an abduction."

"This is bad, but I think we have the opportunity to assuage the damage." Keegan wanted to minimize the social conversation with his good buddy. It had to be business.

Cassell understood the urgency of the matter as he began to digest the proposed private sector solution, but he couldn't help taking a playful jab at Keegan. "Assuage? Really? You've been in D.C. way too long."

The meeting appeared to be between two ordinary gentlemen, perhaps even old friends, chatting and nothing more. But a forgotten memory emerged as Keegan surveyed the hall. As a young homicide investigator he had worked just a stone's throw away from the train station. It would be highly unlikely for someone to happen by and recognize him, but it was still a possibility. But he was now sixty, an elder statesman in the intelligence community. It would take a very perceptive individual to recognize him now.

"The DNI is convinced a private sector solution to the abduction is the sensible way to proceed. He told me POTUS is on board with it, and we are good to go. They also know it is risky to deny it even happened, but the government has long taken the position that we don't negotiate with criminals or terrorists, so this situation could potentially drag on for a long time, with possible tragic consequences."

Keegan was not one to delegate a duty, but he sought to gracefully hand this over to the private sector, someone with whom he had an abundance of trust. For him, it was simply a case of an old friend enlisting a trusted intellectual equal in a global drama.

"My young Kuwaiti attaché is on stand-by to update you with the intelligence you'll need to negotiate the exchange. His name is Will Strain. He will meet you upon your arrival in Aktau, Kazakhstan. And Cassell, the government will abide by whatever agreement you reach with the Bratva."

Cassell's thoughts kept him silent. He knew Keegan had something more to say.

"One more thing," said Keegan, his voice now betraying his confident management style. "Commander Strain's wife is the jump team leader on board the C5M."

"I understand. I look forward to meeting the commander, and I understand how difficult it must be for him, knowing his wife is in the middle of it all. I'll depart tonight for Aktau and meet him in the airport lounge in the morning. Is that doable?" Cassell knew the VIP lounge at the Aktau airport very well, having traveled often to the former Soviet satellite country on company business. He was comfortable with the location and felt it would offer as neutral an operational platform from which to connect with the Bratva as could be had. Not quite U.S.-friendly turf, but immensely friendlier than some of the other "Stan" countries under continued Russian domination. Aktau, he reasoned, was as good as any place for the exchange to occur, and, if necessary, for U.S. Special Forces to respond from nearby locations.

"The Kazakhstan government, though uncomfortable with having to host this global problem, has no choice, but to allow our guys to enter their airspace and occupy the airport should the deal go sour."

"It better not come to that, but I'm glad to hear you have that contingency nonetheless," Cassell responded.

"I will have Will Strain there by 1030 hours in time for your arrival. He will remain in Aktau as your point of contact. We need to resolve this by tomorrow night and put 'the mop back in the bucket' or the private sector solution may be scrapped in favor of a military solution. With so many people involved it will be difficult to keep the lid on this."

"How is Baubles expecting to explain the American fatality?" said Cassell.

"His death will not be disclosed until an exchange is completed, and even then the story will be intentionally opaque. We can't afford for the exchange to become public knowledge. The Russian syndicate has us by the balls. They have executed flawlessly. They also have a cargo plane of their own, access to our C5M, use of a secret airfield in a distant Middle East country, a tactical deployment to gain custody of the service and military hostages, plus a means of escape from Saudi sovereignty. Well, now it's time for a reversal of fortune."

FIFTY FOUR

Prior to the attack on the Twin Towers in New York City in 2001, a chief security officer, or CSO, representing a large corporate institution was typically recruited from a major federal law enforcement agency or one of the larger police departments. It's true that all politics are local, but to be selected for a plum corporate job, the applicant must have demonstrated superior social skills and be acceptable to the corporate security community. He or she must be a "known commodity" to a city's public and private partners; otherwise, his or her ability to effectively perform would be limited.

Most company executives like to be pampered, and they rely on a well-connected CSO to get things done. The executives do not necessarily know the intricacies of personal security, but they do know about, and want, the perks that are enjoyed by someone as well heeled as Cassell. They want access to the silent skill set that can facilitate them and their families through customs, finesse them out of police scraps, or remedy motor vehicle issues. Executives are willing to pay large salaries for someone like this. A CSO's shelf life can be extended when the company provides him with a healthy budget, particularly one that allows him to take care of his police contacts, discreetly sponsoring social events, paying for dinner and drinks.

New York City has as robust a security job market as there is, and it plays host to all of the most powerful, well-endowed international companies. These security jobs are filled by an array of former NYPD, FBI, Secret Service, and DEA operatives. Their reputations speak for themselves, and they usually "play well" with each other. The positions favor those with strong investigative and managerial backgrounds or those with extensive physical and information security expertise. The "super" security positions go to the select few who demonstrate an ability to manage a wide range of safety and security issues. This pool of practitioners is small. Larry Cassell, the former Secret Service director, was part of this elite group.

Cassell's CEO once told a corporate audience, "When this company retained Larry, it got a Cadillac for the cost of a Chevrolet. Having him as our CSO is money in the bank for the company."

After serving as a Saint Louis, Missouri, detective, the desire to go to a federal assignment bit Cassell. He applied for the Secret Service and served with distinction: investigations, protection, and intelligence. A previous president had described Cassell as "the most adept agent on the personal protective detail."

Cassell became the first African American to assume the role of agent-in-charge of the coveted Presidential Protective Division (PPD). Once the talented Cassell met with opportunity, the rest was history. He became the first black director of the Secret Service. His appointment was based upon competence, not politics.

After he served with distinction for several years, word went out that Cassell was retiring. "It's time to make some money and get the kids through school," he said. When it became known Cassell would soon be available, the recruiters lined up. Cassell had just completed a distinguished career, and he didn't relish the idea of being a bodyguard. He found the right position, as chief security officer for a major global credit card processor and associated money transfer business. It was a perfect fit from day one. The salary and bonus offered were good enough to get his kids through an expensive Ivy League school and indulge his loyal bride. "Honey," Cassell said to his wife, "you've put up with me transferring from state to state for the last thirty years. It is now time, and my honor, to give something back to you." He handed her keys to a brand new Lexus 470.

"Is it gassed up?" she said with a grin, then threw her arms around him and hugged him tightly. "You didn't have to do that. I would have been happy with just a mink stole," she laughed.

Cassell, the strategic thinker, had trained his entire career to think in terms of prevention. "If we don't plan to render crisis management unnecessary, then we are not doing our job," he told his staff. It was not that he didn't believe crisis management was an important tool, he just believed spending the dollars up front on prevention was a more prudent and wise investment.

"This is different," he thought as he left Keegan. "I have to go into a crisis management mode to get these people back safely.

FIFTY FIVE

Cassell's flight was about a half hour from the Shevchenko-Central Airport. He looked out his airplane window and commenced to daydream. "I don't feel comfortable flying business class," he had once confided to his wife, Patricia. "I just feel like I'm not worthy, and I'm spending company money foolishly." He laughed softly to himself as he remembered her quick reprimand.

"Oh shush. You absolutely earned it," she admonished. "And when you take me on a business trip you better sure as hell take me business class or you're going to feel awfully silly sitting in coach while I'm in your business class seat."

The Lufthansa flight arrived in Aktau on time. After a brief delay going through immigration, Cassell headed for the international lounge. He was used to the occasional stares from the East Europeans. "They just have never seen such a handsome African American before," he mused to himself.

Flying business class gave Cassell an entrée to use most of the VIP lounges around the world's airports. He had used the Aktau airport lounge fairly recently, and though he was not impressed, he felt it would suffice for the current mission. Upon entering the lounge he presented his business class ticket to the receptionist. She nodded respectfully.

"Welcome to our world class executive lounge," she said to him in broken English. Exuding a genuine sense of pride, she smiled politely and waved him inside. He wondered if she had ever seen the inside of a

Western lounge. Probably not, he reasoned. "She is probably better off not knowing the difference."

On a previous trip to Aktau, Cassell had called home and told his wife the place "was not up to Western standards by any means." But compared to what existed elsewhere in some of the old Soviet Union countries, it was more than comfortable.

To the average Kazakhstani, the new airport, completed in 2009, was a showcase in modernity. The country's oil boom spawned many enhancements to its infrastructure. Aktau airport represented a crowning achievement to the government's desire to complement Kazakhstan's railway and seaport enhancements, showcasing a country on the way up.

Cassell looked around the lounge in search of a location that would give him and Strain an opportunity to meet and speak candidly without being overheard. He reflected on what he had heard about this American hero and looked forward to getting to know him. He furtively glanced about, taking stock of the lounge's appointments.

"So small. So unadorned. Pretty damn bland," he thought.

He relied on surveillance techniques he had adopted as a seasoned law enforcement veteran. To know one's territory, one always measured, especially when approaching the unknown, using situational awareness to one's advantage. As he slowly made his way toward the seating area, the lounge travelers stopped reading or talking to briefly stare at the latest arrival. He knew he was their momentary distraction. A tall handsome African American arriving in a country that had few people of color naturally prompted a few gazes to linger longer than perhaps they should. He smiled and chuckled to himself.

"My wife always knows I turn these moments into events that are singularly about me," he thought to himself, needing to share the humor of the moment with someone, but Strain had not yet arrived.

Having a sense of humor had to be some sort of survival technique, Cassell believed. From where it came he didn't know, but it helped him to cope in a tenses situations. There just might be some validity to that survival technique theory, he told himself, but mostly he enjoyed humor for what it was. He had an internal comic gift to relieve unwanted tension. He loved comedy and nurtured a view of the world through humor. He felt it kept him balanced in a world that often seemed to spiral out of control. The comic in him also had a pragmatic view that transcended color lines, and he liked that. It allowed him to know his white counterparts better, and for them to know him. It worked. His world of friends, black, white, and Hispanic, grew exponentially through his interpersonal colorblind prism.

The lounge's cleaning crew worked their way through the room, pushing their trash carts and trolling for discarded passenger refuse. Two young dark-haired Kazakh women worked meticulously to maintain fresh lounge tables. They never displayed a smile, just a stoic countenance. They were determined to keep the tables debris free. Both were dressed in knee-length grey outer garments, a matronly look, with button-down front collars bearing a red stripe, which gave the outfits an appearance reminiscent of an old Soviet Union order.

Seating inside the lounge loosened up as the receptionist called for the next Lufthansa flight. While half of the travelers gathered their belongings and headed for the gate, the other half shifted seats. Cassell grinned, an inconspicuous acknowledgement that the lounge had suddenly become a much more suitable place to meet the commander.

"Not much for the airline to brag about," he thought. "Very little to munch on. They seem to be big on coffee, juice, beer, wine, and spirits. All the major food groups for these European folks. Their standard fare, cheese and crackers, is tasty, but they're no match for the more sophisticated Virgin Airline lounges."

Cassell wasn't there to eat and drink. With time preciously low, he grew anxious to meet with Strain and receive an update on the latest information concerning the abduction. Only then would he prepare for the inevitable negotiations. He knew with clarity what he wanted, but needed to determine with greater specificity what the hostage takers wanted. He didn't know where the meeting would actually occur—on or off the airport property? In the lounge? Where? There were too many unknowns, he thought. The stage was set for the international drama to unfold. The remaining act would take place in the vicinity of the Aktau airport and would require a matter of hours, not days, before the final curtain, Cassell thought. Above all, he wanted to avoid further bloodshed.

"Additional deaths will only jeopardize the mission and escalate the event to a military resolution," Keegan had told him while at the Newark Train Station. "That scenario will prove exponentially difficult for the United States and Russia," he continued. "Our sources indicate the Russian government is studiously ignoring the situation. And in the aftermath of the 2014 Ukrainian crisis, we don't need to add any fuel to further disrupt our relationship." Cassell viewed the situation as a stark reminder of how international relationships could spiral out of control. "This must be neutralized in Aktau," he thought.

He realized only a few hours were available in which to make contact with the Bratva boss, Belov, and work out the complexities of the hostage-takers' demands. On the surface, it was a simple quid pro quo; gain the release of the hostages and give Max back to them. He knew Bratva to be a sophisticated syndicate, but he was not sure of its global potency. Commander Strain could provide this perspective.

Cassell took a seat in the rear of the lounge. Within minutes, he saw the commander enter. He had never met Strain, but when the handsome commander walked into the lounge, their eyes immediately engaged as he approached him. Strain was not a difficult persona to dissect. At six foot two, with short, cropped blond hair and blue eyes, he had a surety in his stride that evoked character, confidence, and integrity. "There's a lot of information in that walk," Cassell thought.

Not surprisingly, Commander Strain's whole life had been based on discipline. He was trained to move cautiously, and as he entered the lounge he scanned the small room until he locked eyes with the CSO and walked over to him.

Cassell had met his share of Navy SEALS during his career and had frequently worked with them on various international assignments. He liked them all. Back in the 1990s, he had accompanied then-National Security Director Anthony Lake to Burundi and Rwanda to broker a peace agreement between the Tutsis and Hutus in order to avoid a resurgent genocide. He felt great comfort in knowing at that very moment a small detachment of Navy SEALS was positioned nearby, ready to react should something go wrong. He had great respect for their skills, their devotion to duty, and their willingness to give up their lives for a greater good.

"Commander, it is an honor to finally meet you," said Cassell. "Please have a seat."

Commander Strain extended his hand and shook firmly. Cassell's grip did not disappoint Strain. He was aware of Cassell's storied Secret Service career. Strain's wife, Carly, would often quote Cassell's well-known, philosophical sentiments, which she had become fully aware of when he served as the keynote speaker to her Secret Service graduation class in 2004. He spoke of the strength that an agency like the Secret Service possessed, with its 150-year history. The agency, he said, ". . . had bones, and a resiliency to withstand a calamity such as an attempt on the president's life, and still survive as an agency. It's all about morphing into a strong corporate culture, and the Service is blessed to have that sinew, that strength."

"Mr. Cassell, I have heard nothing but accolades about you from my wife, Carly. She speaks about you with the reverence of a devoted daughter. I hope one day I can impress her as much as you do," he chuckled.

Cassell was well known for his mental discipline, which he had demonstrated many times under stressful conditions. The commander had learned from his wife of an incident involving Cassell's reaction to a health threat affecting the president. As legend had it, Cassell had witnessed a fall the president took while attending a local hotel function. The president struck his head on the floor before his detail could break the fall. It was a thud that everyone nearby could hear. Most cringed, expecting the worst. Shaking off the injury, the president told Cassell he wanted to go back to the White House. "No, sir," Cassell had said, "I want you to get examined, and I am going to insist on it."

To Cassell, the fall had the makings of a serious concussion or worse. Head injuries can take a path that leads to death in short order if not attended to right away. The public never heard about this decision to divert to the hospital, but it turned out to be a lifesaving decision. The spontaneous hospital visit validated the experienced agent's concern. The president had suffered a serious injury. The doctors told him that if had not been addressed in a timely manner, it clearly could have resulted in the president's demise.

Carly Strain had also told her husband a story about the president's visit to a political function at a local hotel during which the president had fallen gravely ill from food poisoning. The culprit was a bacteria-laden salmon plate. In hindsight, no one knew the degree to which the president had been affected, but it was an acute episode. The president had risen abruptly from his seat to make his way to the men's room, when he collapsed to the floor in front of a shocked ballroom audience. Cassell broke his fall and quickly discerned that the president was choking on his own vomit. He didn't panic. He calmly directed those around him, his Secret Service colleagues and the dedicated White House staff, to form a protective cocoon around the president as he lifted the president's head to clear his airway.

"Mr. Cassell," said Commander Strain, after repeating what he knew of the story. "Carly said if it had been anyone else, the president of the United States of America might have unceremoniously died by choking on his own vomit."

Cassell laughed off the praise. "Tell your wife it was all in a day's work. There's no way I'm going to go down in history as the agent who lost a president to a gargle of vomit," he joked. The banter had taken some of the anxiety out of the looming meeting with the Bratva.

Cassell was impressed with the commander's demeanor. "Commander, may I call you by your first name?"

"Sir, my best friends call me Will. It's what I am most comfortable with."

"Will, let's see what we can do to get you and your bride reunited. Before you update me with the latest intelligence, let me go with my understanding of the situation."

"Yes, sir."

After Cassell shared Keegan's insights with the commander, the two agreed a draw with Bratva was an acceptable outcome. Strain then wasted no time in bringing Cassell up to date on the intelligence collected while Cassell was in-flight. As military attaché, he was in position to receive all relevant intelligence gathered about the missing flight.

"I am comfortable with the private sector solution and support your strategy. While you were in flight en route Kazakhstan I received updated intelligence of the Antonov's location and the condition of the hostages. I can confirm the one fatality. We are not sure how it happened, but what we have put together from signal intelligence suggests one or more of the agents tried to defend the flight and were neutralized with sniper fire. We believe the body was taken when their plane departed Saudi Arabia and remains with the group. We know more about Bratva's motive for abducting our people and equipment, and it is consistent with the demand made via the FBI website. There has been virtually no indication the press or international news outlets are as yet aware of what has transpired. This seems to be more luck than deed in the wake of so many leaks with this administration. Our people have recently arrived at the abduction site in Saudi Arabia to conduct a forensic analysis. The C5 remains in its original location. The cyanide petard used as leverage to hijack the plane has been found in close proximity to the plane and disarmed. Belov and his operatives meant business. We think he left the petard behind on purpose to demonstrate he really did have the means to take the plane down, and the plane's commander had no choice but to comply. His operatives, two former East German KGB females, were ready to release the deadly ingredient had the plane's command or its passengers resisted. What I find incredible is the Bratva's collective balls. This man, Belov, had no fear his plane would be accosted or be forced down as it departed Saudi Arabia en route Kazakhstan. We had several assets discreetly tailing it and currently have a drone in the air monitoring the Antonov 225. The drone is giving us some pretty good live shots. The plane is sitting in a location not far from here and has been re-fueled. That's about it, sir."

"Tell me more about this guy, Belov. What do we know about his mental state and his desire to get this kid, Max, returned?"

"Sir, two things: Max has already been removed from the Metropolitan Correctional Center in lower Manhattan. DNI Baubles authorized a Coast Guard Gulfstream V to ferry him from Teterboro Airport in New Jersey to here in Aktau. He should arrive within the hour. There was a bit of a delay with the FBI back in New York. Apparently, one of the FBI's criminal squads had been monitoring Belov's email traffic on an unrelated investigation and started to put two and two together, getting wind of something going on. They inquired further with the Joint Terrorism Task Force, but were swiftly rebuffed once the DNI's office became aware of their interest. The FBI was reminded that their email snooping may be illegal in this case, and it would be prudent for them not to pursue the matter any further. The DNI's office doesn't believe the FBI put the totality of the puzzle together or else they probably would have gone to their media contacts and blown this mission up already. If necessary, the DNI will ask the attorney general to have the FBI stand down."

"You would think the FBI would have learned its lesson from that incident in 2012 involving the CIA director's extramarital affair. To look at the CIA director's personal emails without a warrant, or even a subpoena, and then claim it was conducted as a follow-up to protect him from some love triangle was perverse. To make matters worse, one of those 'anonymous' FBI insiders had some sort of relationship to a third-rate trash author who then conveniently leaked it all. Someone should have been held accountable for that."

Commander Strain didn't say a word and remained deferentially respectful to his new mentor.

"Sorry Will, you touched a nerve. It's amazing to me what they get away with, leaking sensitive information to their media buddies."

Strain's eyes never diverted from Cassell's face. He knew about the FBI's reputation in dealing with other law enforcement agencies and the inter-agency rivalries it engendered, but didn't realize it would irk Cassell to such a degree. He thought of the irony. The FBI's interest had piqued after they missed the meaning of the anonymous threat that was received by their own Public Access Complaint Unit. An alert National Counterterrorism Center (NCTC) intelligence analyst detailed to the FBI Joint Terrorism Task Force (JTTF) in Washington had grasped the significance of the message because of its reference to the Secret Service.

The analyst, Mary Samuelson, didn't think there was much to it at first. She thought perhaps it was some sort of West African phishing scam, but she knew better than to casually discard it. Samuelson was not aware other U.S. Intelligence agencies were trying to locate the abducted plane, but she had good instincts. She been an analyst with the JTTF for almost ten years and loved her job. She also had a direct line to the DNI analyst in the White House Situation Room.

"I don't know if this means anything, but you might want to pass it on to the Secret Service for further action," Samuelson had said. "It sounds like it's a West African scam," she had continued, not overly concerned.

The DNI's analyst received the morsel of information and immediately appreciated its significance. He hastily forwarded the threat message up the analytical chain in haste.

"Sir, we know Belov is a major player in international arms trafficking and is certainly well connected within the Kazakhstan government. He's turned many of the officials into millionaires and there is plenty of Bratva cash to take care of the low-level government folks, particularly here at the airport. The government won't be an impediment for either of us. They just want the whole matter to go away. Belov nurtured Bratva members who live here in Kazakhstan with mounds of cash over the years. They have been an effective intermediary for his international arms trading."

"Will, tell me more about his relationship with Max as you know it. Assistant Commandant Keegan told me before I departed the States that the relationship extends to Max's father, the former NHL hockey prodigy."

Strain sketched out Belov's colorful past as best he could in the short time available, but Cassell, knowing he would have to meet Belov very soon, hungered to know more. He wanted more clarity of perception, especially in regard to how Belov viewed the world and those around him. He had enough operational background to move forward with the transfer of Max in exchange for the hostages, but yearned for more knowledge of the differential associations that made Belov tick. The commander didn't fail the CSO. His brief on Belov, particularly his propensity for violence, was thorough.

Closing his eyes briefly, Cassell digested the background information, particularly the points regarding his personal psychology. Why would anyone seek to hold the United States hostage at such great peril? U.S. Intelligence analysts believed the short answer to be that it was done out of a sense of affection and some sort of longstanding sense of guilt. He was willing to risk a great deal of personal reputation and treasure to get Max back. This level of devotion, the psychologists believed, suggested Belov had a father-like affection for Max that had been nurtured over time and was, perhaps, rooted in heavy guilt resulting from Belov's direct order to kill Max's father and mother. Strain added that it was probably the only guilt Belov had ever felt.

"It appears, sir, that when the Service arrested Max for hacking, it was not aware of how important he was to the Bratva, and to Belov, personally. Nor did the Service, or the DEA, know how interested our own intelligence community was in recruiting Max. While law enforcement pursued him, Max had a collateral passion. He took down more Al Qaida websites than anyone else in the United States. The intelligence community believes he did it as a patriotic gesture. Sounds a bit schizophrenic, but his persona is complicated. Early on, we didn't know if Max knew the Bratva had killed his father and his mother, or if Belov ordered the grisly murders. The Bratva had no sense of humor when Max's dad rebuffed them. After murdering his parents, the Russian mob essentially adopted Max, taking over the paternalistic responsibility to raise a Bratva son. Belov knows why the mob did this. As crazy as it seems, we think Belov actually has a soft spot for the guy."

"You mean Belov set up this whole abduction in order to get a 'son' back?" Cassell asked incredulously.

"Yes, sir, that is our belief. But unfortunately for Max's dad, Belov didn't show him any similar family concern. Belov ordered his thug, Alexei, to shoot and kill Ivan Valdimirovich Dostoevsky. And to add insult to the death, Alexei personally gouged out the rose tattoo, a symbol of Bratva membership, which adorned Ivan's chest. As a further sign of disrespect, Alexei stood and urinated on the mutilated corpse. This was an ultimate act of scorn by the Bratva muscle man at Belov's direction. They made his mother's death look like a suicide."

"I suspect when Max learns of the truth he will be one pissed off ultimate fighter," said Cassell. "I discussed a preliminary negotiating plan with Assistant Commandant Keegan prior to my departure from the United States. Do you have an update from him on that?"

"Yes, sir. Pending your approval, the boss suggests we meet with Belov here at the airport to coordinate the exchange and the logistics for getting our assets back."

"Do we have direct contact with him?"

"Yes, sir. We made contact with him via cell phone. He knows you are here to coordinate the resolution on behalf of the U.S. government. He is awaiting your call. He only wanted to know if you were empowered to finalize an agreement that our government will abide by."

"Okay. I'll contact him and suggest he meet us here. The Gulfstream with Max aboard is due in less than an hour, right? So, we want to get this resolved quickly. Would you be okay with being manifested on their plane to accompany it to Kuwait City International Airport? I would like to suggest that to Belov. Also, I plan to promote the cover story that the U.S. plane had mechanical issues while in Saudi and the Antonov came to its aid. Further, that the United States accepted their gracious offer to deliver the equipment and manpower to the POTUS visit. The American media love that kind of storyline and won't be inclined to ask too many questions. Besides, the Bratva will not be inclined to deny it."

"Sir, how do you plan to explain the slain Secret Service agent?" Strain asked sympathetically, knowing Cassell viewed Larkin as one of his own.

"Agent Larkin suffered a fatal head wound as he was inspecting the Secret Service equipment. The plane encountered violent turbulence, and he was forcefully thrown about the fuselage, hitting his head on the metal floorboard. His fellow agents will remember him fondly, and his family will be well compensated. His wife won't have to worry about income. Their children will receive full college scholarships from the Marine Corps Federal Law Enforcement Foundation at a college of their choosing. And, if I do this right, Belov will pay for most of it."

"Understood, sir," said Strain. "This guy is smooth," he thought to himself.

Strain's cell phone rang.

"Commander Strain, this is Mr. Belov. I am sorry for initiating the call, but I am anxious for further discussion on our mutual concern."

"Mr. Belov, I am here with Mr. Larry Cassell from New York who is waiting to meet you. As I previously indicated, it is Mr. Cassell who is solely authorized to work with you to resolve the issue, and he looks forward to doing so as soon as you are available." Strain looked at Cassell to determine if he wanted the phone. When he got a thumbs up he took it to mean keep going.

"Commander Strain, thank you. I understand you and Mr. Cassell are presently in the airport's VIP lounge. I can be there in five minutes."

Strain kept the phone to his ear as he looked about the lounge area to try and identify any of Belov's operatives who might be in place, but he couldn't identify any.

"Mr. Belov, we are standing by to meet with you."

FIFTY SIX

Cassell sat in silence, anticipating any variables Belov might present that could skewer the deal. It was a simple matter of exchanging what each party possessed, he thought, unless Belov balked at the obligations the Bratva must agree to in order to support the cover story.

Commander Strain was the first to see him arrive. As Belov entered the lounge, Strain thought he appeared exactly as expected: a barrel-chested, well-dressed, confident man with a fearless countenance. Strain wondered how many people this fireplug had exterminated, how many had suffered, like Max's father, because this thug didn't like to be told "No." But this was different. It was a dangerous game to be fucking around with Uncle Sam's children. Strain looked over at Cassell, who nodded at him. This game was on.

Belov knew where to go. He walked directly to Cassell's table, as if he were greeting an old friend after a long absence. Cassell extended his hand, feeling hypocritical at expressing any appreciation for the meeting. Strain deferentially moved away and sidestepped closer to the lounge entrance, where he took a seat. Belov immediately lit a cigarette, careful to exhale his smoke away from Cassell.

"I am hopeful we can conclude our meeting on a happy note," Belov said, adopting a measured servile manner. "I am so thankful, Mr. Cassell, that we have been able to meet so promptly. I know it is a burden for you to have had to travel so far in such a short period of time. I am prepared to negotiate in good faith the release of your people and equipment. But before this happens, I must confirm when Max will arrive. Only then, sir, will I be able to repatriate your people. Did you know, Mr. Cassell, that you and I have actually met?"

"I am sorry to say I don't recall our having met, but I am sure it was under friendlier circumstances."

"Ah, Mr. Cassell, you are a gentleman. I am sorry you don't remember, but we met many years ago. In 1983 your former President Nixon visited Prague, Czechoslovakia, while it was still part of the Soviet Union. I was assigned as one of the local security agents to provide executive protection for Mr. Nixon. You accompanied him and were unfailingly professional. You didn't have much to say, and that was fortuitous for you, because I was there to recruit your people. To your agency's credit, no one cooperated. We tried to get some of you to the hotel's third floor to visit with our pretty female operatives, but sadly no one bit the hook. Our profession seemed so much simpler back then. It is my pleasure to meet you again."

Cassell was intrigued that fate had once again placed the two of them together in this time and place, but he was even more fascinated he had been on Belov's radar. He had been with former President Nixon on that trip, assigned temporarily to the small detail that protected him. It was not unusual for the Secret Service to augment the smaller details with field office personnel while overseas. During the Cold War it was not unusual to expect the Russians to try and probe detail personnel, but Cassell found it even more intriguing that Belov was now admitting it.

Cassell sought to regain his focus in order to complete the deal at hand, repatriate the hostages and equipment, and get them home safely. No time to reminisce. He redirected the discussion to the hostages.

"Mr. Belov, an aircraft with Max on board is less than an hour out. He will be secured upon arrival by our people and taken to a location suitable for an orderly exchange. I am not interested in deviating from this plan in any way that will give you pause and delay our respective goals. If I may, let's agree on a story that allows the parties to move forward."

Belov inhaled deeply from his cigarette, holding the smoke in for a few seconds before turning his head to the right to exhale. He began his reply before the finality of his last expiration. "I think I understand, and I suggest the following, Mr. Cassell. We offer to transport your people and equipment to Kuwait City. This will provide us with the account we need—a human nature angle. When your plane went down with mechanical problems our plane was in a position to help relocate its stranded cargo to Kuwait."

"Yes, we think alike. But how do you explain the death of the agent?" countered Cassell.

"A tragic fall while the plane was airborne. Apparently your agent had a stomach virus and became severely dehydrated, and when he got up to use the urinal he got caught up in the turbulence of the plane and lost his balance." Belov reached to touch Cassell's arm. "Your agent fell violently onto the hardened steel grating, the same grating that bore your limousines and helicopters. We let the world know we are sorry for your loss. That's when we offer our services to assist your people to go on to Kuwait. What do you think?"

Cassell was not concerned that Belov had a similar explanation prepared. One that was suggested to Strain only minutes prior, "Probably a listening device," he thought. "Or, perhaps, two experienced operators thinking alike."

Strain moved toward the two negotiators. He looked at Cassell, who gave him a nod to interject.

"Mr. Belov, we want to verify the remaining passengers are alive and well."

"Ah, Commander Strain, you are worried about your wife. She is, indeed, doing well. She handles herself professionally and probably saved more than one life by convincing her colleagues not to overreact. It would be my pleasure to reunite you with her."

Strain maintained his composure. He gave Belov no indication of emotion, although he privately thought, "I don't need you to do anything for me. I will secure my wife even if this doesn't work out. If I learn that you even touched her, you are a dead man."

Belov sensed he may have struck a chord with Strain, but he wasn't certain. "This Mr. Strain is a difficult read, difficult to assess," he thought.

"Okay," Cassell interjected quickly. "We can agree then to have your plane take our people and equipment on to Kuwait. Once we have confirmation the plane arrived at the Kuwait International Airport, Max will be released. I will remain here until to ensure it all happens."

"When do you expect Max to arrive in Aktau?" Belov asked. "I would like the opportunity to conduct a proof of life check."

"He is less than one hour out. We will keep him at a neutral location to ensure his availability to you at the appropriate time. You will be permitted to visit with him."

"Fine. I can agree with that and look forward to greeting him once he arrives. Further, I will need assurance that both Max and I can continue to transit to and from the United States without interference in the future."

"Mr. Belov, I have the authority to sanction all that you request. If you release our assets, you will not be molested should you decide to re-enter the United States. However, there are two more concessions we ask of you."

Belov began to pull a cigar from his inside left suit pocket, buying a few extra seconds to anticipate the additional request.

"Mr. Belov, we think reparations for the family of Mr. Larkin are appropriate. We also want to recover the remains of Agent Larkin and take him back to the United States with us once this exchange is complete."

Cassell anticipated Belov might balk at the suggestion of reparations. Belov had the United States by the balls and knew it, but Cassell pushed the envelope. He guessed Belov would place immense value on his unfettered ability to return to the Brighton Beach area. He surmised the granting of that freedom, coupled with the successful release of Max, might help Belov understand the need to make the Larkin family and the hostages whole.

"Reparations to the Larkin family will go a long way toward ensuring everyone's silence," said Cassell.

"Mr. Cassell, the discussion concerning reparations is quite a surprise and complicates this proposed exchange process. I have no problem releasing the agent's body. It seems to me, though, that you are in no position to ask for money. It is, indeed, unfortunate Agent Larkin had to die, but it was his own doing. True, the remaining passengers were taken against their will in order to facilitate that which we discuss now. So your request is one I may have requested as well. Regardless, I am inclined to agree to some level of payment, but only if those of us involved in this matter are granted full travel to and from the United States without harassment or threat of retaliation. If that can be accommodated, then I would be amenable. Perhaps one million dollars in reparation to the Larkin family as good faith." The advantage shifted to Cassell's position.

"Mr. Belov, with all due respect, the pain caused the Larkin family will be interminable. I suggest you agree to double the amount and let's work to conclude this matter. As I stated already, I speak for the U.S. government and I can assure you that you will have unfettered travel henceforth."

Belov was silent momentarily, but maintained his stare. Cassell wasn't going to waver. Strain observed the negotiations, but knew better than to interfere.

"I will agree to the terms, Mr. Cassell. Let us move forward and have the plan in place in time for the plane with Max to arrive. I will return to my group and await your notification."

Cassell nodded affirmatively but remained ill at ease.

FIFTY SEVEN

At three o'clock Eastern Standard Time, the United States Marshals Service departed the Metropolitan Corrections Center, lower Manhattan, and drove the young hacker to the Teterboro airport, located across the Hudson River in New Jersey.

The two-vehicle formation was standard. Both vehicles were black armored Chevrolet Suburbans. The second vehicle's windows were down. The deputy U.S. marshals inside their vehicle had their guns at the ready, prepared to repel any attempt to wrest Max from their grip. They had been briefed that the mission was high priority and classified and took their responsibility seriously. They may not have known why they were depositing the high-profile defendant at the airport, but they didn't ask questions. He was their charge until properly relieved by the Coast Guard Intelligence team awaiting them. They would get the job done efficiently and without a lot of fanfare.

Max did not yet appreciate what was happening and remained characteristically reticent during the escort process. Once he arrived at the airport his curiosity could not be contained. He just wasn't sure who to ask.

"Excuse me," he said to the person who appeared to be greeting the deputy United States marshal in charge of the detail transporting him upon their arrival. "Where am I going?"

The officer in charge, James P. Fitzpatrick, replied, "It will be explained to you once we get airborne. We will tell you what you need to know."

The escort role represented a first for the well-regarded agency. Asked to reorganize and expand its traditional duties and responsibilities during the previous decade, the Coast Guard had eagerly embraced the new mandate to broaden its scope. The broader mission was driven by the Department of Homeland Security as it sought to redefine its investigative and intelligence apparatus to compete with that of the Justice Department. The rules of the intelligence directorates were being re-written. Despite increasing suspicion by the CIA and the FBI, the new DNI relished the competition and urged the process forward.

DNI Baubles was a maverick who sought to shake things up. "Fuck'em," he once told Keegan. "Let the other agencies fret. Once they find out the Coast Guard is assuming a larger role, perhaps they'll get off their asses and figure out there's a new sheriff in town. Perhaps they can begin to make an effort to be more cooperative with the other directorates. I love the fact I have alternative assets. Thank you, Keegan."

"Let's go," Fitzpatrick told Max. "Once inside, things for you will change." Max followed without hesitation.

Fitzpatrick took Max onboard a Coast Guard Gulfstream V. It was one of several the Coast Guard maintained to support the DHS secretary but it had been tapped to take Max to Kazakhstan. It was a sign of the Coast Guard's growing influence with the director of national intelligence.

The plane's range was extraordinary, well over 10,000 miles, and more than enough to get the celebrated passenger to Aktau without re-fueling. The plane left the airport at 4 pm that afternoon. Its crew expected to arrive at Aktau the next day at approximately 2 pm, Kazakhstan time, a flight time of roughly ten hours.

"This should give Cassell and Strain enough time to work out the details of the transfer," Keegan advised Baubles. "The biggest sticking point in the whole abduction scenario is the death of the Secret Service agent. It will be interesting to learn how Cassell nurtures that aspect."

"Take his cuffs off," Fitzpatrick ordered. Max made no comment. He was the principal passenger, but accompanying him on board the spacious jet were six highly trained Coast Guard, SEAL-trained operatives specifically assigned by Assistant Commandant Keegan, who was highly confident in their abilities.

The Gulfstream V leveled out as it reached its cruising altitude of 39,000 feet. Max had never seen Maine from the air, and as the plane hugged the Atlantic coastline he marveled at its natural harbors. He imagined how fulfilling it might be to be a fisherman on these waters. He had grown up near the ocean off Brighton Beach where the waves during the winter could be treacherous, but this coastline appeared from the air to be even more daunting. He quietly promised himself that should he ever return he would commit to taking a road trip up to Maine and Canada. For now, that vision looked bleak. His thoughts turned to his father, who twenty-five years earlier had arrived in the United States to start his new life. "I want to come back to the country my father adopted," he thought. Tears began to form in Max's eyes. It was a strange feeling. He had never cried before.

Fitzpatrick noticed the poignant moment and thought to say something, but decided to keep his empathy in check. He had been instructed not to engage Max in conversation beyond a short briefing.

"Provide him only with the basics to assure him of his anticipated freedom," Keegan had advised. "This will alleviate any idea he may have to resist while in flight. Just keep it short and to the point. More information will be provided once he arrives in Aktau."

Fitzpatrick formulated a one-sentence statement as he leaned closer to his high-profile passenger. "Upon arrival in Kazakhstan you will be a completely free man and that's about all I can discuss with you at this time." Max offered no response.

The plane left U.S. airspace, passing over the state of Maine and crossing into Canada between northeastern New Brunswick and Nova Scotia. With his handcuffs removed, Max began to feel relieved and a new sense of freedom as the plane leveled out en route to its destination.

While Keegan couldn't share the government's objectives with Fitzpatrick, he did share them with Cassell. "We want to parcel out what we know about his history, giving him enough incentive to entice him to come back home, that is, repatriate him, to work with the United States. He has the potential to be a one-person cyber brigade that can effectively counter the Chinese and Russian cyber threats. Strain will begin the tease once Max arrives in Aktau. He'll offer a package he can't refuse."

Max sat pensively in his seat, grateful the handcuffs were off. The Coast Guard operatives were no longer a threat to him, nor was he to them, as the situational relationship had changed. The Coasties on board would shift from their earlier role in securing Max as a prisoner to establishing a secure perimeter around the Gulfstream V to protect him upon arrival. He was a valuable commodity, at least, until his exchange for the passengers was complete.

The Gulfstream was an hour away from the Aktau Airport. It was about to enter the airspace over the Caspian Sea, the pilots having been instructed to give Fitzpatrick a thirty minute heads-up before the intended arrival and to relay the same message to Strain. Max had fallen asleep and Fitzpatrick did not want to wake him. None of the Coast Guard operatives slept. The mission would be over soon enough, and they could sleep then.

FIFTY EIGHT

"Mr. Belov, as I said before, I speak for the U.S. government when I say I agree to the proposed plan. I will remain here to ensure our commitment. I am grateful you have agreed to the terms, and we can work out the details for the money transfer after the exchange is concluded."

"This is all good, my new friend. I thank you and your young commander for your patience and understanding."

Cassell maintained a verbal and facial discipline. He viewed Belov as an international thug and didn't want to reveal his true feelings. If justice prevailed, this guy should be killed. But, for the moment, he had to play a different role. He was confident Belov had no real affection for him either.

"Mr. Cassell, I have nothing but confidence in your word. I am relieved the United States has agreed to the prompt release of my Max. I am appreciative more bloodshed has been avoided, and again, offer my condolences for the unfortunate demise of the agent. I regret any disruption to the upcoming presidential visit in Kuwait that this matter has caused. I hope the storyline we discussed about using our Antonov to ferry your equipment and manpower on to Kuwait to remedy the mechanical problems will provide your government plausible deniability should the true events of what happened ever become known."

"Yes, Mr. Belov, the anniversary celebration should provide a welcomed diversion from the strife that has plagued the region. These are difficult times for all of us."

FIFTY NINE

Belov's thugs secured the outer perimeter, about twenty meters from the Fixed Based Operations (known as "FBO" and used primarily by private aircraft throughout the world) where the Coast Guard plane would taxi. If Cassell were inclined to leave the airport with Max on board the Gulfstream it would not end well. Cassel knew this, and he knew Belov knew this. He was not about to let Belov exact any vengeance, taking both him and Belov's Russian "son" out in a ball of fury. His job was only to win the successful release of the hostages with zero failure.

What Belov didn't know was shared with Cassell prior to Belov's arrival in the lounge. The intelligence community, aware of Max's cyber prowess and his patriotic leanings in regard to eradicating al Qaida websites, felt it was worth a gamble to repatriate him. There was jeopardy in this, certainly. They were not sure how Max would react once they told him how his parents were murdered and by whom. And telling him too soon could undermine the agreement with Belov.

"You will have to convince him it is true and that he must keep his cool at the same time," advised Cassell. "It will be a difficult sell and could put us all in danger, but the opportunity to do it is now."

Strain stood at attention in civilian garb, a pair of khaki pants and matching waist jacket over a long-sleeved white collared shirt, while he awaited the Gulfstream on the tarmac in front of the FBO. His stance revealed a military bearing, a warrior's posture. His blond hair had grown a half inch since his last haircut, and his six-foot-two-inch frame complemented a thirty-two inch waist framed by well-formed biceps and forearms that filled out the jacket. His imposing stature did not go unnoticed by Belov or any of his people within eyesight.

There were two FBOs at Aktau International Airport. One served the growing number of private passenger planes that transported a new generation of successful Russian executives who sought to develop business relationships with the West. It was the one the Gulfstream would use when it arrived. The Antonov remained positioned at the other FBO across the airport runway, about three quarters of a mile away. That FBO was dedicated to cargo deliveries to and from the former Soviet Union satellite countries. The intelligence community suspected it existed solely to handle the lucrative arms and drug trades in the region. It was where the Antonov remained idle with its valuable cargo. The aircraft had been in place for almost twenty-four hours, having flown in from Saudi Arabia the previous day. The Kazakhstan government ensured both FBOs were on "holiday" and would remain closed until this matter was resolved.

Strain could see the Antonov being serviced. He knew his wife and her colleagues were on board. He thought of the body of Agent Larkin and the heartache his colleagues surely felt with his remains on board. Although it was cold enough in Aktau to keep the body, which was stowed in the plane's cargo storage, from decomposing too rapidly and creating an unbearable stench, that would not be the case forever. "We need to get this plane moving sooner rather than later," he thought.

Strain allowed himself to feel his wife's presence next to him. She was so close; he imagined he could smell her perfume. The "hug" they called it. It meant so much to the both of them. He snapped back to the reality of the situation, resolving to remain focused. "How does he do it?" his colleagues often asked each other. They even teased him about his ability to rise above the physical and mental stresses associated with the job. "The truth," he replied, "is I train for it. Personal feelings have to be held in check." Commander Strain could never betray the calm cool demeanor that others described as superhuman. "Mission comes first, emotion comes second," he was told over and over during his SEAL training.

Commander Strain caught a first glimpse of the Coast Guard plane as it made its initial down flight pattern, vectoring to land. He made out the Gulfstream tail number, N143CS, and grinned. The number was pure fiction. Someone's idea of a subtle jab at the Bratva. The tail number was a combination of the C5 mission and Carly's initials. He wondered who had the temerity to pull that off. "Nicely done, guys," he chuckled to himself.

As N143CS slowed to a halt, the FBO crew placed rubber chocks behind each of the planes wheels. No baggage cart had been requested. No food or beverage service was forthcoming, but a gas truck arrived within minutes to refuel the plane. Commander Strain had issued instructions that the asset should be ready to depart on a moment's notice to take the entourage back to the United States or the nearest friendly country.

Strain's two-way encrypted radio crackled. "Commander Strain, I have the 'package' for you to receive when you are ready. Do you want it now, and do you want it secured?"

Cassell monitored the transmission with the radio Strain had given to him earlier in the day. He would not interject his thoughts. It was now a logistical issue and he would defer to Strain and let him handle it.

"Fitz, it's good to hear you," said Strain. "No, please do not cuff him. Just bring him to me." Strain wanted to raise Max's comfort level as high as possible before he talked with him.

"Roger that, sir," Fitzpatrick said. He retreated to the plane's cabin to retrieve him.

As soon as Max exited the plane, his deep blue eyes met their match. He focused directly upon Commander Strain, whose eyes were as blue and intense as those of the super hacker. Strain had no problem maintaining eye contact. They looked like one another—tall, blond, and muscular. In truth, they could have been brothers. One was an accomplished mixed martial arts fighter and a global superhacker, and the other was an American hero who was trained to save lives, and take lives, and to know the difference.

"Mr. Dostoevsky, my name is Will Strain, and I am with the United States Coast Guard. It is my duty to brief you as to what you can expect next. Do you need anything before we go to a private area to talk?"

"No, I don't need anything." Max wasn't nervous. He only hungered for information. The past week had been confusing. He thought the events swirling around him had little to do with him. He was now just a small cog in the wheel. If he had known how much effort Belov had put into the exchange, he might have had a different perspective.

Strain led the Coast Guard entourage to the FBO's safe room, not far from the lounge, where he intended to have his one-on-one talk with Max.

"I'm not sure how he'll take what I have to say, but I have to get to him," Strain thought. If the effort weighed heavily on him, it was not evident from his countenance. At the Coast Guard Academy his fellow midshipmen had called him "Mr. Steel." Keegan liked him precisely for that reason. He knew the commander would not waver and would remain a strategic, logical, thinker, even under tremendous pressure.

Getting his wife out of harm's way would be a consequence of his first priority: convincing the cyber prodigy to come back home. Safely inside the FBO, Fitzpatrick's men established their security perimeter. One of Fitzpatrick's security detail remained with the plane with a modified MP5 at the ready, contained in a "fag bag," a custom-made container designed to open as the weapon was drawn out to the "ready" position. Ironically, the bags had been designed years earlier to secrete the Secret Service's UZI sub-machine guns. The name for the bag, a generation after it had been coined, was now a political correctness issue. Coasties no longer used the term. In a world of civilian aversion to weapons, hiding their automatic guns in a bag was a smart move. Associating the bag with a derogatory term used in reference to a protected class of citizens was not smart.

Commander Strain arranged to have Max sit directly across from him at a grey metal card table imported from the lounge. A bottle of water and two glasses sat on the table in front of them. No ice. The uncanny resemblance they shared was not lost on either of the poker-faced men. Both were warriors. Though trained differently, they were equally deadly.

"I saw your championship fight on New Year's Eve. You were at the top of your game," said Commander Strain. Max was taken aback by the comment. His desire to remain stoic was stolen by the compliment. Strain had disarmed him immediately without as much as an arm bar and knew he made an immediate entrée toward establishing a rapport.

"Well, that is nice for you to say under our circumstance. I don't know much about what you do for a living, but I did overhear some of the guys on the plane talk about you. Sounds to me like you are a very gifted person and that you work for the United States. You have a reputation for defending our country, and, I think, as some sort of SEAL-trained person. I have no beef with you."

"Mr. Dostoevsky, we don't have a lot of time to talk, but let me share with you what I know, and I'll be as straightforward as I can. The United States had a real problem with you because of your attempts to defraud our banking systems. This, however, was tempered by our knowledge of you as an aggressive anti-terror activist, taking down Al-Qaeda websites at will and unilaterally. The United States recognizes you possess extraordinary computer skills. You may not find that compelling or take comfort in that belief, but frankly, the U.S. seeks your help. We are aware, obviously, of your connection with the Bratva, and specifically, of your relationship with Mr. Belov. The United States is willing to work with you to extract you from his talons, if you're interested." Max sat upright when he heard Strain's mention of Belov.

"Please call me by my first name, Max. I do love the United States; it saddens me I must leave the country in order to remain free. I don't know why your government would want me to assist them, but if that is something that would help me resolve the situation I am now in, I am willing to listen. I take down terrorist websites because they piss me off. I love my country. I am a fighter, and I train hard. They are cowards and hide behind skirts. They kill indiscriminately. Children are of no concern to them. They are not worthy opponents, so I have no sympathy for anything they do. As for helping the United States ward off those who seek to attack us via cyber warfare, that is something I find intriguing. However, I don't know why you would choose to ever trust me again."

"Max, you have an opportunity to be welcomed back as a full-fledged citizen, but only you can make that decision. I am obliged to give you one more detail the U.S. intelligence community knows about you and your relationship with Mr. Belov. But the information is toxic."

"I can handle whatever it is you have to say."

Strain wondered if that were true. The information he was about to share with Max had the potential to strike at his soul and rupture his human psyche.

"Max, Mr. Belov is known to operate the most dangerous criminal organization in the world. You have been part of it. You have known him all your life. He supported your grandparents as they raised you. You have worked for him and made money for his organization. In return, you have lived decently. Your grandparents, before they passed away, raised you comfortably, though they did not necessarily have the means. If your grandparents had known the truth, they most certainly would never have accepted assistance from the Bratva, or from Belov."

"It put bread and butter on our table, paid for our apartment. The Bratva has been good for me, I admit, but I have had in the recesses of my mind concerns about the Bratva, and Mr. Belov in particular. There is something that troubles me, but I am just not sure what it is," Max politely responded.

"Max, Mr. Belov had your parents murdered. This is indisputable. Your dad was an honorable man who refused to forsake the dream he had worked so hard to achieve. He would not compromise his integrity and throw NHL games to give the Bratva the opportunity to win large sums of money on wagers. He had too much love for the game and the team he worked hard to represent. He appreciated the opportunity he had to live in the U.S.A., and he was determined not to yield to Belov's overture and pervert the outcome of the games. For this, your dad paid with his life. He did not know your mom was threatened for simply being his wife. He would have protected her above all else, given the opportunity, but Belov did not give him that opportunity. You have an option to realign yourself with what is good in America and divorce your allegiance from the Bratva. It is up to you. I want to leave you with a way to get back if you desire to do so. Here's my cell number. If, and when, you are inclined, call me. We know you can restore your honor. I think you have it in you to become a silent warrior for our nation. Max, you are still an American."

Max's eyes never diverted from Strain's. "I have always been concerned Belov was something other than what he portended. I have held a deep internal unease throughout my life, beginning with his visits to my grandparents' home. He never touched me, but it was his stare that caught my attention. It triggered a grim emptiness in my soul. I have no love for him though he treated my grandparents and me quite well financially. He was a provider and never asked for anything in return. Apparently, my family had given more than I was aware. I will take your information to heart and begin to figure out my destiny. On a personal note, I wish good luck to you and your wife. Please tell her I appreciate her not hurting my dog, Torre, when she arrested me. I could tell she had an animal lover's concern for her when she and her fellow agents took me into custody. Your wife is a good person."

"How did you know my wife is on the plane," replied Commander Strain.

SIXTY

John Blake arrived twenty minutes early to Magistrate Moskowitz's third-floor courtroom in the U.S. Post Office, a short jaunt from his office in the adjacent federal building. The room had not been renovated in years. The regular visitors, young prosecutors and aging defense attorneys, did not seem to notice. The daily cycle in and out had become their norm.

Blake dutifully checked in with the court clerk, letting her know he was there, which helped to ignite the process of getting in and out quickly. Blake received word from the magistrate's office that Max's petition for a writ of habeas corpus, filed with the United States District Court in Brooklyn, had been reviewed favorably. It appeared Max was to be released from custody. Max's attorney wanted his client freed from the Metropolitan Correctional Center as soon as possible.

The motion challenged the original basis for issuing the search warrant: the data garnered from the use of the Secret Service thumb drive. Max's attorney, Sergey Arkhipova, sought to have the court throw out the information used to support the search warrant and have his client immediately released. He predicated his motion on the use of Agent Austin's thumb drive, which he argued had been used in previous investigations without ensuring its sterility before its use in the extant investigation. The use of a corrupted thumb drive that could have tainted the questioned hard drive could render the warrant defective.

"Your Honor, the original search warrant obtained by the government used a corrupted thumb drive. The Service used the same thumb drive in numerous other investigations without ensuring that information combined in it had been completely erased. Further, the application for the warrant did not particularly describe the specific hard drive the government wanted to search. There is no way to know to what degree they obtained cross-contaminated data from other investigations. This is tantamount to a hospital using contaminated syringes. Your Honor, I am compelled to move for an immediate release of my client."

"Mr. Blake, can you comment on this? If true, then Mr. Arkhipova's assertions are most troubling for the government," said Judge Moskowitz, displaying his patented deadpan stare.

"Your Honor, I would argue the agents didn't even need the warrant, as the cohabitating apartment resident voluntarily allowed the agents into her computer room," Blake responded, not sounding entirely confident.

"Stop right there, Mr. Blake," said Judge Moskowitz. "The computer hard drive is essentially a residence within a residence, and if the application for the warrant didn't specify, in particular terms, the defendant's computer, then the government has a big problem."

"Your Honor, as you are aware, the case agent, Carly Strain, remains out of the country. I submit her absence places an undue burden on the government to have to defend the warrant at this time. I respectfully request a continuance until her return."

"Mr. Blake, you are asking the court to keep a man incarcerated for another week, with the prospect that he remains jailed on flawed information used to support the application for the search warrant. This court is not going to be a party to that reasoning. Have a seat."

Blake sat down. The motion had come before the court unexpectedly, so Blake didn't have time to have the Service's cyber investigators present. Carly Strain's predicament was unknown to most of the courtroom actors. Judge Moskowitz perused the brief prepared by Max's attorney, the judge's eyeglasses perched on the end of his nose as he scanned the information intently. After a moment, he grasped the document in both hands. He slowly looked up, glaring at an empty space somewhere between the litigants and appearing to be in a considered state of mind. Then, Judge Moskowitz began to speak.

"The court rules that the information obtained by the government and used by the government to obtain search and arrest warrants for the residence and person of Maksim Valdimirovich Dostoevsky was poisoned. The fruits of the original warrant were used as the basis for the subsequent warrants, and therefore, render those warrants invalid in the eyes of this court. I am ordering the immediate release of Mr. Dostoevsky. Should the government desire to appeal this decision it may do so, but not while Mr. Dostoevsky remains in custody. Mr. Blake, does the government have anything further?"

"Your Honor, the government respectfully objects and will seek to appeal your ruling. Can the government ask the court to require the defendant to remain in the local area?"

"Mr. Dostoevsky will not have any travel restrictions placed on him," the judge advised.

"Mr. Arkhipova, this court will direct the U.S. Marshals Service to process your client for release today."

"Thank you, your Honor. My client will be pleased with the court's ruling, and I am grateful for your consideration."

"Mr. Blake, I would like to confer with you in my chambers for a few minutes." Judge Moskowitz nodded to both attorneys, stood up, and walked briskly out of the courtroom.

Blake reached for Arkhipova's arm. "Congratulations," he said softly. "Wish me luck explaining this to the Secret Service." He walked toward the judge's chambers. Max's attorney stood alone and answered his cell phone.

"Ah, Mr. Belov. It is fortunate for you to call. I have some interesting news for you."

Arkhipova did not know Max had already been removed from the correctional center by the Marshals Service and taken to Teterboro airport, nor did Belov share with him any information on the ongoing Kazakhstan matter. He knew the government's charade, the illusion of release. His conversation with Arkhipova served to confirm for him that the government was making good on its word to release the Brighton Beach hacker.

Judge Moskowitz took off his robe as Blake walked in. He kept his office dark, giving it a slightly somber, almost brooding appearance. Behind the judge was a replica of a thirty-nine-foot 2006 Yorktown Yacht. The actual boat had a twelve-foot beam and a six-foot draft. It signified Moskowitz's escape from the daily courtroom drama. Blake wondered how a U.S. magistrate could afford such a boat, which surely cost more than $60,000. He thought the judge probably wished he were on it.

"Have a seat, John. I want to thank you for your contribution this afternoon. The record will demonstrate your earnest objection, but we will not see this kid back in this court. It is rare for the executive branch to supersede the judicial branch, but in this case I can understand why the intelligence community needed the assistance. It seems to me a small price to pay to exchange the young man for the agents. It will never be part of the court record. I only hope our Agent Strain and her colleagues make it through the ordeal without further complications."

"Yes, your Honor. Let's hope for the best."

SIXTY ONE

After Belov departed the VIP lounge, Cassell sat pensively for a few seconds before looking over at the commander. "Okay, Strain, looks like you will be taken to the Antonov by the FBO van and allowed to board. Once the plane arrives in Kuwait, your boys will release Max to Belov and his people. What he does after that is not our concern. I suspect the Bratva will have him transported to one of their safe houses somewhere in Kazakhstan and then on to oblivion."

For the first time, Strain allowed himself to think about being reunited with his wife. "I look forward to getting to see Carly. I'm grateful we didn't lose more lives. I'm grateful for having met you. My perception of you did not fall short. You are a cool dude, and I look forward to meeting with you in the future under different circumstances."

"I am thrilled you will soon be reunited with Carly. I hope to see you both back in New York in the near future." Cassell extended his hand. "I wish you a safe trip to Kuwait City." Cassell stepped forward and gave him a man hug. Strain reciprocated with an equal embrace before heading toward the idling passenger van that would take him across the airfield to Belov's Antonov.

Commander Strain sat in the back by himself. The driver said nothing and had not an inkling of the international drama unfolding in front of him. The driver knew the Bratva, and drivers like him, would say nothing, lest they wanted to end up floating face down in Koshkarat Lake south of the airport.

It was 3:30 in the afternoon, ten hours ahead of D.C. time and two hours ahead of Kuwait time. It would take two hours for Belov's plane to arrive in Kuwait. DNI Baubles sat with Keegan in the White House Situation Room monitoring the day's events. Strain sent snippets back to them keeping them informed of his progress. They began to feel cautiously optimistic.

Cassell left his ad hoc command post in the Aktau lounge and walked to the interview room where Max had met Will Strain. Max remained seated at the same table.

"Mr. Dostoevsky, my name is Larry Cassell. I'm here to help resolve the dispute between the United States and Mr. Belov's interests. The plane carrying the U.S. citizens and equipment will depart the Aktau airport very soon. It will take about two hours for it to arrive at its destination. Once that happens, you will be escorted to Mr. Belov's location on the airport facility and permitted to go about your business. Our job then completed, those here with you, to include me, will board the plane that brought you here and depart. Is there anything you need in the interim?"

Max was comfortable with remaining in the visual custody of the Coast Guard. In fact, he felt secure.

"Mr. Cassell, I spent some time in the last hour with Commander Strain. He shared with me some information I have always suspected, but held that truth deep within my heart. I feared knowing the truth could harm me, harm me more than any of my mixed martial arts opponents. I have some soul searching to do, but I want to maintain contact with the commander. Please let him know that."

"Max, I don't know the commander very well, but I do know he is someone with whom you ought to stay in contact. It is ironic you were arrested by his wife, Carly. After having spent a career in the security world, coincidences no longer surprise me. Americans are a forgiving bunch. I think I know where you are heading and wish you the best of luck."

"Mr. Cassell, I have a request. It may seem trivial but . . . my dog Torre."

"We have already arranged for your Torre to be placed with your friend Shorty. When you contact him he will advise you of that fact, but that is all he knows," Cassell interjected quickly. "By the way, the charges against you in New York have been dismissed. It appears you avoided an arm lock." Cassell grinned slightly. Max did too.

Cassell returned to the lounge, which was now completely devoid of passengers, inasmuch as the airport remained closed. The Kazakhstan government publicly announced the airport was closed due to a reported terror threat and would not reopen until the situation was resolved.

As Belov stood by his Antonov to meet Commander Strain, he decided to go aboard in order to see Carly. She had been sitting in a jump seat, staring off in her own distance. The last two days had worn her out, and she was showing signs of exhaustion.

"Agent Strain, I have some good news for you. Your husband, who I met a short time ago, will be here soon. We discussed the events of the past few days and agreed to a mutually acceptable solution. This will include a payment of reparations to the Larkin family."

Belov thought the news he delivered had fallen short. Carly had passed into a trance-like state. What he had to say didn't seem to jar her out of it. He grew concerned. He didn't want the commander to see her like this.

"Agent Strain, I have brought you some hot towels and a new toothbrush and toothpaste to freshen up. Your husband will arrive shortly. Is there anything else I can do for you?" Belov's concern was relieved when he saw a faint smile begin to emerge on her face.

"No, Mr. Belov. I am okay. Can I step outside to greet him?"

"Of course. Follow me."

Agent Strain stood quietly as she saw the white van approach. The oil-induced black exhaust emanating from the tailpipe gave the van a tired grey look, but for her the van represented hope that the end of the nightmare was within reach. Her breathing rose in anticipation of the reunion with her Will. Tears began to well up in her eyes, slowly dripping down her cheeks. She felt a physical relief as the tension she had suppressed over the past two days began to leave her body. The weight of guilt she constrained inside had begun to play on her nerves, brought on by what she had witnessed: the abduction of her agents, the HMX Marines, and the Air Force personnel. She had witnessed the assassination of her colleague, Frank Larkin, the lone ranger who singularly, and some say heroically, attempted to obstruct the Bratva. Now she felt relief. Finally.

The van came to a stop twenty feet from the Antonov's side cargo door. Carly stood at ease. Will stepped out slowly, tactfully scanning the arrival point for snipers, not wanting to let Carly see his concern. Then he found her longing eyes. They moved to cut the distance between themselves, finally engaging in a kiss and embrace. Belov observed the affection from a short distance and turned away, a display of respect for the moment he perversely caused. He waited a few moments for the couple to express their love to each other before ordering engines started.

"Commander, now is the time for you and your wife to board the plane so we can conclude our business arrangement."

"I understand. Will you be coming with us?"

"No, I have to return separately. I wish you and your lovely bride the best." Strain did not show his disgust for the Bratva thug. "Don't foreclose your options," he had been taught throughout his life.

"Will you deliver Agent Larkin's remains to Mr. Cassell soon?" Commander Strain asked in a no-nonsense manner.

"Commander, again we extend our condolences. Mr. Larkin's remains are on their way to Mr. Cassell's location. His body has been properly attended to and prepared for transport back to the United States on the Coast Guard plane. Please have a safe trip to the Kuwaiti kingdom."

Strain nodded. He said nothing more before boarding the plane and took a seat next to his wife. Carly, secure in her web seat, put her left arm through his right arm as he sat down and held on tightly. He kissed her on the forehead and then scanned the interior of the plane. Cavis caught his stare from across the plane's belly. He nodded, indicating all was okay, then sat back as the Antonov accelerated down the runway and took off.

SIXTY TWO

Belov's plane headed for Kuwait City with its valuable cargo. The flying elephant leveled out at 20,000 feet over the Caspian Sea as it waited for the local air traffic control, ATC, to pass them to their international counterpart, which would allow them to move to a higher altitude.

"Roger, sir. Copy 11375.0," replied the Antonov pilot.

The Antonov had been instructed to change frequency for the new controller to handle their flight as the plane left the Aktau controller for the Kuybyshev ATC, until it reached the midway point to Kuwaiti ATC.

"Kuybyshev, this is Antonov 225 heavy."

"Copy that, Antonov 225. You may proceed to 28,000 feet."

As the Antonov leveled out at the new altitude and the pilot was about to relinquish control of his ship to the co-captain, four U.S. Navy F-18s closed in on his port and starboard sides forming a box configuration, a protective formation. He could see the eyes of the pilot in the F-18 to his left.

"Antonov 225 heavy, this is Commander Nelson Keyser, U.S. Navy. How do you read me?"

"Loud and clear, Navy. And what honor has fallen upon us that has your planes in such close proximity?" the disbelieving pilot asked his escort.

Keyser, an Annapolis Academy graduate, had been flying since 2005. Now, he commanded the four F-18s. "Sir, we will be escorting your bird to its final destination, Kuwait International Airport, without deviation. Do you copy that?"

"Roger, Navy. We copy and intend no deviation."

"Copy that. I am also advising you to change your call sign henceforth. You have been designated as W143CS. Do you copy that?"

Keyser's planes flew in choreographed precision. Keyser's group mimicked every subtle movement the largest cargo plane in the world made. The F-18s appeared grossly diminutive, but controlled the Ukrainian's destiny.

"Navy, this is W143CS. Can you advise the significance of our new call sign? Over."

"Negative."

Keyser's mission was a preamble for why the F-18s were in the region. When Air Force One was to enter Middle East airspace, the F-18s would be deployed to provide an escort for the president. This was just a practice run with benefits, paying forward to the U.S. Coast Guard.

SIXTY
THREE

"Look at the size of that motherfucker," remarked Sims as his advance team stood by on the tarmac. The White House advance team attended the late afternoon arrival, as word leaked out there had been some sort of calamity. The Service reps refused to confirm or deny.

Sims and his team were anxious to receive their colleagues on the ground. The jump team was now a day and half late. They would be stressed out and posting assignments were the last thing they needed to consider right now. The prospect put Sims in a difficult position. He felt they may need time to decompress but he still needed them to perform their duties to protect the president. He was one of the few who had been briefed about the abduction, but he, too, didn't know the totality of what had happened. The lost agent had been a friend, a close neighbor back in Annapolis, Maryland. Sims and Larkin had worked together on the president's detail years ago. Sims quietly mourned the loss, but kept it internalized until he returned home.

"This is the biggest fucking plane I have ever laid my eyes on," Sims blurted out, mostly to alter his thoughts and avoid discussion about what led up to the Antonov. Of course the cover story was the C5M had mechanical issues and the Ukrainians had offered the use of their aircraft. To the uninformed that was more than plausible. It arrived with all the equipment. No one who didn't need to know would be the wiser.

"It will be an interesting comparison to see the Antonov 225 sitting next to the C5M when it arrives later today," said Harry Wilde, one of Sims's assistants. Wilde was assigned as the airport security site agent and was tasked to handle the cargo planes' arrivals and departures from the Kuwaiti airport.

"Wilde, make sure we do what we can for the Marines and Air Force personnel when they disembark from the Antonov," said Sims.

"Yes, sir," Wilde responded. "I've got dedicated vehicles for all of them and have arranged to have the Kuwaitis escort their vehicles to the hotels. Also, I have dedicated baggage vehicles so they can depart without having to wait for their personal items. We have it covered, Boss."

Sims gave one of his trademark smiles as a thank you and then turned his attention to the 225's touchdown. It had all the appearance of an asteroid hitting the Earth, but somehow it worked.

Sims, as an experienced Secret Service veteran, possessed clearances most government employees only dreamed about. He had been read-in as to what happened to the C5M, but sworn to silence on the matter. It was an oath he intended to keep. That would be a difficult task for many on board who had witnessed the death of a colleague. Sims had Wilde taking care of the passengers, but he would take personal custody of the commander and his Secret Service bride.

"Wilde, were you able to get a dedicated van for me to put the commander in?"

"Roger that."

"Terrific. I have arranged to get them upgraded at the hotel to a suite with a water view. I want to give them some time before we need Agent Strain to help with the agent post standing briefing."

"Sims, is there anyone or anything you don't think about? You must be running for office."

"Fuck you," Sims chuckled. "I may do something nice for you one day, so don't mess around with me."

Keyser's F-18s peeled away from the Antonov as the mammoth plane entered its down flight pattern and prepared to land. W143CS deployed its landing gear, revealing a grandiose endowment of tire to soften its landing. As the rubber touched the tarmac, a plume of grey vapor slowly dissipated in its wake. The behemoth plane landed safely, its cargo now secure and protected in Kuwait.

"How much do you think it costs them to replace those tires?" asked Wilde.

"Trust me, those boys don't have to worry about money. The sooner they leave, the less evil we will have to deal with," a now serious Sims countered.

As Belov's plane taxied its way to the airport arrival point, Will Strain sent a text message to Cassell, alerting him of the safe return to Kuwait. Cassell knew this was not the final notification. Commander Strain would send one additional.

"I will let Belov know," Cassell texted in return. "Thanks for all you have done."

Commander Strain allowed his wife to disembark the Antonov with her agents. He trailed deferentially. Once he observed all personnel and equipment had been unloaded he sent his final text to Cassell to indicate all had been accomplished according to the agreement.

"The broom is in the closet."

SIXTY FOUR

March 17, 2016, Brighton Beach

The Saint Patrick's Day Parade had concluded and the lower Manhattan taverns were overflowing with Irish faithful. It did not matter many were anything but Irish. On this day everyone was considered an honorary Irish son or daughter and that included the Russian mob. Long ago, Belov had adopted the day as his own. It was one of the rare times he allowed himself to loosen up with a few glasses of Guinness.

The day morphed into a remarkably warm, spring-like Thursday. Belov celebrated his recent return from Aktau on a high note with Irish cheer. Ireland had been one of his favorite countries from which to recruit and nurture KGB recruits, primarily harvested from the IRA, and it was a great place to be for someone with a thirst for liberal amounts of beer.

"Time to get back," he told himself. It was late afternoon, and he had dinner planned back in Brighton Beach. Belov thought the New York City subway system was the best way to travel throughout the city and could not understand why Americans didn't appreciate the system they had. "Shit," he told his friends, "If Americans knew what the underground transportation was like in Moscow, they would never complain about their own. This if a fucking Cadillac compared to our Moscow clunker."

He squeezed his way through the throngs inside the Irish tavern and clambered up the steps and out onto John Street, walking briskly to catch the number four subway off William Street and departing lower Manhattan before changing to the B line. The B dropped him off at the elevated platform onto Brighton's Sixth Street and Brighton Beach Avenue. He could do this blind.

He decided to head down toward the ocean for a walk on the boardwalk to smoke one of his Cuban Trinidad Robustos. Belov only smoked Cubans. He savored the subtle flavor and aroma. He never smoked anything that didn't have great girth and length. "Size matters," he joked to his fellow Bratva members. He lit up, puffing slowly to stoke the cigar.

Biting down firmly on the Cuban, he crossed Sixth Street, not even glancing in either direction. Let others watch out for the Bratva chieftain. He walked over to Fourth Street and turned left, walking past the Miramar apartment building where he lived. He entered the ramp at the end of Fourth Street leading up to the Riegelmann Boardwalk and passed his favorite eatery, the Café Restaurant Volva.

He was slated for an early dinner with his sidekick, Alexei, but first he would take time to savor his Cuban and appreciate an unusually mild March day. Belov yearned for these private occasions to be alone. By nature, he was a loner.

The mild afternoon gave him time to evaluate the recent events in Kazakhstan. At dinner, he would share his thoughts with his cronies and then begin to outline the mob's future initiatives. Belov was pleasantly gratified with what he perceived to be a brilliantly choreographed abduction of the Air Force plane and the successful Kazakhstan exchange.

"I beat the U.S. government at its own game," he said to himself, beaming with pride. "The money I agreed to pay in reparations was chump change. I would have agreed to pay more if they had pushed it. How great is this? An old Cold War operative can outwit the former enemy and continue to live in the lion's den. Ha!"

Belov had not seen Max since Kazakhstan. The brotherhood had him sequestered in the Caribbean, giving him time to get his head together, but mostly, to keep him out of the purview of federal investigators. He arranged for Max to go to an exotic location. Tatiana and Gamera accompanied him. It began with a flight out of Kazakhstan, which took them directly to the small island of Martinique. There, he had Max taken to the French side of the island and ensconced at the secluded and prestigious La Semanna Hotel. "I envision the young man is relaxing, perhaps enjoying the young ladies Tatiana was tasked to send his way," he thought. Privately, he wanted the boy back in Bratva's embrace. "He needs to learn more than just fighting and typing on a computer. I will reach out for him soon."

As he continued his boardwalk stroll, the chieftain's thoughts shifted frenetically. Each draw and puff on his cigar signaled a new topic. His mind raced through a mental checklist. The girlfriend, Tanya, who had started all the problems, was no more. She was butchered and left for the authorities to piece together; never again would she be in a position to compromise Max. The NYPD had her listed as a missing person. They would never find her. Her cocaine connection existed no longer. Belov smiled at the thought of Diablo's mutilated body floating in the Arthur Kill, a half mile from the Driscoll Bridge, just south of Perth Amboy, New Jersey. His penis had been stuffed into his mouth, and the mouth was crudely stitched shut with fishing line. A passing boater spotted the body and reported it to the New Jersey State Police. An open homicide investigation failed to develop any investigative leads. The Bratva would never be connected to his demise. It would probably be viewed as a drug-related murder.

Young Russian mothers pushed their baby strollers along the boardwalk, finding the mild afternoon as tempting as did Belov. Today they escaped the boredom of their bleak apartments to share local gossip while their lily-white faces absorbed the early rays of the year. Belov weaved his way through the maze of strollers, keeping as close to the boardwalk handrail as he could in order to avoid them. One of the young women caught his eye. He demurred, and she quickly lowered her gaze out of respect for the Russian Godfather. He was known throughout the enclave. They all knew not to approach him on the boardwalk unless there was an established relationship. Violating his personal zone risked provoking his wrath. His stroll was personal time, his time to think, and his way to flesh out his schemes before presenting them to the mob leadership. In fact, it was here he carefully developed the Kazakhstan exchange scenario. It took him only a few hours of pacing along the boardwalk. Max's public arraignment in federal court gave him the impetus he needed to piece the plan together and notify the ladies at Ramstein Air Base to execute his abduction plan.

"Ah. I better head to the restaurant."

Belov timed his arrival to the restaurant so he could savor the Trinidad cigar's dying moments. He picked up his pace. Stepping off the boardwalk at Second Street, he headed to Brightwater Court where he made a right, one block away from the Café Restaurant Volva. It was located directly across from the Benderskiy Motel. He had never liked that place. It made him uneasy. Across the street, he saw Alexei waiting for him, not far from the wooden ramp that led to the front of the Café Volva. He would soon follow up the cigar with his daily dose of a sixteen-year-old, single malt, Lagavulin whiskey.

"Today, Alexei pays," laughed Belov. "He never picks up the fucking tab, the little bastard. But today he will."

He took a final puff from the diminished cigar before throwing it onto the street and aggressively twisting it under his shoe, flattening the remainder to a pulp then kicking the debris into the roadway. He straightened his tie, dusted the ash from his sports jacket lapels, and entered the pedestrian crosswalk at the intersection of Fourth and Brightwater Court, just fifteen feet from Alexei. He looked up at him and smirked. Alexei said something, but Belov never heard it. "Alexei is headless," was Belov's final thought. The top of Alexei's head flew off completely; the bottom seemed to dangle down around his neck. It all happened in a second. There was nothing left; no brain matter, no cranium, nothing. The bullet did its job. The thug was gone. His body fell limp to the concrete; the weight of the corpse hitting the ground pinched Alexei's wallet from his rear pants pocket. It bounced a foot away from the corpse.

Peering through his weapon's Leupold Vari-X-dot riflescope, the gunman had taken a full, deep breath then released half of it before squeezing the trigger. He had fired the second of two silent gunshots, both suppressed to reduce the noise and muzzle flash typically associated with the discharge of a powerful weapon. Each shot took less than a second to reach their mark. The bullet that struck Belov's head left him similarly decapitated. His blood flowed liberally from the carotid artery on to the street pavement. It absorbed Belov's cigar ashes in a macabre euphemism; a revenge death has no dignity.

The sniper had been perched at the Benderskiy Motel's third floor window, located a short distance across from the Café. The motel had always made Belov uneasy.

The weapon was an MK-11 Mod Sniper Weapon System, a standard Navy SEAL tool. When used by an experienced sniper, the 7.62 caliber round had a devastating effect. From the distance between the crosswalk and the window, the bullet had hardly expended its potent energy before striking, leaving an obliterated, no longer recognizable target. The bullet was launched through a simple, but explosive process that delivered its destructive load through its barrel's finely honed lands and grooves, at great speed to its target.

The sniper efficiently disengaged and left the scene. He didn't take time to gloat. He placed the weapon in its beige carry bag before he exited the room and made his way out to Brighton Beach Avenue. Within moments he discreetly signaled to a Yellow Cab waiting less than half a block away. The cab pulled up immediately.

The sniper placed his bag on the far side of the rear seat and calmly hopped in next to it. The cab accelerated after the driver heard the rear door close, then turned left onto Seventh Street and was out of the area before police sirens were heard. Once out of the neighborhood, the cab headed west on the Belt Parkway.

The cabbie remained quiet until the taxi had blended effortlessly in the flow of heavy traffic. Finally breaking the silence he turned his head slightly to the right and asked, "How did it go, sir?"

"The assholes are dead," the sniper responded.

The cab driver's face grew solemn. "My son can now rest in peace." In the rear seat, Will Strain looked out the window but said nothing.

Mr. Larkin felt the tears welling up. His son's death had been avenged. He was eager to support the commander in this operation in any way he could, but had been told only that the person who orchestrated the death of his son lived in Brighton Beach.

Will Strain realized he would need to quickly distance himself from the Russian enclave without attracting suspicion, so he had arranged to have Larkin in the area with his Yellow Cab, which could easily transit through the community with ample anonymity. He did not tell Larkin how he planned to eliminate the KGB operatives; he was better off not knowing. There was no hesitation by Larkin in his decision to support Strain and provide a way out of the Brighton Beach. "I would have done it myself, if you had told me who it was."

As Larkin's taxi passed the Belt Parkway's Coney Island exit, the cabbie shouted, "Happy Saint Patrick's Day to you, you snake! I hope you rot in hell!"

Strain cautioned him to celebrate quietly. He trusted Mr. Larkin would keep the matter to himself, but while offering his condolences, he had added a cautionary note: "I am sorry for your loss, sir. Your son was a dedicated Secret Service agent. My wife told me he died a hero, trying to defend his fellow agents. You will, no doubt, be proud of him for the rest of your life. Mr. Larkin, it is imperative that no word of this is ever spoken."

"No worries," said Mr. Larkin. "I have a few of my own secrets that will forever be kept in the deep recesses of my mind. This will be stored there as well, but only after I savor it for a bit. Nevertheless, I assure you I will keep it to myself."

The avenged cabbie traveled east on the Belt Parkway to the Verrazano Bridge, through Staten Island, and over the Goethals Bridge into Elizabeth, New Jersey, where he picked up the New Jersey Turnpike. He exited not far from the site where Diablo's arrest had occurred, then turned onto Ferry Street in Newark.

Brighton Beach was now a safe distance away. The cabbie concentrated on his instructions to pull into the Hilton's arrival turn-around, opposite the Newark Train Station entrance. When he brought the cab to a halt, Coast Guard Chief Petty Officer Patrick McMurray calmly opened the taxi door from the opposite side.

"Good afternoon, sir," said McMurray. "Sir, I can take it from here." McMurray referred to the beige bag containing the sniper's MK-11 and two expended cartridges.

"Mr. Larkin, as I explained earlier, I need you to now transport this man to the U.S. Coast Guard station located on Staten Island. He will give you further directions."

Strain acknowledged McMurray with a firm handshake. Nothing more was said between them. McMurray knew what to do with the weapon once he returned to the station. The MK-11 would be transported out to sea and forever rest in the deepest recesses of the ocean. The weapon would never again be used or seen.

Strain watched the taxi depart and then quickly stepped the short distance to the station. His ticket indicated he would be taking a 6:30

pm Acela back to Baltimore, Maryland. He hustled up the escalator to track three. He wasn't late, but he moved quickly because his wife was waiting for him.

Carly Strain caught his eye as he came off the escalator and stepped into the elevated lobby. She desperately wanted to run toward him, but remained stationary to let him walk toward her on the platform. She had to give Will every opportunity to shake any countermeasures that might have been in place to track him.

As she engaged his eyes, he gave her a soft smile, which indicated to her it was now okay. Carly put her handbag on top of her luggage and raised her arms to embrace the approaching love of her life. He placed his arms below hers and hugged her tightly, kissing her tenderly on the lips. She leaned her head to the side and smiled at him. "I love those lips," she said. He kissed her again as the Acela arrived.

The Strains boarded the train. They were now only hours from their home on Maryland's Eastern Shore. The commander said, "When we get back to Oxford, I will show you how much I've missed my Carly."

EPILOGUE

The patrons at the Café Restaurant Volva slowly emptied onto the boardwalk as word of a shooting spread throughout the community.

A gaggle of rubberneckers soon congregated. They leaned over and attempted to get an angle that would allow them to view the unidentifiable faces below. It took a few seconds for the gawkers to digest what they had seen. Some quickly turned away, while others continued to stare at the macabre scene. Their heads were gone, obliterated by the power of the sniper's rounds. Alexei was lying only a few feet away.

The influential and powerful Bratva crime boss lay dead in his own neighborhood, prior to dusk, having just enjoyed the last puff from his Cuban cigar. His body remained only a few feet from the next meal he never ate. The deceased chieftain, a competent and efficient killer himself, was now displayed unceremoniously on Brightwater Court, his blood draining to the side of the street and engulfing the cigar ashes he had just spread about upon the macadam seconds earlier.

His demise would shock the Bratva syndicate. A new mob organizational structure would emerge, but not until internal and feudal bloodletting had occurred. This was the nature of the mob's command and control hierarchy. Some of the emerging contestants would surely die before the new Bratva power base was established.

Later, Max received a phone call. "Hello, Max. This is Commander Will Strain. The director of National Intelligence will have you flown to the Washington, D.C., area on Monday. We are scheduled to meet with him at 1300 hours—sorry 1 pm—and then travel to the National Security Agency in Maryland for your orientation. My boss, Assistant Commandant James Keegan, will join us. I look forward to seeing you again."

"Yes, I am anxious to move forward with my new life and to work with you as a friend and not a foe."

"You bet, Max. I understand Mr. Belov is no more. Sounds like the memories of your mother and father have been avenged."

"Yes, I have heard. It came as good news to me."

Commander Michael Mudd and his flight crew were assigned to pick Max up at Andrews Joint Air Base. Max had arrived earlier in the day from an undisclosed Caribbean safe house. Mudd's non-descript Blackhawk Helicopter departed Joint Base Andrews, ferrying Max to the secure landing zone near Buzzard's Point, a short distance from the former U.S. Coast Guard Headquarters.

As Max sat on the starboard side of the helicopter, wearing a headset that allowed him to hear the radio traffic, he gazed out the chopper's window. What he observed gave way to a slight smile then to a full-faced grin. Standing next to Commander Strain, and directly in front of Agent Strain, he saw his trusted buddy Shorty, who held Torre's leash. Mudd circled the landing zone to give Max a broader perspective of his arrival point.

Mudd briefed Max over his headset. "Looks like you have a greeting party."

Max felt honored the pilot of the aircraft took the time from his flying to say that. He didn't know how to respond, so he just savored the moment and nodded, hoping the pilot would recognize his gratefulness.

Torre sat on her behind, not alerting or reacting to the approaching aircraft, a position that was to be short-lived. Commander Strain arranged through his wife to have Shorty and Torre transported there in time for the arrival. The familiar faces, he reasoned, would prove fruitful in raising Max's comfort level. It had been predetermined that Shorty would not be "read into," or briefed, as to what Max's future held.

The handlers had no problem with the presence of the friend and the dog. Next to Torre, Shorty was Max's most loyal buddy. Strain had argued they would play a vital role in allowing Max to begin a new life away from the Brighton Beach crowd, at least for the short-term.

The small greeting party was close enough to the zone to witness Mudd's smooth landing. Within seconds of a wheels-down landing, a young "Coastie," Coast Guard landing zone operator, opened the hatch door from within and bounded out to secure the steps.

Max was next to disembark. Torre saw him, and with her tail wagging excitedly, broke from Shorty's grip and ran toward his master. Carly and Will Strain both smiled in amusement. The terrier would accomplish what no one else could, even Shorty, who had struggled to keep up with Torre to embrace Max first. It appeared to Carly that Shorty and Torre were almost competing for Max's attention. She chuckled. "Will, look how cute this is."

"It is so great to see you guys!" Max shouted joyously. He gave Shorty a brotherly hug, while trying to keep one arm around his loyal canine. The gleeful Torre tried to lick Max on the lips, while Shorty began to tear up in happiness at seeing his best friend once again. He was especially happy he didn't have to share the moment with Tanya. He had heard she may have been killed, but he did not know the details and didn't dare ask. He liked this Strain guy, but he wondered briefly why Max suddenly had all these new friends. "Max will explain all this when he feels like it," Shorty thought and was okay with that.

Commander Strain waited briefly to allow the reunion to work its magic, then approached Max. "Good to see you again, Max. I hope you have had time to relax and think about your new job. Let's get you all inside where we can have some lunch."

He pulled Max off to the side, away from Shorty and the others. "We have some folks ready to sit down with you, Max, to go over our next assignment."

"Does that mean you and I will be working together?" Max asked. "If it does, then I am extremely happy to be here."

"Yes, we will be working together. Do you speak Spanish? Ha!"

Carly marveled at how much they looked alike, almost like brothers.

ABOUT THE AUTHOR

Mr. Sloan served more than twenty-five years as a Special Agent with the United States Secret Service. During his distinguished career, he held numerous positions of increasing responsibility to include being the Special Agent in Charge of the Baltimore field office where he oversaw complex financial crimes investigations and security arrangements at Camp David. Prior to that, Mr. Sloan was the Special Agent in Charge of the Major Events Division where he managed security systems for the U.S. government's designated national security special events, including the United Nations General Assemblies, the NATO fiftieth anniversary celebration, and the Salt Lake City Winter Olympics. He managed all security aspects leading up to the 2000 presidential campaign. During his career, he had been responsible for the security of President William Clinton and managed an international financial crimes task force. Since retiring from the Secret Service in 2001, Mr. Sloan has traveled extensively as a corporate security executive representing Western Union and the New York Stock Exchange. He is a recognized authority on identifying physical security risks and designing programs to protect employees and company assets. He received his bachelor of arts degree from Villanova University and his master of forensic science from George Washington University.